By the same author

The Devil May Care

Captain Ninja

Sins of the Fathers

Empathy

SHARD

John Richmond

Published By
John R. Richmond
Johnrollinrichmond@hotmail.com

First Published 2011

ISBN: 978-0-615-41154-5

SHARD

JOHN RICHMOND

For Bob:

Who taught me to commune with the dragons in my basement... and anything else lurking down there.

Chapter 1

WILL TWO-BEARS McFarlan shook his head and sighed, "Damn, that's a great line." He scanned the first sentence of his favorite novel again, flicking over ant letters: *The man in black fled across the desert and the Gunslinger followed.* Clean, clean, squeaky clean. He knew every character as well as his own family, every plot twist as well the planes of his own face, but his breath still caught at the end of that sentence. Any further and Will would amble the blasted alkalai with Stephen King's brave and terrible gunslinger until they were done. One more word and he would plunge again into the shifting deep of imagination. And, here there be dragons.

He closed his eyes, let his breath out and—

"Hey! Sheriff!" *Sheriff* sounded more like *shurf.*

Will's head lolled back, mouth slack. He called over his shoulder, "Whaddaya need, George?"

Silence from the holding cell in the back. There was just the one cell—a relic with bars instead of chicken wire and plexiglass. Will tended to think of it as *George Rhodes' Weekend Retreat.* He'd considered having a plaque made.

Will cocked an eyebrow and a lock of too-long hair slipped from under his Kentucky Wildcats cap. "George?"

Silence.

Will gave *The Dark Tower: The Gunslinger* a long look and put it down on the scorred and gouged surface of a desk twice his age. He swung a pair of red Chuck Taylor All Stars tennis shoes down from the corner of said desk and thought about strapping on his .375. Not because he would ever need a weapon of any sort when dealing with George Rhodes—even on one of his bad benders, George always greeted Will with a sloppy hug—but more for effect. It wasn't one of Roland of Gilead's infamous sandlewood revolvers, but it was the right shape and size. Will liked to think of the big six gun as his pet cybernetic dragon. He'd even named it Smaug after Tolkein's famous scaley horror. Instead of strapping on the iron, Will clunked it down into the top drawer and slammed it shut. He squeaked down the short hall and stood in front of the cell. The door, of course, was open.

George Rhodes had been first in his class at Blue Ridge High, quarterback for the Blue Ridge Razorbacks and captain of the chess team. By the age of twenty-four, alcohol had stroked the shine out of his eyes like a child pets the fur off its favorite teddy bear. It had been a long, treacherous affair, but booze loved George and George loved booze. The only problem, according to George, was that it was a dysfunctional relationship. The love was real though, and that was worth fighting for. George's six foot-three frame used to run two-thirty of solid muscle. Will stood looking down at a broad-built skeleton draped in gin-soaked rags. It smiled at him and cleaved another chip off his heart.

George's brow tented over sunken eyes. "Sheriff?"

"You rang, George?"

"I did? Did I?"

Will walked into the cell and leaned back against the bars, cool through his Janes Addiction t-shirt. "You did, buddy-roo. Need something?"

George slurred through a bad Brittish lilt. "A Bombay Sapphire and Tonic would be the tops, my dear Sheriff."

"I'll bet," Will said. "And you know it's *Constable*, Georgie. I hate it when you call me Sheriff. Tommy Ward and his deputy dawgs are up at the County Courthouse. You know it as well I do."

"Sorry, dude."

"What's up?"

George belched. Really it was more of a poison sigh. "Hmm?"

Will waved his hand in front of his face. "Last chance, Georgie. I have a tower to run down, a man in black to climb."

"You readin' that fuckin' thing again?" George held his hand up—gnarled blue branches under the loose skin—and examined it. Was this his? Oh, yeah, fingers were for counting. "How many times?"

Will waved him off. "Like four or five."

"You'd think there were only a hunnert books in the world, *Constable*."

"That's not true, man. I read all the time."

"I'm sayin'. What I'm saying is that I know you read all the time. It's just that you been reading the same damn books since we were kids." For a moment, the gin glaze swapped for the glaze of memory as George first came upon little William Two-Bears McFarlan leaning up against an oak with his nose in a dog-eared copy of *The Once and Future King*. He chortled and muttered, "Threw my football at you."

"Huh?"

George squinted up at Will, a suspicious buccaneer. "Wass' the last thing you read?"

"Today's New York Times on-line edition. Apparently, the rich are getting richer and the poor are getting fatter."

"Yeah, yeah. What's the last book, *novel*, you read?"

Will pivoted an ankle so he could look at the five-pointed star on the side of his shoe. He favored Chucks because of those stars. Reminded him of a badge. "Fine," he said. "It was *Fantastic Voyage*."

"How many times you read that one already?"

Will smiled, triumphant. "Only twice, so bite me."

"Including this last time?"

"Okay, three times."

"You suck, Sheriff."

Will splayed his hands. "What do you want from me, Georgie? I like what I like."

"You always order the same thing when you get Chinese, doncha'?" He jabbed a finger at Will. "Never get something new."

Will crossed his arms. "Chinese restaurant. Shard don't even have a McDonalds."

"Always getting' the General Tso's Chicken." George shook his head; long, greasy blonde hair, already fading to gray at the temples, hung over his brow. "Never takin' your shot on the Hunan Beef."

"You sound like a drunk, Georgie."

"Truly? Why do you suppose that is?"

"Gimme' a break, Georgie." Will sighed and dropped down on the bunk next to his oldest friend. Old springs screeched in protest, metal snakes that would one night eat through their cotton cocoon and bite. Will made a mental note to order a new one before he had to get George another tetanus shot. "Nothing's happened in this town since The Fire. There's like, what? A population of thirty-three now?"

"Peterson and his daughter packed up couple of days ago."

Will started. "Greg Peterson took lil' Shell? They're gone? Shit, man, see? That's what I'm talking about. There's nothing here. You gotta' at least let me read what I like." He looked at the star on his other shoe. "Doing what makes us happy is the only thing to keep out the bats, George."

"You gonna' get me that gin tonic, then?"

"The Fire" was the result of the Shard Mine explosion of 1994. A build-up of volatile gases (and a company looking to save a few thousand dollars a year by ignoring a safety measure or twenty) had doomed the once booming town of Shard, Kentucky. The cough and roar from the earth had been bad enough, eating five miners alive—men who lived and loved in Shard. The aftermath had been worse: the main coal seam took to smoulder. Sulphurous smoke seeped non-stop from cracks in the earth. Any pore from underground to the surface bled stinking devil's breath.

The mine shut down, the chains scraped over the tunnel head-caps and the town began to die. Within a month of the accident half of Shard had moved on, rolling out over roads that split like melon skin in hot sun. After a year, the fire slipped along the fuse of coal seam, poisoning one acre after another. One night you could go to bed, hoping the seam might zig instead of zag under your lot, only to wake with smoke drooling up through your bathroom sink. An idyllic Appalachian mountain village with an unemployment rate of less than one percent and a steady growth rate fell back into the emerald forest, sighing its last smoky exhale.

Every now and then the ground would shudder and thud as a new mouth opened to sing the earth's dirty song. Sink holes that glowed weak orange at night, and gurgled pale, gray-yellow vapor in the day pocked the town. In spring and summer, creeper vines found purchase and dragged down while they decorated. In fall and winter mildew bloomed between boards, painting white siding black then freezing in coagulated colonies.

Twelve years gone now. Twelve-hundred citizens. Some thirty-three left. Greg Peterson and his daughter Shelby Grace gone. Thirty-one. Huddled in the last unburnt corner of town was Tooley's Grocery, the elementary school, the town hall and jail. The rest was row after row of empty, smoking streets—eddies of ash in the gutters. The mine offices loomed over the asphalt grid, a brick sore on the side of the mountain. Red, angry flesh of the world beneath it all. Shard.

"Which one of you is the prisoner?"

Will Two-Bears McFarlan and George Rhodes looked up at a compact young woman with electric blueberry hair. Her arms were bare to the shoulder save for the tattooed sleeves, writhing in faded color and mysterious symbol. She wore torn black jeans and motorcycle boots scraped to the steel on the toes. Neither of them had ever seen her before in their lives.

Chapter 2

ERICA MENDEZ STOOD in her most comfortable underwear, a black sports bra and matching thong, and surveyed the clothes laid out on her bed. On the left, three pairs of designer jeans, four custom blazers, and underthings boiling in a pile of lace and spaghetti straps. On the right, blouses for a week along with her oldest Armani suit. Nearly everything was custom-made, tailored, altered. Her body was a collection of custom-made, tailored and altered musculature. Her hair was long, deep chestnut with highlights labored over by talented brushes.

Looking at Erica was like looking at a computer simulation of an attractive young woman. At first sight, men were often momentarily puzzled, but then they would circle. Their approaches were seldom direct—afraid to get cut on those honed edges. For the brave few who offered to slay a twenty-dollar martini in her honor, she served them back to themselves in shreds, never having spoken a word. The deep black of her eyes and the intelligence that crackled within them was more than enough to do the wet work. For those foolish enough to continue pursuit, Erica might employ her extensive verbal arsenal (she wasn't the youngest female litigator at Miller, Seay and Summerstein for nothing). The eviscerations were surgical and deadly. She only told the truth.

A car horn blared in the street ten stories below her apartment on 98th and West Park. In the winter, the resevoir shone cobalt through the bare trees in Central Park. It wasn't as big as her loft in the Village had been, but she was a grown-up now and she was never going to make partner unless she worked, played and lived like a grown-up. Miller, Seay, Summerstein...and Mendez. The green of the park foamed in through the window and into her mind. Yes, this had been the right choice. Smaller, but it wasn't like she used the apartment for much more than a place to catch a few hours of sleep between billable hours.

Erica padded across the hand-carved Persian rug, placing her feet so the ridges in the carpet filled the space between the pads of her toes and the ball of her foot. She trailed her hand along the Chinese armoir, hand-lacquered, and slid into the bathroom. The lights sensed her body heat and bloomed. She leaned into the mirror. Her father's face overlay her mother's—second gen Puerto Rican beat cop over fifth gen Irish Public Defender. A collection of ambitions and expectations, a duality of over and under through which Erica emerged. She blinked long lashes, chemically darkened, and tried to see herself. Erica grabbed her bone-handled brush and began to stroke her hair into submission.

She stopped and twisted her left arm down and in. Her triceps were just the tiniest bit watery. Time to switch protein shakes. The one with which she'd been breakfast dosing for the past week had been an experiment and it wasn't working. She'd go back to the old formula. She flexed and twisted, checked her tummy, reminded herself not to frown lest the stress tattoo her brow. Her own fault. The old protein shake was more expensive and Dad always taught her that you got what you paid for. Mom's voice rose up and admonished that only a horse's ass paid full price for anything.

Erica looked into her own eyes and restrained the urge to Tae-bo the shit out of the mirror. She imagined herself a moment into that future: bleeding and staring at an Erica Mendez caught in a web of shattered glass.

The phone rang. That would be the cab for the airport—seven and one half minutes early.

"Fuck," she said.

* * *

ONE HOUR AFTER checking her bag and claiming her ticket (and that was *with* the security fast-track option—fucking JFK) Erica slotted herself into a business class seat and opened her laptop. Provided the glorified bus drivers in the cockpit were able to get wheels up on time, she would touch down in Lexington in one hour and fifteen minutes. Provided the Morlocks who toiled under the airport got her bags to her on time and the rental car trogs didn't fuck up her reservation, Erica would arrive at her final destination just in time to tuck into what would most certainly be a horrific excuse for restaurant food so laden with transfats a coronary would not be unexpected.

"Coffee, miss?"

Erica looked into the red-rimmed eyes of a woman twenty years older and ten pounds heavier than she. Her skin was orange tan, her hair crackled with CVS-brand blondness, and pink lipstick flowed into the cracks around her mouth. It moved. "Miss?"

Erica restrained a wince. Her mother's mouth had done that in her fifties, wrinkling into itself like an anus. Erica threw a brilliant smile and raised her voice an octave. "I'd love a glass of Orgeon pinot noir."

The attendant's lips quivered around her own smile, but held it, held it. "I'm not sure we have that. Would a merlot do? Dear?"

Erica knew five people—three through her work, two through her father—who would throw acid in this woman's face for a hand job. If she used her mouth, they'd probably ruin the stew's credit rating as a bonus. Ugly and poor... Shit, the woman was a stewardess in her late forties, she was already there. Erica sighed. "Bourbon. No ice."

She opened a folder on her computer desktop labeled "vacation", exposing several sub-folders. She hovered her mouse arrow over the one titled Blackstone Energy & Mineral, opened the file titled "Background_Location_Mine_1". Her computer thought about it for an instant longer than Erica would have liked before opening a graphics reader. A satellite photo resolved. Erica leaned in and squinted. It looked like a kelly green quilt thrown over a bed full of bodies. In the middle, the circuit board of a small town: angled street wires and red, tin roof microchips. The bedspread ate away at the edges of the circuit board, a foliage acid bath. And everywhere the blurry lens of smoke.

Erica had volunteered to research this stamp of waste in the Appalachian Mountains. Sure, she would just parachute right in, check out the town's infrastructure, the political environment, and assess the ramifications of scraping it off the face of the earth. There were no corpses under that rolling green blanket, but lumps of anthracite and pockets of natural gas. Not bodies, money. Hordes of treasure piled high. Never mind the smoulder. With full-on mountain-top removal you didn't worry about things like collapse and explosive firedamps. You blasted off the upper layers, stubbed out the seam and pulled in the revenue. It was what was left of the little town that really demanded her expertise. Sure, she'd go in and check it out. Sure, she'd get a feel for the place and see what it took to relo the denizens. It'd be fun to get out of the city for a while. She'd even use her vacation time.

Erica zoomed in on the town courthouse like a controlled skydive and hover. She could already smell the sulphur, hear the podunk accents and sprung banjos, feel the eyes of the inbred and moonshine-addled fumbling at her breasts and hair. She glared at the screen, absorbing the photons and cooling them dead. A single word adorned the bottom of the map: *Shard.*

She looked up at the quivering lips of the attendant.

"Bourbon," she said, setting down a plastic glass full of ice and a tiny bottle of Jack Daniels. "That'll be five-fifty."

Erica produced a crisp twenty. "Keep it."

The attendant's smile crystalized, the bill crinkled and she moved on.

Erica looked at the cup full of gray ice. She leaned forward and dumped it in the seat pocket in front of her. Jack Daniels was Tennesee whiskey not Kentucky bourbon. Coal was potential revenue not dead bodies. She slugged down the Jack, denied the shiver and straightened her seat as the turbines began to whine. Erica took a last look at the glowing satellite map and shut her computer.

She closed her eyes and leaned back, the cheap leather enveloping her shoulders, the electric dark enfolding her mind. She saw deep forest and hills and imagined the elbow of an old oak tree filled with spiderweb; there was nothing caught in it.

She opened her eyes and stared out the window at the hard, rolling tarmack. "Shard," she whispered. "Fuck."

Chapter 3

DARWIN'S BOWL OVERFLOWED with two days worth of kibble. That the beagle would be missing for long stretches at a time—running the woods in an ecstasy of forest smells—was nothing unusual. But even if twelve-year-old Childe Howard (known to most of Shard as "Kiddo") hadn't actually *seen* the dog, his food was always eaten.

Kiddo stared down at the small mound of brown pellets. "Mom?" he called over his sunburned shoulder. "Darwin hasn't eaten in a while." Kiddo waited the obligatory three seconds. He imagined his mother in her office down the hall, tilting her curly blonde explosion of a head just so, her wireless lenses a double mirror of the computer screen in front of her. It always took a couple of tries when she was writing. The first attempt was just a primer, a flare on the horizon of her unconscious. Kiddo nudged Darwin's bowl and caused an avalanche of kibble. He thought about ants and Pompei.

Kiddo grinned. "Yo, Loraine!" She *hated* it when he addressed her by her first name. "Your only son's dog is missing."

Down the hall Loraine Howard blinked and actually saw the words floating on the monitor in front of her. When she was in the zone, she didn't see anything except the scene under construction. If she was typing and aware of the words on the computer, she wasn't writing, not really. Drove the kid *crazy* when she went deep like that and ended up ignoring him. How long had he been calling her this time? At least once; Childe never resorted to her first name unless he was just this side of ticked. And her lovely son was almost never ticked. It's probably why it bugged her so much when he called her Loraine. It meant something was wrong.

She hit "Ctrl" and "s" and shouted, "Sup', buttercup?"

Childe rolled around the doorjamb, careful not to knock into the six-foot stack of books leaning there. Loraine's office was filled with these literary towers. They were like seaweed spires growing from the ocean floor, and the casual observer might connote an un-packing still in progress. Thing was: Loraine's office had looked just like this in Hollywood, too. The only difference was what came through the windows. In So. Cal. they threw heliographs from passing cars and shouts and honks from the drivers within them. In Shard, the windows threw shifting green shadows and the ratchet-song of summer cicadas.

"You really gotta' stop calling me, Loraine, Childe, my child."

Kiddo channeled Dirty Harry, "Yeah? What're ya' gonna' do about it, punk? You feel lucky? Well, do ya'…*Loraine?*"

Without pausing to check the title, she grabbed the closest paperback and lobbed it at his head. Childe yipped and ducked, but his gawky elbow caught a book tower and brought it down all over him. "Yahhhh!" he cried, and crumbled beneath it. He immediately "died" with a long and mournful death rattle.

Loraine jumped to her feet and ran around the desk. She barked her ample right hip but didn't lose momentum. Timing was everything in a situation like this. She knelt by her son and cradled his blonde head, hopelessly kinked like hers. She channeled Miss Scarlett, "Mah son, mah onlah boyah! Speak ta' me!"

Childe opened his eyes. "Your accent sucks, dude."

"Oh, yeah?" Loraine let his head thunk down on the books.

"Ow, man, hey!"

"Don't call her your mother 'man'," Loraine said, pulling them both up. "Just because we moved to the sticks doesn't mean you can lose your West Coast manners."

Childe thought for a moment. "Ow, dude?"

"Better." She grabbed him in a hug and smelled his head. He wasn't quite to the wet puppy stage, but by the end of the day her lovely boy was going to be one mighty stinky boy. "Now, what's so important you gotta' bother your mother in the middle of her next Oscar-winning screenplay?"

Childe pulled away, but not without a return squeeze. "Don't you have to have won an Oscar before getting a 'next' one?"

"You want to clean up the tower of Babel you just knocked over?"

"Okay, okay." The play fled his face, drawing the open, easy features into the points Loraine never cared for. Childe had looked like that for a year after his father left them. "Darwin's been gone for a while."

"The Amazing Ninja Dog? How can you tell?"

"Seriously, mom. It doesn't look like he's eaten anything for like two or three days." The rind of a whine edged his voice.

Loraine kept the rebuke out of hers. The only reason he was a little whiny was because he was scared and Childe wasn't normally a fraidy cat. Matter of fact, he was a little too cavalier for her tastes from time to time, running around the woods and the empty town with just the beagle for company. Maybe it was a testosterone thing. Would've been great to have a man around the house to help her with that kind of thing. Would've been even better if said man was the kid's father. Jerk. She took a breath. The screenplay could wait.

"You wanna' go look for him?"

Childe's shoulders dropped a little. "Thanks, Loraine."

She leaned forward and kissed a freckle on the end of his nose. "Booger."

* * *

DEEP IN THE woods, Darwin was in trouble. At the bottom of a natural bowl caused by the subsistance of partial mine shaft collapse, the sturdy Beagle fought for his life. Trees ringed the hollow like spectators, hushing and sighing as the scene played out. High in the shifting green, a cluster of black orbs reflected the drama below.

Darwin's left back leg was caught. He could smell his own blood, which was BAD. He could feel the emptiness of his tummy which was also BAD. But the real BAD, the *NO*-BAD was the howler pack that encircled him. They looked like dogs of a sort, but were not like him. They didn't smell like houses or boys and boy-mothers. They smelled like dirt and woods. They smelled like hunger and flies and shit. One or two of them smelled like sickness. And they sounded like the broken sirens on the giant flash animals that used to roar by the old house in the dry place. These forest dogs were longer in the leg and snout than Darwin was, but not as heavy in the middle.

Darwin could also smell their fear of him and that was GOOD. The forest dogs reeked of fear; it was an undercurrent to almost all of their other smells. Right now, fear of his jaws crushing their weak spines and tearing their thin bellies was enough to keep them back in a growling circle. But over time their fear of starvation had swollen. It pulsed like a red swarm of angry gnats. Soon it would be greater than fear of his teeth and the forest dogs would charge him.

Every so often, their crazy, hungry, terror-rage would explode and one of the forest dogs would snap at his brother. They would roll in a ball of spikey limbs and triangle teeth, then fall away from each other like wet leaves in a November wind. Eventually, they would all frenzy at the same time and boil in at him. Darwin would be able to kill one or two but in the end there would be too many. And his little doggie belly was so empty.

Darwin had about twenty boy and boy-mother words and word combinations in his mental vocabulary, most of which dealt with his behavior and food. He didn't know the name for the metal mouth-thing that had bitten his back leg around the ankle. He didn't know that some well meaning human had placed it long ago in an effort to trap the forest dogs that had been killing neighborhood cats and stealing the odd chicken from time to time. That had been when Shard was full of humans. Now, the forest dogs had taken back the woods and ran the town with near impunity. But without the trash from the humans, their smaller pets and livestock, the forest dogs had little on which to feed. Darwin would be like a huge TREAT for them, like what he got when he was a *VERY* GOOD BOY.

A flash of boy memory floated through his mind, a smell that said *Childe*. Darwin whined and gave a cracked whimper of a bark. His throat was dry and the full-bodied beagle barks he so loved to voice sounded like a trombone run over by a truck. For a moment, he thought about just stopping. In as much as he could consider, Darwin thought about laying down, putting his head on his paws and closing his tired brown eyes. The forest dogs would come in and have him. He was never going to see his boy again or the boy-mother. There wasn't much point.

One of the forest dogs sensed Darwin's thinning resolve and lunged. It moved with a sly, jerking grace, pretending to be in one spot for an instant then injecting itself into the kill zone just below Darwin's snout. Darwin spread his front legs and angled his head down. He was already lower to the ground by design than the rangy forest dog and was able to dodge under its snapping teeth. Darwin growled a strange canine roar (had Childe seen his beloved pet he might think twice before inviting him onto the couch again) and shoved his own jaws at the forest dog's throat. The metal mouth-thing threw pain up his back leg and hauled him back. Had it not been attached to a short length of chain, Darwin would have torn out his attacker's throat.

The forest dog recovered her place in the shifting ring of her fellows. Darwin showed her his teeth. *These are what just missed you.* The forest dog bared her own. *These will tear you open. These will feed my pups.* A soft summer breeze soughed through the canopy. A few fat green leaves floated to the ground.

The forest dogs grew quiet; those in front of Darwin lifted their noses over his head. Again, the scent of his boy, but stronger now. Darwin turned around and now all the animals looked up at the rim of the bowl. Climbing headfirst down the boney trunk of a venerable sycamore was a human boy. He clung to the bark with insectile prowess and righted himself on the ground with a deep bend to his lower back. Darwin's head tilted to one side, one long ear flopping over. Was that his boy? It looked like his boy and the smell was the same, but the way he moved and something else... He barked a question.

The boy lifted a gawky wave and smiled, the sun glowing through his corona of curls. The forest dogs sent up a chorus of growls and yips; one of them sat back on his shit-stiff haunches and howled. They would not be denied their windfall feast. The smallest of their number had not tasted meat in a week. The boy made no sound and took a step down the slope.

Darwin lurched back. This was wrong. Why wasn't Childe making the word sounds? Why wasn't he calling DARWIN? Why wasn't he shooing the forest dogs, calling them BAD and *NO-BAD*? The little beagle could feel that the attention of the forest dogs was off him, but he still couldn't flee or reach them to bite. What if they attacked the boy? Darwin whined and yapped but the boy took another step toward the circle.

Two of the forest dogs peeled off from the group and pounded up the side of the bowl, scrabbling for purchase in the leaves and roots. Their growls melted into slavering snarls as their snouts skinned back. Unmindful of the tearing fire in his back leg, Darwin lurched forward against the metal mouth-thing and was held fast. The forest dogs were going to kill his boy! He charged forward again and again was held fast, his wound gouged deeper. Fresh blood pumped over his fur and slicked his footing. He barked and barked. One of the forest dogs nipped his tail from behind and in his fury Darwin whirled back on himself and caught the beast in his strong jaws. His teeth crashed down on the forest dog's snout and splintered its nasal bones and the lower orbits of its eye-sockets. The blood in his mouth was bright triumph.

Darwin turned back in time to see something he couldn't understand. Childe was holding one of the forest dogs by the neck, dangling it at his side as if he were examining a ragged coat. The other lay dead at his feet in three large pieces connected to each other by sinew and intestine. The forest dog in his grip snapped and flailed, saliva flying and legs gouging air. Childe painted it with cold fascination.

The three remaining forest dogs streaked up the ridge. Childe moved almost faster than Darwin could register. He pulled his victim close and bit down hard on the back of its neck. An instant later, he dropped the limp animal and faced the other attackers. Without looking, Childe lept up and back and clung to the trunk of the sycamore. His arms and legs contorted so he was gripping the tree while facing out. The forest dogs stood up against the bark and commenced their rowdy complaints a few feet below.

Childe grinned through huge teeth and spat a long ropey substance. It enveloped the head of one of the forest dogs, but before it could pull away, Childe reached forward and began to reel it up toward him hand over hand. The last bit of strengh ran out of Darwin and he lost consciousness watching the forest dog writhe and wrench at the end of the giant string. The voice of a gentle boy-mother, a voice he had never heard before, whispered *good boy, brave Darwin,* in his head. He followed it down into sleep.

* * *

TWO MILES AWAY from where Darwin had caught his leg in an old beartrap, Loraine and Childe Howard walked a narrow deer path. This wasn't exactly a Park Service trail and they were deeper into the woods than she would have liked, but it was the kid's dog. They'd look until they couldn't.

Were it not for the grave nature of their hike, Loraine would have been loving the walk. The woods were gorgeous. Or, if you liked Frost, *lovely, dark and deep.* She hated Frost, though—sanctimonious prick. Maybe it was just that Childe's father, Jordan, had loved Frost. Anyway, she was definitely going to make a point of spending more time in the forest. She took a greedy breath and tasted verdant, cool earth, and emerald air.

She watched her son move in front of her with a steady gait, dodging under the odd spiderweb, electrified silver-white in a lucky bar of sun. Like a lot of city dwellers, the idea of getting lost didn't really occure to Loraine. It was like any other path, you just walked backward along it until you ended where you began. That and the fact that she was marking every fith tree trunk or so with a blaze of distrubingly orange lipstick; "Radioactive Rita" she thought it was called.

Loraine held her hand up in front of her, fingers tight and pointing to the side. She squinted and stacked her other hand on top and then again. She'd seen this trick on the Survival Network and used it whenever she could. You stacked your hands from the horizon to the bottom edge of the sun. Each finger was approximately fifteen minutes. So, four hands from the horizon equalled four hours. If they hadn't found Darwin yet, they'd start back two hours before sunset.

Childe looked at his watch and stopped. He faced his mother. "Sun's going to set in about four hours," he said. "We should probably head back way before that."

Loraine smirked. "Show off."

"What?"

"Nothing. Nothing. You're right."

"You were doing that thing with your hands, weren't you?"

"Quit smiling at me, punko, or when we find your dumb dog we're eating him for din—"

A long howl drooled through the trees.

Childe's eyes widened. "What the hell was that?"

"Watch that mouth, mister." Loraine scanned the forest, eyes darting into the dark spaces. "It was a coyote. Shit."

"Watch that mouth."

"Yeah, yeah." She breathed long over her teeth. "You know what, kiddo?"

"Aw, don't say we hafta go back! It's just a coyote. They hate people! It'll be okay."

"I know they're not big fans of human beings, but they're on the comeback in this part of the country. I read it in National Geographic."

"The one that's been on the coffee table for, like, ever? I read that same article. That's how come I know they're afraid of people."

"Do you also remember the bit about how that's changing now that people are moving more and more into their territory? Do you remember about how they're actually going after small pets and—." Childe's shoulders rose up around his ears. She put her hands on them, the smell of insect repellant and sweaty boy rose into her nostrils. "Honey," she lied, "I'm sure Darwin's too big."

Another series of howls and alien canine noises richochetted through the trees. It was impossible to tell distances in these woods. The hills rose and fell like waves and bounced the sound all over the place. They could be five miles away. They could be just over the next rise. And there were abandoned mine tunnels all over these hills. What the hell had she been thinking coming back here as cavalier as her son and his dog on a summer romp? A drop of sweat rolled out of her hair line. A fat fly droned. It was suddenly hot and very damp.

"We should go," she said. Loraine looked over her son's head into the green halls of the forest. Shadows shifted and twigs cracked. "We should go now."

Childe yanked free of her grip and bolted down the faint trail. "Childe Jordan Howard!" she shouted. "Get your ass back here. Right! Now!" But the boy was already twenty yards away, bounding like the deer that had made the trail. She started after him, huffing and puffing, her forty-seven-year-old lungs dry and hot. She watched his red and white striped t-shirt recede and began to feel real fear for the first time that afternoon.

Childe stopped. A moment later, Loraine pelted up next to him, breathing hard. She planted her hands on her thighs and leaned over, heaving for air. "What were you…thinking?"

"Mom?"

"Running away from me like that?"

"Mom."

"Not listening when I called after you. If you ever do that again, young man—"

"Loraine!"

She opened her eyes and straightened up. "Oh. My. God."

Slung between the trunks of two large oaks was the biggest spiderweb Loraine had ever seen in her life. It was easily twenty feet across and the strands were *thick*. They shone in the shifting sun like cables spun of peuter-silver alloy. Suspended in the center was their dog. His little tummy moved in and out with his breath in a peaceful sleep. There was more web around a patch on his lower back leg. "Darwin?" Childe asked. The beagle opened his groggy eyes and his tail began to wag. The whole web shimmered with the motion.

Chapter 4

THE MAN IN black fled across the desert.... Will Two-Bears McFarlan closed his eyes and saw the great white hardpan stretching to meet a cloudless blue—a perfect binary of land and sky. He took a deep breath and opened his eyes. The next line of text swam into focus.

And the phone rang.

Will looked at the plastic box studded with lights and numbers on the corner of his desk. When it made that annoying chirping noise, he was supposed to stick the horn-shapped thing with the cord up against his ear and say "Shard Police. Constable McFarlan here." Instead, he quick-drew his .357 and pointed it at the phone. "Do that again," he said. "I dare you."

The phone rang again.

Will pulled back the hammer.

The phone rang again.

Will pulled the trigger and got an unsatisfying "click" as the hammer fell on an empty chamber. He only loaded the huge revolver when he was on the firing range. Said firing range was actually an empty quarry just outside of town. Will leaned forward and used the end of the barrel to push the "speaker" button.

"Shard Po-leece. Constable McFarlan here."

A smirking female voice filled the room. "Howdy, Prisoner. It's Amy James."

"Oh, hiya, Amy." Will clunked the pistol down and grabbed the handset. The image of the petite punk-rock-girl with blue hair and tattoo sleeves flickered just under his consciousness. "What can I do for you?"

She had rolled into town during George's last bender—some kind of geological survey specialist. Amy had shown Will permits granting her access to the mine and given him a quick tour of the RV she rode in on. It was half mobile laboratory and half living space full of equipment and monitors. *Doctor* James (she was as Ph. and Deeded as you could get) explained to Will and George (who had staggered into the office proper to make coffee and listen in) that she was in Shard at the bequest of an energy company called Blackstone. They wanted to know if the seam and remaining gas pockets under Shard were viable, and if so, was there a way to get at them.

At first, Will had trouble wrapping his mind around this twenty-something woman with the wild hair and body art as any kind of scientist, but once she showed him the RV and started talking in a manner reminiscent of his old geology teacher, he bought it well enough. Besides, like any good cop (even small town ones, maybe *especially* small town ones) Will possessed an uncanny lie-detector. She was on the level about her reasons for being there. And, blue hair aside (hell, maybe because of it) pretty darn cute to boot.

Her permits were in order and so he gave her directions to the old mine headquarters building on the ridge above town. He promised to check in on her every now and again and was considering asking her to have dinner with him if the first "check in" went well. He had been planning on heading up there the next morning, but here she was calling him.

"I have a little problem, Will."

He could get used to her saying his name. "What's the situation?" *Situation* was a cop word. He rolled his eyes at himself. "What's up?"

"A woman and her son wandered out of the woods a few mintues ago. They had their dog with them, but the dog's been hurt. She says her name's Loraine Howard?"

Will sat up. "Yeah, you said her son's there, too. Kiddo?"

"He said his name was Childe. Like the poem I guess?"

Childe Roland to the Dark Tower Came. Will smiled. He'd liked Loraine right away when he learned that she had named her kid after the inspiration for Roland of Gilead. And Amy James knew that poem, too. "So what's going on?"

"Well, I guess they got a little lost looking for their dog and," she paused, "saw something that shook them up pretty badly."

"Are they okay? They're not hurt?"

"No, no, they're fine."

Will could hear the papery rasp of a hand pressed down on the receiver and then Amy's voice was back. "Will, Mrs. Howa—okay, Loraine—wants to talk with you for a sec'."

"Put her on, Amy, thanks."

"Loraine?" he said. "Y'all okay?"

Will listened as the tinny voice leaked out between his ear and the phone. It shared his office with dusty evening sunlight and silence. Every now and again Will spiced the mix with a "Yup." or a "Nope." and a series of "Okay, what else?" A square of orange sun had crawled an inch across his desk by the time he said, "I better come out there. Stay put."

* * *

AMY LEANED AGAINST the RV, a hand-rolled cigarette hanging between her lips. She smoked and watched the boy pet his dog while the beagle lapped from the bowl of water she'd fetched for him. Loraine sat on a folding chair under the RV's roll-away awning next to a plastic table strewn with rock samples, each sporting a tiny white tag—evidence of Amy's first three days of work. The cup of tea Amy had brewed for her sat un-sipped next to a sample of low grade anthracite shot through with a vein of some lighter colored stuff.

Amy didn't know how to talk to either of them. It wasn't that they didn't have anything in common. Matter of fact, they had plenty in common. Amy had gotten her Ph.D. at the School of Mines in Colorado and then had taken a job with Blackstone at their So. Cal. offices. Turned out they were practically neighbors when the Howards still lived in Hollywood. As a rule, Amy wasn't terrific around kids, but they didn't freak her out or anything. And Loraine seemed pretty cool. Writers, if anything, tended to be more accepting of the blue-haired, tattooed set. She'd known a couple from L.A. and they were all at least a little punk rock down deep, even the ones who didn't know it. Small talk should have been easy. It was just that Loraine and her kid were completely fucking crazy.

An hour earlier, Amy had been swabbing off the samples she'd collected with ethyl alcohol so the spectrometer in the RV lab could get a cleaner reading. The sun had swelled into a huge orange ball just over the tree line. The parking lot outside of the abandoned mine headquarters building was crazed with cracks and fissures bleeding up fountains of weeds. The August cicadas were scratching out their *ree-ree-reeeeeee* serenade and the air was infused with cool, organic smells. The big square states out west where Amy had grown up and spent almost all of her life didn't make smells like this. The Appalachian forest was verdant and peaceful in a way even the mountain woods outside Durango were not—older, secret.

Loraine and Childe (cradling the beagle like it was a baby he'd just rescued from a tenement fire) had come stumbling out of that emerald verge and called out to her. A startled shriek had spiked Amy's sternum, but she'd held it back, feeling the burn and tingle of stress chemicals distill in her muscles. A moment later, she was offering them a chair and listening to a deluge of babble about giant spiderwebs, coyotes and strange feelings of being watched. She'd nodded through it all, getting the water for the dog and tea for the human, finally giving up and calling Shard's version of Andy Griffith.

Now, she stood and thought about rolling another nail even though she was only three drags into the first one. The smoke was a fragrant, thick blue in the deepening gloom. Amy'd been thinking about firing up an altogether different kind of hand-rolled cigarette and smoking the sun down before the woods belched the Howards and their *Scooby-Doo* meets *Tales From the Darkside* story. It could have been *such* a nice evening.

The silence was punctuated only by the undulating cicada opera and the slurp of a thirsty dog until Childe finally broke it. "I like your hair," he said.

Amy blinked, focused through the smoke. Good looking kid, a little gawky, tall for twelve, but he'd bloom okay she guessed. "Thanks."

"Why blue?"

Amy glanced at the boy's mother. Loraine was smiling into her tea and keeping out of it. In fact, Amy had the distinct impression that she was somehow recording the scene. She tugged a short hank over her forehead and crossed her eyes to look at it. "Dunno," she said finally. "Guess I just dig on the Smurfs."

"Like instead of Smurfette you'd be Punkette?"

Amy could feel the smirk rising. She already liked the little smartass. "Maybe I'd be more like the one who had the tattoo, though, right?" She flexed a painted biceps and a respectable bulge rippled through a section of vines and jungle birds.

Childe's eyes widened. "Handy," he said. "His name was Handy-Smurf, but he only had the one heart tattoo. You got like a million." He looked thoughtful. "Naw, I think it ought to be Punkette." He stuck out a tennis shoe and nudged his mother's foot under the table. "What do you think, Mom? Punkette?"

Loraine threw a wink at Amy. "I think you're pushing it is what I think, Kiddo."

Amy dropped her cigarette and stubbed it out under her work boot. She leaned forward and grabbed a baseball-shaped hunk of gray rock off the table that sat a little away from the others. It had a rubber band wrapped around the middle. "Check this out, bud." She underhand tossed it to Childe who snatched it out of the air.

"What it is?"

"Ooh, I know what that is," Loraine said. "Take off the rubber band, right Amy?"

"Yep. Just don't drop it when you do."

But instead of a simply ripping open the mystery, Childe paused and held the rock up to this nose. He inhaled and then stuck the tip of tongue out, tasting the lunar-like exterior.

"Childe Howard!"

"No, no, it's okay,"Amy said through a half smile. "That's how the pros do it, too. Go ahead, Kiddo." It was an easy nickname to roll into. And then to Loraine, "It's been cleaned already anyway."

Childe slipped the rubber band off the rough sphere, but held the two the halves together in his fist. He turned over his shoulder and placed the rubber loop on top of Darwin's head like a little crown. The beagle shifted his eyebrows, but left his weary head on his paws. Childe turned back and split the rock. "Awwwwwwesome!" In each hand he now held the hollowed-out half of a geode. Spiky clutches of crystal reflected the light in a mellow Beaujolais. "This is so cool."

"It's amythest, right?" asked Loraine.

"Yep. Pulled that guy out of a creek about a mile back into the woods." Amy threw a glance into the inky edge of the parking lot. "I guess you'd call it a *crick* out here, though, right?" She looked back at Loraine. "Actually, from what you said you two probably had to cross it to get here."

Loraine tried to remember their panicked flight through the woods after pulling Darwin free of the giant web or whatever it had been. (She was now questioning herself even more than their new friend must surely be.) They'd lost the trail almost immediately in their dash in spite of her careful lipstick trail blazing. Ridiculous, ignorant risk to have taken with her boy. She could hear Jordan in her head yelling his dissaproval for such an air-headed stunt. Shouldn't someone who spent so much of her time ignoring her husband in favor of writing and research have more common sense? They had come to a shallow creek (crick) after some time—perhaps had even been drawn by its chuckling—and splashed through it like runaway slaves evading the hounds. It stuck in her memory mostly because of the sense of relief she'd felt after crossing that liquid line. Vampires weren't supposed to be able to cross running water. Maybe it worked for all kinds of beasties. Foolish, her rational mind told her, but nonetheless, she'd felt safer after they'd crossed.

"Old stories," she muttered, "old tales, old wives."

"Sorry?"

"Oh, nothing. Just babbling," Loraine said, now finally tasting her tea. Orange something or other. Sharp in her stress-dry mouth. "We did see the creek, but didn't stop to pan for geodes."

"Crick," said Childe.

"Cricket," said Amy and rubbed one shin against the other. "Reet-reet, reet-reet."

Childe looked at her. "You're weird."

Loraine was staring into her tea again.

"Yeah, well, you're short."

"I'm almost as tall as you!"

"*Almost*, shorty." She fake-scowled at him. "You can keep that alien asteroid if you want."

Childe beamed. "Really? Awesome! Thanks, Amy."

"Yep." Amy caught the doggie lifting one ear just as a low rumble began to overpower the cicadas. "Sounds like a motorcycle," she said.

"That," Loraine said, "would be our dear Constable Ursa-Duo."

"Ursa-Duo?"

"Greek for Two-Bears," Childe said, eyes crackling over the geode. "Mom likes to show off."

"He's right, I do."

"He's got a scoot, huh?" Any lifted an eyebrow not unlike Darwin a moment before. "I likes me some motorcycles."

Loraine threw her another wink.

* * *

TWENTY MINUTES LATER, the sun was down, the mosquitos were fierce and the RV was full of people. Amy was scraping at samples in the back; the *ruck, ruck, ruck* of her work hypnotic background music. Will had just finished questioning the Howards in the driving area, sitting on a short stool between and behind the two swiveling captain's chairs. Childe was planted behind the steering wheel. Will couldn't imagine a greater terror than this twelve-year-old boy, clever as he may be, piloting a vehicle the size of a small house. Will was looking over the scrawl in his pocket-notebook when Loraine spoke up.

"Will, I know how it must sound." She laughed. "Jesus, that's bad dialogue."

"Sorry?"

"That sentence would never survive a first edit if it were in one of my scripts."

Will sighed and closed the notebook. "You're okay, Loraine. I don't think you're nuts. I think you and Kiddo here just had a real bad scare and maybe got a little confused. I've lived around here my whole life and these woods, especially when it's starting to get dark, can get massively freaky."

Childe sat forward. "So you don't think there're any coyotes?"

"No, no." Will held up a hand. "I *know* there're coyotes." He pronounced it KY-oats. "Since the mine closed they been creepin' back more and more. And even when Shard was in its glory days, they'd still snatch the odd chicken or randy tom out on the prowl."

"But the other stuff," Lorain said.

Will pulled off his cap and a fall of hair so black it was almost blue belled around his head. Loraine tried not to giggle at his horrendous hat-hair, but it wasn't all that hard. Young Constable McFarlan was plenty easy on her eyes. Were those eyes and everything below them ten years younger—well, Amy James wasn't the only woman in this RV who liked her some motorcycles. He ran his hand through his hair and looked at the stars on his shoes.

"The other stuff," he started. "I've been thinking a little about that as you went over everything. Here's what we know: Neither you nor your son're crazy or taking hallucinogenics, right?" Loraine had the urge to make a joke about writers and magic mushrooms, but let it go. Will went on. "We also know that you two have only been in this part of the world for a few months, i.e. you're not terribly familiar with the flora and fauna."

"What's that mean?" Childe asked.

"That we don't know jack about those woods or what's in 'em, boy o' my heart." Lorain offered. "Right, Constable?"

"Right. And finally, the spider web. Now, I've seen orb weaver webs back in the woods this time of year and even into early fall that are near as big as you describe." His eyes sparkled. "They're really neat, actually. Scare the bejesus outta' me, but cool in a Discovery Channel kind of way."

"You're not suggesting a little spider caught a forty pound dog?" Lorain said.

The scraping from the back stopped.

"No, what I guess happened is that Darwin was really caught up in some vines or something like that and this big ol' orb weaver web got all dragged into it. You two were a little freaked out already what with the coyotes howling and being a little lost, right? Isn't it possible your brains just kind of supplied the scary details?"

Loraine stared down at this handsome young man with the Kentucky accent like honey dripped over his words and wanted to give him a good whap upside his head. Sure, sure, the wacko writer from the "Other Coast" and her imaginative little boy had themselves a little episode in the woods. Sure. Bullshit.

She took a deep breath. "Constable, I don't believe in giant spiders outside of bad horror flicks from the fifties and Peter Jackson movies. I am not prone to hallucinations, mass hysteria, alien abduction, or belief in Sasquatch."

"C'mon, now, Loraine. I wasn't saying—"

She pointed at him and he sat back on his stool, a student reprimanded for talking in class. "My son is not prone to hallucinations, mass hysteria, or alien abduction."

It was out of Will's mouth before he could stop himself. "What about Sasquatch?"

"Oh, I'm *totally* tight with Big Foot." Childe beamed. "But Mom's right. It wasn't vines, Constable Will. It was a big Spider-Man spiderweb. We didn't just think it was, or whatever, because we were scared." He leaned down and stroked Darwin's velvet ear. "And besides, what about this bandage thing on his back leg? It's spiderweb, too."

"Kiddo, I'm guessing that he just ran through part of that big, but normal, web I think you two saw and got a bunch of it on his leg." Will squinted and leaned forward. "How come you didn't take that off him?"

"It's stopped his bleeding," Loraine said. She sat back and crossed her arms. "Childe looked under it when we found him and there was a pretty decent gash. That *normal* web stuff is making it better."

"Well, that's good luck," said Will. "Spider web is a natural coagulant. The old folks all up and down the Appalachians have been using it for centuries on cuts and things like that. Something to do with the proteins. There're certain mosses that are good, too."

Loraine just stared at him.

"I'm not going to convince you, am I?" Will asked.

"Doesn't look that way," Loraine said.

Will put his hands on his knees. "Okay, I'll trek on back there first thing tomorrow and see if I can't find what you saw. You said you marked the trail up to that point from the back of your house with this orange lipstick, right? I should be able to follow it well enough. I'll take my camera and we'll put paid to this once and for all. Deal?"

"That sounds fine," Loraine said.

"Constable, Will?" Childe asked.

"Yeah, Kiddo?"

"Take your gun, okay?"

* * *

FROM THE EDGE of the parking lot, the RV looked like the coziest of mountain cabins. The muffled voices from within blurred to indistinction by the time they reached the boy standing

27

at the border between woods and asphalt. Curly blonde head tipped to one side, he seemed to be listening or daydreaming. Gore and bits of brown fur ringed his mouth. His eyes were inhuman black saucers. He inhaled long and deep through his nose, scenting the humans and the brave dog. He smiled. The dog would be fine.

Chapter 5

THE FLIES BUZZED, describing lazy helixes and figure eights over a pile of week-old bodies. The flesh-drunk cloud of shifting emerald and black droned over a faint crackling—the second generation mining paths to the light. Ricky Dunbar—*Trickie Ricky* to those who knew of his beginnings as a tina hustler in the Castro—gave birth from a split in the bloated flesh of his left cheek. He'd been fine-faced, edged just so around softer features, his whole face suggestive of full lips turned up sly. After a week on the floor of this farmhouse outside of Ricochet, Montana, Tricky Ricky had become beautiful in an altogether different way. The rest of the gang—two men and one woman—had joined him in his new aesthetic.

Across the room, through an almost visible stench, squatted an old couch. Long arms spread along the back, naked and bone white, shot through with a relief of cerulean veins. Black-leathered legs crossed at the knee, the lambskin creaking once a minute or so as the wearer respired. Were it not for the telltale expansion of accordion ribs, one could assume this to be a fresher member of the gang. Behind great round sunglasses his face was etched marble, thin mouth pressed closed. He hadn't desired a growth of beard since taking this seat seven days ago, so a shadow had not broken his cheeks, as the maggots had broken Ricky's. His hair, long and black as his leather shanks, painted his shoulders and along the length of his arms.

A questing botfly corkscrewed away from the mound and landed on a black-laquered fingernail. All cellular activity ceased. It fell into the pile of flies drifted in a rough outline around the figure on the couch. He, or it, for beneath the leather pants he was smooth as a manequin, sighed. Another one bites the dust.

"I am the dust," he muttered.

A thousand flies pattered down in a short, grey downpour. The couch sitter enjoyed the silence for a moment, letting it crash against the shores of his skull. He slapped his knees once and lurched to his feet.

He would have been tall, over six feet, but his spine curved at the top, humping his torso over in a question mark. His arms and hair hung forward and swung as he loped across the room past the gang. His boot nudged a protruding elbow, or something—it was already getting hard to tell—and the mound released a rude breath from some secret orifice. His pencil thin eyebrow rose. The machinations of the human body never ceased to amuse.

He rounded a corner into the bathroom and found himself in the mirror over the sink. The bathroom was spotless. Even the grout beneath the toes of the claw-foot tub was bleached white. The bad air from the living room had penetrated the entire house on a molecular level, but he could still smell the tang of mildew cleaner in here. Twyla, the female section of the mound, had been a cleaner when she was high on crank. Since that had pretty much been her constant state, Ricky had banished her to the bathroom.

Most of the rest of the house looked like it had played host to a troop of transients, camping out instead of really moving in. Soiled sleeping bags like cast off larval carapaces snugged against the corners of the bedrooms. Used condoms crystallized at the bottom of empty Jack Daniels bottles. Cigarette butts were as numerous as dead flies, foaming out of beer can ashtrays. Under the smell of corruption was the chemical knife of the meth lab they'd set up in the kitchen. And the bathroom, the squeaky clean bathroom with its Windex-clear mirror.

The man-thing curled his long fingers around the sides of the sink and leaned into his reflection. He reached up and removed the saucer sunglasses. His eyes were huge, nearly as large as the sunglasses and darker, all pupil. The light in the small room seemed to dim as they sucked at it, the scoured tiles greying as if a shadow passed over the sun. He blinked lashless sockets. His lips skinned back over a bushel of cannibal teeth. His voice rose out of his throat, deep and dry, buzzing.

"I am so bored," he said.

He blinked again, longer this time and when he opened his eyes they were normal sized and yellow brown. His squinted and a few days' crop of stubble shaded his jaw. He took another grain from the million-year hourglass of his existence and checked his reflection; he would pass. It was time to go back to his begininning on this plane. Time to go back to the mother-cut. Back to Shard.

Chapter 6

ERICA SLAMMED INTO consciousness, her breath coming in short bursts, her heart thrumming. Early morning sun electrified the perimeter of the windowshade, a neon square in the dark. A green LED flickered on the smoke detector on the ceiling. Old, moist cigarette smoke, engraved into every surface, wrinkled her nose. She was in that shitbag chain motel outside of the county seat about forty miles north of Shard. The only sound was her breath. Something had yanked her out of her Ambien-induced yuppie-coma. Erica listened, an animal in the dark sensing danger.

The digital clock flicked through a couple of minutes to 6:14AM. Hell with this. She'd had a bad dream or something. It was just another hotel room in another town, another assignment, another step. It wasn't a half-suite at The W, that was for damn sure, but there wasn't anything to freak out about; a normal room—shitty, small, redolent of bulk-purchased cleaning products and short-term human habitation.

Erica lay back in the dark and stared at the blinking LED. She started thinking about her day. She'd gotten in too late the previous evening (ass-fucked by MapQuest yet again) to get any work done at the courthouse. With no cell signal to speak of, she had finally surrendered and pulled off the single-lane blacktop at the first habitation she'd seen in thirty miles of aimless wandering. The doublewide trailer had sloped so deeply in the middle that it looked like it could fall in any day. A short woman, roughly as wide as she was tall, had answered the door and looked everywhere but at Erica. (Not her fault, really, the poor thing had the worse case of walleye Erica had ever seen.) She got proper directions, thanked the back-woods cliché who gave them, and got back into the rented Subaru Outback. The Motel 8 loomed out of the darkness several turns and dark, tree-walled roads later. Had it not been for the walleyed woman, Erica might have driven around in circles all night on that labrynth of back roads. The thought frosted her skin more than the car's air conditioning.

The young woman at the front desk assured her that the courthouse wouldn't be open until tomorrow at 10 A.M. and didn't she just have the most beautiful hair! How'd she get it all wavey an' streaky like that? Where was she from? New York! Manhattan! Really? What was it like? Were there just, like, a billion people there? Was she afraid of terrorists? There was this one time? When she and her sister, Olivia-Jean? Had been up to the Walmart in Lewiston? And they'd seen these Arabic guys in turbans? It had really freaked them out. Did Erica want a wake up call? She was in room 124.

Erica needed records, deeds, avenues of infiltration and opportunity. She wanted at least three plausible legal strategies for relocating every last pathetic hold-over in Shard. The lower the cost to the Blackstone Mineral the better. The simpliest, of course, would be to just buy everyone out. There couldn't be more than a hundred people still living in that smoke hole, if that, and their homes were virtually worthless. They should thank Blackstone for buying them out at a dollar per square foot, but you didn't make partner for following the most obvious course of action. Erica wanted a way to get the people of Shard off their land for nothing. Hell, maybe she'd find a way to make all those rednecks pay Blackstone for discounted relocation assistance.

She smiled and stretched her legs; her silk harem pants a luxuriant armor against the course hotel sheets. They probably had a thread count of about, oh, one. She should think about getting up and taking a run and shower before heading to the courthou—

A loud buzz, like a cicada caught under a papercup broke the silence. Erica sat up. Jesus, what the fuck? It came again and this time she noticed the movement behind the window shade. That's what had woken her up, some kind of pissed-off insect. It buzzed again, thrashing against the window and the shade. Erica wasn't afraid to swat a bee or whatever (flying bugs she could deal with, it was spiders that wigged her out), but this thing sounded *huge*.

She had to do something. If she just sat there in the dark the little monster could get out and start flying around the room. Jesus, it probably had been while she'd been sleeping. Erica reached over and fumbled for the lamp by the bedside table. She found the neck and moved her fingers up the cheap brass to the switch. Her hand closed over a spikey lump that jumped to life like a joy buzzer. She flinched and pain stabbed through the webbing of her thumb and index finger.

"Owoohshit!" she screamed and rolled away off the other side of the bed to the floor. She pulled her hand between her breasts, fighting panic. There was a bee in here and it had stung her. That was all, she was okay. She wasn't allergic or anything. How the fuck had it gotten from behind the shade to the lamp so fast? Slowly, she reached up and found the lamp on that side of the bed. With iron will she forced herself to feel up the neck for the switch. It was nearly statistically impossible that she would find another bee in the same place as the last one, but her hindbrain was screeching at her not to do it. She jerked away when her fingers touched the protruding switch, but she controlled herself and clicked on the light.

Erica shrank down on her haunches. "Dios mothah*fuck*," she whispered. The ceiling writhed with the biggest wasps she had ever seen. No, hornets, these could only be thought of as hornets. They were each about the size of her thumb and blue-black. There had to be near a hundred of them sprayed across the waterstained plaster not six feet above her head. The light seemed to wake them up a bit. A few detached and began to float around the room, cruising black helicopters.

Erica's will descended like a lead-lined curtain. Her skin cooled and breathing slowed. She had to get out, but if she bolted for the door it might goose the hornets into attacking her. God, they were huge, *huge!* No, no, she was cool. She was okay. They were just a bunch of fucking back-water bugs that had a nest in the motel she would soon own through the lawsuit she would file as soon as she got the fuck back to New York. She exhaled and began to crawl across the carpet toward the door. Details in the carpet seared her eyes—the acne scars of cigarette burns, the rorschach patterns of ancient stains. Oh, look, that one looked like a woman being stung to death.

Sensing her motion, the rest of the hornets took wing and filled the upper two feet of the room like a flashover in a housefire. The hum was loud and harmonized. It invaded Erica's mind and pulled at her eyelids. The door seemed so far away. Everything hummed. Maybe she could just lie down on the carpet.

It smelled dusty and a little bit like asphalt. She could just press her humming head onto the humming carpet and hum for a while.

A motion caught her eye at the corner. She watched a large grey-brown house-spider stride out from under the bed a few inches from her hand. As spiders went, she'd seen bigger, but it was enough. She yanked her hand away and exploded toward the door on all fours, hammering her knees and the heels of her hands across the floor. The humming smoke turned into a growling storm cloud. She yanked at the door, but it wouldn't open more than a couple of inches. Fragrant summer morning wafted through the gap. Tires sighed on the road. She had to get out! Erica yanked and jerked, but the door wouldn't move. *Cool it, chica,* she thought, *it's just the chain.* Erica reached up and unlatched it, then whipped around the door, closing it behind her.

Quiet poured over her.

The buzzing from those hornets had been *infernal.* She wrapped her arms around herself and hugged. Erica closed her eyes and counted to ten; she dug her fingernails into her arms with each count. She opened her eyes and looked out on the little parking lot. Dew quicksilvered the windshield of her Subaru. A songbird perched on a powerline across the road like a comma on an otherwise empty line of notebook paper. She took a breath, another, another. The air smelled of deep green and high summer. Okay. Okay.

Erica turned around and jumped. "Holy shit."

The window was coated with hornets, black and sharp as obsidian chips, but safely on the other side of the glass. Erica covered her mouth and felt her eyes go wide. Her hand complained and she examined the angry red welt. She could actually see the fucking hole the stinger had made. Oh, she was so going to sue the hell out of this place. Had that little redneck skank who'd checked her in last night known her room was infested? Maybe she'd thought it would be funny to teach the big-time city girl, (the Spic, perhaps) a little lesson?

Erica shook her head and stared at the writhing mass. The hornets flowed around and over each other, dragging pendulous abdomens, great poison factories, behind them. They cleaned their antenna with garden-shear jaws and sucked at the light with oil drop eyes. Erica took a step toward the window and they froze, becoming a framed poster of hornets. It wasn't that they slowed, or just a portion of them stopped crawling—they ceased all motion, not a wing tip twitched. She felt as if she were dreaming. Erica reached out and flattened her hand against the glass. The world silenced. Then, very low, Erica heard a ticking like miniature hail blown against a tin roof. She squinted and looked close. Where her hand touched it, the hornets were stinging the glass.

THE MOTEL OWNER stood behind the counter like a pudding with delusions of humanity. "I'm sorry, miss," he said. "We just couldn't find no bees in your room."

Erica had been standing in what passed for a lobby at this fistula of hell for the past twenty-five minutes, in her pajamas, arguing with a man who smelled like eggs and took her about as seriously as a page ripped out of a porn 'zine. "That's probably because the swarm of prehistoric fucking *hornets* fucking ate them."

"I'm sorry?" No light behind those watery peepers, nothing.

"Not half as sorry as I am," she sighed, and pinched the bridge of her nose. Uhg, her own morning breath pounded up her nose. Lovely. Couldn't be worse than the way this yokel smelled. "Listen, for the millionth time, maybe they went back to their nest—wherever the hell that was, in the ceiling or whatever—but when I woke up there were at least fifty or sixty enormous black hornets in the room." There had been more like two-hundred, but fifty or sixty sounded less hysterical. She held up her throbbing left hand. "See this? I didn't ram a spear through my own hand, pal." *Pal*, that was one her father's. Whenever he'd slam some punk up against the patrol car, he'd call him "Pal". Erica wanted to do that, slam this fat bastard's face straight down on the counter. Instead she held up her palms in surrender.

"Fine," she said. "Fine. I just want to check out."

"Well, okay, but don't you want to go back to your room and collect your things?" He scanned her body for the fortieth time. "Your, um, clothes and sundries and all?"

Erica paused. Twenty minutes ago she wouldn't have set foot back in that room for a partnership at the firm, but now curiosity itched behind her forehead. She reset her face to pleasant mode. "Yes, of course. I'm just a little flustered, I suppose. Listen, sir, could you maybe—while I'm collecting my sundries—call ahead to Shard and book me a room?"

He leaned a hip against the counter, a wedge of hairy belly flowing over the lip. "Shard, huh. You, uh, got folks there?"

"No."

"Well, they had a motor court but it closed down a long time ago." He chuckled and a ripple traveled his flesh. "Pretty much *everything's* closed in Shard."

"Well, where else is there to stay in the general area?"

"Other than here?"

"Yeah, other than here."

He rubbed his cheek. "Well, miss, I don't think you'll have much luck. There's Mechanicsville about fifty mile up County 31, but other than that…" he opened his hands and trailed off.

"And there's nothing in Shard? Nothing at all? A B&B, something?"

"Well, there is a boarding house down there. The Rhodes family used to run it, but I think there's only the son there now.'

Erica brightened. "Do you think he'd rent me a room?"

"Might do. Might do."

"Do you think you could call him while I go get my things?"

"Nope."

She raised her eyebrows and imagined stabbing a railroad spike through the flab of his neck. She could almost feel the hot gush on her wrist. "Nope?"

"No phone." He showed her his teeth. Still had most of them.

ERICA STOOD IN the door of her room and watched the owner's daughter, a sallow teen with stringy hair, make the bed. He'd been so huge and she was like a greased pipecleaner. She turned with a start when Erica cleared her throat.

"Oh, miss, you gave me such a scare!"

"Sorry," Erica said. Here eyes were everywhere, every shadow seemed to jump and crawl.

"I got the room all cleaned up for you," the girl said, "in case you changed your mind about leavin' us?"

"You didn't see anything? Find any of the hornets I saw?"

The girl tugged the bedspread up and fluffed a pillow. "I found a big old spider, but we're in the woods here. You're gonna' have them. They don't hurt nobody, though. He was all curled up dead, anyhow."

She thinks I'm crazier than a shithouse rat. That one was one of her mother's. When had they become hers? Erica crossed the threshold into the room. "No," she said. "Thank you. I'm going." Erica popped the handle on her slick, black suitcase and wheeled it into the bathroom.

She was waiting for herself in the mirror, dark circles framing eyes that were a little too big. Had the wasps been a dream? Could it have been something so pedestrian, so weak? She planted her hands on the side of the sink and pain flared. No, she'd been stung by something. Maybe it was the sleeping pills and the stress mixed with an adrenalin dump from the sting. Maybe there had only been one hornet and her mind had produced the others. Maybe, maybe…maybe she was just going to wash her face and get the fuck out of here.

* * *

GEORGE STOOD IN front of himself, hands on the sink, mouth open. His reflection had a coated tongue and the shirt he'd passed-out in last night hung off boney shoulders. His eyes felt like wooden ball bearings painted to resemble a person's. He squinted. The paint was peeling. Metallic-blonde wisps hung down over his forehead. The guy in the glass looked about forty, maybe forty-five. Today was George's thirty-fourth birthday. He pointed at the older fella in the mirror.

"You need a drink, dude."

A triple fall of bells wafted into the bathroom. The old dude in the mirror lifted an eyebrow. It came again. Doorbell. Right. George tried to imagine who might hate him enough to ring his doorbell first thing in the morning. (Well, okay, it was around ten, but "first thing" was a relative term.)   That ancient excuse for an elementary school teacher, Missus Najarian, gave him the hairy eyeball every time their paths crossed, but other than that his enemies list was pretty short these days. There just weren't enough people around Shard to hate him. Besides, George was the kind of drunk who really only hurt himself. He didn't tend to take it out on others. The bell again and it now had an insistent tone somehow.

George ran the tap (got water instead of smoke—another good day in Shard) and rinsed out his mouth. Moisture infused his tissues and brightened his mind a bit. He splashed his face and toweled off. The bell. "Comin'!" he shouted, and winced at his own volume. Nothing was louder than your own voice. He moved through the cool scent of oil-soap and old, clean linens that pervaded the Victorian his parents had left him.

The house was in good order. George lived a disposable life, eating from cans and prepared trays of microwaveable fuel. There were no empty bottles lying around, drawing miniature dust devils made of fruit flies. Open the oven, now, and you'd find your Beef Eater and Bombay. George, like dear old Mom, was a hider not a cooker. And he actually enjoyed doing laundry. Lots of time to sit n' sip in between loads so his clothes were clean and folded.

The top half of the wide front door was a stained-glass depiction of the Arc Angel Michael menacing a naked couple as they fled the garden. Mother's little reminder that sexual congress was sinful. In spite of those baleful glass eyes, there had been a fair amount of squeaking bedsprings in Rhode's Boarding House during the wee hours of George's childhood. Blue and red painted the sharp planes of his face as he reached for the crystal doorknob.

He blinked three times, carefully, deliberately, to make sure he wasn't seeing a gin fairy. When she spoke, George was convinced—The Most Beautiful Woman in the World was standing on his doorstep. A strange emotion heated his face. Up until the last few years it had been the undercurrent of his life, but this was first time in at least the last half decade that George Rhodes had felt shame.

Erica waited a moment, another, but when the zombie in the doorway didn't say anything, she asked, "Is this the boarding house?"

George straightened up to his full six-foot-three. A fiery belch ratcheted up his gullet. If he opened his mouth he would douse her with used gin fumes. George nodded and smiled. He bowed his head and stepped to the side, welcoming her in like any good Southern Gentleman should. Erica paused for a second, peering into the shadowy throat of the house. It was this or sleep in her car. She conjured a smile and walked in. George exhaled his belch into the morning air once her back was to him and closed the door on it.

Erica looked around the foyer. Mouldings gleamed and the wide floorboards stretched away to meet the tumble of a large staircase. The air was clean and something in her midsection relaxed with the first breath. She wished she'd known to come here first. "You have a lovely home," she said, turning to find George with his back to the scattering stained glass. He seemed a little less freakshow now. It looked like the sunlight had really been punishing him. And it smelled like he'd had a serious party the night before. Well, there probably wasn't much else to do in this shithole town. "You do let rooms, right?"

"Yup," George thought fast. He couldn't talk to her like this. "Would you like to sit down in the parlour for a moment, Miss…?"

"I'm Erica Mendez."

"George Rhodes, ma'am. Would you excuse me for a just a quick second? I'll be right back, and we'll get you settled." George didn't wait for her answer. He zipped into the parlour, motioning toward a chaise longue in a large bay window, and disapeared around the corner. He was up the kitchen stairs and into the bathroom before Erica even had a chance to take a seat. She heard him close the door.

George was waiting for himself in the mirror, but something was different. The eyes were real now, not some dollmaker's approximation. He yanked himself to the side as he opened the medincine cabinet. There it was: two birds with one swig. George grabbed the big bottle of green mouthwash and drank down half of it. Now his hands wouldn't shake *and* his breath wouldn't peel the paint off the walls. He grabbed the clean shirt hanging on the back of the door and buttoned up on his way back down stairs.

Erica had pulled aside the heavy drapes and sat in a bolt of sun. She turned toward him and smiled as he walked into the room. George blinked again and grinned.

"What brings you to Shard?"

Chapter 7

WILL WALKED ALONG the deer trail, daydreams flowing over his mind as coins of sunlight flowed over his shoulders. The coal seam ran under his boots. A whiff of sulphur mixed with the black-tea smell of rotting leaf-litter. The seam must be deep here, or the smoulder would fill this part of the woods with smoke. Closer to the main shaft the sticky coal smoke had stripped the trees and turned the sky white, but this was still forest. Will took a long breath.

There was every chance these woods wouldn't even be here if the mine hadn't caught fire. Mountaintop removal was the name of the game these days. These lovely woods would be little more than heaps of slag. He shamed himself for thinking it, but sometimes Will Two-Bears wondered if The Fire hadn't been a good thing.

His people, the Cherokee, had husbanded the forest with fire. Every so often they would set a blaze to clear the undergrowth and open up the woods for easier hunting. This forest, like most in the Appalachians, had already been logged a few times long after most of the Cherokee had been frog-marched west. The trees shading Will's baseball cap were only about fifty years old. Maybe the fire would keep the logging companies at bay as well. Will stepped over a fallen log. How long had it been since a lone Cherokee hunter had walked this forest?

He smiled to himself. *His* people. What a load of shit. His mother had hitched off the reservation in Southern Virginia when the casinos started sprouting like questionable mushrooms. She'd found work waitressing in a little mining town a few months later and met his Irish Catholic father. Charlotte Two-Bears had been used to ignoring the soot-smeared miners with their grabby hands and racist bullshit about redskin this and Pocahontas that. But Jack's McFarlan's eyes—blue diamonds in the black dust—had been kind and quick. He'd always called her ma'am and meant it. If Will had ever had any *people*, it had been his folks.

Dad was six years in the ground now, Mom four. The explosion at the mine hadn't taken Jack's life, just his job. It was the job itself that took his breath away, trading black dust for pink tissue. Again, maybe The Fire had been a good thing. If Jack had been allowed to keep working, Charlotte and Will might have had even less time to enjoy his quiet presence and quick, kind eyes. Will might have had more time with Mom before the depression got her. The death certificate said complications from diabetes but Will knew better. When they put Jack under the soil, Charlotte got burried too. She just kept walking around for a couple of years before she realized it.

Will squinted up into the sun. A person or ghost walking with him would have been forgiven for thinking he was about to cry for a second there. He decided to smile and spit over his left shoulder instead. Jack and Charlotte were under the ground on the other side of town behind the clapboard Methodist Church. The seam had sent a tongue of smoke and heat under there a few months after Charlotte went in. One day—if it hadn't started already—the ground would subside and the dead would rain down into the forge. Either way, Mom and Dad were under the earth and Will was still walking it. *Keep your thoughts in the sun, William.* That's what Jack had told him when Will asked how his father could stand working down in the dark all day.

A dry stick snapped underfoot. Will stopped and looked down. Not a stick, a bone. He picked it up and turned it over. Probably a femur. It was big but not too big. Too big would have been human big. This was only dog or... "Ah-ha," he said to himself. "Here's at least some of your coyotes, Kiddo."

Will held the bone in close, catching the dusty mustard smell from the break-exposed marrow. It was stripped clean, gleaming almost, and there were no teeth marks. Another coyote hadn't done this. The only other predator around here large enough to take out a coyote would be a bear and that would definitely leave teeth marks. The marrow was still viscous, so it couldn't have been ants or beetles; a bone gets all dried out by the time the critters are done with it. Will supposed a person could have killed it, but why go to such trouble to clean a single bone and then just leave it?

A crow called and Will looked up. The forest floor rolled out in front of him like slow ocean, broken by icebergs of granite. The afternoon air began its daily struggle with the oncoming cooler evening, tossing the trees and shifting the light. Everything seemed to move. Will caught a slash of bright orange on the trunk of a venerable sycamore. His lips quirked in a sideways smile. "Radioactive Rita," he said.

His father stepped out from behind the tree. His crow-feather hair stuck up like it always did after he took off his hardhat at the end of the day. His face was war painted with coal dust and his eyes shone bright as sapphires.

Will's breath solidified in his throat. He dropped the coyote bone and felt it bounce off the rubber toe of his left sneaker. That was his Dad, Jack McFarlan, not thirty feet away. It didn't *look* like his father. It was his father. His father was dead. Jack McFarlan was six years in the smoking dirt. He couldn't be standing there because his lungs had silted up with microscopic flecks of anthracite and he had died. Will had held Mom's hand and they'd thrown dirt down onto the coffin. There had been pebbles in it and they'd rattled on the pine.

"You," Will whispered and stopped.

Jack McFarlan closed his eyes and tipped his face into the white light, then looked back at Will.

"Keep your mind in the sun," Will said.

Jack looked at him and smiled. He slipped back behind the tree and disappeared.

"Oh, *hell* no." Will didn't think—he ran. "Dad!" The tears were already blurring the forest in front of him. "Daddy!" Will focused on the slash of Radioactive Rita and pelted over the leaves. He stubbed the shit out of his toe on a sycamore root and roughed his palm on the bark as he ran past it. His .357, *Smaug,* bashed against his hip. There! Jack was just cresting the next rise. How the hell had he gotten so far so fast? Stupid to ask questions. Just run. Dad was dead. None of this made sense, so Will pumped his arms and bared his teeth. "Dad!" he called. "Jack! Jack McFarlan! Wait! Stop!" Jack rolled easy in his old denim over the hill between two black oaks and passed below Will's sight line.

About a minute later, panting and slicked in sweat, Will looked down from the top of the rise. The forest flattened out below and fanned into a hollow before breaking at the base of a granite outcropping. When he was little, the kids had all called that the "Castle Wall". The grown-ups had called it Out Shaft Six for the tunnel opening that stared out like a blind, cyclopean eye. A thread of yellow-gray smoke dribbled up from the top. Jack McFarlan stood in the entrance. He tipped Will a wink and walked into the dark.

Will straightened up. He needed to just stop and think for a second. He hadn't taken drugs or fallen and injured his head. He was awake so no dreaming. That left two possibilities: One, he'd gone crazy somehow. Two, that really was his dead father who'd just walked into a vent shaft for a mine that had been closed down for over a decade. Will clenched his fist. He was being fucked with. He didn't know how or who or what was doing it, but someone was playing some kind of sick game.

He pulled *Smaug* and opened the cylinder. Will reached into his jeans pocket and came out with a handful of very large shells. He loaded a few teeth into his pet cybernetic dragon and flicked its jaws shut. Jack McFarlan was dead, and his son William was going in after him.

As he made his way down the slope, Will muttered to himself in a mock-whine, "Oh, no! Don't run up the stairs, big-titted starlet!" He stopped at the open maw of the shaft. The heat wasn't too bad, but there was definitely some smoulder down there. The tang of sulphur was much stronger. "The killer's calling from inside the house." Will pulled a penlight from his belt and the beam sliced into the dark. It picked out rocks and leaves...and boot prints. He thumbed the safety off *Smaug*. Thing was: big-chested starlettes never carried huge handguns. Maybe he was more the skinny-babysitter-who-has-to-save-the-innocent-children type.

"This is Constable McFarlan of the Shard Police Department," he warned. He thought a moment; a code 22 would work. "You are tresspassing on private property. I'll give you a three count to come on out." Will waited two beats, "Didn't think so. Okay, I'm coming in there. I'm armed and totally freaked out."

Will walked into the cave straight-backed. The tunnel was high here, fully bored and supported with healthy steel girders. He had a good three or four feet of clearance off the top of his cap before the smoke condensed into an upsidedown stream. He could smell it, but he wasn't breathing it much. The lamp of the world faded behind him as he stepped farther in—ten feet, twenty feet, fifty feet. Will stopped.

"Fuck am I doing?" Real cops could call for back up before running into an abandoned mine after their dead fathers. Real cops had partners and clever little radios. Will had a cell phone in his back pocket with a dry battery because he'd forgotten to charge the damn thing again. Not that there was much signal to be had in Shard anyway, even when a body wasn't halfway to hell inside a mineshaft. *Smaug* was getting heavy. Will took a deep breath. "Hello?" Nada. Shit. Okay, what was he going to do? He could go on into the deepening dark and probably get lost after the first turn, or he could back right the hell on up and get himself into some light.

William.

"Daddy?" The gloom ate the echo. Will squinted his eyes shut—darker in his mind, but it was his dark—and shook his head. "You ain't my Daddy," he whispered. "Jack McFarlan's in the ground."

You're in the ground, William.

Will opened his eyes. He was being huckstered. That voice (was it a voice, had he actually heard anything?) wasn't coming from his father. Down is down and up is up and the dead don't come back. "Whoever you are," he called, "I'm not buying this horseshit." He calmed at the sound of his own voice, but his gun hand shook. The low light greased *Smaug's* spine. This was the first time he had ever drawn his weapon on duty. Will eased the safety on and holstered the little dragon. Bad things happened around guns. Ultimately, every single one came off the assembly line looking to put someone down.

He took another step, his Chucks silent on the dusty rock. The shaft sloped down and the heat from the smoulder fought the earth's tendency to cool. The pen torch was a strong MagLite LED, but it only gave him about twenty feet of his immediate future. Will followed the waffle-prints of workboots for another couple of minutes. Whoever this crazy bastard was, he was going to get them both into some serious trouble if he didn't stop soon. Even if the seam was mostly burned out here, it meant that the integrity of the tunnel had burned out with it. Will panned the white circle up the walls. They were scraped and gouged, chipped.

This part of the seam had played out even before The Fire. The company should have closed this shaft a long time ago. Well, they'd never been known for their safety record.

Will slid up on an opening in the wall, an offshoot shaft. It was smaller, only about man height and three feet wide. He threw the MagLite beam into it. The floor angled away at a forty-five degree angle. Will tracked the light up. No smoke here, just the slatey breath of the earth. The boot tracks continued on down the main tunnel without a pause for this tributary. That was fine with him.

Will turned around. The tunnel opening was a salad plate of grey light. When it shrank to the size of a quarter, he promised himself, he would turn back. He followed the boot tracks another twenty feet or so and stopped again. He couldn't quite believe what he was seeing. The tracks curved into the wall and stopped. He hunkered down and examined a couple of tracks back. Maybe this guy had backed up in his own footprints? They were perfect. You could pull that kind of ruse in snow, but in thin rock dust it would leave a trail, a blurring of the original track. So what in hell? Barring the whole ghost theory—to which he *did not* subscribe—it would appear that his quarry had walked through the wall.

"Heh, *quarry*," he smirked. "I'm the hillbilly Sherlock Homes." Will dragged the light up the wall. The spot shone on a band of moist clay about five feet off the ground. There was a boot print embossed in it pointing toward the roof of the tunnel. Will whipped the beam onto the floor and then back to the print on the wall—same boots. "My dear, Watson," his accent was crap, "I do believe we're pursuing Spiderman."

William.

Will turned around as a silhouette stepped between him and the rough circle of daylight. So he *had* gone down that side tunnel, but how in hell had he gotten past? Will glanced at the boot print on the wall. Bullshit, bullshit, bullshit. He put his hand on the butt of his gun.

"Hold it, buddy!"

The silhouette tipped its head to one side.

"Don't you—" It zipped into the side tunnel. "Shit."

Will's heart was hammering in his ribs. He could go back now, call Sheriff Ward and his boys up in Roundtree and come back in force. He imagined the conversation and sighed. *Why in hell had Two-Bears McFarlan bothered Tommy over some drifter or trail camper walking into an old shaft? He looked like who, now?* Okay, this was stupid. He was freaking himself out over nothing. This guy probably was just some hiker or nature lover who'd fired up some high-test Northern California nature and was screwing around. Constable McFarlan would now apprehend said nature-loving jerkoff and put an end to this foolishness. George would just have to sleep it off at home tonight; his cell was going to be taken.

Will trotted over to the mouth of the side tunnel, flashed the penlight into the gloom and walked in. The cool dank closed around his neck and shoulders. The MagLite beam grew solid, plasmic in the total dark. The rabbit hole ran down and away. "I sure hope this is fun for you, asshole." He walked for another few feet and stopped. Fuck this. He was going back. The ground gave way and Will dropped into nothing.

WILL'S HEAD HURT. He sat up and winced. His ass hurt, too. He groaned and probed his forehead for stickiness. No blood, but his noggin hadn't pounded like this since the last time he'd tried to keep pace with George over a bottle. The light wasn't bright, but he squinted. How long had he been out? How long he had been…where was he again? Will looked around and gasped.

The walls bristled with amythest. Great angular columns of wine-colored crystal bloomed from every inch of the huge chamber. He craned his neck but could not find the ceiling. What he could see was illuminated by the crystals themselves. Soft purple glowed and pulsed from their cores. Will flatened his palm against the floor. It flowed like flashed-cooled metal across the room to a great mound of layered crystal. It looked like a pile of quartz with what could only be emeralds heaped upon it. The irregular emerald bulk pulsed in time with the walls.

Will stood, hissing as pain flared from his ankle. Jesus, had he fallen as far as that ceiling was high? He was lucky to be alive. And this place, this place was… He turned in a slow circle, taking in the phantasmagoria. A gigantic spiderweb radiated out from one corner of the chamber, its cable-thick anchor webs attached to crystal pylons. Will sucked air. Loraine and Childe had been right.

47

Chapter 8

"WHAT IS IT you think you understand about life?" The Wasp Man pinned the last survivor of what the local papers would call *The Jamie Blue's Bar Massacre* against the wall with an extended finger. His fingernail had already burned a tiny crescent through the cotton of Jamie's t-shirt and was presently rewriting the chromosomes of the skin cells underneath. If the Wasp Man didn't decide to kill him, the resulting blue-black spot on his chest would. Really, he couldn't make up his mind about it. This one had put up a decent fight. The Wasp Man reached down with his other hand and squelched a loop of his own intestine back into the gaping wound in his gut.

The bartender winced, every atom of his big ol' boy biker frame wanted to pull away from this skinny freak. The room was decorated with leather and denim clad pieces of people. What could only be the torso of Pete Margolis from the Easy O Ranch hung impaled on a dusty elk rack over by the juke—Jamie recognized the shirt. The freak had literally taken everyone in the room apart. Jamie had watched it happen from behind the bar in slow motion—it had been like that in Fallujah, too—as this, this *person* unmade everyone in the place. By the time he'd loaded up the Eagle and put one into the bastard, everyone (and there'd been at least a dozen bikers and ranch hands in for a lunch break brew) was well beyond dead. Guy was some kind of martial arts super-champeen or some shit and on speed to boot. You couldn't take a hit in the belly from a Desert Eagle .50 and keep walking and talking. You just couldn't…unless you were this guy.

He'd just walked in like any other biker fresh off the road, grabbed himself a stool and waited for Jamie to amble over and take his order. Jamie was short a leg below the knee from an IED and he took his goddamn time taking anyone's order. His fucking

48

bar, his fucking pace. Besides, he moved well enough. He rolled up in front of the freak and said, "What'll do you, son?"

"Son?" A pencil thin eyebrow rose. He looked at Jamie through those huge goggle sunglasses made him look like some faggot rockstar and rasped, "I've never been anyone's child."

"Makes no never mind to me, buddy. You want something to drink or chew on?"

The freak had looked over at the man on the next stool, a Salvadorean migrant worker paying attention to his steak and eggs and little else. "I'd like to drink a cup of his blood and chew on a bowl of his brains." He tipped his head to the side. "Please."

The Salvadorean gentleman's straw cowboy hat rose and swiveled. "You got a problem, guero?" A couple of the other ranch hands slid up behind him. One of the bikers pushed back from her table, legs tensed.

"Son," Jaime advised, "stand up and just walk on. That's what's best."

The freak looked up and Jamie saw himself doubled and darkened in those lenses. The thin lips beneath them said, "Walk on down the hall, perhaps?"

That's when the pool cue had splintered against the back of his greasy head. Thing was, he had to have seen it coming in the mirror behind the bar. And as fast as he was, he could have stopped it.

Now, Staff Sargent James Litz, retired, stood with his back against the bricks in a room straight out of a horror movie. Everyone but him was dead and it had happened so fast. People he'd gotten drunk—and gotten drunk with—every Friday and Saturday night for years were splashed all over his bar. For one self-disgusted moment, he wondered if the lower half of Pete Margolis had his wallet in his back pocket—ol' Pete owed Jamie two hunnert bucks.

Carnage was nothing new to him. He'd seen the kind of real terror that humans can inflict upon one another. He'd put bullets in women and children, not because he'd wanted to, but because they were standing in front of men who would end him and his men in the next instant. He watched women birth fire from under their burqas and chadors while the evening call to prayer warbled over the city streets.

The Wasp inhaled his thoughts and repeated, "What is it you think you understand about life...son?"

Tears cleaned tracks through the blood spatter on his cheeks. "I...," he started. The Wasp's eyebrow lifted. "I..." Jamie stared through those smoked lenses into something hollow and ancient, mine shafts into the freak's head. "Nothing."

"That," the Wasp said, "is an honest answer."

He pushed back from Jamie. His belly was fine; his yellowed wife-beater wasn't even singed. The freak showed Jamie his back and walked toward the door. He stepped over a decapitated head with a straw cowboy hat still screwed down tight over the brow and paused. He turned, picked up the head and held it next to his ear. He addressed Jamie, "Manny was an avid soccer fan. He had plans to start a local team with the other migrant workers." The Wasp dropped the head and caught it on his knee. He hefted it up to his other knee and then caught it on the toe of his boot. He stared at Jamie for a moment then lofted the head straight at him. It whoofed into his stomach and thudded to the floorboards. Jamie moaned and his bladder let go a warm gush down his thighs.

"Goooooaaaalllll!" The Wasp shouted over his shoulder as he slouched into the afternoon sun.

Out front, he threw a leg over a low-slung custom chopper with chrome highlights and midnight black paint. For a moment he slumped in the saddle, the cosmic whirl between his ears full of the call to prayer over tinny speakers. He felt the grit of yellow sand. He tasted gun oil and smelled cordite. He looked up as a gunshot rang out into the parking lot. The call to prayer cut out and only the faint whiff of tar and open Montana sky filled his nostrils. So much for Staff Sargent James Litze, retired. The road stretched out in front of him, a black ribbon holding down the golden grass on either side. He kicked the bike alive. That hadn't been boring at all.

Chapter 9

FOR A LONG time, neither George nor Erica said anything as they walked. Content to stroll through the afternoon on the empty streets of Shard, the ease of silence between them was itself a wonder. George had promised her a walking tour of his town. He would make sure she didn't wander somewhere dangerous. It wasn't always easy to see the trouble spots. Some places the ground was solid and safe, other places would swallow you up with little more than a whoop and rush of flame. He'd offered to show her around over the really excellent breakfast he'd prepared earlier that morning.

ERICA CAME DOWNSTAIRS after a quiet night. Bed-and-breakfasts had never been her first choice of temporary accomodations; she preferred the sterility and anonymity of a corporate four-star. Something about sleeping in a stranger's actual residence was too intimate, as if she owed them something other than payment for a night's lodging. But when she clocked down the kitchen stairs, drawn by the aroma of eggs and toast, she began to grant that B&B's might have their advantages.

George (no worse for wear after a shot, a beer and a cup full of wintogreen breath freshness) busied himself at the stove. "Don't have a newspaper to offer, I'm afraid. But there's a copy of one of my favorite magazines on the table there," he called over his shoulder. "Coffee's in the silver decanter. I've got French toast warm in the oven and my dad's famous scrambled eggs and cheese coming off the fire in another minute."

Erica's smile surprised her. "Well, good morning then."

George glanced over his shoulder and in spite of the bathtub medication felt his heart give a lurch. Just a pair of jeans and a tight fitting black sweater. Just your basic fall outfit. No big deal. Basic low-key make-up, nothing jazzy. Medium hoop earings.

Hair down and catching the ambient light in gorgeous little brush strokes that set off the highlights in her almond-shaped eyes. He was staring.

George turned back to the eggs. "I usually eat in here, but if you'd like me to set you up by yourself in the parlour, that's fine."

Erica sat down and poured herself a cup of coffee. "No, no, please sit."

George served them eggs and too much toast, poured some fresh-squeezed and sat down. He felt incredibly awkward eating his breakfast and sharing a newspaper with a strange woman—a strange woman who cleared his head more than a radioactive cup of coffee. (He'd been up and preparing their breakfast hours earlier, as keen to greet the day as a kid on Christmas morning.) After a minute or two he blurted, "Is this weird for you?"

Erica put down the magazine—*The Week,* to which she subscribed herself. "You mean just eating with a stranger like this? Not at all. Saturday mornings I always eat breakfast at this little diner down the street from my place. They only have a counter and two tables, but the food's so good strangers don't mind sharing the space."

"You told me Manhattan yesterday, right?"

"Ever been?"

"Every week." George picked up his own magazine, *The New Yorker.* He opened to an article. "*Goings on About Town* says that, apparently, MoMA held a fundraising gala and Giuliani's second wife showed up already soused."

Erica smirked. "So, no, then."

George smirked back. It was like his face just wanted to do whatever hers was doing. "Actually, I went when I was a kid. There was a chess championship and I had won the state finals, so I got to stay in a youth hostel off the park with a bunch of other nerds." He sat back. "I remember it being overwhelming and dirty and scary as hell and wonderful. At the risk of sounding utterly un-cool, I'm a little in awe of anyone who can live in a place like that. Must take a yard of guts."

"It does."

"You ever get tired?"

Erica sighed. "I can't remember a time since grade school when I haven't been tired, Mr. Rhodes." That was more personal information than she'd revealed about herself to anyone in almost as long.

George winced. "You must never, ever call me Mr. Rhodes again, okay?"

"All right," she said. "George, what can you tell me about your town?"

"What do you mean? Is this why you're here? You a writer or something?"

"Not at all, I'm a lawyer."

"Bom! Bom! Bom!"

"Cute."

George warmed at her use of the word "cute" to describe an action of his. "You must be working for one of the big mineral concerns."

Erica kept herself from showing surprise. George Rhodes was not what he appeared in the slightest. "That's right. I'm here to assess the situation."

George barked a laugh. "You mean to find out how much it'll take to buy us all out."

Shit, so much for stealth. Erica, note to self: don't underestimate rubes just because they're rubes. "At this point, I'm just trying to get the lay of the land."

"Want a tour? I'll answer any question you ask."

"Honestly?"

"You mean about me offering a tour, or answering your questions truthfully?"

ERICA AND GEORGE meandered up Main Street, the empty shops and store fronts rolling by, afternoon sun in their busted glass eyes. A cocktail party of mannequins dressed in scanty gowns of cobweb tracked their progress. The old style marquis over The Gem Movie Theater was empty, its lettering stolen decades before. A pall of faintly acrid smoke marked the sunbeams between buildings. The asphalt was fissured and buckled. Every so often a vent of sulphurous steam hissed through a crack.

"God," Erica whispered. "It's eery."

"Oh, I dunno'," George said. "I think wastelands are kind of beautiful in their own way."

Erica wondered what it must be like to think of the town you grew up in as a wasteland. "So, there's a fire just below the street here, really?"

George pointed to a short pipe growing from the sidewalk. It was flaked with red paint and breathing a steady stream of yellow-white. "See that? Fire hydrant. Pressure blew the top right off." He chuckled and shook his head. "I think that's easily one of the best visual gags I've ever seen in my life…and I like Mel Brooks movies."

"I don't get it."

"A burning fire-hydrant? Seriously? That's not funny to you?"

Erica smiled and bowed her head. "Ah, I get it. Yeah, I guess."

George reminded himself that he had half a lid full of booze and that things were a little funnier to him than most folks. Walking through the smouldering corpse of a town might not be a laugh fest for Erica.

They walked in silence for a minute or so and the shopfronts stopped, bookended at the end of the main road. The road began an exchange; clumps of weeds and grass like islands in the frozen asphalt thickened into a meadow that stretched the size of a football field before slipping into the woods. The land dropped and rolled like glacial moraines or ancient Indian burial grounds.

"What happened here?" Erica asked. "It looks like the ground just swallowed everything."

George stopped and stuck his hands in the back pockets of cordoroys. (His butt hadn't gotten any less bony, that much was for sure.) He blew out an easy sigh. "That's pretty much what happened."

"How do you mean?"

"Apparently, the seam… The coal seam? It was really thick here, so when it burned out it left a huge cavern of empty space. When you mine out coal or any other kind of ore it leaves a space, right? So, in mines—well, responsible ones anyway—they shore up the empty space with big girders to hold up the land above."

"But they couldn't do that with the fire?"

"They tried at first in a few places, but it was all too unstable and probably just too much work. There are a hundred burn-out caves and tunnels, a thousand." He shrugged. "Town was royally fucked by then, so the company just cut its losses. It's what finally scared off most of the people. An older couple, name of Findley, was burnt alive when half their house slid into a burning sinkhole opened in the backyard." He was quiet a moment, pensive. "They found what was left of them kind of welded onto their bed. That was when the greater exodus really got underway. I was about fifteen, I think."

Erica threw a sidelong glance at George. He was smiling, sardonic and sunny, but there was a sour smell under his words. He might just toss off comments like that and the one about Shard being a wasteland like it was no big deal, but he was angry. Erica knew that particular emotional odor better than any other. She turned toward him.

"Why do you stay?"

George squinted out over the field of blonde summer grass. "I'm not entirely sure." He crossed his arms over his chest. "You know I'm a drunk, right? You must've caught that already."

Erica's father had loved whiskey as much as he'd ever loved her or her mother; she caught it the moment George opened the front door. "Yeah, I figured." She added before he could reply, "But you're obviously functional, good at getting by, anyway." Jesus, the enabler speaks! All hail Princess Enabla! (Erica's mother was the proper Queen, but Erica was still heir apparent.) She shook her head. Stupid, poisonous old ways. What was wrong with her? "Why'd you tell me?"

"It's going to take you a while to figure out how to get the rest of the Shard holdouts to vacate." George looked up into the sky as if clocking the time of day by the position of the sun. "That means you're going to be a resident of The House of Rhodes for a few days. I just wanted you to know I got this problem."

"You ever get violent?"

George faced her, held her deep brown eyes with his washed-out blues. "Never." Of course, he wasn't counting his liver in that equation, but he figured she wasn't asking about inwardly directed violence. "The last time I raised a hand to another human being was in high school. Got in a fight." He shook his shaggy blonde head and smiled.

Erica saw the handsome man, the clever quick grins and easy confidence, under the alcohol-boiled skin. "Over a girl?"

"Ha! No. It was over some dumb injun didn't have the sense to run from a bunch of even dumber rednecks. Small-fry tried to take on half the football team. I tried to play hero like the great jackass I am." He barked a clean laugh. "God *damn*, did we ever get our asses kicked. You'll meet him later—he's the law around these parts. Hauls my gin-soaked butt into the hoosegow about every other Friday night." Although, this Friday George had the idea he might be behaving himself.

"He arrests you that often? You must hate him."

"Will? Hell no, he's my best friend." George jerked a thumb down a side street. "C'mon, we'll mosey over to his office and say 'howdy'. I'll tell him you're my dinner date for this Friday night and we'll watch his jaw drop."

They started walking and Erica said, "That was pretty slick."

"What?"

"Asking me out on a date like that."

The tips of George's ears burned so hot, he thought she must be able to hear the blood coursing through them. "Well, I was just kinda thinkin' that you... If you didn't have anything you were already—" Erica was smirking. Her shoulders were hitching up and down. "What?" he demanded.

She belted a laugh. "That's the first time anyone's asked me out without showing off their stock portfolio or offering me a six-figure job in as long as I can remember." She touched his arm. "George, I'd love to have dinner with you on Friday."

George's throat parched and his guts screamed. His temples throbbed. His nerves demanded booze. An image of the intricate stained glass on the front door of his mother's house came to mind—Adam and Eve chased from the garden—and shattered. He looked at Erica and the cacophony muted, the shards settled. "Know what?"

"Hmm?"

"I think you're going to be here for longer than you bargain for."

She cocked a razor sharp eyebrow, "Dinner going to be that good?"

"Nope. Well, I mean sure, but that's not what I mean." They stopped in front of a block of razed houses, the scorched stone foundations the only remains. The stink of brimstone itched in their noses. "Look at this place. If we were going to leave... No,

56

strike that, if we were *able* to leave, don't you think we would have?"

Chapter 10

WILL COULDN'T LEAVE. No matter which way he turned, the strange cavern was as smooth walled as, well, the bowels of the earth. If there was a way to climb out it was behind the enormous, shimmering spiderweb. There was a declavity behind it that ate the light. He didn't want to think about what might be back there. He could feel... He wasn't going back there.

Will might only be a small town constable, but he'd put his cop radar up against the best big city detective. What he was picking up from the rest of his surroundings was weird. He should have been freaking out in only the most major ways, but instead he felt curious—even a little excited. The fact that he held a handgun reknowned for punching holes the size of pie plates didn't hurt. He took a breath and stepped toward the pulsing emerald heap in the center of the cave. His footfalls threw hollow, metallic echos as if he walked across a huge tin drumhead. "Curiouser and curiouser," he muttered.

"Indeed, Alice... Welcome."

For a moment the voice felt as if it originated from inside his skull and radiated out. Will shook his head like a sneezing dog. He listened. Nothing. That feeling of being fucked with was coming back strong now.

"Hello?" He pulled the hammer on *Smaug*, the clicks distinct. "I don't know what's going on and I don't know who you are, but I'd suggest you cut the shit—like yesterday, man!" Kentucky dripped over his words, stretching the vowels and clipping the corners off the consonants. His accent was always stronger when he was emotional; he *hated* that. If anyone knew better it was him, but like many people Will associated a heavy southern accent with ignorance, not authority. He calmed himself and took another step forward. "Now, why don't you come on out and we'll talk."

The mound of emeralds flashed as if charged. Will froze in his tracks as the emerald heap began to unfold. Sharp angles rearranged and climbed over each other. A tower of green stone fell upward and took familiar, terrible shape. Wings flared, the size of frigate sails. A spiked tail stretched away like a long road. Talons long as Will was tall flexed and gouged the steel ground. A huge black pearl, old and deep, blinked open and fixed the little constable where he stood.

Will's vision swam and sparked on the edges. He was going to faint. He shook himself again and refused to let it happen. The great *(don't think it, don't think it or it'll mean you're crazy)* dragon looked at him. It felt like being stared down by a mountain, a planet—no, a star that's gone out and spins dark in the heavens.

"I am older than some stars, Constable, but your thought was lovely."

Will's throat clicked. The dragon was talking to him, its voice like passing weather fronts.

"You're afraid, but there is no danger." Its head, an emerald-chip spear point the size of a small car, tipped to one side. "You know this."

Will concentrated on breathing. His head felt like it had detached and floated above reality on a ballon string. Breathing was solid. One breath after another. Cool air in, warm air out. Jesus, he could *smell* the fucking thing—hot glass and ozone. He wasn't seeing this. He wasn't here.

"You will believe what you see or not. Either way, you must decide."

It was right. He didn't feel like he was in trouble, just a little nutty. A giddy smile bubbled up from his guts. "I named my gun after you." He held out *Smaug* like a kid looking to have his favorite baseball glove autographed.

The dragon flared its mouth slightly and treated Will to a chilling display of teeth. It was like a giant chunk of emerald had exploded into a thousand jagged shards and the dragon had caught them in its jaws. "Not after *me*, little constable. I came before the Englishman's fiction."

And suddenly, they were having a conversation. "You've ruh-read Tolkein?" Will stammered. "You read?"

"I know every tale that has ever seen paper and every story yet to be scribed as if the ink were my blood."

Will realized he was still holding out his .357. With a deft thumb and spin he made it safe and holstered the weapon. "Sorry about that. Kind of rude of me, I guess."

"Do you trust yourself, William?"

The sound of his name was a firm hand around his mind, turning his face to the light of reason. It substantiated him. Will's shoulders dropped, his hands unclenched. "I don't get this. I should be so *scared* right now, but I'm not."

"You do not fear because you understand truth. If there was something to fear, you would know it."

Will jerked a thumb over his shoulder toward the massive net of spiderweb. "Yeah, well," he half-laughed, *"that's* totally creeping me out."

"Well," the dragon chuckled, an avalanch of temple stones, "in that your senses do you justice. Yïn means neither evil nor good. She acheives both."

"Huh? What's a Yïn?"

"Turn around, Constable."

The back of Will's neck stiffened with goose bumps and his shoulders rose. He turned, his hand dropping to the butt of his gun. His father sprawled in the center of the web as easily as he would recline on a couch. He winked and Will sucked in a breath as Jack McFarlan's torso began to bulge and darken. Four tips of rib bone punched through his shirt on either side. They stretched into a quartet of spikey legs and found balletic purchase in the web. Jack McFarlan's eyes divided like cell nuclei and became eight drops of emotionless blood. His hair pulled in as his features smoothed and tinted obsidian. His teeth pushed from gums of tallow, the canines elongating into chitinous garden shears. A sinsister drop of clear fluid bloomed at the end of one mandible. Will's father had become a spider the size of a pony.

A sigh slipped over Will's teeth as he fell into a deep, merciful faint.

UNDER VELVET BLACK, Will heard the lilt of a young girl, heavy with Appalachian molasses. "You revealed yourself too soon for our little constable, *Yahn.*"

No, not "yahn". It was the accent, even stronger than his. *Yïn,* she'd said. Yïn was that thing his father had turned into. A giant spider. Fucking *Shelob* for the love of God. Will's eyes fluttered open and the great cavern swam into focus. A dull throb warmed the back of his head where it had hit the metalic ground. He sat up blinking, hands splayed out behind him.

A girl of no more than seven or eight was standing a few feet away from him. She was dressed in a clean but worn gingham blouse that looked like it had been handed down over at least two decades. Her jeans were dark and tough, patched at the knees. She wore emerald green Chuck Taylor Converse All Stars just like Will's black ones. Blonde pig-tails sprouted from either side of her freckled face, clipped in place with plastic dragons. A black labrador (maybe with a little Irish Setter thrown in) sat next to her, favoring Will with a dopey doggy grin. The pair could have come from any of the surrounding mountain hamlets that still dotted this part of the Appalachians. Made sense—Will had been shooing kids like this away from the abandoned mine since he first strapped on the gun.

She tipped her head to one side, pigtails flopping. Her jade eyes squinted. "You okay, Mister Will?"

Will shook his head. "Do I know your family, honey? How'd you get down here?" He looked around the cavern. "I must have knocked the hell—," he checked himself as her eyes widened, "heck outta' my head when I fell."

"Nah," she smiled. "Y'all just fainted." She scratched the lab behind the ears and set its tail to thumping. "Yïn *(Yahn)* just went and showed her little old self a little too soon. What with me being my big old impressive self and then her pretending to be your Daddy an' everything, it was just too much for you. Kinda' overloaded your mind is all."

Will stood up. "What are you talking about, kiddo? What's your name? You know you're not supposed to be running around down here. You could get hurt." He chuckled and rubbed the back of his head. "Kinda' like me, I guess."

The girl sighed. "William," she said. "Stop trying not to believe, okay? It's counterproductive." She gave the dog a gentle flick to the ear. Will's lips pressed tight as its fur lengthened and the black bled away. An instant later the black lab/setter mix was a great Arctic Wolf. It still favored him with an affable doggy grin, but Will found its teeth somewhat more disconcerting. "You understand now, William." It wasn't a question.

Will's gun hand itched, but he kept it away from Smaug. "I, uh… Shit, I'm still here. *You're* still here. Still real."

She smiled an almost full smile. It looked like the tooth fairy had come for a visit. Nice touch. Will sucked in a breath as she changed. Her transformation was more graceful than Yïn's, less visceral. It was as if she were a cloud of vapor in the shape of a girl, and with a breeze of will, she dispersed and reformed. Will exhaled like he'd been gut punched. He was standing before a woman so beautiful that tears pricked his eyes. Her head was hairless and exquisitely shaped. Her skin luminesced with a bluish-white glow that Will associated with a back-lit diamond. Her naked body flowed with a dancer's musculature and was at least seven feet tall. What really caught his attention, though, was the spread of ash-colored wings that feathered out behind her.

"An angel," he whispered. "That works."

"Sometimes, William," she chimed in a voice that was a chorus of several voices masculine and feminine. Will noticed the speaker was neither. Its legs joined in a smooth V of flesh below its belly. "I have worn this guise many times."

Will's face was bathed in the light cold-burning off the angel. "What is this?" he asked. "Oh, shit! Have I died?"

The angel tipped its head to the side, a characterization Will recognized carried over from one form to another. "You live, William."

"I—"

"Hush now, and your questions will be answered."

"Just your name, then," Will blurted.

Frustration bent its brow for only a moment—a cloud-shadow over a field—but Will's blood chilled. At its feet, the wolf's tail ceased its lazy wag and it looked up at its master.

"You may call me Dampf."

William was a child of the mine. A "damp" or "fire-damp" was a build-up of combustible gases. The official investigations were never conclusive, but the Shard Fire was always supposed to have been started by an explosive damp. The word "damp" comes from the German for "vapor"—*Dampf.* Will nodded and kept his mouth shut.

"Before rock was solid and water knew to flow down hill, beings of mutable substance danced over the skin of the world. Neither angels nor demons, they existed in a swirling balance of will and intent, light and dark. All was chaos and all was balance. The world existed as a single note. I would sing it for you, William, but your body would not survive."

The angel paused and nodded at the wolf. Yïn's fur drew inward and coarsened. Her legs extended and her tail whipped into a long, fine spray of black. Her paws fused into hard, dark hooves. A grand Arabian mare, slick with a blue-white sheen on her black flanks, tossed her mane and whinnied. Will shook his head and resisted the urge to put his hands on his hips and say "Hoo-wee!" It would have been a little too Kentucky even for him. That and he had never been more afraid to speak in his life.

Dampf, too, commenced a change. Again, it was as if a puff of wind blew it away and another reformed it. A second later, Dampf stood defiant. Its skin was forge red, lines of keloid scar striped its cheekbones and banded its huge biceps. Dampf stood with heavy arms crossed over prodigious breasts, veins pulsing in its forearms. A mane as black as Yïn's streamed from its heavy brow and down its back. Horns—more blades of black glass than bone—sprouted from its hair. A thick tail snaked around its thigh and spiraled down its leg, ending in an arrowhead. It raised hands tipped with blackened triangular chips to the ceiling and stretched. It lowered its arms and caressed its body, purring in a voice that was all shadow.

"The skin of the world hardened and rose like a tide to envelope the First Ones. Beings of flesh then dragged themselves from the mother pools and walked. The First Ones were content to stay beneath and maintain the balance." Its eyes glowed orange. "But one formed who destroyed the balance. A Wasp coalesced in an eddy of dark will, wrapped itself tight in malice and began to sting. The sting infected others and the darkness grew. Here." It stamped a cloven hoof into the floor and a blue spark shot. "Under *this* mountain a hive swelled and the Pompiliad grew strong." Great leathery wings spread behind it, wafting Will's hair over his shoulders. "The Pompiliad and its young dug and chewed and tore a rent in the skin of the world. They gathered, curious, from the inside of this cunt under the mountain, sniffing the air and the smell of flesh beyond."

Will was so transfixed by this apparition and the imagery its story called forth in him, that he didn't notice Yïn's final transformation. When Dampf paused, Will glanced over and caught the spider staring at him, mandibles scissoring. He yelped and jumped back a step, hand snapping to his pistol. He calmed himself. Now was *not* the time to lose it. It hadn't eaten him before and he didn't sense it would now. Not that he believed for a second that it didn't *want to*, just that it wouldn't. Dampf didn't want that. Out of the corner of his eye, Will caught the disintegration and reformation of the great emerald dragon. Dampf had once again found its first and truest form.

The dragon stared down at him, quiet for a moment. "I set The Fire."

It was like a slap. Before he could stop himself, Will shouted, "What?"

Dampf tilted its massive head. "Had I not, you and your kind would all be rotting in the bowels of Wasps, or playing host to their larvae. The skin of the world would have sloughed off and a great war would have ensued." The dragon snapped its jaws shut with a sound like a hundred chandeliers spontaneously shattering. "I sealed the rent with fire, the wasps still below. As long as it burns, they will stay where they belong.

"Yïn and I stand as guard and watch over the burning portal, to tend the smoulder."

Little William Two-Bears McFarlan glared up at the demon responsible for the death of his town and ultimately his whole world. He was the guard and the watch over a smoking trash midden because of this nightmare and its hideous pet. He had been lured from the light with a cruel yank on his emotions and then tumbled head-long into temporary insanity. In short, he had been royally, *royally* fucked with. It was all a big sell, a great big preamble to something, a flashy movie with tons of CGI, but it all came down to priming his mind for one thing.

"What do you want from me?" he demanded.

The spider jittered up and down on its spindly legs. Will had the distinct impression that it was laughing. He spat on the ground in front of it. It froze and Will saw himself reflected in eight red spheres.

"Brave constable," Dampf said. "You are right. We do need your help. A single Wasp escaped through the rent, the original. It has wreaked its petty havoc over the years, but caused little imbalance in the grand scheme."

"And now?" Will asked, already knowing and dreading the answer.

"The Pompiliad returns."

Chapter 11

CHARLOTTE NAJARIAN KNEW for certain, for dang certain, that she would go the rest of her life without ever hearing a word of thanks from the miserable brats attending Shard Elementary. She was fifty-one and three fourths (though she'd pass for ten years older) and probably had another ten or fifteen years, may the Risen Jesus protect her, before retirement. That meant another ten to fifteen years of swollen ankles from standing in front of a steadily diminishing crowd of mouthbreathing imbeciles. The fact that it was summer vacation for another few weeks *barely* gave her any relief.

She kneeled in her garden on a fine August morning and tended her peonies, her boney backside in the air and her straw hat swinging back and forth like a jerky radar dish. The dang deer— always such a bother to her tomoatoes and just about anything else that would bud—had given her beloved plot a pass this summer. At least she had that to be grateful for, but it wasn't providence, no sir. It was the ten or so bars of Irish Spring she'd hung in an alien perimeter around her yard that kept those pesky deer at bay. Strange thing, but she hadn't seen many deer at all over the past few months and Shard was normally lousy with them. Oh, she'd put in her complaints to the Constable, but that William Two-Bears McFarlan was a no good. Just look at that long hair of his and you could tell he didn't deserve the job. He'd asked her what she wanted him to do about the deer infestation (*Tics, Constable, tics! Limers! It's a public heatlh emergency!*) and when Charlotte suggested a mass poisoning campaign, he'd had the temerity to ask her what she had against Bambi.

"A no good," she muttered now to her cukes. "A no good Cherokee." She checked over her shoulder. The yard was empty, of course, as was the street. She could hear a couple of mouthbreathers shouting and whooping it up down to the park on the corner, but that was far enough off that no one would catch Charlotte in her political incorrectness. "A no good injun." She showed her teeth to the carrots. "Worse'n a nigger, if you ask me." She finished with a nod. One of the children, probably that Patty Wilkerson trollop (always lifting her skirt for any boy over the age of eight), gave a delighted summer screech.

Charlotte cast her squint up and down Rhodes Street. And wasn't that just a pip: naming this fine strip of Victorians and spreading, venerable oaks after that no good Rhodes family? Maybe they had been something approaching respectable back in the days when she herself had been known to lift her skirt a time or two on the playground (not that said memories even existed inside Charlotte's mind), but it had been a long time since. For the nonce, the Rhodes Family was comprised solely of one George Rhodes, town drunk and Charlotte's greatest disappointment.

She remembered the big blonde boy in her K-6 classes quite well. Young George has been as far ahead of the other children in his brains as he had been in athletic abilty. She'd had real hopes that one day George Rhodes would come back from college, finely degreed, and take over one of the top administrative spots at the mine offices. But no, he'd chosen sin instead of success. Such a shame, such a shame. And now there was that—she checked up and down the street again—*spic woman* boarding at the house. If Marabelle Rhodes could know that a Porto Ricci, or whatever she was, was sleeping under the same roof as her poor lost boy... Well, it was good she was under the ground, and in the arms of the Risen Jesus.

Charlotte grunted and—again checking the street—let a fart slip as she moved over to her rows of squash. They wouldn't be in until the fall, but the first vine shoots were coming up. Thinking of autumn reminded her of the desks in her single classroom at Shard Elementary and her contented, somewhat lofty expression darkened. She stabbed the earth with a trowel. A drop of her sweat ran down the metal barrel and magnified the letters C. NAJARIAN as it headed for the shovel end. One of her greatest pleasures in life was engraving her name on her possessions. She'd started with a few school supplies—her scissors were always walking away—and it just took off from there. Now, just about anything she owned that was small enough to be carried and hard enough to take the vibrating point of her engraving gun bore her name. Charlotte levered the trowel, yanked a dandelion and sighed. Fall always fell too soon.

To even call it an elementary school was incorrect. Only one room was even used and in it Charlotte taught a five-student menagerie—all that was left of the children of Shard, Kentucky. There was ten-year-old Patty Wilkerson, the skirt lifting trollop; twelve-year-old Howard Sams, the fat boy (and wasn't there always one of those); Patty's younger sister, eight-year-old Madison (well on her way to an illustrious career as a professional nose picker); sixteen-year-old Tommy Ray Dalton; and finally the new hope, Childe Howard. And, no, she would never refer to him by his nickname, Kiddo. It was repugnant, though he seemed to like it.

To even call it a teaching job was also something of a misnomer. Charlotte hardly taught anything at all anymore. She was a babysitter. The school existed to keep the brats of Shard on a leash during the day. Oh, she ran them through a few lessons here and there, but mostly she had them stick to their respective text books. Her lesson plans were exact copies of the ones she'd used for years. She spent most of her classtime with her nose shoved deep in the crack of her favorite stories, the *Left Behind* series. Every now and again, she would raise her eyes to silence a giggle or whisper, using the opportunity to wonder which of her mouthbreathers would be chosen when the Rapture finally came. She might have picked Childe Howard (he was such a quiet, attentive and bright boy) but for the fact that his mother was a Jew and that stain followed along the mother's bloodlines. Well, perhaps she and the rest of the righteous would be able to put in a good word with the Risen Jesus when the End Times came.

A loud buzz burst in Charlotte's ear. "Hai!" she screamed and her legs pistoned her up into a crouching sort of hop. She flailed a hand at what could only have been a fat honey bee or cicada—the sound was of a *heavy* insect, deep and dronning. She stood up and backed off a pace from the plot she'd been tending. The smell of hot sun on rich earth and wet grass filled the air, thick and sharp. The brats up the street shouted to each other from farther off. The August blue of the sky spiked between leaves of deep jade from the oak across the street. She was not usually afraid of bee stings or insects; a lady couldn't garden if she was weak in the heart about such things. But now she cradled her elbows as gooseflesh covered her arms with crepe paper. It was eighty degrees and she was cold.

Someone was watching her; had probably seen her funny little jump and screech. She whipped around, but the cool shade of her pin-neat porch was empty. During the years when the town was still a success story instead of a footnote, her daddy would sit on the porch on fair days and watch Charlotte's momma tend this same garden. Butch Najarian would drink his beer and smile. Every now and again he would let out a ringing belch just to let his wife know he was still staring at her behind while she rooted in the soil. She'd call him a "pig" or a "gopher" over her shoulder, but always with a grin in her voice. Charlotte would laugh fit to split when her daddy burped like that. Her mother hated it when she did, but the giggles wouldn't stay down.

Butch Najarian's lungs had gone pitch and he went into the dust when Charlotte was still in her teens. Not three years later, her momma was struck with Legionnaires. The doctor said it could have been the garden what killed her. Something about microbes in the soil. Happens more than most people might a thought, he'd told her, as if the ignorance of other people was supposed to make her feel better about her mother's last days of delirium and shitting the bed. And now she was standing here shivering in high summer sun, giving herself the creepy-crawlies because a big old lazy bumble bee had mistaken her hat band for a landing strip.

"You're being an empty-headed imbecile," she nearly hissed at herself. "Garden's not going to tend itself. Get to it, woman."

Charlotte bent back down, her knees sending off cannon shots, and slipped her hands back into the cool earth. She reached behind her for her trowel and when she brought it back around a huge black hornet was perched on the back of her hand. Her breath caught for a moment as she just stared at it. It's body was at least three inches long, armed at the front with manfibles like tiny garden shears and at the back with a stinger that looked like the tip of a knitting needle. Its delicate wings fluttered, fluttered like chips of bluish mica on a furtive breeze. And then it stung her, gouging its spear between two prominent veins in the notch of a couple of tendons. The flare of pain was a bolt of white phosphorous.

Charlotte opened her mouth to scream and the wasp flew in. Her hind brain spoke before she could think better of it and she closed her teeth with a click. Her eyes bulged like twin cue balls as the animal forced itself over her tongue and began to quest down into her throat, all roving spikes and needles. She clasped her hands at her neck. (A passerby might have been forgiven for wondering why the local school marm was trying to strangle herself.) Her left hand had already ballooned into a grotesque clown's glove, the dusky blue veins now black and standing out on the red flesh like wire. That dark liquid slipped up her arm and into her heart. The big muscle burned with the poison and seized. Charlotte fell on her back, paralyzed with pain and weakness. Even as she died she could feel the wasp behind her breastbone, working some secret with its clever, spikey parts. Her last moment was filled with the cobalt of the deep August sky. Beyond was the starry vault of infinity.

Twenty minutes later, a pair of antenae peeked between Charlotte's cyanotic lips almost as if she were spitting out a cherry stem. They were followed by the triangular head, worming back and forth to break into the world. A moment later and the large hornet slipped from her mouth and crawled to the wide expanse of pale forehead. It began to clean its antennae and legs, drawing each through its mandibles, tasting blood and other nectars. It dried its wings in the sun and waited. In the near distance, it sensed a cool, dark place under the house. The rest of the swarm would come now. It would need their help to drag the host under the porch.

Chapter 12

THE GRANITE SLAB angled gently from the forest floor, forming a natural platform about the size of a twin bed. Early afternoon sun caught it in a bolt of white light and the rock flected the heat back like a slow-feed capacitor. Amy James lay naked as her many tattoos would allow (sleeves up both arms, black lightning bolts on her ribs, chakra point color wheels, wings on her ankles) and soaked up the light. As far as she was concerned there was no better way to get a nice summer tan or spend her lunch hour. Bathing suits, as a rule, sucked.

"I am an iguana," she said to no one, stretching the vowels as she stretched her limbs. The rock was a bit scratchy on her bare butt and shoulders, but the contrast between it and the soft air was kind of interesting. Truth be told, everything was kind of interesting after a couple of post-lunch tokes. She wasn't soaring, but her feet weren't exactly planted either.

On any other project Amy never would have considered lighting up during working hours. The Shard survey was boring her to fucking tears, though. Over the past few days she'd been tramping through the woods, covering enough of the terrain around the mine to have formulated the basis for her report: Shard sat on a typical hunk of Kentucky granite shot through with anthracite deposits. A first year geology student could have figured as much and without a semi-portable mass spectrometer and diamond bladed rock slicer. Hell, anyone with a pair of eyes could have figured it out because all it meant was that this place was a coal mine in the mountains. Blackstone's Business Development Unit wanted her to ascertain if the Shard load could be further exploited. If she could have some time down one or two of the old mine shafts, she might be able to figure all that out for the suits, but Legal expressly forbade her to do anything of the kind. Too dangerous. Energy companies like Blackstone were already hemorrhaging revenue from decades of lawsuits over black lung and injuries due to safety violations. They didn't need to worry about one of their geologists getting fricasseed down in a big scary coal mine.

"Pain in my ass," she sighed and shifted said ass off a small tooth of rock. Sweat was now pouring steadily off her and darkening the rock. She was going to end up leaving an Amy stain when she'd had enough sun. She giggled. Amy stain, Amy James. Almost rhymed. The Police would probably have considered it a decent enough couplet. Some of their rhymes were rediculous. Like that one about coughing in *Don't Stand So Close Me*? Man, that had been terrible. Hadn't Sting been an English teacher, too?

Speaking of police, it had been three days since the handsome young Constable had stopped by her place to take the statements of the Howards and he still hadn't asked her out on a date. He had wanted to, she could tell that much. What's more, she wanted him to want to, but he either hadn't picked up on it or... "What?" she thought aloud. "Scared?" Nah, didn't fit. Two-Bears McFarlan didn't put off pussy vibes.

Amy rolled over and lay her head over her folded arms. The forest streched out in vibrant jades that faded to an almost blue-black in the deep tunnel of trees. The soil smelled of strong tea and hot summer dust; her rocky beach chair of ancient rain storms. The pink triangle of her tongue slipped out and sampled the granite: Mmm, nice vintage: Pleistocene. She sighed and closed her eyes.

No, Will Two-Bears wasn't afraid, but there was some kind of reservation. He was waiting for something. For her to make the first move? If that's what it took to get a decent meal and possible orgasm from the local hottie, that was fine by her, but that didn't feel right. Maybe he was waiting to get a better feel for her. She was admittedly, purposefully, not your average Ginger Geologist and that often threw people, even if they had checked her out the way she'd caught Will checking her out when they first met.

She remembered staring down at him and his friend, George, in that open cell. Will had given her the once over in a way that stood out. Most people lingered on the neon signs of her hair and ink, but he had spent no more time or attention on those facets of her than he had her shoes or t-shirt. It was her face he kept coming back to. She got the idea he was recording her, storing her up for further reference. In another person, it might have been creepy. In him? Well, he was a cop right? Andy Griffith or not, it was his job to pay attention to people.

The wind picked up and the forest was full of sound. (Harbinger of a summer thunderstorm, perhaps? They came up fast and nasty in the Appalachians.) From the darkness behind her eyes, the wind hissed through the leaves and snapped the odd dry twig. The red-orange light on her eyelids dimmed. Cloud over the sun? She squinted one eye open. "Huh?" She opened them both and peered into the trees. She hadn't had enough weed to start seeing things. Amy's college roomate at the School of Mines in Colorado had been prone to light hallucinations whenever they *partoked of the smoke*, but that was never Amy's thing. Her brain caught up. Not hallucinating meant she really was seeing Will Two-Bears McFarlan stagger out of the trees across the clearing.

She sat up on the rock, mind clearing with the adrenaline that came with being caught naked out of doors by the local constabulary. Well, it was one sure way to make the first move.

Will walked with his head down and had almost smashed his knees into her rock when she said, "Hi, uh, for lack of a better word."

He looked up and Amy noticed his condition. His clothes were dusty and torn in a couple of places and he was he was covered in spiderweb. His eyes were far away and his lips were parted. He reminded her of those pictures you always see of people wandering around after a bomb has gone off. Her embarassed grin melted and she pressed an arm across her breasts. "Will, you okay?"

His eyes cleared and then snap focused on her's. "Amy?" Certain now. "Amy." He looked around the clearing and then took her in on her rock, "You look like a mermaid."

AMY'S RV SMELLED like Orange Pekoe tea and quartz dust. They sat at the little fold-down table she used for a work surface and meals. Will warmed his hands on a steaming mug emblazoned with the words: *Colorado School of Mines: Up Yer Shaft!* It was eighty-five degrees and humid outside but he was cold to his bones. Amy had helped to clean him up, disinfecting a few scrapes and brushing the spiderwebs off. Will had endured it like a child who's taken a tumble off his 3-speed, hissing in a breath at the iodine sting every now and again, but otherwise silent. So was Amy; she wanted to ask him what had happened, but whatever it was had spilled over the edges of his mind. After sitting for nearly five minutes without a word or even a glance down at his tea, her patience and curiosity were being replaced by serious concern.

Shock was nothing new to Amy. One of her shoulder tattoos was a cover for an ugly patch of scar tissue earned when her old Harley decided to zig instead of zag one wet day on the way home from school. She'd literally bounced off the asphalt (leaving a smear of her shoulder on the road) and over the guardrail. Amy had been lucky that the shoulder and a sprained wrist were her only injuries. In a fog, she'd walked down the road and called for help at a gas station but it hadn't really been her. The real Amy had stayed at the scene of the crash, flipping through the air over the guardrail again and again. The one who walked and talked to the the pump jockey at the Exxon had been an automaton, shock sub-routines running at maximum.

That was Will's deal—his bod might be sitting about thirty-six inches from hers (now fully clothed, thank you) but Amy knew he was still walking those fathomless woods, flipping over his own guardrail. But it shouldn't go on forever like this. He needed to download. You could do a lot of harm holding onto a trauma for too long and a lot of good starting the repairs as soon as possible. She reached out and encircled his hands and mug with her own rough palms. The A/C was blasting but he shouldn't have been as cold as he was.

"Will?"

He raised his eyebrows, but kept his gaze on the tea.

"What happened to you?"

He didn't answer.

"Sheriff?" She squeezed his hands, a hard pulse. "Hey!"

Will made eye contact, washed-out blue, bleached. He muttered something.

"What?" she asked.

"It's Constable," he said a little louder. "Tom Ward...the Sheriff's up at the County Courthouse." He sounded like a man talking in his sleep.

Amy didn't want to yank the information out of him, but needed to keep him engaged. If she was aggressive he might run the other way. She sat back in her seat and planted one booted leg up on the bench. "What's the difference? Is Constable like a deputy or something?"

"Hm?"

Firmly, "What's the difference, Will?"

"Oh, ah, a deputy works for the Sheriff. That'd be Si Smalls and a couple of other guys."

"You don't work for the Sheriff?"

"Shard's in his jurisdiction…" His eyes had gone dull again.

She wasn't letting him slip back. "And? But?"

"Hm? Oh, yeah. Shard's under his general jurisdiction, but I'm the prevailing law officer for what's left of the municipality."

"So he's like the President and you're the Governor?"

"Close enough, I guess." He came up almost all the way. Talking about the normal, familiar parts of life was like laying the planks on the bridge back to reality. He tilted his head to the side. "Amy?"

"Yeah?"

"How come you were naked?"

She colored. "Bother you?"

Now, it was Will's turn to blush. At least it made him look human. Another minute and she was ready to classify him as a new type of chalk. "I, uh, no it didn't bother me," he said. "Nice ink, by the by."

She sat forward, "What happened to you, man?"

Will sat back, surprised by her sudden change in tack. Amy's tone was still gentle, but insistent. He took a breath and spread his palms flat against the table top.

"Have you ever seen something, or experienced something that you knew didn't happen?"

"I'm not sure I get you."

Will frowned. "Okay, say you had a dream where you were— I dunno—a fairy princess with magical powers."

"Gem."

"What?"

"Gem. I always used to pretend I was Gem from *Gem and Holograms*."

"I dunno know that one." He shook his head as if to shoe a fly. "Don't matter. Anyway, pretend you woke up from a dream where you were Gem, except that when you woke up you were still sure you were both Gem *and* yourself. How do you deal with that?"

A scowl dragged down Amy's brow. "So, you're saying that you're sure not what's real?" Her mouth quirked into a smile. "You shroomin', Constable?"

"Ha, that'd be great. At least then I'd know what was what. I could put all the weird shit down to the psilocybin and accept everything else."

Amy loved it. His repsonse didn't guaranatee anything, but it certainly made it sound like the good constable was experienced in a Jimi Hendrix kinda' way. She was digging him more and more. "Seriously," she said, "you go for a hike and find something funky in them thar woods?"

Will patted *Smaug*. "I don't get screwy on anything when I'm on duty. That whole altered reality thing doesn't jive all that well with large caliber firearms."

"Not even beer?"

"Never." He ran his hands through his hair, knocking his old ball cap off. "Ah, man, I don't know how start."

Amy put her hand over his. "Try the beginning and we'll figure it out from there."

Her touch set off a thrum from his toes to his nose. Will hoped the blush he could feel creeping up his neck wasn't visible. He felt like a cartoon character that'd just eaten a hot pepper, filling up red from the bottom like a thermometer. It wasn't like Shard had a big dating pool. And now, what? Was he going to tell her what had just happened? This morning he'd been thinking about how to ask her to have dinner with him. Was he really going to include her in the insanity he'd just witnessed?

"Ah, hell," he said. "Started when I saw my dad walking in the woods. He's dead by the way."

"SO YOU THINK I'm completely crazy, right?"

Amy sat back and put her arms behind her head. She looked up at the ceiling of the darkening trailer. They were either going to be hit by a summer storm or time had slipped during Will's story of giant spiders and shape-shifting dragons. She looked at him for a long enough enough time that the color began to rise in his cheeks and said, "I think that you probably are messed up somehow or another, yes."

Will sighed, "Shew, that's wonderful."

"Seriously?"

"What, that I'm nuts or had a hallucination? In a word, hell yes." He laughed. "Listen, I'd much rather put down what happened as a concussion dream than as real. Concussion means I don't have to worry about a big demon-dragon-uh...*thing* and its freaky pet spider. Which, by the way, really seemed to want to eat me. Did I mention that?"

"You did."

"Now I don't need to plan my life around a battle with a wasp-creature who's coming here to end the world. I can get that pedicure I was looking forward to on Wednesday." He shook his head. "Now that I hear myself say it like that, it's amazing I was ever confused. Must have been the knock I took when I fell."

He was speed-talking, and from a man who was a slow southern-drawler to begin with, the effect was that much more pronounced. Amy let him go. He was babbling himself right in a way he hadn't during the initial story telling. That had been more like listening to someone recount a dream, slow and stammering through impossible situations that seem real only moments after waking. This was his version of getting the shakes and crying.

"I suppose I should get myself on up to Lexington and load up into one of those MRIs. Have my brains scanned for any real harm. You shouldn't ever have one of those, you know. They're supposed to hurt like hell for people with tattoos."

"Not anymore. If your paint's less than 20 years old, you're good. New ink doesn't have all the heavy metals the old stuff used to."

"Oh, okay, well, great. I won't have to worry about that because I'm paintless, but I should probably have one just to make sure I'm not bleedin' into my brain or anything. Then maybe I should get like a full neurological work up."

He went for a little while longer, Amy nodding along and waiting for him to peter out. She didn't believe that his episode was due to any concussion. First of all, he saw his dead father *before* he went into the mine and fell. Unless he started the walk in Them Thar Woods concussed, it didn't make sense. Second, he just didn't have that big a dent in his noggin. And his pupils were fine. He'd look like a big cat on ketamine if he'd hit his head hard enough to hallucinate as freely as he described. Third...well, shit… he just didn't seem the type to go nuts all of a sudden. She didn't want to think that about him.

But she wasn't going to tell him that. Amy *wanted* him to think that it had all been a hallucination or dream, at least for a while. At least until she had time to do a little investigating of her own. It was the description of the dragon's chamber that got her. If even one tenth of what he saw was actually there, it would be the largest diamond and emerald deposit in the northern hemisphere. There were only two diamond deposits of any size in the lower forty-eight United States—northwest of Ft. Collins in Coloraddo and Crater of Diamonds in Arkansas. If she could discover another it would make her career. Even better, if she played her cards right she could lay claim to it, but that would be tricky. She'd have to find a partner to go in with her who would have to pretend to "stumble" on the find him or herself. They could then buy what was left of the mine and exploit the gems for themselves.

"So what do you think?"

Amy focused. "Huh?"

"About dinner tomorrow." Will smiled. "You were totally just spacing out there, weren't you?"

She laughed. "Caught me. Sorry. What'd you say?"

"Aw man, you're going to make me ask you out twice? That's hard."

She narrowed her eyes. "I'm a hard woman."

He swallowed. "My friend George seems to have made himself a new friend. He asked me over to his place for dinner with them tomorrow night. Wanna' be my date?"

Amy crossed her arms over her chest. "I don't know," she said. "You put out?"

Will looked genuinely confused. "It's been so long I'm not even sure."

Chapter 13

DARWIN'S CLAWS CLICKED along the warm August pavement on what used to be Shard's main street. Where there was still glass, storefronts reflected a young boy with curly blond hair and his sturdy beagle. Darwin's leg had healed up almost overnight and the spiderweb bandage had dropped away. The Amazing Ninja-Dog started howling in his beagle basso to be let out into the world again and finally Loraine Howard had capitulated. She'd admonished Childe to stay out of the woods, feeling every bit the worried mother straight from a Grimm's Fairy Tale. The way they'd found Darwin and that giant web still hung in her mind (Or rather, her mind still twisted in the web.) Just so long as he minded himself and stayed out of those woods. She didn't care what Constable Will had to say about it. So Childe and Darwin had rushed into a warm summer day.

His first steps out of the house had been electrified. Childe might not be able to go into the woods, but they surrounded the entire town. Whatever was there (Giant spiders? Coyotes?) was all around them, too. He felt a species of mingled fear and adventure, but tempered by a lifetime of normalcy. While he was only twelve, Childe Howard had been around long enough to have lost most of his magical-thinking. Didn't matter what you saw the day before; comfortable reality always comes rushing back in. It wasn't long before he was just bopping along in his usual, lonesome daydream.

It would have been cool to run into Howie Sams. The other kids busted on him a lot because he was pretty porky, but Howie was Childe's age and smart. (He'd actually earned enough money day trading on-line to get an X-box, which was totally dope.) The other kids were all a couple of years older or younger. At least he had Darwin to keep him company. The makeshift leash (a twenty-foot length of clothesline) tied to his collar earned the Kiddo a few reproachful doggy looks from time to time, but Loraine wouldn't have let them out without it.

Childe kicked a rock and it skittered over the pavement before bouncing into the gutter next to a smoking crack. The air burned with the usual back-of-the-throat tang that was Shard's breath this far into town. Some days the fumes were stronger than others, but today wasn't so bad. The thunderstorm the day before had pulled most of the mean out of the air. Childe's brow was dry and Darwin was barely panting. It was a perfect day to be a twelve year-old explorer.

They walked over to the sidewalk outside the old movie theatre. If there was any one building in Shard Childe wanted to check out it was that one. Man, that would be awesome. He could just imagine the empty seats and the cool, mildewy smell, the secret, scary echos the big space would make—it would be like a big cave. He could turn it into a neat clubhouse and he and Howie could hang out. Maybe they could invite Patty and Maddy Wilkerson, even if they were younger…and girls. There was no way he'd want to bring in Shard's only teenager, Tommy Ray Dalton.

Tommy Ray insisted at knuckle-point that all the other kids refer to him as T.R. At sixteen he was already well over six feet, but probably only weighed in around one-sixty or so. His skin had this freaky yellow white tinge because he tried hard to stay out of the sun whenever possible. Tommy Ray's parents both worked at the same factory almost sixty miles outside of town and he was the only child. During the year, Tommy sat quietly in class, reading his textbooks and making sure to have filled in all the blanks in his workbook. He was very polite to the teacher and the other grown-ups, but Childe and the rest of the kids in Shard knew better. You didn't want to get caught in one of the school's empty halls with Tommy.

Howie told Child about one time when he stumbled on Tommy Ray in one of the empty sections of the school. When it got toward the end of the year, Howie didn't like to play outside with the other kids during recess—the heat and what his momma called "baby fat" didn't make for a good mix. Intead, he would recede into the one of the empty classrooms with his lunch and a good sci-fi novel. One day he looked up from his book, cookie crumbs on his shirt, to the sound of a low rhythmic banging out in the hall. Howie had gotten up and gone around the corner to find Tommy Ray repeatedly smashing his forehead into a locker. Howie had called out to him. Tommy Ray had thought himself alone and actually snarled as he spun around. In the darkened hall, his eyes and teeth seemed very bright. In a deep, flat drawl Tommy Ray had said, "Forget this or I'll slit you open like a pig."

If Childe and Howie ever did start up a clubhouse or a hideout in the old movie theatre, T.R. was not going to be on the guest list. "Got that right," Childe said out loud. Darwin looked up from his sidewalk snuffles. "Wasn't talking to you, boy. Just broadcastin'." That was one of his mother's. Loraine talked to herself a *lot*. She said it was a writer thing. Kiddo thought it was more likely a Loraine thing. He smiled. The Childe reflected in the ticket-taker's booth (a little darker, a little dustier) smiled back. He sighed. Man, it would be so cool in there.

Darwin gave a gentle tug on the leash. Something farther down the sidewalk smelled an awful lot like woodchuck piss and he *really* needed to check into that. If memory served, that particular stretch of sidewalk belonged to him.

* * *

T.R. WOULD KILL someone by the end of that summer. He'd decided just that morning while lying in bed. Daddy and Momma had slammed the screen porch door on the way to work (just like they did every morning) yanking T.R. into consciousness. The thought was there waiting for him: *I am going to committ murder.*

For a few minutes he just laid there, one arm behind his head, the other absently squeezing his morning hard-on. How would he do it? More importantly: who would it be? His father, Gene, or his mother, Martha Jean, would both be likely choices. Everyone in this shitberg town referred to T.R.'s folks as "The pair of Jeans". His folks even thought it was funny. On the rare occasion when either of them was home instead of catching overtime at the Maytag factory in Riectherville and a shitberger would happen by and inquire as to T.R.'s parents' overall state, the conversation normally included back and forth not unlike, "Hiya, Gene. Martha Jean. How you all feeling today?"

"Oh, well, I'm a little blue," his daddy would say.

"I'm feeling kind of faded, myself," from his momma.

And everyone would laugh just fit to split.

T.R. gasped and released his dick from a painful death grip. There was choking the chicken, but he'd been about to break its neck. He rolled out of bed and pulled on a pair of black combat pants, festooned with nifty pockets for the storage of all kinds of interesting and useful things. He lifted the window shade and recoiled from the blue-white sunshine. He cracked the window and pulled the shade most of the way back down before plopping down at his computer.

T.R. nudged the mouse and lit a Marlboro. The box took fucking forever to wake up but the price had been right. The city had paid for the used computer because T.R. was the only student in Shard who needed access to college level AP courses and that wasn't going to happen under the tutelage of that walking root ball, Mizzzzz Najarian. (Maybe it'd be her?) As his dear, sage father liked to say about every three and a half fucking seconds, "Beggars can't be choosin' a fuckin' thing in this world."

Daddy would know, too. The Dalton's were as dirt poor as just about everyone else in Shard. When T.R.'s grandmomma finally kicked off a few years back, she'd left them with the family house and the property taxes to go with it. Sometimes, usually after a seventy-hour week, Daddy would muse about burning the grand old Victorian to the ground so they could up and move away. Finally get out and get a decent start somewhere that wasn't dead. They wouldn't have to travel sixty miles each way to a shitty job in a washing machine factory that threatened to close three or four times a year just to make barely enough money for food, gas and taxes on a house that no one would ever buy. But Momma wouldn't have it. The house had been in their family for generations. Her great grandpappy had built it and okay, okay already Martha-Jean, just get me a beer and shut yer fucking pie hole.

The computer beeped and T.R.'s eyes swam into focus. He opened four browser windows and filled each one with a different on-line newspaper. He liked to compare coverage of a single story by several different media outlets. One man's terrorist was another man's insurgent was another man's freedom fighter depending on the last name of the tired old fucker who owned the printing presses. That got old after a few minutes and he switched over to his favorite porn site, weirdasiansluts.com. He watched a grainy video of a skinny woman with a funnel in her rectum, mewling and moaning while another woman poured eels into the funnel. His cock didn't stir. Hell with it. He'd seen this one a buncha' times already anyway.

T.R.'s brain was fast, feverish at times, and the AP courses held his interest for short stretches. Chemistry was his favorite. If he could ever get his hands on a quantity of ammonium nitrate, well, let's just say they would finally get some fireworks in Shard for the next Fourth of July. The fuel oil part of the receipe was easy to get but since Oklahoma City, the Feds tracked any purchase of ammonium nitrate over a few pounds.

He was just so bored. The world was out there, strange and violent and beautiful in its chemical spill way, but he was never going to see it unless he got out. College wouldn't happen unless he got a scholarship, but no one was going to give a full ride to a white male. He just wasn't special enough. Hell, even the rich kids were getting turned down by schools they could pay for because they weren't black enough, Native American enough, handicapped enough, etcetera.

T.R. sat back and stared at the ceiling. The smoke from his cigarette rose in a dirty vine and coiled. He could still make out the ghost of old glow-in-the-dark stars, long painted over, from when he was little. When he was seven, he'd taken hours to lay them out in a night sky that was accurate to the real one, using the star map that came with the package. He'd lie in bed and look up at those green radium stars, imagining what life would be like on other planets. Or, what another life would be like on this one. Now, they were just outlines under a layer of yellowing latex paint.

Who would it be? Who would it be? His parents were just too cliché, besides part of T.R.'s motivation for the act would be the horror it caused. He wanted to see the looks on the faces of the other shitbergers after they found the savaged corpse, especially his parents. And it would be savage. No mere disappearance would do; we're talking evisceration and creative flesh arrangement. The act itself was as much a symbol as an outlet. T.R.'s kill would be a sacrifice to the universe, a payment for his escape from Shard. He would send a body into the void so that he might be delivered out of this one.

He stubbed out the cigarette and rubbed the heels of his palms into his eyes. It just wasn't coming to him here. His bedroom just wasn't the right environment; probably the stupid-rays eminating from the rest of the house. Well, he had a place. Shard was full of unused corners and caves. When his subconscious threw up the victim's name he would drag the supplicant to his own special cathedral, and T.R. Dalton would take his time. No one would hear the screaming or disturb them. He'd give Shard one thing: when you wanted to do evil, it didn't get in your way.

* * *

"DARWIN, YOU DUMB dog!" Childe shouted. "Loraine'll will totally unmake me if I go into the woods." The last statement had been to himself as Childe watched the shifting emerald shadows close around his dog's wagging tail. Whatever he had scented where the sidewalk ended and the smoking meadow began had gotten into the beagle's brain and set him off. Darwin had shot across the hummocky field, zigzagging around plumes of yellow smoke and disappeared into the woods on the other side. Childe shifted from tennis shoe to tennis shoe and stared at the useless length of closeline, the knot at the end unraveled. He bunched it up and shoved it in his pocket. The air was acrid with sulphur and the sun slammed down, shimmering the air over the meadow. Darwin barked a single happy yap, muffled by the trees and distance. "Crap," Childe said, and trotted off after him.

He knew better than to be in this field. The seam wasn't far below and you never knew when the ground would give way. One minute you could be strolling along looking to collect your annoying dumb beagle who always gets you in trouble, the next a flaming mouth could open beneath your Keds and chew you right up. Except it wouldn't be chewing. You'd cook. When Childe first met Constable Will, he had warned the boy to stay away from any area where there was a lot of smoke. Aside from the dangerous fumes, a heavy amount of venting meant the seam was close and burning hot. Will had told of a young girl back from Shard's earlier days who had fallen through the thin crust in such an area. She'd had survived by clinging to a tree root, but when they pulled her out, her poor legs had blackened and shriveled to sticks. And now here he was.

Childe looked up from his footing. The dark edge of the woods didn't seem any closer. He imagined he could feel the crackling of the fires below, vibrating just below the soil. A tuft of grass compressed under his foot and he let out a little yelp. Not falling, dummy, it was just soft there. He let out his breath. His eyes stung and watered. Why did they move here again? Oh, right, so he could grow up somewhere safe in a real American town, not in Psychosexual Sin Farmtonville—one of Lorain's favorite names for Hollywood.

Darwin let out another volley of doggy shouts. They were playful, excited. He barked like that when he and Childe were playing chase, but they were getting farther and farther away. Childe started to jog, sweat rolling down his face. A minute later he crossed the threshold into the gray-green halls of oak and maple. The air was at least ten degrees cooler and stripped of most of the steel mill smells. It took his eyes half a minute to adjust to the gloom. As they did, an old deer trail materialized, cutting through the undergrowth and Childe set off again.

The forest closed in and rushed past in flickering antechambers. Other deer trails branched off, but Childe kept to his original path. Darwin was this way. He just knew it. In fact, it was almost as if a voice in his head were telling to keep on straight, he was almost there. He stopped short at a wall of holly bushes that was so regular and impenetrable it could have been part of a hedge maze. Childe panted his breath back and walked along it left then right. The holly wall ran in a rough circle for a long way, a couple of hundred feet he guessed. That meant—he scrunched up his face—it was at least sixty feet or so through the middle. Man, this thing was weird. A big stand of one kind of bush or tree wasn't so off, but all perfect like this? Darwin barked again and something russled deep in the center of the spikey mass. "Darwin?" The beagle yapped back, but in a "come and play" tone.

How was Childe going to get through this? It seemed he had had forgotten his chainsaw again. The same voice in his head (Was it his? It *sounded* like his, but felt…apart) told him to get down on his hands and knees. He crawled around a short way to the right. A tunnel. Clear as day and as perfectly formed as the rest of this crazy thing. It was just big enough for a slim boy of twelve to wiggle through on his tummy. Just like playing commandos. Keep yer' head down, dogface! Halfway through he saw a flash of doggy legs go zipping by and a smile rose on his face. A second later, a clutch of what looked like those dominatrix boots from the shop windows back in Hollywood, or like varnished walking sticks clattered by.

Childe froze. He couldn't tell what those things had been, but it couldn't have been good. An image of the giant web came to mind and something deep below his rational mind tore loose and started to scream. He dug his elbows into the dirt and began to scramble backward. His feet plunged into spiky growth. The tunnel had closed behind him. He tried to push through, to heck with some scratches, but the holly was too dense. In fact, he could feel it advancing up his calfs. No, this wasn't possible. It was sealing off the way out! If he didn't move forward the thorney bushes would encase him. Childe shot forward, but his feet were caught in a tangle of sticks and roots. The panic rose up in his throat and he made a little mewling noise. That's what did it. He heard himself and was disgusted with the weakness in that sound, the early surrender. He yanked and tugged, the dusty soil filling his nostrils. With one great explosive jerk he shot forward, losing his shoes to the tunnel as it healed up behind him.

Childe tumbled into a large clearing about fifty feet across. And before his mind could process anything else, he felt a ridiculous moment of pride in himself that his math had been right when you took the thickness of the walls into account. An instant later he was mashing his back into the holly, scratching the hell out of his shoulders and not caring, trying to move as far from the scene in front of him as possible.

A spider. A spider the size of a horse. A spider as black and shiny as one of Loraine's old vinyl record albums. A spider with twin clusters of crimson eyes and slashing mandibles as big as your forearm. A spider balancing on jointed, graceful spike-legs...*was playing with his dog.* It was unmistakable. Darwin was down on his front legs, his ears forward, his beagle butt and wagging tail high in the air. The spider moved in jerky little dodges, then froze, then moved back, the javalin points of its legs thudding into the ground with a staccato Childe could feel in his sock feet. Darwin followed, jumping in and then back. Every now and then he would give a delighted bark. Childe played with him like this all the time.

Childe whispered, "Darwin, c'mere boy," as if by keeping his voice low he could somehow hide from the monster. Darwin wasn't interested. They had begun a new game. The spider would gently knock him to his belly with one outstretched leg, and Darwin would roll over, then jump up and run around and around the hulking arachnid barking with joy. Childe put an edge in his whisper, "Darwin! Come!"

The dog looked over and obeyed. Had Darwin been a human kid he would have slumped his shoulders and dragged his toes in the dirt as he walked over to his master. Childe crouched down and pulled the dog to his chest. He ran shaking hands over his dog as if searching for the terrible wounds those legs and jaws must be capable of rending. The spider stared at them, reflecting the boy and his dog in those eight red spheres.

Fear tears began to cloud Childe's eyes. *Never hurt you, boy.* Came into his mind. Again, in his own voice, but different, apart. *Darwin is my friend. He fought the coyotes until the last. He's a good, brave dog. Are you a good, brave boy?*

Childe squeezed his eyes shut and whimpered, "Mom."

Darwin whined. Childe opened his eyes and Loraine Howard was standing across from him. Her eyes were as big as saucers and full of blood. She blew him a kiss. Childe sucked in a gasp as she twisted and melted back into the spider. The monster turned in a dainty circle and sort of hunched down on its front legs. Childe blinked. Had it just bowed? What the hell was going on here? Was he dreaming? Darwin licked his face. Uck. No, way. There wasn't any dog breath in dreams. The spider was looking at him again. "What do you want?"

Are you a good, brave boy?

"Is that you? Is that you in my head?"

Childe's mouth dropped open as the spider pulled in four of its legs, the other four turning into human arms and legs—familiar arms and legs. An instant later, Childe was staring at himself. The spider-Childe touched a finger off his brow and spun back into the spider a second later. Darwin barked and wagged his tail. The spider's mandibles scissored, a decidedly creepy sight, but Childe got the impression it was laughing. And like reaching into your pocket and finding an unexpected twenty-dollar bill, a laugh bubbled up from Childe.

You are *a brave boy.*

"That is you! You're talking in my head, aren't you?"

The spider affected another bow.

"Did you help Darwin the other day, when he got hurt?"

The spider morphed into a pefect Darwin, right down to the wagging tail and jaunty doggy grin. It changed back just as fast.

"Holy shit."

Its mandibles scissored.

A hundred stories raced through Childe's head. Hans Christian Andersen and the Brothers Grimm wrestled with Tolkien for space in his mind as he tried to classify and clarify. Andersen won. If it had been Tolkien or the Grimm boys, that big sucker'd be picking Loraine Howard's boy out of its garden shears by now. "So, like, what are you? Like a fairy or a goblin, or something?"

Something. Old One. Djinn. First One.

"You don't look so old."

The spider flashed into a quasar about five feet across, burning and rotating in the air across from Childe before morphing back. Childe who had grown up with visions of *Star Trek* holodecks and holographic computer displays found this easier to process than his mother would have, but it was still a little jarring.

"I get it," Childe said. "I think."

Darwin rolled over showing his belly, allowing Childe to stroke him into a lazy doze. These were the dog days of summer after all. Childe stared at the spider. Now that he wasn't as afraid, his curiosity began to hammer. Once, he'd caught a great big house spider (although "great big" were now terms he would no longer apply to this particular memory) under a water glass and had stared at it close-up. This what-ever-it-was (*First one. Djinn*) seemed pretty much the same…just, uh, huge. Well, the house spider had been brown with a couple of black stripes on its back. This thing was as black as coal.

"Do you live in the woods?"

The spider stabbed a leg into the soft earth.

"Underground?"

It bowed.

"Like a gopher?"

The spider began to morph into a gopher with great buck teeth but kept its legs. The spider-gopher ran around in a little circle then frantically burried itself in a hole. It changed back, mandibles blurry with scissoring. Childe laughed, too.

"You're funny."

The spider bowed.

Childe's brow screwed up. "What're you doing here?"

The spider didn't move for a moment, then just as Childe was about to ask another question, it morphed into a clanking suit of armor, then halved and became two identical suits. Each had a poleaxe at its side. Childe's mouth opened and the armor crossed their poleaxes in a tall X. "You're a guard?"

The spider changed back and bowed.

"Hey," Childe asked. "How come you don't just tell me stuff in my head? How come you show me everything?"

Hurts to talk.

"Oh, sorry."

It raised a foreclaw.

"So what're you guarding against, or from, or whatever?"

The spider fixed Childe with those multiple eyes and for a moment, the boy's fear raced up his veins like liquid nitrogen. This time it took its time on the change—slowly melting into a lanky human figure. Its black carapace flowed into black leather. Its multiple red eyes merged like drops of magnetized mercury into two black lenses. Its bristles condensed into long greasy hair. When it was finished, the killer from Montana stood motionless before Childe. The boy looked for a long time, taking in the sharp bones and sunken cheeks, the long fingers and ragged nails, the fish-belly skin. He found himself whispering again as he asked, "Who is he?"

The man's arms split up the middle, becoming four as his legs elongated and thinned. His back humped and his sunglasses compounded. His waist narrowed to a thread and chitin shears punched through his lips. Delicate, veined wings sprouted from his shoulder blades. The crotch of his leather pants bulged then burst through with a cruel obsidian stinger. A moment later a seven-foot wasp hung a couple of feet off the ground under twin blurs that blew and tossed the holly leaves. The wings buzzed low and made Childe want to cover his ears. Just as it was becoming too much to bear, the spider returned.

Childe just breathed for a moment, one hand over his chest like an overwrought debutante. Darwin peeked out from under his paws. "So, he's like you? He changes."

The spider raised a foreclaw.

"But he's bad. I could tell that. He's bad."

The spider morphed again, this time into an old-fashioned, ornate scale. One plate dragged the ground, piled high with bones, the other high in the air. The spider returned.

The Pompiliad comes.

"What? Here?" Childe suddenly wanted a stick or a rock to hold. "Can you keep him away?"

The spider just looked at him.

"So what do..." Childe began and stopped. Darwin lifted his head and cocked an ear. "What *is* that?" A humming not unlike the sound the great wasp had made, but smaller, harmonized was growing near. The light grew dim. Childe looked up. The air over the little clearing was dark with hornets. There must be a thousand, each as big as a man's thumb. The swarm whirled, moving in and through itself like sentient smoke. The spider crouched.

Go.

Childe felt the holly give behind him as a new tunnel opened. Darwin was growling low in his throat; he felt hot and his muscles were tense and hard under Childe's hands. "No, boy. *No!*" But Darwin wanted to move in close to the spider. He wanted to fight. The buzzing from the swarm had become a din. Childe began to feel it seep in between his ears, making him sleepy. It was such a hot day. He could just lie out on the cool earth here.

CHILDE HOWARD, RUN! GO!

Childe's head snapped back so hard it felt like being smacked. The spider had reared up on its back four legs, it's mandibles dripping fluid that steamed and sizzled as it hit the ground. The swarm was coalescing above it like a storm cloud. A tentacle of wasps rode the air down and wound around the spider. The great arachnid batted it into decoherence, but the wasps regrouped. Two more tendils smoked across the clearing toward Childe. He wouldn't get through the tunnel in time. Even if he did, the wasps would follow and have him. They would sting him to death in that tight, dark space. Childe saw his own frantic face reflected in the crimson eyes of the spider.

Suddenly, the spider was all red, covered with hundreds of bright little black eyes. Triangles of bright red were everywhere. Even the legs were made up of shards of red, dotted with black eyes. Childe blinked and the spider exploded into a flock of cardinals. The boy and dog were enclosed in a cloud of flickering blood. The cardinals wheeled and dove, snapping at the wasps, crushing their heads and thoraxes in their smart little beaks. There were nearly as many birds as insects, but they never so much as brushed a feather against each other, their flight was so coordinated. A cardinal fell to the ground in front of Childe, a wasp riding its belly, digging in its stinger again and again. Another fell and another. The voice came again to Childe, but different now, shattered. *Run while I dance with them.*

Childe didn't need to be told again. He shoved Darwin through the tunnel, feeling it close up behind him as went. When he reached the other side of the holly wall, he picked up Darwin (the solid beagle seemed to weigh nothing) and pelted down the deer trail, sure that he trailed a pennant of buzzing, poison needles. He burst into the bright sun at the meadow, the heat and fumes plowing up his nose. He put Darwin down and they ran together for the buildings across the grassy, smoking expanse. Perhaps they could find shelter inside.

When they reached the sidewalk, Childe couldn't run anymore. A wicked stitch seared in his side and his breath was whistling. Black spots danced in front of his eyes. He doubled over and threw up what was left of his breakfast. Darwin stopped a few yards up and barked at him to get a move-on. Childe straightened and looked back. No wasps. He listened. Other than the roar of his own blood there wasn't a sound. Not even the chirp of a cardinal.

Childe walked with Darwin back up the street, sweating in torrents and trying to catch his breath let alone his mind. It had all happened; he was sure of it. He was sure of two other things as well: One, he had to get his mother and leave this place. Two, she would never believe him. After another minute or so passed, a third thought occurred to him: He was needed here. *Are you a brave boy?* Those suits of armor had been empty. Was he expected to put one on? His mind's eye ran over the giant scales.

Whose bones had heaped the heavy plate? There had been so many.

* * *

EYES PEERED FROM the dusty glass of the ticket taker's booth as Childe Howard trudged past the old movie theatre. T.R. kept perfectly still as the new kid and his mutt walked by. Well, there it was. He knew that if he came to his special place, his cathedral, the focus of his summer project would present itself.

* * *

IN THE HOLLY, a pile of red and black death as high as a young boy's knees lay still. A stuttering swarm, much diminished, smoked over the forest floor away from the battleground. In the other direction, a seven-legged spider limped back to the dark mouth of the mine. Underneath, the great dragon sighed with a weariness like gravity.

* * *

THREE HUNDRED MILES from Shard, a wasp that looked like a man twisted open the throat of its chopper and grinned down the distance.

Chapter 14

ERICA WALKED THROUGH the woods and thought about George Rhodes and the merits of comfortable shoes. She had a couple of hours before dinner and he had shooed her out of the kitchen. ("No Rhodes ever accepted help in the kitchen from a house guest.") He'd suggested she go for a stroll in the woods at the end of the street. There was a hiking trail that looped up the bluff to the old mine offices and back. He'd loaned her a pair of his mother's old walking shoes. Not the height of fashion, but let's face it: there was no such thing as a fashionable tennis shoe—not to a woman like Erica. The Keds were a little loose but nothing a double pair of socks couldn't fix. And an extra layer of fabric between her toes and the inside of another person's shoes didn't bother her at all.

The four-o'clock sun was just beginning to take a serious slant, throwing strange, shifting disco lights through the canopy. There were bugs, but they were lazy, drunk on August heat and the deep green of the forest. An easy breeze dragged a hand through the trees and Erica was reminded of the sound newspaper makes as it tumbles down a quiet street. She took in a great breath of air. Something in her was unclenching.

Shard wasn't what she expected at all so far. Erica had been sure it was going to be a mix of *Deliverance* and *The Road Warrior*. But where she thought she'd find industrial waste and devastation, she found a ghost town in repose, folding back into the mountain. Where she thought she'd encounter uneducated simpletons, she met brilliant, complicated George Rhodes.

George was a drunk. She got that. She also got that he hadn't taken more than three drinks their whole day together. She wasn't fooling herself, he needed to fix every now and again, or the pain came on him. But he wasn't swimming in it either. When he had first answered the door, he'd just come up from a deep dive. Now, he seemed to be keeping to the shallows. She knew why. What she didn't know was why she was encouraging it. She was here to murder this place the rest of the way.

What would a man like George think of Manhattan? Would he flourish there, follow his intellect into the pursuits available to someone with his kind of intelligence? He might not be sporting an MBA or a JD, but he was the kind of person who stood out. That was how you made it in New York. You had to be something special. George was something special. She could help him get his start, and then…

"Really, Erica? Seriously?" She sighed at the sound of her own voice and sat down on an old log. She flicked a ladybug off the knee of her jeans and noticed a chip in her nail polish. She was already coming apart, changing, slipping back into the mountain like everything else around here. A waft of sulphur tinted the air for a moment, riding a shift in the breeze as the day lost its heat an hour at a time.

She waved a droning fly away and the air sweetened, filtered through tannin and water-heavy leaves. That clutch in her solar plexus ratcheted down another notch and she closed her eyes. Orange and black, webbed with retinal blood vessels, shifted, shifted. A twig cracked and she opened her eyes to find a deer foraging a few yards away. It was a fawn, finely muscled and glossy. Erica froze, but it sensed her. The deer lifted its elegant neck and regarded her. For a long time they looked at each other—dark city eyes to dark forest eyes. "Hello," Erica said, expecting the deer to run, hoping it would not. It dropped its head and cropped a fern.

Erica sat with her hands in her lap as the forest moved and lived around her. The fawn nosed through the undergrowth, never more than a few yards away, flicking an ear at the odd mosquito. A tear slipped from Erica's eye and patted down, a small dark circle on her jeans.

* * *

AMY JAMES CHECKED her watch. She had another forty minutes or so before she had to meet the yummy constable for dinner at his friend's place. God, was she really going on a double date with the town's lone lawman and his most reliable customer at the jail? Yup. Was she also snowing him a little while she went behind his back to treasure hunt based on a wild story about giant-spiders-and-dragons-oh-my? Yup. Multi-tasking was indeed one of her specialties. Having her cake and eating it too was how to win, and she could have it if she wanted it. Besides, all she was doing at this point was tramping around in the woods a little bit. If she happened to find the shaft opening Will had walked through chasing his dead father, and she just happened to locate the horde of diamonds and other precious gems he'd described, well, all the better.

There was the berm humping up the leaf-littered floor like Will described—a giant anaconda taking a giant siesta under a giant carpet. She crested it in motorcycle boots and a cornflower-blue babydoll dress. The dress was ridiculous and one of her favorites. She was being very careful not to get it dirty. Treasure hunting or not, she still wanted to look hot for Will. He made her, well, feel kinda goofy. She stopped on the little rise and there it was, complete with the thin stream of yellow smoke rising from the top of the opening: the shaft.

Amy walked in close and the smell burned her nose. Man, what was she thinking? She knew better than most people how dangerous it was to go screwing around inside a condemned mine, let alone one that was fucking on fire. Her ambition burned back. Hell with it. She started in and stopped as the cornflower-blue caught in the corner of her eye. She'd ruin the dress if she went in there with it. Well, easy enough remedy to that problem. Amy slipped the dress over her head and hung it from a sapling growing just to the side of the entrance. She pulled a little mag-lite from her boot and paused, imagining what she must look like from behind—a young woman scrawled with tattoos, wearing men's tighty-whities and a lacy blue Victoria's Secret bra, complete with chunky black motorcycle boots. Amy spun, penlight held like a light sabre, but there was no one there. Her tattoos crawled with goose flesh.

"Am I really this dumb," she said to herself. The tunnel before her hollowed her voice and ate it. She shined the flashlight in and around the walls. The supports were still in place and looked sound enough. She took a step, another. The heat wasn't too bad and the smoke was sticking to the ceiling. She shone her light up on the zero-gravity stream of black that boiled along the roof. Amy checked over her shoulder. The breeze tugged at her dress and a flag of jaunty blue winked at her from the opening. *All's well out here, babe! How's the mouth of hell treatin' ya?* The opening was close, she was okay.

Amy kept walking, panning the beam around the walls, looking for the... There it was the, the crack in the side that Will had gone through—that Will had chased the ghost of his father through. She splashed the powerful little Mag-Lite into the gap. The floor angled down at about 30 degrees, the walls a good three feet apart. The overall shape was circular and fairly regular. She reached in and ran her callused hand along the skin of the wall. It was pebbly. The fumes were strong here, really acrid. She coughed and looked up. Sure enough the stream of upsidedown black was thicker here and closer due to the smaller bore.

She stuck her head in and squinted at the wall. Something in the texture had her hackles up. Patterns were forming up in her head, she knew the feeling. A little more data, just a little more. She spat on the stone and wiped it with her hand. Her palm came back covered in soot from the coal smoke. Amy shined the light at the clean spot and sucked in a gasp. The stone was crystaline and yellow-brown. Her heart started to pound. She turned and spat on the opposite wall (hard to get enough saliva now), cleaning it with her hand as she had before. Holy shit, more of the same. It was a ryolite pipe—what happened when molten rock from under the mantle, under terrific pressure, thrust up through the surface.

She couldn't believe it. You didn't find these in America in more than a couple of places. You sure as hell didn't find them in coal mines. You found them in Africa. You found them in diamond mines. Amy forgot her fear and walked farther into the pipe. She wished she had a tank of water and hand pump. If she bet right, this whole structure was like the inside of that geode she'd given to Kiddo the other day, except it was full of yellow diamonds instead of amythest. She was so excited she didn't see the hole that Will had fallen through. One heavy, booted foot came down on nothing. Amy yelped, and jammed her hands out, the sharp walls biting into her palms. She arrested her fall, one foot hanging in space, the other on solid ground. The Mag-Lite was not so lucky. She watched it tumble down and down and down, illuminating the sides of another pipe, a throat of pure emeralds the size of her gaping mouth.

* * *

ERICA AND AMY were both distracted during dinner but got on well enough. The conversation around George Rhodes's bright kitchen table was easy, and the wine flowed. The menu was simple—venison and steaming cornbread with fresh greens from the garden—but presented with flare and skill. The men laughed and talked, ribbed each other and were joined by the women. Amy liked Erica—she was a bitch and sharp as the rocks in a ryolite pipe. Erica liked Amy—she was funny, cared fuck-all for the niceties and was quiet at the right times. George and Will were pleased as punch with themselves and each other.

Chapter 15

CYRUS MACCOY LIVED outside of Shard proper but considered himself a citizen. His cabin, moss covered and silvered with age, slumped at the base of a natural granite wall. You could walk right by it and never realize it was a home, which suited Cyrus just fine. His still was over the ridge on the other side of the granite knob near a clear stream; the chuckling water echoing off that great rock lulled him to sleep each night. Cyrus had watched his Pa stumble around more and more as the whiskey blind came on him, and so never took a drop himself. But, the family business was the family business. To his knowledge he was the last of the family, so the still was all he had left. Sure there were other MacCoys, and *Mc*Coys maybe, but no one that he was close related to, nowhere around Shard anyway. He was alone in his woods.

The same fair summer evening that found Will and George, Erica and Amy strolling post-dinner through a town burnt orange with sunset found Cyrus MacCoy tinkering with his still. He fiddled a bit with the tubing between the burner tank and the furnace, coating the joints with a soapy mixture that would bubble if there were any leaks. There were always leaks, but nothing too bad. The high-pitched voice of his old Pa crackled at him, raw with drink. *Ain't no such thing as a safe still, boy. Bitch'll turn and bite cha', you give her half a chance.* Then the old man (he was always old, even when Cyrus was barefoot in biballs) would lift a greasy flap of hair and show off the scar that wormed along the side of his head and over his ear. The ear itself looked like a twisted mushroom. Pa had died crazy and blind; his mind and his eyes fired out by white lightning.

Cyrus's hands were filthy except at the finger tips where he rubbed the liquid soap into the creases of pipe and tubing. A cluster of soap bubbles bloomed at the join between the burner tank and the outflow hose. He squinted a brilliant blue eye at the leak and then looked up into the canopy, tossing easy in the evening breeze. Oh dammitalltahell. He'd have to bank down the fire and unhook half of everything to fix this. When he did that he was likely to find ten more things needed fixing and that meant going to town for parts. Did he have enough lightning jarred up for a run so as not to waste a trip? He looked up again. Wasn't going to happen tonight, too late now. Get some dinner then. Tomorrow for the bitch still.

Back in his cabin after a meal of canned chili (oh, was his little house going to smell like the ass end of a bull come sun up), Cyrus sat at his little desk crammed between a wall layered with stacked mason jars on one side and canned goods on the other. He bent over his ledger, squinting in the hiss of a forty-year-old Coleman lattern. *Never write your dealings down. Law can read, too, you know.* Cyrus had heeded Pa's advice to an extent, kepping his ledger in code. Each mason jar was a "brick", moonshine whiskey was "mortar" and every dollar was a "pebble".

Cyrus and his Pa and his Pa's Pa on back had been running moonshine since before The War Between the States. Buried deep in the soft soil at the base of the granite knob was a copper-lined chest full of money, some of it printed with the likenesses of those generals on the losing side. Now in his fifties (he guessed), Cyrus could retire in style if he wanted. He could even afford to move into that fancy Rhodes rooming house for the rest of his days. Have someone else do his cooking and cleaning. (Well, to be honest, he'd never done much of either anyway.) Hell, he could even move away from Shard itself, nasty sulphur-smelling ashtray of a place. But the hoard never felt quite full enough. Just another few runs in his old International Harvester pick-up. Just another few dozen bricks of mortar and he'd have enough pebbles to put a bullet in the Harvester and the bitch still alike. He glanced over at the old, but gleaming, possum gun leaning by the bed.

Truth be told, there wasn't any reason to code his dealings. The Constable trooped on up here every couple of months or so, just to see how Cyrus was getting on. He knew well enough what Cyrus brewed on the other side of the ridge. Everyone knew; it was how he stayed in business. Most every house in Shard and the surrounding hills—even up to the county seat—had an empty mason jar or two that smelled more like lightning than put-away peaches. Cyrus was like a backwoods milkman. Constable Will just warned him to keep his shine away from young folks and drunks like George Rhodes. (No worries on either. Cyrus was afraid of kids and Rhodes never touched the whitelightning, cottoning to his gin.) Other than that, the young lawman would check to see if Cyrus needed anything, if he was safe, healthy. Had he seen any coyotes? Were the other hill families doing all right? Cyrus always offered to pay his "taxes" to the Constable (as traditional as the rest of it) and Will always refused. Told Cyrus that information and responsibility were payment enough.

Cyrus always had plenty of information for Will. He was the only person making rounds through Shard's suburbs: the clutches of shacks and cabins and even a few doublewides the hill families called home. There weren't more than twenty souls living back in the woods, and, truth be told, that was fine with Cyrus. Maroons most of them. The women was too short and fat (cept' maybe that Maggie Owens girl and she was only fourteen) and the men was all stupid and drunk. All right, that last part was mostly his doing, but if he didn't sell it to them they'd just beat on their short, fat wives all the more. Wasn't as if they had jobs. Most of them scraped by on garden plots and hunting. Lord knows how the fat ones got fat. Good old Cyrus always knew their doings though, and Will liked to know them too.

Cyrus blinked and sat back, his old chair creaking, threatening, holding. He rubbed his face, the gray stubble on his cheeks rasping in the stillness. He pulled a corncob pipe from his shirtpocket and filled it with homegrown tobacco from those self-same Owenses, delivered by their too-young-for-him-to-be-thinking-about-her-that-way daughter. He got up and stood in the open door of his little cabin, the pipe a censer in a cathedral of old trees. The air had gone all purple-blue and a few fireflies lit their behinds at one another. One would go off and then a string would follow like bulbs on down a line into the dark. Blink, blink, blink—deeper into the woods they went. Cyrus counted them: one, two, three-four, five…six. His teeth clamped down on the pipe stem. There was a woman standing back in the shadows looking at him.

He narrowed his eyes and despite the growing darkness touched a sun-visor hand to his brow. The pipe suddenly smelled like roasted shit. "Hello?" he called out. "Who is that?" Cyrus looked over his shoulder into the cabin. His gun was loaded and one long stride away. He turned back and she was now a couple of yards from the cabin, standing just outside the trapezoid of light the lantern flung out the door. Cyrus dropped his pipe. "Lord a' mighty, lady, you gave me start!" He laughed and shook his head. "A man can get a little jumpy out here by his onesome." He peered at her in the gloom. Her face was pale and framed by black hair that looked like it hadn't felt a brush in a few days. He couldn't see her eyes. "You, uh, out here on your own, too?"

She nodded.

"You looking for a jar?"

Another nod.

"Course' you are," Cyrus said, shaking his head. "Why else would you come out here by yourself, cept' to liven up a dull night. Am I right? Sure I am." He turned around and waved a hand over his shoulder. "C'mon in and I'll get you fixed up." He walked over to the desk and with a grunt slid the left corner over about a foot. He opened a trap door in the floor and pulled out a sloshing mason jar full of clear liquid. Even with his meticulous storage (his product tended to evaporate in a hurry otherwise) the fumes poked fingers up his nostrils that were almost as familiar as his own.

A footstep scraped the floor behind him. The corners of Cyrus's mouth perked. Finally he could get a real look at this lil' lady customer. Maybe they could have a sampling before his mysterious visitor disappeared back into the night. "Now how was you fixing to pay for this here order?" he said, turning around.

Cyrus breath caught, "Oh, it's you." His heart (and prick) sank. He wasn't getting a thing from the town's dried-up old school marm. "Something wrong Missus Najarian? You feel sickly? You don't mind my saying so, you don't look very well."

Charlotte Najarian's clothes and hair were filthy. The creases of her elbows and the folds of her neck were lined with dirt. A purple-black stain flowed up her arm from her hand, following her viens and bringing them into sharp relief against her white cheek. The fingernails on that hand were black. The fingers on her other hand looked as if something had been at them. Her eyes were on him, but cloudy, empty. In the close confines of the cabin her smell enveloped Cyrus and he winced.

Out of manners, Cyrus forced himself not to cover his nose with the back of his hand. He took a step toward her and almost put his hands on her shoulders before thinking better of it. Whatever she had might be contagious. "Here," he said, "sit yourself down on the bed here." He was already going over what to do for her. He would have to leave her here and go for Constable Will in the Harvester. Much as he hated to drive the two leaf-covered ruts he thought of as the Woods Road after sundown, it was what a man did. This poor lady was sickly something awful. Could it have been a critter bite? Her hand did look, well, *chewed.*

"How'd you ever get yourself all the way out here?" he asked busying himself by his camp stove once he got her set down on the bed. "I'll make you some tea. The Owenses gave me a packet of root tea—don't ask me what kind of root—but it always makes me feel better when I'm feeling poorly."

Cyrus turned up the heat on the stove and prayed the water would boil soon so he could get the tea steeping. Anything he could do to fight the stink coming off this poor woman would be a blessing. Maybe it was blood poisoning; that might explain the dark coloring on her other arm and her veins all showy like that. Would that explain the smell, though? Once a person had that gassy, sweet odor coming off them, well, flies made more sense than doctors. The reek actually intensified, making his eyes water. *"Sweet Jesus,"* he mutered, breathing through his mouth. He turned around and she was standing right behind him. "What are—?" he began.

She opened her mouth wide, wide, too wide and extended a long gray tongue. Perched on the end, like a tiny diver at the end of the board, was the biggest hornet Cyrus had ever seen. It was thick as his thumb and shone blue-black like a wet piece of coal. Charlotte pulled her tongue and its rider back into her mouth. "Oh. My. God," Cyrus said shaking his head slowly back and forth. He took a step back and bumped into the wall of mason jars. They jangled like dream music. Charlotte smiled and darted at him, pressing her stinking body against his with uncanny strength. Mason jars fell and exploded. He opened his mouth to scream and she clamped her lips over his. Cyrus MacCoy's eyes bulged as something sharp and buzzing passed between them.

Cyrus lay still on a carpet of broken glass, a web of black veins radiating from his lips and neck. He died with his jaw clenched and set. Charlotte stood over him, swaying gently, her mouth unhinged and tongue dangling. The forest hissed with the night winds every so often, but no animals called. After twenty minutes, a muffled buzzing stirred behind Cyrus's locked teeth. A moment later, the triangular head of the wasp scissored its way through his cheek. It pulled itself through the hole and took a moment to pass its legs and antenna through its mandibles. It flicked itself into the air and alighted on Charlotte's tongue. She hauled the wasp back into her mouth.

Charlotte shambled over to Cyrus and threw him over her shoulder like his near two-hundred pounds were little more than a rolled up doormat. She pivoted and walked out into the night with her prize. She would take him home and together they would wait in the crawlspace under her porch. There was room. She'd been digging.

Chapter 16

WILL SAT IN his mother's favorite old rocking chair and watched Amy James sleep. Dinner at George's had been a blast. They'd stayed up drinking, telling their stories and playing Trivial Pursuit. George, of course, trounced them all, but Erica gave him a run for his money. George hadn't drunk any more than the rest of them the whole night and Will was pretty sure his best friend had laughed more in a single evening than in the year leading up to it.

Will rocked in the dark and thought about Erica. She was good for George, but he wasn't sure how good she was for Shard. And what would happen to George when she was finished here? There was something between them, something big and true, anyone could see that, but would it be enough to survive when it came time for her leave? Amy stirred, rolled over and sighed something in her sleep about ryolite. At least that's what it sounded like. One tattooed arm lay stark against the sheet in the moonlight.

The sex had been amazing. Will had been a little nervous at first. It wasn't like he couldn't get himself out of Shard every so often. He had a couple of women he dated on and off in Lewiston and another in Somerset, but it had still been the better part of six months. He'd reached the point in his life when sex was something that left him empty if the emotional connection wasn't there, and had begun to resign himself to the excentric old bachelor model. Nothing wrong with being on the lonesome—he enjoyed loneliness to some extent—but Will was wired to love. Amy had surprised him. With all her tattoos and crazy hair he'd been sure she would be a wildcat in bed, but she'd been slow and gentle. It was he who had lost control (to her delight) and went all howlin' wolf. The moon streamed through the window over his shoulder and brushed her cheek with blue-white.

Is this where it starts? Would he look back in a few years and remember this moment as the one when he fell in love with Amy James? No. Some question stood on his heart. There was something she wasn't telling him and…the other thing—the concussion dream, the hallucination, whatever you wanted to call it. It wouldn't leave him be.

In the two days since he'd come back out of that hole in the ground, he'd been running from it, telling himself he hadn't seen it, that it didn't happen. It was just like Amy said: he'd fallen and banged himself up and his bruised brain had thrown some scary at him. That was it. But the cop in him wouldn't let it go. Amy's explanation would have worked just fine, but he'd seen his father *before* he fell. But it wasn't his father. It was some kind of demon watchdog that looked like a spider most of the time, but could look like anything it wanted to. *Yïn.* The dragon had called it, Yïn. Dragon. Jesus. Will leaned back in the rocking chair and closed his eyes.

Dampf was waiting there in the dark, wafting through its different forms: the little girl, the celestial angel, the obscene devil, and the towering dragon. Will Two-Bears McFarlan lived a great part of his life in his imagination, the pages of books his stepping stones into other worlds. He could tell the difference between make-believe and reality. He couldn't un-know what he knew. The dragon and the spider were real. They had pulled him underground because they wanted his help.

"The Pompiliad returns," he whispered in the dark.

Amy moaned and thrashed in the sheets, grew still.

Will tried to imagine it, the Wasp. Why couldn't demons be bunny-rabbits or fuzzy little puppies? He closed his eyes and tried to see it, but for some reason all he got was an image of his motorcycle. Will got up and stood over Amy. He brushed a stray lock of cobalt hair off her forehead and stared a little at the swirls on her shoulder. There was enough here to love, wasn't there? He walked out of the room. Give it some time; he'd only just met her.

Will walked out the front door without bothering to put any clothes on. There probably wasn't another living soul even awake in Shard right now, let alone about to walk by his house. The August night was cool, but with just enough moisture to give it a velvety feel on his skin. His Indian Chief leaned in the driveway. There was a tiny spec of bug guts on the tank that needed cleaning, but other than that it was as gorgeous as always. Now, there was a love he didn't have to question. It had been his dad's bike and now his, the family sword rumbling down the generations.

Will sat astride the bike; that one rear shock squeaked its usual welcome. He put his hands on the grips and closed his eyes, *The Pompiliad.* A flash of road blurring by under a front tire. He opened his eyes. Just the driveway and his little rancher with the neat row of box hedges out front. Will closed his eyes again. A horizon line, dead flat against a night sky sprayed orange with sodium light. Will scowled, what was this? Were these his thoughts? They felt *injected.* A city now, rising along that pin straight horizon. Great towers serrated with glowing windows and crowned with blinking antennae stretched up as the asphalt roared underneath him. He knew this city even before he passed the big green highway sign. The black tower, like a pyramid stretched long, with two great white horns, stood out in his memory from movies.

WELCOME TO CHICAGO
THE WINDY CITY

Will opened his eyes. It was getting close, eating the miles between the plains and the rolling Blue Ridge Mountains. How long until he heard the sound of another motorcycle echoing through the woods? Would it stop to eat or sleep? Or, would it wait until it got to Shard to feed? He wrapped his arms around himself. "Get a hold of yourself, gunslinger," he said. The shake in his voice was not a comfort. Goosebumps tightened his skin and his scrotum squirmed on the leather saddle.

There was no use telling himself this wasn't happening, or that it was some kind of dream. He knew what he knew. There would be no running from this into denial or craziness. Will let go of himself and gripped the handlebars. He was Authority, the Law, and there was no one else to take this job. How far was Chicago? Maybe eight hours. Will squeezed the front brake, expecting to hear that mousy little squeak and getting it. He'd fix that one day, but tonight it was like the voice of the Indian, telling him he wasn't alone. Would it really be here in eight hours?

Will breathed in the night air, cool, full of green and lavender. Frogs and crickets sang, the woods shushed and creaked. A whiff of sulphur found him and like the squeaky brake reminded him where he was and what was under him. He had more time. Shard wasn't ready to receive the Wasp yet. He didn't know how he could know any of this, how he could see these things in his mind, or how he could feel so certain about the time he did or did not have, but there it all was.

Will stared up at the stars, slow wheeling through the night toward dawn. Orion stood on the shoulders of a big oak, stretching his bow. Will wished his father was still alive. He needed some help. He swung off the bike and walked to the front door. He turned to survey the night one final time before heading in to bed…and froze.

His father was sitting astride the motorcycle.

No, not his father. The eyes were huge, black, anti-stars. The spider—Yïn. It tipped Will a wink and touched its index finger to its brow. *You have time to prepare. Gather your forces.* A smile split his father's face. *The Pompiliad gathers his.* The image of the road, Chicago receding in the side view mirror and the giant electrified intestines, pipe and tank and tower, of Gary, Indiana flashed in Will's mind.

Will shook his head and the images cleared. "Get out of my head," he said and turned to walk into the house. He stopped with his hand on the doorknob. "And get *the fuck* off my bike."

* * *

"GIANT SHAPE SHIFTING dragons and spiders, huh?" George said, sipping a fumey cup of coffee. Will could smell the gin in George's mug even over the gourmet French Roast he'd had delivered all the way from Lexington. Even so, in these last few days George seemed to be getting a handle on his alcohol problem, dosing down. Will looked at his best friend across the kitchen table.

"I know exactly how it sounds," Will said, keeping his voice low. The light coming through the windows was ashen, not yet full dawn. Erica was still asleep upstairs and George was half asleep in front of him, his hair corkscrewing off in several directions. "And I know how someone saying 'I know exactly how it sounds' sounds. You must think I've gone off my fucking nut." Will paused a second. Loraine had said that same thing to him the other day when she told him about finding Darwin in the web. And what had he done? Not believed her. Shit. He was an asshole. Nothing worse than figuring that out for oneself.

George stared into his coffee mug and thought about adding another half shot of gin. He didn't. He looked back up at William Two-Bears. Will's eyes were red-rimmed with purple bags under them and were a little too wide and white, but he didn't look crazy. George knew crazy. Up until just a few days ago he and mental illness met every morning in the bathroom mirror. So what did that leave? Will could have had a hallucination or a dream. He could have been sleepwalking. Or as Amy suggested he could have gotten a concussion when he fell through that hole. Jesus, what the hell was he doing down a shaft anyway? Everyone in Shard knew well enough to stay out of the damned mine, even the kids.

"Say something, man." Will said. "You're making me nervous."

George took a deep breath and ran a hand through his hair, spiking it up even crazier. "You're not nuts, I can tell that just by looking at you. Not any more than usual, anyhow."

Will blinked. "You believe me?"

George sipped his coffee, grimaced. "I wouldn't so much as call it belief, friend of mine. I mean, how on earth could I possibly wrap my gray matter around what you just told me?" He held up a hand before Will could say anything. "I'm not saying that what you said isn't true. I also have to wonder—*have to*, Will—if you had a somnambulistic episode or something like that. You know people have been known to drive cars and everything while they was sleeping. Hell, some folks get fat because they can't stay out of the fridge while they're dead to the world."

Will clenched a fist on the table. "You think I haven't been over that? I had myself convinced that I saw what I saw because I hit my head." Now that he thought about it, Amy was the one who convinced him of that. "But I saw my father *before* I hit my head and blacked out."

"You sure it couldn't have been someone else, man? C'mon, Constable, you're a cop for Christ's sake. Figure it out."

Will sighed. He needed to be patient. It had taken him three days to come around to believing and he had been the one who actually witnessed everything. He couldn't expect George to just cotton to his story over a single cup of coffee at 5:30 in the morning. "I know, I know." He sipped his coffee. "I been over this and over this. And I sure as hell didn't have a concussion when I saw him, or it, that fucking spider-thing tonight." He took on the rhythm of a witness reciting the facts at the scene. "I left Amy in the bedroom 'cause I couldn't sleep and walked outside. I sat on the Chief and had a kind of, I don't know, a kind of vision, I guess—saw where the Pompiliad was."

"The bad guy?"

"Yeah, the wasp thing. And then I got up to go back into the house, turned around and there he was sitting on the bike." He paused a moment. "My dad."

"And you told Amy?"

"Not about last night, this morning, whatever…no, but I ran into her the first time when I had just crawled out of the mine. That was after Dampf."

"The, uh, the dragon?"

"Yes, the *uh, the dragon.*"

"And what did Amy think of all this?" Now George had taken on the cadence of an interrogator—just the facts, ma'am.

"She was sure it must have been a concussion dream, too."

"Uh-huh, uh-huh, and how was the sex?"

Will looked up.

"She as much of a hotrod as her detailing might suggest, Constable?"

"Aw, shut up, man," Will said, but both men were laughing.

After a minute, Will sat up straight. "I got it."

"Oh, shit. You got what?"

"I'll show you. When it gets a little lighter, we'll just go back there with some gear and I'll introduce you." Will sat back.

"I don't think so, Constable."

"The fuck you mean?"

"I'm not going spelunking with you into a burning mine."

"That part of it wasn't even smoking," Will lied.

"Yeah, and what are you not even smoking, Señor Two-Bears?" George put his palms flat on the table and took a breath.

"Listen, aside from persuading me that you ain't gone on a trip to Wackeyland Farms, what do you need me to see this so bad for?"

Will thought of those towers of pipe and sodium light outside of Gary; he could almost feel the rumble of the alien motorcycle under him as it ate the miles. He thought of Dampf and Yïn: monsters, nightmares—they were the good guys. Will looked at George and admitted two hard things, "I'm scared, Georgie. I'm scared half to death and I need some help."

George looked into his friend's face and sighed long and tired. "I'm a little claustrophobic."

"The main chamber's really big."

"You said it's all full of diamonds and shit, right?"

"It's a fucking dragon horde, George."

"Right," George said. "Well, I'm taking one."

Will didn't argue. Outside, the sun threw a burning leg over the horizon and hauled itself into Shard.

Chapter 17

THE WASP ROARED onto the breakdown lane of highway 20 about three hours west of Toledo. Fallow fields of long grass stretched for miles, tossing in the breeze. A chalky blue pick-up truck skimmed the horizon on some farm road to the south. Dawn grayed the air. He could be back at the source, the mother cunt from his world into this one before the sun touched the other side of the sky. But it wasn't yet time. If he faced the dragon and its dog now, he would lose. His agents were at work, he could feel them, see through their faceted eyes as they enlarged the swarm, but it wasn't enough. It would take a thousand more just to beat the spider, let alone the dragon. There wasn't enough meat in Shard to make that many wasps.

A redwing blackbird flared like a match and settled on a barbed-wire fence a few feet away. The Pompiliad allowed it to draw his eye and scanned the land beyond. An empty barn with a sagging roof hulked about a quarter mile off the highway. He thought of Shard, thought of the outrider swarm and felt through them. The balance of power still favored the dragon. "Time," he whispered and the blackbird's tiny heart shriveled like a raisin. It fell into the grass where ants would find it and take it apart.

The Pompiliad blew a kiss at the fence. Rust stained the wire and ran along its length like blood poisoning. It infected the wood posts and they rotted in the space of a second or two. The motorcycle pushed through that section of wire like wet tissue and crushed down the grass in a line for the barn.

Inside the barn: strong smell of decay, wet grass, ammonia from the guano-painted beams; dawn light gassed through the many chinks in the walls. The Pompiliad guided the big chopper into the middle of the wide dirt floor and killed the engine. For a moment, he slumped in the saddle, greasy hair hanging around his face. He smelled the air, past the obvious natural odors. He inhaled sharply—there it was— someone had died here. He swung a long leg over the bike and got down on all fours, smelling the dusty ground like a bloodhound. He paused where a support beam grew up out of the floor. His tongue snaked out and tasted the earth. Right here. Images fluttered through his mind: a highway, the cocked thumb of a teenager, a slowing car and a wide smile. The Pompiliad crunched the grit on his tongue and considered. Still here.

He scrabbled at the hard-packed dirt, breaking his ragged nails and shredding the tips of his fingers. The earth came away an inch at a time and soon he was pulling aside strips of rotten clothing. A new smell rose with the gathering light, mildew and old, wet trash. His fingers tangled in a mat of long, blonde hair. "Yessss," he hissed and yanked, the resulting crack disturbed an owl far above. He held up a brown skull with dirty Barbie-doll hair, the jaw bone still attached by a piece of dry sinew. He brought it up to his face and slid his long black tongue into the mouth, running it over the gritty surfaces, tasting death.

For a long time after, the Pompiliad sat cross-legged in the dirt, the skull in his lap. He stared off into the worlds between worlds, stroking the long platinum hair. A large gray spider wandered over his knee, froze and tried to bite him but its fangs couldn't penetrate his leather jeans. He glanced at it and the spider flared into quick flame and was gone. It broke him from his reverie. He bent low over the skull and whispered something into its ear hole. He got up and walked to the open barn door, holding the skull by the hair like a lantern. He swung it back and forth, a sensor in a church, and spoke into the clear August morning.

"Find my servant. Give him my message."

* * *

THE SCREEN DOOR slammed, but T.R. had been up at his computer until past two in the morning, so the sound did little more than roll him over in his dirty bedclothes. He dreamed he was strolling down 5th Avenue in Manhattan by the Metropolitan Museum. T.R. had spent hours virtually roaming the streets of Manhattan using Google Maps Street View, but in his dream he felt rough sidewalk under his bare feet. He slept naked and was so on the street as well, but his arms swung freely and he walked right out in the middle of the street. As with Google Maps, the people and cars were frozen in a three-dimensional still-frame and only T.R. could move.

He strolled past a blurry woman walking her blurry dog; some small, yellow-colored thing. T.R. touched it and drew back at its warmth. He stood and planted his foot on the dog's side. Its heart fluttered against the sole of his foot and he grimaced. T.R. gave a good shove and the dog toppled over like a cheap lawn ornament. He walked on to another woman, closer to his age.

She was blurred out like all the people on the street. It sort of looked like she was made out of colored sand and the wind had eroded her features. He could make out her rack, though. She was one of those high-toned work-out honeys out for a run in tiny jogging shorts that had some slogan or brand printed across the back so you had to stare at her high ass to read it. T.R.'s cock jumped as he looked both left and then right. Legions of stone New Yorkers watched him as he cupped her breast. Like the dog, her heart fluttered in her chest. His dick throbbed in time with her pulse and he squeezed her tit, hard. Her heart began to hammer. She could feel him. These people were frozen, but they were aware. T.R. took a step back, eyes wide. He could do anything he wanted to these people. He was God here!

He walked around behind her and yanked down her little shorts. He was panting now, his cock was dripping. What a way to lose his virginity. He hoped she was a virgin, too, that would make it awesome. There was a little blurred out tattoo on her right cheek. He bent to inspect it, but couldn't make it out. T.R. got of whiff of her: fresh sweat and some kind of feminine lotion or soap. What was she feeling right now? Was she just jogging down the street in her world aware of him as just a breeze or pressure? Could she feel it now as he pushed his penis against her?

The tip of his dick touched her lower back and a black mark bloomed on her skin. T.R. yanked himself back as the mark spread, flashing over her pretty curves and blackening her entire body. Even her pony-tail, frozen in mid swing, was dark as ink. T.R. poked her with his finger and she collapsed in a heap of slag. Holy hell, had he done that?

He ran over to a blurred sand-sculpture of a tall man in navy-blue suit, one hand pressed to his head, mouth open. It was hard to tell but this guy looked like he was on a cell phone call. T.R.

touched his arm and stepped back. Nothing happened. Maybe he had to touch someone with his cock to turn them to dust. He looked down at his wilting erection and had another thought. T.R. touched the man's face, skin to skin, and watched as the black stain appeared. A moment later, business dude was a pile of dust at T.R.'s bare feet. Why didn't it work with the dog? The fur maybe? T.R. ran over to the little capsized yellow lump and touched its side—nothing. He touched its nose, wet and cold, and the dog disintegrated like the others.

T.R. straightened and looked around at the hundreds just within his sight. He thought of the thousands, millions in this city—*his* city. It was a shame he couldn't actually fuck anyone without turning them into a pile of dust, though. That pretty much sucked. Wait, maybe if he used a condom? First drug store he passed, he'd find out. Well, if he couldn't bust his nut right away he could stimulate his brain. He walked toward the Metropolitan Museum of art, naked butt flat and a little cold. He snared a hot dog right out of street vendor's hand, "Thanks, Abdul," and walked up the stairs.

The Armory drew him like a needle to true north. T.R. stood in front of the Samurai Kitanas with his hands pressed against the glass. The blades were so fine they glowed as if electrified. This had to be where George Lucas got the idea for light sabers. Man, he'd do just about anything to have one of these things. Imagine getting to use a five hundred year old Samurai sword to lop off the head of that little brat, Childe Howard. He knew just how he'd do it, too. T.R. would tie up that ugly fucking beagle so it had to watch its master get his cute, curly blonde noggin lopped off. No, wait, he'd tie up Childe and stab the dog to death, nice and slow, in front of him. And then he'd kill the boy. T.R. picked at a zit on his chin. Maybe he'd run here, to New York, and disappear afterward. If only he could get that sword.

He was just wondering what he could use to break the thick glass when he caught the reflection of someone nodding behind him. T.R. covered his crotch and froze. Squinting into the glass, he stammered, "Uh, hi. I'm lost." Whoever the hell it was didn't answer, just kind of rocked back and forth. "Someone, ah, someone stole my clothes." And then to clarify, "Because this is New York." Still no response, just that pendular rocking. The hair was weird, too, really light and sticking straight up like some kind of punker or something.

"Listen," T.R. said, "I know I'm not supposed to be here, but if you could just maybe help me get some clothes…" he trailed off and turned around, hands still cupping his privates. "What the shit?"

Across the wide hall, flanked with suits of medieval armor, a huge black knight stood with its arm raised. T.R. could tell it was as empty as the rest of them from its open visor, but someone had hung a human head by its long hair from an upraised fist. It looked kind of like the knight was holding a lantern at the end of an extended chain. That sure as hell hadn't been there when he came in. Someone must have sneaked in behind him and done this while he was gawking at the kitanas. T.R. padded over the cold marble on tip toe and stood a few feet in front of the swinging head.

The skull was browned and stripped with age, but the jawbone was still attached by a little piece of tendon or something that hadn't quite rotted away. One of the lower front teeth was a little crooked, but the rest were white and tombstone straight. The eye sockets were empty, but it felt like the damn thing made eye-contact with him every time it swung up on its arc. Up and back, up and back, up and back. T.R. began to rock forward and back on his feet a little, pulled and pushed by those blank eyes. His jaw hung open a bit just like the skull's and his eyelids drooped. He became dimly aware that his cock had grown rigid, the muscles in his groin contracting in time to the swinging skull.

It spoke: "Tommy Ray Dalton." The voice was a grating bass. T.R. could feel the thumping syllables in his skinny chest. He rocked back and forth with the pendulum head, back and forth. "You are the chosen."

A sleepy smile spread T.R.'s lips, still greasey from his hot dog. "I knew it," he mumbled. "I *always* known it."

"Soon I will be among you, and the world above the world will be taken back." The jawbone never moved, the voice issuing like one from a megaphone. "You will prepare the way."

T.R. was swaying, almost pitching forward and back, his feet remaining planted, his legs straight. "Prepare the way." His brow furrowed, "What am I supposed to do?"

"You will know at the appointed time."

"Yes."

"And you will be rewarded for faithful service."

"Rewarded." T.R's eyes squeezed shut as his cock exploded into orgasm. He seemed to come for a full minute, the pleasure so intense he couldn't even moan. When the warmth and muscle convulsions passed, he opened his eyes. Instead of ropes of white spattering the marble floor, ribbons of thick blood made strange art at his feet. The skull had stopped swinging and a line of blood dripped from the mouth where T.R.'s cock had spit its ejaculate. It looked like it had been feeding.

* * *

THE POMPILIAD DROPPED the skull in the grass and brought a heavy boot down on the temple, crushing it. He turned his back on the gathering dawn and slumped back into the shadows of the old barn. His servant would prepare the way, skew the odds a bit more in his favor and then he would ride into Shard. He had been waiting a hundred-thousand millennia, another day or two wouldn't matter. The Wasp found a pool of darkness in a cluttered corner and nestled in. A passerby might mistake him for a jumble of twisted lumber or old machinery. He was still. His eyes were open.

Chapter 18

WILL AND GEORGE stood at the base of Castle Wall and stared into the maw of Outshaft Six. The sun shone straight down but it was a little chilly in the shade. Fall was already on its way into the mountains; by midnight it might be down in the low sixties. There wasn't even the slightest puff of breeze and a reedy line of gray-yellow smoke spilled over the lip of the entrance and dripped skyward. The throaty smell of sulphur was very strong today.

"You lied about the fire not being here, Two-Bears," George said, checking his flashlight and the length of blue and red striped climbing rope slung over his shoulder.

Will's cheeks colored a little as he adjusted his gunbelt. *Smaug* needed to be within easy reach. If all went well there wouldn't be any shooting, of course, but having the huge revolver at hand just felt better when going into a burning hole in the ground with the express purpose of talking to a dragon and its pet giant fucking spider. "Yeah, well, I figured you wouldn't a come otherwise."

"You're right, you half-blooded injun dickweed," George said. "*But*, I'm far too intrigued not to try this." In reality George's only real concern was proving to his best friend that there were no dragons or giant spiders living in the mine. If it took a little afternoon cave-crawling to do that, fine. They used to do this all the time when they were kids anyway, right? The only difference now was that they'd be a little sore the next morning. That and Will would see that he really did have a concussion dream or what-have-you and abandon all this end-of-the-world-final-battle hoo-hah. It was disconcerting as hell when a man with a gun that big started talking like a hobbit.

George clapped Will on the shoulder a little too hard, "Ready, Tonto?"

"You're not going to leave off the Indian shit are you?"

"You kidding? You're making me walk into a burning hole in the ground and I'm almost sober. Lead on, kemosabe."

Will gave a grateful smile. "If I knew how to speak Cherokee, I'd be calling you motherfucker or something right now."

"What do you think 'kemosabe' means?"

They switched on their lights and sprayed cones of dusty white into the dark. George squinted and said, "Yeah, I can just see that side opening you were talking about." Will was concerned with their feet. "There's another set of prints, here." He squatted down. "Shit, there's two more, Georgie, lookit this." George hunkered down and Will pointed to the different tracks in the dust. "These're mine from the other day and these," he glanced at George, "these are my Dad's, or that thing pretending to be my Dad." Before George could say anything, or worse, nothing, Will pointed to a set of boot prints that were smaller. "These here are new, though."

"You're just like an injun scout or something; I'm impressed." George laughed. "All joking aside, I really kind of am, Constable."

"Then shut up about that injun shit, will you? We prefer The Noble Native Disenfranchised. Anyway, see how these new ones are a little smaller?"

"Kid?"

"Maybe. He'd be a teenager at least."

"Your spider pretending to be someone else?" George said, half humoring Will.

Will didn't catch it or ignored it. "I dunno'." He pulled the coil of rope off his shoulder and motioned toward an old support beam that looked to be in pretty solid shape. "Let's tie off on that. If memory serves the drop down to the big chamber is only a few feet in.

Will had been expecting a straight drop through the rocky floor into the chamber below, but they found something more a like a chute that angled at about forty-five degrees. They were able to slide on their butts a foot at a time until Will's boot stuck out into space. "Okay, hold up," he whispered over his shoulder, his voice echoing as if they were inside a large soda can.

George stopped a couple of feet behind him and shined his light around the inside of the natural shoot. "This looks like regular old granite, but did you get a look at the walls up top before we dropped down here?"

"Talk a little quieter, Georgie, Jesus."

"Sorry, man, I'm just excited." George stage-whispered. "The walls were mostly ryolite up there, Constable." He waited.

Will checked his climbing harness, tugging here and there. "Uh, huh."

"You numb-shit, you know what ryloite means in a formation like that? Will, we're probably inside a volcanic pipe. There could be diamonds down here." George was talking fast now. "I read this article about how there are only a couple of places in the continental U.S. that have diamonds. It takes a seriously heavy operation to sort through all the crap to find the diamonds, but if we did this right…"

Will looked over his shoulder. "What?"

"Well, it wouldn't make sense for us to mine the diamonds ourselves, but we could stake a claim and then sell it to a mining concern. Shit, your new girlfriend could be our agent in this."

"Turn your light off for a second."

"What? Are you listening to me, Two-Bears?"

"Yes. Just do it, George."

George clicked off his flashlight and Will did the same, a second later their eyes adjusted. A weak green glow filled the tunnel. George whispered, "There's light down there."

"Yep." Will slid over the edge of the tunnel and hung in space, swinging like a worm on a hook. The light was low, but he could still make out the vast chamber with its glowing emerald walls. The metallic floor flowed frozen beneath him about twenty feet down. The diamond horde lay in the center.

"Oh. My. God," George said, his head poking out of the hole in the ceiling.

Will smiled inspite of himself. "C'mon." He let out some rope and slid down until his All Stars hit ground. Will's hands were sweating inside his gloves and his fingers shook as he unhooked himself. That spider was in here; he could feel those eight black eyes on them. He was invited last time and Yïn could barely keep from attacking him. What would be like now that they were dropping in unannounced? He patted *Smaug* and hoped hollow points would be enough.

119

George touched down and let out a whoosh of air. Will turned to him and tried not to laugh; his friend's mouth hung open like a seven year-old boy confronted with a shiny monster truck. George turned in a slow circle, gasping and jerking every time his eyes filled with some new wonder. "Is it…? It's all emerald, isn't it? How's it glowing? Oh my God, Two-Bears." George froze and pointed at the massive pile of diamonds in the center of the chamber. He grabbed Will's arm. "Holy shit."

"I know," Will said. "Still think we need to involve a mining concern?"

"I think we can just fill our fucking pockets and be done with it."

Will was playing it cool—someone had to keep his shit together—but it was hard not to gawk just as much as George was. He wasn't coming up from a blackout this time around and only about a third as terrified. The place was magnificent. He found himself stilling the urge to run around and shout. He wanted to run his hands over the glowing walls and pick up the gems in the diamond bed. This was every little kid's dream come true.

Except for the part about the monsters.

Will put his arm out in front of George like a mother holding her kid back at a busy street corner. He thubbed the snap off his holster and dragged *Smaug* out, resting the .357 against his leg. George looked at him. "What?" Will stared straight ahead. George followed his eyes. "What the fuck?"

A seven-foot tall bottle of Bombay Saphire Gin walked around the base of a large natural column, and by "walked" it kind of clunked from one side of its bottom rim to the other. It stopped in front of the diamond bed and did a little a twirl. George gawked; Will thumbed back *Smaug's* hammer.

George half-turned his head toward Will but kept his bulging eyes on the sentient, economy-size bottle of his favorite gin. "Are you seeing…?"

"It's Yïn."

"It's *gin.*"

"She's fucking with us. You."

Will took a shaky step forward and pitched his voice into cop mode. "You can cut that shit out, now. We're here to talk to Dampf."

For a moment, nothing happened. Will's blood pulsed in his ears. George swallowed a mouthful of dry spit and his throat clicked so loud it echoed. The clear liquid in the bottle colored dark. (In the low, green light, it was impossible to tell, but Will was sure it had turned to blood.) The clear glass tesselated with scale and wings and a tail burst forth. A moment later, a dragon made from the very gems in the walls stood before them.

"Holy shit," George whispered.

Will muttered over his shoulder, "That ain't Dampf."

"B-but it—."

"Dampf's taller. This thing's only ten feet high. Dampf's a freakin' four-story hotel." He turned back to the smallish dragon. "Cut the shit, will you?"

The dragon's eyes flashed red and split into eight half-spheres. A second later, Yïn stood before them, mandibles scissoring.

"Ohmigod," George hissed. "Will! Will! Shoot it! Ohmigod, Will!"

Will backed up a step and put his hand out. George grabbed it in a sweaty death grip. "It's okay, Georgie," he soothed. "If it was gonna' hurt us, it could've done a while back. We're good. We're good."

George grabbed Will's arm and yanked him in close. "Its mouth!"

"I know."

His breath was coming fast and shallow. "Looks like it wants to eat us."

"I know," Will said, "but I'm pretty sure that's what she does when she's laughing."

"She? How do you know it's a girl? Did you turn it over?"

A voice thundered from behind, "All of her kind is female."

George squeezed Will's arm once very hard and let go. Will turned around and sucked in a great rush of air: towering, undeniable, dragon. "Dampf," he said. "This is George Rhodes." Will turned to George just as he went down like a heap of rags.

Will knelt by George and checked his breathing. He'd be all right—just passed out was all. Will stood up and said, "Does everyone you meet just faint?"

"The boy never lost consciousness."

"The boy? Childe? Kiddo? You've seen him? He's seen you?"

"Yïn saved the boy's animal. Yïn and the boy are bonded."

"But he hasn't met you, yet?"

"He will if he must."

Will squinted when the dragon spoke. Dampf's voice was like strong wind in his mind. *Smaug* was getting heavy. He looked over his shoulder. Yïn hadn't come any closer. Will holstered weapon. "Don't you want to know why I brought George here?" At the sound of his name George stirred, a nonsense syllable slipping over his lips. "Can you change into something a little less, uh, huge?" Will asked. "Like you did with me. So, you know, he can wrap his brain around you two in stages?"

George sat up slowly and stared at the dragon. He looked back over his shoulder and took in Yïn. The slightest shiver vibrated through his shoulderblades. "I'm okay, Will."

Will offered George a hand and pulled him upright. "You sure, man?" But he could already tell George was more curious than afraid. "Yeah, fine," he said and took a step toward Dampf.

"Uh," George smiled, "greetings."

Dampf lowered his head: a bow. George grinned and clapped his hands together. He turned around and waved to the giant spider across the chamber, "Howdy!" Yïn's mandibles scissored and she dipped on her front legs. "So, ah, Will's told me all about you. Sort of."

Will grabbed George's elbow. "What are you doing?"

"What? Ow. I'm just talking." But George's eyes were a little too white and his skin was hot.

"You're freaking out, Rhodes."

George jerked away from Will. "Of course I am! What am I supposed to do? At least I'm freaking out cordially. I can't believe you brought me into this. Why the fuck couldn't you have kept this to yourself?"

"George Rhodes," Dampf boomed.

George spun around and stood ramrod straight.

"The Constable brings you to us because he is alone. Would you stand with him?"

George stared up at those celestial black eyes. There were eons in there. He could smell gin that wasn't there and he wanted to urinate. He tore his gaze away from the towering insanity in front of him and looked at Will. Stupid red baseball cap, screws of black hair sticking out the sides, those cheesy goddamn Chucks. Probably had some paperback he'd read forty-five times in the back pocket of his jeans. Dumbass old six-shooting cowboy gun on his hip. Look on his face that said, *"I hate this. I'm scared."* But Will was going to fight when the time came. Will was going to protect them all. Will had brought him into this because he was afraid to do it by himself. Would George stand with him?

"Can we get me a gun, too, please?"

* * *

GEORGE SAT AT his mother's kitchen table—the house never actually felt like it was his even this many years after her death—and contemplated a full bottle of gin. Two hours had passed since Will dropped him off at his house. "Need some time to get my head around this," was all George had said. Erica was at the county seat doing some research in the library, so it was just George, the gin, and the house making the odd click and creak as the afternoon strolled through. The last of the ciccadas ratcheted outside and every now and then he caught the far-off call of a kid shouting at summer to slow the fuck down.

The smell of juniper was very strong in the kitchen. Hell, he could practically see the air ripple over the open bottle like heat coming off pavement. If he drank that George would be raving in minutes and end up either on the floor, the street, or in Will's holding cell. He could see himself in the glass, pale, elongated, warped—perfect reflection. He'd seen a pair of demons today. Or Gods, depending on which side of the theological isle you fell: The First Ones.

Dampf had started The Fire. Like a real God, Dampf had made Shard the way it was with a puff of his molten breath—all to keep the bad ones from coming through, the wasps. And now the one that got away was coming home. George knew a thing or two about Pompiliads. They were fascinating insects and arguably the most brutal. They hunt other bugs and inject their eggs along with their poison. The poison paralyzes the victim (often a spider) and the wasp carries it off to its den, or burrow. Over time the egg hatches and the larval wasp eats the host from the inside out,

123

emerging full-grown. The host is alive and paralyzed through most of this. George tried to imagine what it would feel like to be crammed down some dark hole and eaten from the inside out. He shuddered and reached for the bottle.

It burned his nose as his lips touched the glass. He held it for a moment and thunked it down on the table. A dollop of gin splashed cold on his writs. He could just go, leave. He could maybe go with Erica back to New York. Things hadn't progressed as far with them as they had with Will and Amy—at least, not physically—but she liked him. And they were good for each other. George had slowed his drinking way down and Erica seemed so much less... *fractured*. They could leave tomorrow. Hell, they could leave today when she got back. George could imagine himself at some job in a suit, doing suit things, or walking in Central Park with the most beautiful woman in Manhattan while Will and the others were crammed down some dark hole and eaten alive from the inside out.

George got up and walked to the front door, gin forgotten. He stood in front of the stained glass scene of St. Michael chastising Adam and Eve. They had eaten from the Tree of Knowledge and so knew about the heavens and the earth, innocence lost. It was terrible to know. Summer sun glowed through the glass and fell in George's eyes, complicating them. He opened the door and walked into the light.

Chapter 19

ERICA WAS LOST. The Subaru wagon bumped and crunched over a gravel mining road that was but one in a maze. They seemed to have been laid down with all the precision of tossing a bunch of unraveled yarn onto a map. Speaking of maps, the one spread out on the passenger seat was next to useless. She'd realized that fifteen minutes after she'd turned off the main road. Erica had passed the same intersection with the big double oak four times now. Thank God it was still daylight; if she lost the sun she was royally fucked.

Technically she was still inside the Shard Township limits; at least she thought she was. She'd spent all morning and most of the afternoon with her nose buried in books and survey maps (one going as far back as 1843) trying to ascertain Shard's exact borders. After that, she hit the tax and census records, her goal to find every last legal inhabitant and property owner in Shard. If her records were up to date (and she seriously doubted that) there were forty-five living souls in Shard—thirty-one in town and fourteen in the surrounding hills—and Erica had to convince all of them to leave. Blackstone Mineral was the largest client her firm had ever secured. She was certain that if she could clear Shard of complicating factors and then buy up the remains in Blackstone's interest, they'd make her a partner.

What she was not certain of was her location. The map said that this little unmarked red line squiggled about a mile and a half in, crossing that little squiggly blue line. She had splashed through a wide creek some time ago—props to the all-wheel drive—and at that time had seemed to be on track, but had since zagged when she should have zigged or whatever the fuck. "Dammit!" she hissed and hit the brakes.

Erica turned off the engine and got out of the car. Today she graced the empty woods in a sharp-collared blouse with matching oversized cuffs and fitted black suit pants. She'd bought herself a pair of low pumps at the Shoes-4-Less four miles down the main strip from the county library that were at least the right color to match her outfit if hideous in their own right. (She was not about to wear George's mother's old tennis shoes any more than was absolutely necessary.) A pair of redwood frame reading glasses held back her glossy hair. Erica leaned against the car and closed her eyes. She listened: wind ran its hands through the canopy, tree trunks creaked and groaned, birds called, her heart beat and her breath slowed. She smelled the clean rot of old leaves on the ground and the bright green of new leaves as yet unfallen. Erica opened her eyes and that green rushed in. "Okay," she said. "Let's find these shit-kickers."

She spread the map out on the hood of the Subaru, the engine still ticking beneath it. She traced a red fingernail along the red line she was pretty sure she was still on and figured out her problem: the map was bullshit. Half these roads weren't even on it. Her stomach rumbled. She'd forgotten to eat lunch while she was at the library.

Erica put her hand against her tummy, trying to soothe the animal trapped in there. She wished she were sitting at George's kitchen table, eating one of his amazing tuna melts. (She'd probably already put on three pounds since she got here, but it wasn't like she was going to find a GNC with her favorite protein supplement.) George would putter around the kitchen cleaning up and she'd daydream or chat with him. He was brilliant. There wasn't much about which George didn't have a considered opinion. The other day she'd asked him how he knew so much living in such isolation and he'd laughed and asked her in a turbo-charged accent, "Y'all never heard a' that intraweb thingamajig?" There were also close to a thousand books in the Rhodes house—novels, non-fiction, even textbooks—and Erica had the idea that George had absorbed most of them.

The breeze shifted a bit and a whiff of barbecue tinted the air. Oh, that was just evil. She was starving. Erica had to be close to habitation. The dry stick of a woman behind the librarian's desk had told her that she'd find a few cabins and a double-wide or two back here. She must be closer than she thought. Well, hell with the map, she'd just follow her nose. Erica walked on the down road about a quarter mile, the smell of cooking meat yanking at her complaining stomach. The wind shifted from time to time, but she was getting closer. A corner of trailer came into view as she rounded a sharp bend.

It was a village of sorts. A few cabins tacked together with sheets of plywood and tin, a couple of double-wides with faded siding. Everything had a coat of road dust paint. Trees had been cleared on either side of the road and there was even a little fishing pond. A couple of rusted pick-up trucks squatted next to one of the trailers and there was another hulk that might have been a car at one time sinking into the weeds around its tireless wheels. A single wood pole stood sentinel at the road's edge, thin black wires webbing out from it to most of the buildings. Another thicker wire ran off into the trees. They had electricity at least. The open areas were mowed and neat except for a few plastic toys that might have been donated. There was a shiny red wheelbarrow that was someone's pride and joy—not a spot of rust on it. And a wooden horse with wheels that looked sturdy and homemade. Where the hell was everybody?

A crow cawed and Erica jumped. Jesus, she was freaking herself out. "Hello?" she called. "Is there someone here?" She had it all figured out. She'd claim lost city girl and prevail on their mercy. (Lies worked best when mixed with truth.) Once she'd established rapport with the natives she'd trade them their land for a song—maybe something by Hank Williams. "Helllll-oh-oh!" What the hell? It was the middle of the day and it was obvious that at least some of these people didn't have jobs. School was still out, so where were the kids?

Erica walked over to the double-wide with the trucks parked out front. The screen door shrieked as she pulled it open. She knocked gently on the peeling wood door, shoulders hunched. No answer. She knocked again, louder. Nothing. Erica turned around and the let the screendoor slam behind her. She stared at her reflection in the windshield of the powder-blue pick-up. It was one of those old ones from the fifties or whenever. An American Corn Picker? Something like that. She put her hands on her hips and her stomach protested its emptiness again. Oh, yeah, the barbecue. The smell of sweet, cooking meat was just pervasive enough that she'd kind of forgotten about it.

Erica walked around back behind the double-wide, but there was no smoking grill. She turned west to head across the little grassy area toward the largest of the three shacks and something caught her eye. Erica turned and froze—a blaze of crimson splashed across the white siding of the trailer. There were several black dots moving around on it and Erica whispered, *"Madre de Dios,"* when she realized they were flies. "Hello?" The flies buzzed, drunk on protein and sugar. A large bluebottle droned past her ear on the way to the feast and snapped her out of it. Someone might be hurt.

She walked quickly over to the other doublewide and yanked the screendoor out of her way. She rapped three times and then twisted the doorknob. The door opened easily and she stepped into the gloom of a tidy kitchen area with linoleum floors that were old and brown. She could already tell that no one was home. This place, this village was still. The handle of a good kitchen knife called to her from a rack over the sink and she grabbed it before heading back outside.

"Hello!" She shouted as she banged out into the lowering afternoon sun. No greeting, a warning. That was a "hello" that said try to paint my blood on the side of some redneck tornado magnet and you'll have another thing coming. Erica didn't do scared very well. Now, pissed off? Pissed off she did great. If there was someone hurt around here she would find them and help the shit out of them. She stomped over to the nearest shack and almost tripped over a discarded shoe. It was a man's workboot, the kind rap artists wore (if not the brand), but this one was scuffed and well used. These were good boots; even the cheap ones were too expensive to leave just lying around. Erica prodded it with her knife. "Ah, shit." There was a drop of blood on the toe: a bright red period at the end of someone else's sentence.

She clomped onto the rickety porch and shoved through the screen door, "Hey! Is there someone here?" The shack was a single large room—wood stove in one corner and a sink with a believe-it-or-not portable, apartment-size dishwasher connected to a garden hose that ran through a small window. Across a green rag-rug, a couple of beds squatted in opposite corners; a child's crayon drawings were tacked up over the smaller one. It reeked of barbecue here. The air was a little blue with fragrant smoke. They must be out back. There were having a barbecue and couldn't hear her they were whoopin' it up so much. That was all. (How come she couldn't hear them a-whoopin?) Erica turned and walked out.

She hooked a hard left as she hopped off the porch, her grip on the knife knuckle-white.

At first what she saw behind the shack/cabin didn't register in her brain, like looking at an MC Escher drawing. Her mind got the component parts well enough, but the configuration was all wrong. There was an old oil drum, blackened from years of use as a trash and leaf incinerator. A man in coveralls was bent over at the waist, his upper half disappearing into the drum as if he'd dropped something and had leaned in to get it. There was a fire burning in the drum. She could hear it crackling, feel its heat, and see the smoke now that she was standing a few feet away. She could smell the...

"Barbecue," Erica whispered and dropped the knife in the grass. She put a hand over her mouth and nose and turned around. A man in filthy clothes stood next to the road. Erica started and wheezed out, "Help. Can you help me?" She gestured over her shoulder. "This man...he—" She squinted, something was wrong with this guy. He was more swaying on his feet than standing and his mouth was hanging open in a dark "O". Erica trotted over toward him and stopped. No barbecue smell here. She coughed and put her hand over mouth and nose again. Rot, sharp and active. This guy had something. Maybe they all did. Maybe someone was trying to burn the body of a, a what? A plague victim? And couldn't finish because he was too weak. That explained it...sort of. Erica's breath was rasping fast and hot over her teeth. Her heart was fluttering down in the pit of her stomach and the back of her neck tingled as if she were completing a circuit. "Are you okay?"

Cyrus McCoy was far from okay. His face was gray with bluish rings around the eyes and lips. There was a ghastly hole in his cheek that wasn't fresh and wasn't even pretending to heal. His eyes were cobweb-white cataracts. His clothes were torn away on the left side of his abdomen and hip. The flesh underneath looked mauled, the edges burned and dotted with tiny black spots. No breath inflated his lungs. No blood moved through his veins. He reached for her.

Erica kicked hard and high, a nonsense word that could have been, "Ya!" exploaded from her diaphragm. It was pure reflex action, muscle memory from Body Combat 3.0 classes at the gym. Her heel connected with Cyrus's forehead with a wooden *thock!*

and his neck snapped back. He staggered a few feet and refocused those empty eyes on her. His brow drew down and something like a smile bent his wide open mouth. Erica screamed. Erica ran.

She pounded hard over the grass toward the most permanent looking structure—the doublewide trailer. If anything would have a phone and a door heavy enough to keep out another...person...it would be that. She whipped around the corner with the bloody hand print, noting now the perforations in the siding, tiny black dots in a spray pattern. Her mind was trained to pick-up detail, find patterns and use them to her advantage in the courtroom or judge's chambers. Those tiny spots were birdshot from a shotgun. Someone had taken a chunk out of the sick man behind her and it had splashed onto the trailer. What the fuck had happened here?

She yanked open the screen door and slipped on the brown linoleum. Heat shot up her inner thigh and in a detached sense she knew it would hurt like the devil tomorrow if she didn't stretch later. The thought brought a screamy little laugh as she fumbled with the lock and chain on the front door. It was a single piece of wood, what was referred to as "solid core" in B&E cases. That was good. It took an axe to get through one of these, or a really good kick if you didn't have a deadbolt. There wasn't one. This was probably the first time this door had even been locked at all.

She risked a look through the small diamond shaped window centered high on the door. He was still out there and shambling toward the trailer. "Fuck me," Erica hissed. She'd left her cell in the car, but it wasn't like it had gotten any signal since she left the county seat. She scanned the walls but there was no phone. Maybe in the back. Erica ran down a short hall way and tried the bedroom door. The knob turned, but it would only push in a few inches before something stopped it. She pushed harder, convinced that a phone was sitting on the bedside table. One more good shove and she burst into the back bedroom, knocking over the small, sprung recliner that had been pushed against the door.

Erica clutched a fist to her chest. A woman lay sprawled across the bed. Erica could tell it was a woman because she had breasts and was wearing a housedress. A shotgun bisected her body along the meridian, its barrel ending where the woman's head used to be. Behind her on the wall...art.

Thud!

Erica whirled. That man was at the front door, trying to get in.

Thud!

She looked around the room for the phone, but ha-ha, there wasn't one.

Thud!

Jesus, it sounded like he was hitting the fucking thing with a tree trunk. The whole trailer shook. He was going to get in. He was going to get in and touch her. "And what, Erica?" she asked herself. "What?" She was panicking. This guy was obviously sick and needed her help. It looked like someone, maybe this crazy woman on the bed, had even taken a shot at him. Something horrible had happened in this little village and this poor man was the only survivor. He needed her help and she was running away like a freaked out little kid.

Thud! Crack!

Help, her well-toned butt. Sick or not, this guy wasn't looking for Cipro. He was looking to hurt her.

The door was giving way. She could hear him tearing it to pieces—sounded like a bear tearing apart a wicker chair. Her mother would kill her for acting like this. Erica straightened, even as the sounds of his footsteps on the lineoluem reached her ears. She wasn't some stupid cow who just waited for trouble to find her. She was a smart girl and smart girls thought first, then acted. There, a window in the corner next to the...art. She had it open and had hoisted herself mostly through it when she felt fingers close in a manacle around her ankle. Erica threw herself forward and yanked out of his grip. She tumbled to the grass with a yelp. Her wrist was sprained, but she'd worry about that later. She stood up and risked a look behind her.

He was framed in the small window, sticking his tongue out at her like an insolent child. Erica blinked. There was a huge black wasp perched on it. Its wings fluttered and Erica took off. She didn't stop until she was sitting in the Subaru, cranking the engine, her breath coming in hot little gasps.

* * *

THE GOOD CONSTABLE was about fifty pages into *The Dark Tower: The Gunslinger* when Erica burst into his office like a hurricane gust. Will was getting used to the little mental sputter he always seemed to have in the first few seconds whenever he saw Erica—she was just that beautiful—but he didn't have it now. She looked wild, a horse in a thunderstorm. Before he had even begun to process her words, his danger meter went into the red and the internal alarms went off. He got up and went to her.

"Erica—."

"Don't touch me. Something bad happened in the woods." She wrapped her arms around herself. "Just...," she took a deep breath and closed her eyes. "Can I steal your chair a minute?"

Will nodded, "'Course, siddown." She did and he scooched his butt onto the corner of the desk. "You want some water, somethin'?" He was throwing his accent on a little heavy, but that usually had a calming effect on folks. He hoped it would not have the opposite effect on a city person. "Can you tell me what happened? Does anyone need help?"

She looked up at him, eyes showing too much white. There was a smell coming off her like electricity and fresh sweat. "I went to talk with some of the people in the woods," she said, receding into memory. "I got lost and found, like, a sort of a village?"

"Big white trailer?"

"Yes, yeah. Some cabins, too." She blinked. "And toys."

"Yep, the Owens live in the trailer. Rick Becket and his boy Luther stay in one of the cabins. What happened, Erica?"

"I'm not sure."

"Just take it a step at a time. You were driving around back there," he'd have to chide her later for doing something so foolish. Even he got lost on those mining roads from time to time, "and you got turned around until you found the trailer. Then what?"

"I smelled...something."

She told him the rest of it, her words catching on her teeth at first then flowing over in a great gush of story.

Will shook his head slowly back and forth. "He was just bent over in the oil drum? You sure it was burning? Oh, right, the smell." He made a face and Erica actually smiled. Will stood up. "Okay, I want you to call George. He'll come get you."

Erica sat up straight, the chair squeaked. "Where are you going?"

"I gotta' go collect Cyrus. Sounds like he's finally gotten a taste for his own medicine."

"I don't understand."

"The man you saw, the 'sick' one? That sounds a lot like Cyrus McCoy. He's our local moonshine fairy." Will rubbed his jaw. "He don't normally cotton to the stuff himself, but it sounds to me like he's gone and burned his brains a little."

"Just burned his brain a little? Are you kidding? What about those other people? They're dead, you hick."

Will looked at her.

"Sorry," she said. "I'm freaking out."

Will put a hand on her shoulder. She flinched but let it be. "I know and you should be."

"What are you going to do?" she asked.

"I'm going up there and I'm going to take care of it. All of it." He moved around the desk and pulled open the drawer. "'Scuse me a sec'."

Erica's eyes widened as he pulled out the biggest handgun she had ever seen. Light ran along the steel for a country mile and the barrel had a maw like a train tunnel. *"Maricon,"* she whispered.

Will gave her a sideways smile and strapped on the gunbelt. "Now, you call George. He'll come get you, but I need you to stay here with him until I get back. It's not gonna' be fun, but—."

"You need me to identify this Cyrus guy."

"Right," Will said and started walking toward the back door. There was an old Jeep Cherokee waiting out there. He only drove it when it rained or he needed to haul something. Looked like he was going to have to haul a person.

"Hey, Constable!"

Will turned, "Hmm?"

"Make sure you Mirandize him," Erica had gone hard again, thinking of that woman on the bed. "I don't want that fucker walking on a technicality."

Will gave her a broad grin. "Why counselor this is the South. We do everything by the book down here. Really."

* * *

133

WILL STOOD NEXT to the oil drum forty minutes later. Its rusted sides were still radiating heat and that barbecue smell lingered, but there was no body. The splash of red still marked the Owens's trailer—that hand print a crossing guard's stop signal—but there wasn't anyone inside. The blood and gray matter on the wall over the bed and the upset furniture were the only evidence of foul play, but enough to justify Will calling in the Sheriff's department and county forensics. But he wasn't going to do that.

Will walked back over to the Cherokee, the big engine ticking, and leaned against the side. He crossed his arms and scanned the tree line. Someone—most likely Cyrus—had come up here and...what? Gone after these people. They fought back and it looked like Lizzy Owens took a shot at Cyrus with her quail gun before eating it. Will couldn't be sure who the man in the barrel had been, but it was most likely Bill Owens or Rick Becket. God only knew where the kids were. For that matter, God only knew (God and Cyrus) where the bodies were either. The grass was tramped down all over the place from the ruckus—pre and post Erica's part in it—but the drag marks were unmistakable. They led to where a pick up truck had been parked not long ago; its old-fashioned balloon tires left distinctive tracks in the dirt.

This was the first battlefield in the fight for Shard. Will still didn't believe the Pompiliad had arrived, but it would very soon now. Something was preparing the way. Just like Dampf had recruited him, the Wasp was building up his own forces. Will gave one last look over the compound; his eyes rested on the discarded work boot. He spat on the ground and got in the jeep.

Back in town, the sulphur smell was strong. Will rode with the windows down and grimaced. He didn't usually notice it, like wearing a pair of glasses and forgetting they're on your face. (He actually saw George do this once and stone cold sober, too. He ran around his house looking for his reading glasses, grumbling to himself, while Will sat at the kitchen table snickering.) Now he was noticing everything: the edges of the gutters along the roofs of houses, the depth of the bark in the oak trees along the lane, the faded blue International Harvester Pickup truck almost hidden around the back of Charlotte Najarian's house.

Will stopped the jeep. "Holy shit on a stick." That was Cyrus's truck. Will gripped the steering wheel and stared at the old Victorian. It looked fine. Empty, but fine. Maybe Mrs.

Najarian was out? Bullshit, it was a beautiful afternoon on one of the last few days of summer vacation. She should be in her garden with her big rear in the air, cursing the town's kids under her breath and decapitating dandelions. What the fuck was Cyrus's truck doing there?

Will was stalling. His hands were sweating and his ass felt heavier than a fifty pound sack of cement. He looked over on the passenger seat. *Smaug* sat waiting. Will put his hand on the gun and felt better. He smiled to himself. Funny how a .357 Magnum filled with hollow-points could bolster a man in times of need. Hell with it, he'd charge the place.

Will surged out of the jeep, *Smaug* at his side, and ran up to the back of the Int'l Harvester. He peeked in the bed. There was liquid in the corner by the gate that might have been blood or motor oil. Will sniffed. Ah hell, barbecue. He set his shoulders and took a breath, if he was going to do this, he had to do this. Will walked as slow and easy as he could up to the front door and rang the bell. Nothing. He listened for someone opening a window or the back door. Nothing. He gave a staccato of loud knocks and waited. A bluejay scolded him from the big oak on the corner, but nothing else. Will tried the knob, but the door was locked.

"Okay," he said. "Here we go." He threw his shoulder into the door, aiming for the groove between the frame and door itself. The door popped open with a minimal splintering of wood. Most locks were bullshit. Without a deadbolt you might as well just not even lock it. And that there was strange. No one in Shard locked their doors. You just didn't think to do it, not even Charlotte Najarian.

The hall was cool and dark and had a smell like vaporub and microwave dinners. Will knew right away there was no one in the house, but the hair on the back of his neck was up. Something was all kinds of wrong here, or had been. The house was empty now. He walked through the whole thing anyway, checking each room—the closets and under the beds—and finding nothing as he knew he would. The soft squeaks of his Chucks on the immaculate hardwood floors made him jumpy and *Smaug* felt like it weighed about a hundred pounds.

Ten minutes later, Will walked back out to Harvester and popped the hood. He yanked the spark plugs and walked back to his jeep. For a few minutes, he just sat there and thought, waiting for something to come. It felt like there was a wet wool blanket over his head, suffocating his considerations.

Under the porch, cloudy eyes watched the jeep drive away. Slack faces turned to track its progress like night flowers following the moon. When it was safely around the corner, they returned to their work.

Chapter 20

T.R.'s BRAIN WAS beginning to itch. It had been four nights since his strange dream about New York and the Metropolitan Museum and with each passing minute, the tension behind his eyes increased. School would start in another few days, but he couldn't imagine himself sitting in class, pretending to enjoy the lessons, kowtowing to that old pussbag of a teacher. He couldn't imagine not going Columbine on everyone. But he would have to wait. He had been chosen.

He rolled over in his bed and threw an arm over his eyes for all the good it would do. He hadn't slept more than a few hours. Every time he closed his eyes he heard a low buzzing. He couldn't quite place it, but he knew that damn sound. The first night it happened he'd spent a good forty-five minutes searching around his room for whatever critter was making the noise, but to no avail. By the time the sun rose, he'd given in and realized it was coming from his own head.

Sometimes, he would drift all the way off, but the dream would come—that mummified face dripping with blood, rocking back and forth—and he'd catapult back into consciousness, heart pounding and cock stiff as a fence post. And that was the other thing: he couldn't get off. It had been four days since his last orgasm, and for a three-to-five-time-a-day man that was a real problem. He could yank at it until his arm got sore and the skin chafed, but for nothing.

He couldn't eat much either. T.R. had lost close to five pounds off his already wiry frame. His cheekbones were rising into relief and his eyes were sinking like feral animals backing into the shadows. It's not that he wasn't hungry, everything just tasted rotten. He'd even nagged his mom into making his favorite chili the other night, but it was like spooning in mouthfuls of hot dog turds.

He knew what he had to do to end his torment. That was more obvious than ever. T.R. had to take a life, a human life. But he had also been chosen by the...by the what? He sighed in the dark and whispered, "The Outrider." He had to wait until it was time. He wasn't sure who it was going to be, or how he would do it. Hell, maybe it would be more than one person. T.R. sat up in bed, the moonlight counting off his ribs. Maybe, it would be *everyone.*

He swung his legs off the bed. He had to go. The house was suffocating him, his room, his skin. If he couldn't do what he needed to do to end this...this *constipation* he could at least get out. He could walk. T.R. slid into his greasy jeans and laced up his boots. He knew just where to go.

T.R. WALKED SHIRTLESS down the empty main street. The glass storefront of Paulson's Drugstore—through which he'd never quite had the guts to toss a rock—reflected his passage. The late August air pulled goosebumps out of his skin, but he didn't mind. The cool felt cleansing. T.R. stopped in the middle of the street, shoulders slumped. The moon threw his shadow out in front of him. His shadow-head brushed the end of the asphalt where the meadow rolled away like a frozen silver ocean. A whiff of sulphur burned on the air, mixing with the bouquet of honeysuckle and smelled like some kind of strange tea. T.R. breathed in deeply and imagined drowning in that grass sea.

Maybe that would be best—his death instead of the death of someone else, of many someones. Maybe he could just eat the end of Daddy's deer gun or get in a nice hot bath with a good sharp knife. T.R.'s teeth began to buzz faintly. He wanted to swat at the air around his head, but there was nothing there. His mind was full of...full of what? He ground his teeth and squeezed his eyes shut, rocking a little on the broken street. *"Fuck, fuck, fuck, fuck, fuck,"* he whispered.

His shadow began to flicker and dance. T.R. spun around. A shaft of blue/white light was pouring out of the door of the movie theatre, juttering and flickering. It hit the back of the ticket-sellers booth and split into two bolts like paths. T.R.'s fists clenched. Someone was in his temple, his cathedral. His skin got hot. He stomped over to the theatre and walked inside.

Row after row of moldering seats sat empty as always, but the screen was filled with light. It was an old silent picture, like those funky old cowboy movies or those ones with that Tramp guy. How in hell people had actually liked that shit was way, *way* beyond T.R. Even more beyond him, was how in hell it was playing here, now. The scene was an old-timey shot of some shop-lined street bustling with people. The women wore pointy lace-up boots and frilly dresses cinched tight at the waist. Some of the men wore bowler hats and natty suits, some outfitted in bib-overalls. A pick-up truck with wooden slats for sides and big bug-eyed headlamps puttered down the muddy street. It had to be the early twentieth century. T.R. squinted through the grainy film and stained movie screen at the sign on a shop window: Paulson's Sundries.

"Shard," he breathed.

T.R. clumped down the aisle. He turned and peered up at the projection booth but there was no one up there, no stuttering shaft of light, no click and whir of a projector. Could it have been coming from behind the screen? No, there was nothing back there but canvas covered brick. He turned back to the movie screen and watched as everything began to speed up. T.R. eased into a seat, grimacing at the puff of mildew as it groaned and accepted his weight. The people were little more than blurs now, the days and nights flicking by and becoming a gray in-between. The wooden sidewalks rolled up and concrete squares grew in like machined toadstools. More glass window fronts appeared and signs popped in and out again. A steady stream of traffic flowed down the hardened street. Cars parked for an instant began to smooth out along their edges, less similar to wagons and more like the sleek road boats they would become.

A sense of foreboding chilled the wonder out of T.R. as fissures began to appear in the tarmac. One window after another either cracked and fell away or was boarded up. It was like watching a face rot in stop-motion as an eyeball fell in, a tooth fell out. The time-warp camera began to slow, the days and nights delineating themselves again into second or two-long intervals. After a few moments a night scene settled. The camera panned along a street that bled smoke from a hundred cuts. A lone figure stood with his shirtless back to the viewer. His upper body swam up out of the baggy combat fatique pants, the knobs of his shoulders and spinal column in stark relief. Hey, that was T.R! Those were his narrow shoulders and he'd recognize those badass shitkickers anywhere. T.R. focused on the nape of the neck—just a tiny patch of vulnerable skin—and felt a sting of pity. He was just a boy, alone and in pain, in the dark.

As he watched, the skin over those bony shoulders began to ripple, the knobs of spinal column stretched and humped over. The hair turned liquid black and oiled down over the shoulders. The figured turned to face the camera.

"Outrider," T.R. whispered.

The Pompiliad's great black eyes chilled through the screen at his servant. T.R.'s mouth hung open and his cock sprang to painful attention. The Pompiliad's head tilted to one side, and something like a smile twisted its thin lips. Puffs of dust sifted down from the old theatre speakers as the room filled with the sound of its voice.

"You have endured much."

T.R. could feel tears rolling out of his eyes, but his voice was steady, awed. "Yes," he said. "My head, it's…"

"Full of wasps."

The buzzing churned back behind his eyes. T.R. grabbed fistfuls of his hair and suddenly it ceased. He hunched his shoulders and slotted his eyes left, right. He looked at the man on the screen. At least he thought it was a man, he couldn't quite tell. The body was male, no titties or anything, but the face seemed suspended between sexes. Sometimes the brow was heavy and a moment later it rounded out. Constant subtle changes made it hard to know and hard to look at. T.R. kept his eyes on the lower corner of the screen. "Did you do that? Make them go away?"

The buzzing roared back. Where there had been a group of ten wasps trapped in his skull before, T.R.'s mind now filled with a swarm of a thousand, biting, stinging. His legs struck out and he pitched into the aisle. T.R. grabbed his head as if he could keep it from exploding and rolled on the gritty floor. The pain was intense, but the feeling of being *chewed* from the inside was the worst. Had he a gun, T.R. would have ended things then and there without hesitation. He managed to squint up at the screen and whimper, *"Please."*

Silence in his mind fell like a hammer and T.R. cried out with the surprise lack of pain. Were it not for his ridgid penis, he would have unloaded hot piss into his pants. He lay panting, crying. He wanted to die so much.

"Your life," the Pompiliad boomed, "is not yours to take."

T.R. rolled over and bathed in the gaze of his master.

"You are chosen. You have work."

The image on the screen blurred out as if the camera lense had been twisted. When it was twisted back, the Pompiliad had been replaced by a young woman with caramel skin and expensive streaks in her hair. That was the city woman staying at the Rhodes house. She'd been asking everyone questions about property value and possible relocation. She had stopped by and talked with the Jeans last week.

She threw a flirty smile at T.R., but when she spoke it was with the grating bass of the Outrider. "Save this one," she said. "She belongs to me."

The focus greased out again and then George Rhodes stared out of the glowing screen. The detail was incredible. T.R. could even see the broken capillaries next to his nose. He could practically smell the drunk old bastard's breath. "This one dies under your knife, but not yet."

T.R. wrapped his arms around his skinny ribs. "Please," he said. "When?"

George gave him a look that was equal parts amusement and pity. The screen blurred out again and two faces swam into clarity: his parents. "Sundown," they said in harmony. "Begin with us at sundown. Then take us to the teacher's house."

The screen went out and T.R. was plunged into silent darkness. For a long time, he lay in the dark and listened to the rustlings of mice in the theatre seats. At one point, something with more than four legs crawled over his outstretched left hand, but he didn't mind or move. He lost track of time in the absolute dark and after what felt like hours the rows of hunched seats began to resolve in colorless light. He waited another minute to be sure it wasn't his imagination. Dawn. His parents would be awake soon. He had to hurry.

T.R. emerged into the faintest beginnings of morning and stood at the entrance of the theatre. Overhead the stars were fading as the sky turned blue again. He drew in a long breath of sulphur and mountain mist. It was a new day in Shard.

Chapter 21

YOU DIDN'T GET more prepared than Amy James was on this fine morning. She laced up her combat boots and ran her eyes over the bundle of gear leaning by the front door. In her pack she had rope and pitons, a serious heavy-duty flashlight, a helmet with its own smaller light, her lunch, a camera, and a gallon of distilled water. Her favorite rock hammer hung off a loop on the side of the pack where she could get to it easily for taking samples. She had a bowl of oatmeal warming her tummy and a cup of nuclear strength coffee heating her veins. She was ready.

Dawn sprayed pink light over the weedy parking lot outside of the old mining office where her RV squatted. She wrinkled her nose at the sulphur smell. You'd think she'd have gotten used to that by now, but it seemed to punch her in the nose every morning. How the hell Will (a wicked smile twisted her lips as she thought of him) could live here was beyond her.

She'd miss him when she left. They weren't going get to married or anything, that kind of spark wasn't there, but he was definitely worth keeping in the stable. Hell, if she got her way, she'd own most of this town in the coming months anyway and that meant spending a fair amount of time here setting up a new mining operation with her shadow partner.

More and more, she was thinking it should be Erica Mendez. They'd all played nicey-nice at George's house the other night, but Erica had impressed Amy as someone with whom not to fuck. And she had the legal expertise to make it all happen behind the scenes before her law firm or Blackstone had the faintest idea what was going on. While the fat-old-white-guys were jerking each other off under their boardroom tables, women like Amy and Erica were out on the frontier trying to make things happen. It wasn't fair that the bosses got all the shares while people like Amy and Erica got a salary. Amy smirked—she was rehearsing the speech she would make to Erica. Damn she was excited, though.

She pushed through the membrane of leaves at the border of asphalt and forest and clicked on her flashlight. A deer trail snaked away into the woods toward the shaft head about half a mile in. The air temperature dropped a few degrees and she zipped up her jacket. It would be even colder down in the cave, unless the fire was close. It had been warm in the shaft that first time she'd walked in a little ways in, but Will's description of the main chamber sounded like a separate cavern. Depending on the geothermal gradient, the temperature would drop inside the cavern and probably hover between fifty and fifty-five degrees.

Unless the fire was there, too.

She'd been trying not to think about it, but it was the main danger of this exploratory adventure. Amy didn't have any breathing tanks and if she ran into an eddy of coal smoke or lost her way and the chamber filled, she could suffocate fast. There was every chance that there were unexploded fire damps still down there that the fire hadn't yet set off. Things could be going along hunky-dory, she could strike a spark with her rock hammer and get flushed out of the hole on a plume from hell.

Amy adjusted the straps on her pack and jumped a shallow stream. It was almost September and by the chill in the air, she had little doubt that trickle would ice over at least once before October. Mountains had always fascinated Amy. Going to school in Colorado she had gained an appreciation for them. She understood why ancient people revered mountains. Every culture that knew mountains had stories about the strange creatures and spirits that roamed on and in them. Perhaps it was that proximity to the firmament—what was a stairway up for us, was a path down for them.

A branch cracked behind her. Amy whirled, the rock hammer in her hand before she even knew she was reaching for it. There was nothing behind her on the deer trail. And that was probably all it had been: a damn deer. She was freaking herself out a little, thinking about spirits and mountain creatures. There was nothing more dangerous in these woods than Amy James. Even the coyotes Will told her to be careful of would shy away from her. The only thing to really worry about was poison ivy and "Giant spiders," she whispered to herself, pushing a small branch out of the way.

Which was, of course, total bullshit. She could sympathize with Kiddo and Loraine—it's wasn't like Amy hadn't had a good scare once or twice in her life—but what they swore to have seen just wasn't possible. Amy shook her head and smiled. They were nice enough people, but the Howards were dumbshits to buy into their own fear. Anyone who got off on scaring themselves got whatever they deserved. Reminded her of the Bush Administration and all the horseshit about Code Orange and duct tape on windows.

The light was coming up now, the first gray washing in through the canopy, bleaching away the contrast from the flashlight beam and the darkness. Amy's stride stretched out a little and her boots crunched over fallen leaves and twigs. All this mountain air and greenery put her in a singing mood and she lifted a clear, strong voice:

"It's a holiday in Cambodia,
It's tough kid, but it's life.
It's a holiday in Cambodia,
Don't forget to pack your wiiiiiiife."

She hummed the rest of it as she crested a low moraine. There it was: the granite wall like the base of some medieval fortress. The mouth of the mine shaft yawned open, the line of smoke drooling up from the top lip. The smell of sulphur and coal smoke shoved at her, stronger than the when she was here before. Amy wrinkled her nose and coughed. She was doing this. She set her shoulders and marched toward the opening.

Amy stopped and shone the heavy flashlight into the dark tunnel. Everything was as it had been the other day except—she squatted down and squinted—there were more footprints in the dust. Fuck. Someone else knew about her find. Had Will come back? Had he brought someone? What if they had already taken samples and had the same idea she had? Amy stood and felt the pull of potentiality; turning back meant one life and going forward a very different one. The pull of the new was too great. She'd think about who was here and what it meant later. Today, right now was for getting a look at that main cavern and maybe taking one giant motherfucking step into her future as a very rich person.

She disappeared into the shaft.

TEN MINUTES LATER, Amy hung in space like a giant spider herself, twisting at the end of her rope line and not breathing. The cavern was vast, stretching out for hundreds of yards. Stalagtites and stalagmites that had reached for one another and joined together over the centuries held up the ceiling like columns in an ancient temple. Low light emanated from the rocks themselves. That could be from some kind of fluorescent mineral; something from the zeolite group maybe. But where the hell was the UV coming from? Those suckers didn't glow without UV. It all looked like emerald, but it couldn't be. Emerald crystal didn't form up like that.

Amy dropped down the rest of the way and hit bottom with a grunt. Wait a minute. She stomped her foot. The ground was metallic. It was like walking around on a big tin drumhead in here. "What the fuck?" she whispered. How could a formation like this even happen? Volcanic activity was the only possibility. This cavern was a huge bubble in a magma intrusion. That also explained the ryolite in the little tunnel off the shaft. But the floor was like refined iron. This wasn't supposed to happen in nature.

Amy unhooked herself from the rope and switched on her flashlight. Its beam shoved the gloom aside and a white circle of light slid over the columns, the ceiling, the floor... Amy almost dropped the light. "Holy Mary, fuck me twice." There was a pile of white crystal growing out of the floor about twenty yards away, roughly in the center of the cavern. These had to be Will's diamonds, the dragon's bed. Will had also said the dragon first appeared to be a second heap of emeralds layered on top of the diamonds, but she couldn't see any evidence of that. And of course she wouldn't. That any of his concussion dream was real was more than far out. That the part about the gigantic pile of precious stones was real, well, she'd just have to buy him a shiny new tin star when she owned this town.

Amy forced herself not to run, but couldn't help a little skip in her step as she approached. Her foot steps echoed off the floor and walls; it sounded like she was wearing tap shoes. She tried to keep her heart from racing. There was every chance that these white crystals were quartz, not diamonds, but something in her didn't buy that, couldn't. She crouched at the base of the pile and reached out, almost afraid to touch them. She shone her light on the stones and her head went swimmy. These sure as hell weren't quartz. The edges were rounded, but polished as if something had dragged a rock blanket over them time and time again. She set her light on the floor and pulled out her rock hammer. She spun it around with a flick of the wrist and wacked the point into the crystal. A hunk about the size of a tennis ball cleaved off the main mass and fell to the floor, throwing weird snare-drum echoes around the cavern.

Amy pulled a rock loop out of her pocket and picked up the crystal. She couldn't tell if the weight was right for diamond—she'd never held a gem the size of a child's fist before. She fit the rock loup to her eye and held the stone over toward the flashlight. Her breath caught and she sat back hard on the floor. "Oh. My. God." What she had in her hand alone would fetch millions. She looked at the pile—it was a circular mound maybe twenty-five feet in diameter and about four feet high in the middle. And that was assuming that it *wasn't* the cap to an igneous intrusive pipe that could go for a mile or more into the earth. Even if only five percent of the mound was diamond she'd have more money than she could ever spend in her life. Amy James would become one of the richest women in the country overnight.

Now, all she had to do was steal it.

You could just go with what you have in hand and still be fucking rich. Two little vertical lines etched her brow as she frowned. That sounded like her internal voice, but it wasn't what she wanted in the slightest. Even if she did leave with the massive hunk of diamond she had chipped off the pile, it wasn't like she had the faintest idea where to fence it. If she tried to legitimately sell it to a jewelery wholesaler, or whatever the hell you were supposed to do, she'd have to explain where she got it. Blackstone would end up with the gem and the mine. No, she needed to get the rights to this place first. If she was going to beat the company, she had to think like the company and steal everything on paper, nice and legal. Amy pulled her pack off and shoved the gem inside. If she was going to get Erica's help she'd at least need a visual aid.

A new sense of urgency pushed her back to the dangling rope. The hairs on the back of her neck were up. People were supposed to feel like this right before they got struck by lightning. She attached a couple of ascenders to the rope and shined her light up at the hole in the ceiling. Amy blew a long whistle—that fucker was *up* there. She webbed up and wrapped her hands in the acenders. They'd make it easier…but she needed to stop whimpering to herself and get moving. Fifteen minutes later, she was drenched in sweat as her boots disappeared into the hole.

* * *

SILENT MINUTES PASSED in the cavern. Enough time, at least, to ensure the raider was gone. A boulder in the wall cracked and sprouted a long, jointed leg, another, another and another. Yïn shifted from rock to spider and clattered down to the floor. She focused her many eyes on the hole that had shat that thieving woman and hissed. Venom dripped and scarred the metal floor. One of the huge columns of rock began to blur and shimmer as if seen through hot air. A great pair of wings erupted from either side, a long tail thudded down like a fallen tree and eyes glowed in the dark. Yïn faced her master. *You should have let me.*

Dampf folded its wings and peered down at its little demon. *We need the constable. She is bonded to him.* The dragon craned its jagged head over to inspect the diamond horde. It bent in and listened. They were closer: the Pompiliads swarmed on the other side of this thin wall between worlds, now one brick thinner. Dampf reared back and inhaled, pulling in nearly all of the available oxygen. Yïn scuttled away into her corner and balled up tight. The dragon roared a downpour of phosphorous-white fire onto the diamonds, sealing over the missing chip. The flames ran dry and the molten diamonds threw an orange glow around the cavern, sunset underground.

* * *

AT THE EDGE of the parking lot, Amy stopped and cocked her head. That was strange, it didn't look like rain, but she could have sworn she heard thunder.

Chapter 22

GEORGE COULDN'T SLEEP. It wasn't from worries, though he had plenty, nor garden variety insomnia. George sipped coffee at his kitchen table and shook with cold while sweat dripped off his brow. The edges of things—the oven, the counter, that green ceramic frog cookie jar that'd he loved since he was seven—all seemed too defined, even a little luminescent. His skin crawled and his guts ached. He wanted to throw up, but couldn't. More than anything, he wanted a drink but George was done with that.

A strange woman from New York City had come to stay in his house. She was abrasive at times and unabashedly at work to destroy what was left of his hometown. When she walked down the kitchen stairs in the morning as he was cooking breakfast, his heartbeat matched the tread of her foot on the risers. When she sat across the table from him and scowled over whichever online newspaper filled her laptop screen his cells aligned to point at her true north. When she walked by and threw a passing, casual hand on his shoulder, all the blood in his body fought to be under her palm.

When she had called him earlier that day from the police station George knew something had happened. Erica didn't do needy, but there was some catch in her voice, some signal that said *I can't handle this.* George had come and brought her back to the house and they'd talked it over. Not at the kitchen table, but in her bedroom—Erica snugged down under the covers and George sitting by the side of the bed. She'd given him all the details of her encounter, her eyes far away and her fingers gripping the edge of the quilt. She asked him if he thought she was crazy. He'd said no. She asked him if he believed what Will said about it being some redneck juiced out of his mind on moonshine. George had said yes. She grabbed his hand and asked him if he would stay until she was asleep. He'd sat on the edge of the bed until his legs cramped, but didn't leave until her breathing slowed and her eyes went into REM.

That had been hours ago and dawn was on its way. It had been almost twelve hours now since his last drink. Granted, he had already cut way back since Erica came to stay with him, but this was the first time in many years he'd gone this long without the oily juniper burn in the back of his throat. He shivered and almost dropped his cup. He was bone tired. Blue black night sat outside the kitchen window. An early dawn bird chirped. George hoped a cat would eat it.

He wasn't even sure why he was even doing this. It wasn't like she was going to stay with him. It wasn't even like they'd shared a kiss. Will and Amy had already gone to bed, but Erica and George (stupid to even think of their names coupled like that) hadn't even held hands. What could he possibly offer a woman like her? And even if she did develop feelings for him, what then? She would never leave her firm and come live in Shard. George couldn't survive in a place like Manhattan. It would suck him dry. George shivered. He realized the tenor of those thoughts had sounded an awful lot like his mother's voice. "Wonder if I'm hallucinatin' a little," he said. His voice was hollow and had a funny little echo to it, the auditory equivalent of a halo. The DTs these were not—he'd already cut back enough to keep that from happening—but this was some badass withdrawal.

The echoing quality of his voice reminded him of the cavern and everything that was going on just beneath the skin of this strange little town. Had old Cyrus really gone on a white lightning roller coaster ride? It wasn't the most unusual thing in backwoods Kentucky, but it didn't feel right either. George wondered if it wasn't somehow tied to that other one. What'd that, that *dragon* call it, the Pompiliad? He shuddered and shook his head. What if what Erica saw had something to do with the Wasp? Jesus, thinking of it that way didn't help matters; put an image of a giant black hornet in his mind—buzzing around town like a helicopter, impaling children, old ladies and small dogs with its stinger. And had he mentioned lately that he'd really like a fucking drink?

Motion flickered in his peripheral vision and George looked up. A face hung in the kitchen window, pale skin framed by long colorless hair. The mouth gaped and the eyes were glazed over. George made a "Buh!" sound and shoved back from the table.

One of the chair legs caught on the rag rug by the sink and spilled him to the floor. George jumped up like a jack-in-the-box and grabbed a long knife off the rack over the counter. When he spun around the face was gone.

For a moment, George just stood and stared at the pre-dawn light splashing up against the window glass. Had he really seen that, or was it just a really nasty gin blossom? He had to find out. George gripped the knife with shaking hands, the light along its blade jittered and jived like it was electrified. He walked down the dark front hall—not thinking about it just moving—and stopped at the glass front door. The Archangel Michael glared at him. George looked at the flaming sword then down at his turkey knife. Yeah, uh-huh.

He whipped open the door and cool dawn air rushed in and over him. He flared his nostrils and caught the scent of something gone bad, sweet trash left in the summer sun mixed in with the usual coal burn. He looked left and right, nothing but stillness on the street. Even that fucking bird was quiet. Nothing to it, but to do it. George stepped off the front porch and strode around the house, knife held at the ready. God, he hoped that hadn't been some stupid kid playing a prank because he was about to scare the living Jesus-jumped-up-and-gone-to-meeting-Christ out of them. Now that he thought about it, that face had reminded him of a kid, Maggie Owens. But he could be wrong. He didn't have much occasion to get out to their little village and the Owenes didn't get into town all that often either. Maggie'd be about fourteen now he guessed.

George rounded the corner and stopped. There was nothing there but kitchen window and the flower patch underneath. He'd just turned the earth there the other day while Erica was on one of her library trips and had been looking forward to planting mums when the fall got on a little more. That smell of rotten fruit and bad soil was stronger here, but even that was wafting away as the morning breeze came up and night and day swapped the sky. George walked over and hunkered down. The adrenalin caught up with him and a little moan escaped his mouth; his head was just fucking killing him. Oh, shit. Footprints. Embossed in the fresh dirt like little accusations. Whoever had been standing out here gawking in at him had been shoeless and about the size of a fourteen year-old girl.

George felt like he had to pee. And throw up. And have a drink. Maybe all three in no particular order. A thought pulled his balls up tight: what if she was still out there watching him? George scanned the yard and even up into the high oaks, nothing but grass and empty branches. The light was coming on stronger now and gravity was beginning to yank at his bones. His shoulders slumped and he loosed a massive yawn.

"Little early for gardening, ain't it?"

George whipped around and threw the knife. It landed flat in the grass about four feet out and well off to the left because George had no idea how to throw a knife. Will Two-Bears McFarlan stood with crossed arms, frowning and shaking his head.

"We need to get you a gun, son. That was sad."

George stared at him bug-eyed and panting. "I think I peed a little."

WILL SIPPED HIS coffee and said, "Really? Cold turkey?"

George poured himself a fresh cup and sat opposite his friend at the kitchen table. "Yeah, well, sort of." He was coming off shy, but that was all right. As much as he put his best friend through with his drinking down the years, George had every right to some humility. "I've been cuttin' down over since," he paused, "over the last week or so, so's it's not quite so hard."

"Still kickin' your ass, though, ain't it?"

George smiled. "Why you look downright concerned, Sheriff."

"Blow me. You should be sleeping, not drinking more coffee."

"If I could sleep, I would." George blew on his coffee. "Besides, if I were all snuggled up in bed I wouldn't have been awake to see the Maggie Owens fright show. You're one to talk anyway, Vilhelm. What the hell were you doing stalking around my house this early? You've got a thing for me, just admit it."

Will took off his red baseball cap and ran a hand through his hair. He felt like dogshit. "I've been up most of the night. I close my eyes and start dreamin' dreams I'd rather not." He got quiet a moment. George could feel he had something to say and just let the time spin out. There was no such thing as an awkward silence between brothers. "It's started, George."

151

"I, uh, I kind of felt something."

"Yeah?"

"Yeah. When I picked up Erica at the station and she told me about what happened—well, I sorta just knew it wasn't about old Cyrus getting a drunk on. He doesn't even touch his own stuff anyway, does he?"

"No, you're right he doesn't. I guess I kind of told her that to calm her down."

George chuckled. "She knew you were bullshitting her. I mean, she got it. She understood why you fed her a line, but it didn't work. She was scared, Will, really freaked out. I think she's not used to be being scared, like it's an alien emotion to her most of the time. Half the reason she's all off kilter about this is because she wasn't in perfect control of herself."

"I went up there, to the Owens place."

"Uh-huh, and?"

"That body Erica said she saw? The one in the burning oil drum? It was gone, looked like it'd been drug off. Cyrus's truck was gone, too. Erica said she saw it, but when I got there it was gone."

"It's that blue I.H., right?"

"Yup. I saw it when I got back into town, though. Parked in around the side of Charlotte Najarian's house."

George drank coffee and raised his eyebrows.

"So, I checked out the truck and there was some, ah, residue in the back that *could* have come from transporting a partially barbecued Kentuckian. When I knocked on the door, there was no answer so I kind of decided to do the probable cause thing and go in for a look."

George couldn't help but smile. "I never got the nuances there with probable cause. How do y'all know when it applies, Constable?"

"Pretty much whenever I feel like it does. Anyway, so I went in, but the house was as quiet as a tomb."

"Nice choice of words."

"Yeah, lately my mind keeps running in that direction for some odd reason."

"So where's old Charlotte? Shit, Will, where're the Owenses or Cyrus for that matter? What the hell is going on around here?"

Will stared at the table. "I told you. I think it's started."

"Yeah, but what's that mean, man?"

"I don't know, Georgie. It just feels like things are happening. You know how you always know the fire's right there under our feet, chewing away at the seam? It kinda feels like that, like I can feel it all happening just out of sight."

The two men were quiet a minute, sipping their coffee, musing. George said, "It's recruiting."

"Huh?"

"The spider and the dragon recruited you, Will. Then you recruited me. I think the Wasp thing is doing the same. They're gathering their forces."

"You know how you said Erica don't like it when she feels out of control? I don't much care for it either." Will sipped his coffee and made a face. It was cold. He got up to pour some more and when he turned around George had a look on his face. "What?"

"Why can't we leave, Will?"

Will sat back down. George's eyes were showing a little too much white for his liking.

"We could just get lost and start over. Shit man, the only reason we stay here year after year is 'cause we're afraid of something different. We could just pack up our shit and haul ass on outta' here. Let these creepshow cocksuckers fight it out on their ownsome."

"It ain't like I never thought of that, Georgie. But you remember what Dampf told us—we don't stop it here, it'll open the portal thing and the rest of them'll come swarming out. We're talking about end of the world type shit."

"Can't we at least get some help?"

Will pushed back from the table. "What do you want me to do, man? You think I should call up to the county seat? Get Tommy Ward on the horn and see if he can't spare a few deputies to fight the second coming of a race of demons from another dimension? How's that call going to go, do you think?"

"That's exactly what I'm suggesting you do. You can't handle this on your own. We can't."

"You're not thinking this through to the end of it. We could call in a hundred guns—fuck it, get the National Guard involved and make it a clean thousand. Know what would happen? We'd

153

win, but they'd know about the doorway or portal or whatever Dampf and Yïn are sitting on down there."

"So what?"

"You're scared, George."

"You're goddamn right I am, but I still don't see why getting everyone from Tom Ward to Dick Cheney's private ninja army on our side is a bad thing against all this. So what if they know about the portal?"

Will sighed long and tired. "They'd start administrating, George. They'd start testing. They'd bring in NASA, the CIA, the NSA, the League of Extraordinary Fucking Gentlemen… They'd bring them all in and they'd end up doing what we're trying to keep from happening." George winced. Will nodded. "Now you see what I'm talking about?

George's eyebrows bent up almost comically. "The officials would succeed where the Pompiliad failed. They'd open it."

"You get why we gotta keep a lid on this."

George put his head on the table with a thunk. His voice came up muffled and stuffy- nosed. "I'm so unhappy."

Will snorted. "You could always drown your sorrows…in a nice warm glass of milk."

"You're a bad man."

George's head popped up.

"Yes?" Will asked.

"I have to get Erica out of here. I'll tell her there's been an outbreak or something."

"Holy shit, George, no. You can't do that. You can't do anything that's going to get more people down here."

"It's not safe here!"

"Think about it, man. She leaves and tells someone about how Ebola has come to Kentucky we're going to have the guys in spacesuits down here in about a minute flat."

"What if I just tell her that Cyrus has gone overboard and that she's gotta go until you catch him?"

Will crossed his arms. "Think it'll work? She seems awful tough to me."

George smiled a little. "She is, but she was also awful scared. I think we might be able to convince her to leave until this is over."

"If it ever is. We don't win, I get the distinct impression that there's not going to be anywhere anyone can go to get safe."

The sun was full up now and light sweapt the night from the kitchen. It looked like it was going to be another gorgeous late summer day in Shard. George stared out into the bright yard and thought of his mother. Every now and again he wondered what stage of decomposition her body was in down under the old Methodist churchyard. The fire edged that property. Would the dry heat kill the bacteria in the soil and preserve her, or accelerate the process? The dead were supposed to rise during The End Times—that's what she had believed, and preached. A bird twittered a welcome to the day. George squinted as if in pain. "I *hate* that fuckin' bird. Wish I had a bazooka."

"Oh, that reminds me," said Will. "What're you doing later?"

"I was going to try to scare my only houseguest out of town and then just, you know, shake for a while, maybe vomit. Why?"

Will flashed an enormous grin. "Wanna' learn how to use a machine gun?"

Chapter 23

CHILDE HOWARD STARED into his cereal bowl and yawned. Under the table, Darwin lay across Kiddo's feet, stealing their warmth without an ounce of remorse. Loraine padded by on the way to the coffee maker and kissed her son's head between corkscrews of hair. She poured herself a cup of high-octane sludge and looked out the kitchen window into the woods. A bluejay perched on a branch and scolded the world because the world was drab and the jay was *pretteh, soo pretteh.*

"Mom?"

Loraine turned, "Yes, my son, my boy, my light?"

"What's evil?"

"Whoa," Loraine held up her hand and took a pull from her coffee mug. "Okay, try that again."

Kiddo smiled a little. "Seriously, what's evil?"

"That's a pretty heavy thought for a twelve-year-old."

"How come you're not answering?"

He'd lopped off the 'g' in 'answering'. Her only boy was turning into a Kentuckian. Loraine pulled out a chair and plopped her butt down. "I don't know, Kiddo. Maybe because it's not such an easy question to answer."

"The crazy religion people on TV and on-line talk about evil all the time. They all pretty much say that the other people—the ones not with their church or whatever—are evil."

"Uh-huh," Loraine said. "And what do you think of that?"

"They're all bozos."

"Indeed, bozos."

"Some of 'em even talk about it like the Devil's this monster that's waiting to get us if we do the wrong thing."

"And what do you think of think of that?"

"I used to not think there was one."

"Used to?"

156

"Yeah, I figured that it was like one of those fairy tales that have messages hidden in them. You know, to teach kids stuff?"

"Morals."

"Right, that like if you told someone that the Devil was going to come get them if they didn't go to church or whatever that you could get them to go more often."

"Well, some of those fanatics—bozos—believe that." Loraine sipped her coffee. "But there are a lot of people out there who think that organized religion was all started as a way to control people. Back in the olden days priests were as powerful as kings, sometimes even more powerful. They would tell the people all kinds of garbage to keep them under control and keep the money coming in. They even had this thing where a person could buy a kind of get out of hell free card."

"Seriously?"

"Oh, yeah. It was called a Plenary Indulgence. If you paid enough money, one of the big priests would write up a slip of paper forgiving you for just about any sin."

Childe stared back into his cereal for a moment. "So, does that mean there are more rich people in heaven than poor people?"

"Your logic's dead on, boy o' my heart, but I'm willing to bet that if there is a heaven it's the exact opposite." She looked at her son. He looked so much like his damn father when he was troubled. "What's going on, Honey? What's with all this evil stuff?"

Childe thought of that day in the woods. Magic was real. Monsters were real. Something bad was coming. He was glad Darwin was on his feet. "Mom?"

"Yeah?"

"If you're killed by an evil thing, does that mean you go to hell? Like if a vampire kills you by sucking all your blood you come back as one?"

"Who have you been talking to? Is it that Charlotte Najarian?" Loraine scowled, she knew she should have home schooled him; it was just that she wanted him to make friends. That and she could barely handle her times tables let alone the quadratic equation.

"I haven't been talking to anyone," Childe said. Which was technically true because the spider couldn't talk out loud.

"Is it because of what happened in the woods when we found the Amazing Ninja Dog?" She broke eye contact to sip her coffee. "Because you know what constable Will said about that: It was just a big spider web, probably an orb weaver just like what we looked up on-line." They had found examples of enormous webs on the Internet and if she stretched her mind a little bit, she could believe that what they saw that day was just a particularly impressive example. It felt a hell of a lot better than the alternative.

"I dunno', I guess it's that." He gave her a smile he hoped would disarm her. "I was just wonderin' was all." He took a bite of cereal and opened his mouth. "See food."

Loraine sat back. "You should give it a few more chews, I think. Makes it a little mushier. Close your mouth, disgusting child."

"Gahhhh."

She gave him a look and Kiddo's mouth crunched shut. He chewed behind a big old grin. "So," Loraine said, "you've got what, three more days of summer vacation? What's on the docket for today?"

"I think me and Howard—"

Loraine held up a finger. "Howard and I."

"I think *Howard and I* might bum around a little, maybe play some X-box or something."

Loraine genuflected. "Use the farce."

"Always."

* * *

THIS WAS GOING to be a big day for T.R. He peeled himself out of bed and walked to the bathroom. The Jeans had banged the screen door on their way to work less than an hour ago. Usually, that meant he had another few hours in bed during summer break, but sleep was a buzzing, painful joke now. He gripped the edges of the sink and stared at the wraith in the mirror. His eyes were bloodshot and sunken. His skin was sallow, marked by the occasional eruption of dark red acne. There was a ripe one on his chin, but he didn't care. Let them cover him. He was a monster. Might as well look like one.

He had about nine hours to figure out how to kill his parents. T.R. was tall like his father, but hadn't yet filled out. His mother came up to his nose and ran about one-forty. She'd be easier to handle, but not by much. The only way to take them would be by surprise or with a gun. He had a decent .22 rifle in the closet from back in the days when his daddy used to take him hunting. There was that time the two of them had perched in a tree stand for the better half of a cold October day—Tommy Ray had been maybe ten years old. Tommy's gloves were too thin and his fingers started to hurt. Daddy had held them in his big rough hands and breathed hot air on them until it was better. They didn't see a single deer that whole day, but had come home rosy cheeked, hungry and happy. T.R. blinked at the face in the mirror. Was he crying?

He wiped an arm across his face and walked down the hall. Pictures of young Tommy and his proud, serious parents hung along the wall. Every year they made him drive an hour each way to the Sears to get those damn things taken. T.R. peered at himself at age eight—big head, stupid bowl cut, bad striped shirt. His mother's hand was draped casually over his little shoulder. She had pink nail polish. He felt another hot tear push out and splash his bare foot.

T.R. grimaced and let his head fall back. How was he going to do this? He looked back at the picture and gasped. It had changed. It showed a young boy cowering behind a half-opened bedroom door. His mother sat up in bed frozen in mid-yell, her face all sharp angles, one breast flopping out from behind the sheet she used to cover herself. His father was charging across the room at him; below his hairy belly his erect penis jutted like a javelin. T.R.'s head started to buzz. The next picture down the line was of him even younger, standing in the downstairs parlour with a big wet patch on the crotch of his jeans. He must have been five or six here. He remembered it now: This was the day that he pissed his new Toughskins. His mother had been visiting with a friend and made him stand in the parlour while they finished their coffee because he was a bad boy. Every now and then one of them had looked over at the bad boy and made a tsk of disgust. Tears had rolled down his face like rain but he never made a sound.

The buzzing grew louder, a platoon of wasps crawled the gray matter tubes behind his skull. T.R. slid down the wall and hugged his boney knees to his chest. He rocked back and forth and waited. After what felt like a year the buzzing quieted and he stood up. His mind was clean and cold again. He dared a look at the portraits on the wall. Normalcy had returned to the pictures but his hesitation had not. The gun then.

"It doesn't have to be quick, though," he said to himself.

* * *

AMY JAMES WALKED with a jaunty little skip down George's street. Her backpack bounced along behind her. It was easier to be jaunty without the combat boots. She'd eschewed them today in favor of a pair of bright green Chucks just like Will's black ones. (Maybe if they ran into each other later they could screw wearing just the Chucks. She laughed at loud and a crow cawed at her from the crown of a spreading oak.) It was a gorgeous summer morning, about seventy-five degrees and clear. The weather in these mountains was so gentle compared to the Rockies, but the Appalachians were much older, settled. In geological terms the Rockies were still in their adolescence—all full of piss and vinegar. The Appalachians were in their dotage.

She stopped in the middle the street and put her hands on her hips. She scanned the surrounds in a 360° swoop. These gorgeous old Victorians might surivive her plans, but if that remarkable diamond pipe had thrown arms up into other sectors of the mountain and the surrounding hollows, Shard was gonna get scraped clean off the map, gorgeous Victorians and all. If not, maybe she'd buy George's place or that blue one with the screened porch and the nice gardens. Who lived there, she wondered. And did that awesome antique pick-up truck parked out back come with it?

She was getting ahead of herself. None of her fantasies would come true unless she got a partner to run some serious legal interference. Thus, this little trip. She strode up George's front walk and rang the bell. Oh, cool! She hadn't noticed the stained glass door with the violent bible scene the last time she was here. She was squinting in at the leaf covering Eve's crotch when the door opened.

Amy straightened and smiled. "Just the woman I was hoping to see."

"Not like this, I imagine." Erica ran a hand through tangled hair. She'd only just rolled out of bed still wearing her clothes from yesterday. "George isn't here. Well, he is, but he's dead asleep. I think he was up all night."

"Yeah? Good party?"

"No, nothing like that. He's just not feeling too well."

Amy caught something there, but let it go. She whipped off her backpack and unzipped it. She plunged both hands into the swirling elbows and emerged with a bag of Starbucks Sumatra coffee and a big ziplock bag full of blueberry muffins. "Just baked them myself this morning. The blueberries are from the woods near my rig, if you can believe it, and I've been saving the coffee."

"Ohmygodcomein."

Ten minutes later they sat at the kitchen table eating warmed-up muffins and blowing steam off strong coffee. (Erica had slipped upstairs and into a crimson silk bathrobe. The last night's clothes thing just wasn't working for her.)

"These muffins are awesome," Erica said. "You made these?"

"Uh-huh…What's funny?"

"Oh, you just don't seem the domestic type."

"Now don't judge on appearances alone. The James women are all badasses in the kitchen. It's a genetic thing. Like cancer."

Erica swallowed with visible pleasure. "I'm going to have run twenty miles to make up for the pounds I've put on since I got here, but damn these are good."

"What are you talking about, nutcase? You're a supermodel stick."

"And you are one hot little suicide chica. Show those tattoos to our friendly neighborhood constable yet?"

Amy leered. "Every last one of them." She sipped her coffee and peered over the rim. "You and the innkeeper seemed to have a little som'in, som'in going back and forth during dinner the other night. What's up there?"

Erica sat back and pitched her voice lower. "That obvious?"

"What? You got crush on him. What's the big deal?"

"I'm here on business and that's going to be over in a week or so."

"So? I'm probably leaving, too, but I'm still having fun where I can find it."

"Probably leaving?"

Amy waved her off. "More girl talk now. Business talk later."

"I'm afraid there's not much to tell." Erica glanced over her shoulder toward the back stairs. The door was closed. "George has been a perfect gentleman. Frankly, it's getting kind of annoying."

Amy darkened a little, hesitated. "You, uh, you're not worried about the drinking thing?"

"Noticed that, did you?"

"He wasn't all over the place or anything. In fact, he holds it really well, but he must have polished off a couple bottles of wine all by himself over dinner, and when I met him he was in the holding at cell at Will's jail."

Erica sighed. "I *am* worried about it. I'm sure that's why he hasn't tried to push our friendship into anything more, but I think he's stopping."

"Really?"

"Yeah, he's had less and less every time I've been around him. In the last couple of days, I only caught him taking these little medicinal sips from a flask every couple of hours or so." She sat up a little straighter. "I'm not stupid, Amy. My father had a problem and I know very well that George could be putting away gallons behind my back and covering it up. Career drunks are great at that kind of thing, but I'm just not getting that feeling from him."

"You think he's doing it for you?"

"I hope not."

"Because you're leaving."

"It's that, yeah, but you know you also just can't do something like that and tag it to another person. That has to be for yourself or it messes up all kinds of stuff. I mean, as soon as I'm out of here, what's he going to do if all this is for me? He'll have lost his reason for not drinking and start right back up again, and probably twice as hard."

"What if you had reason to stay in Shard? A professional reason."

"I can't imagine what that would be. Most of the properties around here are abandoned and have technically become public domain because of that and the safety issues. Blackstone can just buy those up from the county for a buck a piece. And most of the people who still live around here are practically begging to get out."

"Really? The people I've run into have seemed really happy here. I can't imagine Will wanting to leave."

"He's different, true, but I've been doing a lot of knocking on doors and most of these hicks—you'll pardon the expression—would take a small settlement to get moving on. They won't tell you that on the surface, Southern pride maybe, but I can feel it. I just have to get the right angle." She mused a little, going into full Mendez business mode. It was like Erica had a chess computer hardwired in her head that had just whinned into life. "I think tax relief might do it. A lot of these houses pull more tax value than the people here can afford to pay. Combine that with relocation to an area with a decent chance of employment and they'll go. Anyway, whatever angle I use, my part in this should be over in another week or so, so I really don't have a reason to stay."

"What if I gave you one?"

"What do you mean?"

Amy sat back. She affected chilly ease, but if her hands hadn't been wrapped around her coffee mug they would have been shaking. "We both work for the same master, right?"

"Well, Blackstone's one of my firm's largest clients, but there are several—"

"Not really what I'm talking about. We both work for men who pay us money and dictate our limits. They say jump, we jump, etc."

"Okay, sure."

"And we do this because they control the purse strings, right? If you could have an almost unlimited amount of money, you wouldn't work for these people, right?"

Erica smiled and squinted at this funny-smart punker girl. "Where are you taking me with this?"

"Gimme' a second, gimme' a second." Amy smiled and sipped her coffee. The caffeine was medling with her natural jitters now, giving her a nice little high. "Just answer me una pregunta: How much money would it take for you to quit?"

"I know the figure exactly, as a matter of fact."

"This," Amy said, "does not shock me. So how much?"

Erica laughed; it lit her like wildfire on a hillside. "Fifty million."

Amy laughed with her, but her heart was racing, racing. "Oh, is that all? Why that number?"

"Because I could sock away half of it and live very, very well on the interest alone and use the rest toward a foundation, toys, travel, what have you. Fifty mill is a nice sustainable number without drawing too much attention to oneself."

Amy just stared at her.

"What?" Erica asked. "You're freaking me out a little."

Amy placed both palms flat on the kitchen table. She had this crazy little gleam in her eye. It wasn't a warm glint, but like the light off the edge of something metallic. She measured each word, "What if I told you I had maybe five percent of your magic number in my backpack right now?"

"Amy, I don't..."

Before Erica could finish Amy reached down and pulled the softball-sized diamond out of her bag and smacked it down on the center of the table. The room rang with silence.

Erica looked at the opalescent rock. It was almost perfectly spherical and milky white. "Go ahead," Amy said. "Pick it up." Erica reached forward and wrapped her fingers around it. It was cold and heavy. She held it close to her face. "I don't get it," she said. "How's this worth a million dollars?"

"It's not yet. You have to cut it first."

Erica's eyebrows furrowed. "You mean it's—."

"A fucking diamond, yeah."

Very slowly, Erica placed the huge stone in the middle of the table. "Um."

"Yeah, um." Amy was sitting forward now, gripping the edge of the table.

"Where?"

"The mine. I went into one of the shafts a little way and found this cavern that's completely independent of the shaft system itself. It's about twenty meters below it. There's a ryolite pipe that's capped off with these."

"Wait, there's more?"

"Baby, there are hundreds this big just on the surface of that deposit."

"Hundreds? Surface?"

"Okay, imagine a tube that starts way down beneath the mantle. You know what that is?"

164

"Yeah, the crust thingy."

"No, the mantle's beneath the crust. The crust floats on it. It's all magma. Anyway, sometimes it'll throw up these fissures through the crust like a pipe and when the magma cools it becomes rock. Sometimes the conditions are just so and you get ryolite deposites which sometimes means you get diamonds. I found ryolite and kept going. Further into this cavern I found there was another ryolite pipe and it was capped with diamonds like this one, all fused together. I've never seen, or even read about anything like this."

Erica brought her mug up to her lips. Her hand was shaking and she forgot to drink. "How much do you think is down there?"

Amy leaned forward. The muscles in her shoulders made her tattoos swell and roll. "If it's just the cap, we're talking hundreds of millions, maybe into the billions with almost no removal cost. Shit, I used some rope and a goddamn hammer to get that one."

"If it's not just the cap?"

Amy sat back now; she had her. "If that deposit actually reaches down into the pipe, or other formations exist under the mine, there could be tens of billions. It could easily be the richest diamond deposit in the world." She sipped her coffee for effect. "It's all in the mine."

"What are you going to do?"

"Not me, we."

"What do you need me for?"

Amy took a breath. Saying it out loud was another thing all together. "I need you to help me steal it. All of it."

"What?"

"I want to own the mining rights for Shard. That's the only way to get at the heart of that mine's potential, but I can't legally file a claim because I'm under contract to Blackstone. You could, though."

"I can't see how that would work, Amy. My firm's under contractual obligation to Blackstone Mineral. I'm here for my firm."

"No you're not." Amy cut her off. "You're here on vacation. You said so yourself at dinner. They didn't send you here. You came on your own time to make points so you could further your career working for a bunch of fat, old white guys."

165

"So, you're thinking that technically I could make this discovery and lay a claim. You'd be what, a shadow partner?"

"Yes," She didn't wait for Erica to question further. "Here's how'd we do it: I file false reports to Blackstone. The mine's played out. What's left is small potatoes and slag. Not worth the money, time and manpower to strip out. The fire makes the thing just too complicated."

"They'll buy that?"

"Sure. Most geological investigations come up bust. That's why they send in the experts first," she thumbed her chest, "to make sure they're not just pissing up a tree. Blackstone doesn't actually own this mine yet, they've just filed a 'claim of interest' at this point, but they'll yank that as soon as they read my report. It costs money just to have one of those temporary claims."

Erica sat forward a little on her chair. "So then what?"

"Right, so I file the report. They tell me to pull stakes and send me on another assignment. But on the way, I disappear. I'll pull onto some country road somewhere, torch the rig and walk away. Young women go missing every day in this country and since I'm not a six year-old blonde girl, I probably won't even make the news."

"Meanwhile," Erica jumped in. "I just happen to stumble upon this huge discovery and discreetly file a claim. We pull out the stuff on the cap?" Amy nodded. "And use the money from that to finance the rest of the operation. Once things get big enough to bring in outsiders, you go back into the shadows." Erica stopped and put her hand on her chest.

"You okay?"

She smiled and fluttered her hand a little. "Yeah, I'm just breathing really fast." Erica reached for the stone again. She held it close, almost cradling it. A million dollars right there in her hands and billions under her feet. She could not only retire, she could become one of the most influential people on the planet with that kind of money. She could work as little or as much as she liked. She could have a family of her own. She could continue to practice law pro-bono back in the old neighborhood. With that kind of money, she could do anything she wanted. She had no illusions about what money could and couldn't buy. Love, no. Time and freedom, yes. The stone weighed against her lap and began to take heat from her body. Erica realized with a little embarrassment that she was becoming flushed, as her mother called it, down there.

She looked at Amy. "Let's do it."

Chapter 24

WILL PRESSED PLAY on the old CD player boombox he kept in the office. Johnny Cash wafted over his desk and down the hall, between the bars of George Rhodes's (former) Weekend Retreat, filling every nook and cranny with a balance of grit and remorse. Will opened an old standing closet but instead of clothes he found heavy wire mesh locking away a rack of high-powered rifles. There was a single twelve-gauge pump shotgun and below that, an insectile M16. Will grabbed a little cleaning kit and the M16.

He lay the rifle out on his desk and just looked at it a minute. It was a simple design, rugged and vastly improved upon since the days in Vietnam when it made its debut. Back then, this kind of rifle was as likely to jam in a firefight as shoot, but Tommy Ward had bequeathed this one to Will just last year with the promise that it was "fresh out the fac-tree". Four things to remember: 1. Slap in a clip. 2. Pull the bolt. 3. Click off the safety. 4. Pull the trigger. If the selector switch was in single fire, it meant one bullet for each trigger pull. If it was in autofire mode, you just held that sucker down and rocked out at about 13 rounds per second. The rounds themselves were a measly .223 calibre—not much more than a pellet gun—but there was a good two inches of powder behind each slug, so it packed a serious wallop. The barrel didn't come with the usual rifling, so when the slug left the gun it tumbled. When a tumbling slug hits a body it has a tendancy to boggey around inside awhile before coming to a halt. Get shot with an M16 in the shoulder, there's a chance it'll blow your foot off and make wet confetti out of everything in between.

And he was going to give it to the town drunk.

Will sat down with a squeak and rubbed his face with his hands. He really didn't have much of a choice here. George needed to be armed. Something was coming. Shit, something was already here. Just because Will hadn't seen anything first hand, didn't mean it wasn't so. Cyrus had gone nuts, old Missus Najarian was missing and his truck was parked out back of her place, and everyone up by the Owens's place was gone, too. All that aside, he just wanted someone next to him that he could trust, someone with a big old fucking gun. Will reached forward and started to disassemble the rifle.

His thoughts roamed the situation as his hands roamed over metal. He checked the weapon, it was clear and unloaded. The simplest weapon to use would have been *Smaug*, but George wasn't strong enough for the recoil. The first time Will had fired it, the big pistol had exploded like a bomb and kicked back so hard he smacked himself in the head with it. He'd had a long, straight line of purple skin on his forehead for a week after that. (George had called him "Chief Stripey Head".) Will pulled the pins holding the M16's upper and lower receiver, yanked the charging handle and set it aside. While he wiped the receiver with an old rag, he considered the shotgun for George. He had experience with that type of gun, hunting with his moma when he was a kid, but it had been years and you had to work the pump, racking in a new shell every time you wanted to fire. It looked all easy in movies, but it wasn't fast enough for Will's taste. The M16 really was the best option. Will reached into the trigger mechanism with a cotton swab and smirked—besides, George would have more fun with the machine gun. Who wouldn't?

* * *

THE SLAG HEAP was like the surface of an alient planet: a small maze of moranes made up of solidified coal slurry and trash rock at the base of the mountain on the other side of town. Of the few residents left to Shard, almost no one ever came here. Not even the weeds had much chance of taking hold in the ruined ground. What wasn't destroyed over top was burning underneath. The fire had split the skin of the earth in a hundred crazy cracks and seaped steam skyward. The entire place was a good ten degrees warmer than the surrounding area. Still Will caught George shivering every now and again.

It had been a good three days since George quit and he looked much better. The color had begun to flush his cheeks and his face was starting to fill out again. Will knew enough about addiction not to expect it to be a lasting phenomenon, but hoped. George hefted the M16 like he was going to shoot pool with it. "Now, it's the little end that I point toward the bad people, right?"

"Shut up, George. I'm uncomfortable enough even showing this weapon to you, let alone teaching you how to use it."

George blew a kiss at his friend, but got his attitude on straight. He was just a little cranky and even when he was in the best of moods it was always fun to yank Will's chain. "Sorry, Constable. Okay, what do I do?"

Will took a breath. "Right. So, first pick your target. Start with something easy." He scanned the rock pile walling them in to the north. "See that reddish rock yonder? One looks like a triangle?"

"Come with me under the shadow of that red rock," George muttered.

"What?"

"Nothing, you just reminded me of what we're doing is all," George said. "I see the one you mean, go 'head."

"Line the rear site up with the front site and flick off the safety, but don't look at the rifle while you're doing it. I want to make sure you can hit that switch and the fire selector without needing to look."

"I do know how to aim a rifle, Two-Bears."

Will held up his hands. "All right, all right. You go ahead and take a shot then."

George found his target, hunted around with his index finger a few seconds and flicked off the safety. He took a deep breath and held it. *TA-TOK! TA-TOK! TA-TOK!* The M16 came to life in George's hands like an angry animal, spitting and smashing into his shoulder. It tried to squirm out of his grip with every ejected shell casing. A trail of little impact craters and dust puffed up and to the right from the rock he was supposed to hit. He let go of the trigger a second after pulling it, but already half the clip was spent. For a moment, he just stood in the ringing quiet, the echos of gunfire crashing off the hills and silencing the birds.

"You doing all right there, Rambo?"

"You could have warned me."

"Oh, I'm sorry," said Will. "I thought you said you knew how to handle a rifle."

"Maybe not quite so much."

"Maybe not. Now, you want a few pointers?"

"That would be nice, thank you, Sheriff."

They spent the rest of the morning and well into the afternoon blowing the slag pile to hell and scaring away even the mosquitoes. When they were through, George had learned to pluck the *corners* off his targets at a hundred feet and score direct hits at a hundred yards lying on his belly. He'd got the knack of countering the kickback and the M16's tendancy to want to spin around and take his face off. Most of a crate of ammunition was empty and he had the distinct impression that by this time tomorrow his shoulder would be a gorgeous mosaic of color. But he was decent with the machine gun.

George took one last shot at piece of mica that had eluded him all day and *finally* sent that little fucker to hell. He made the gun safe and popped the clip. It was empty anyway. Will was packing up their lunch cooler and collecting shell casings. "Will?"

Will kept his eyes on the ground. You got a discount on ammunition when you returned enough of the things. "Uh-huh?"

"You feel like you can trust me with this thing?"

"You did great, Georgie. I wouldn't say you're ready for SWAT or anything, but you handle that sucker pretty good."

"I mean, you think I could take this home with me?" George was thinking of Erica's story about Cyrus and of that face in the kitchen window.

"That was always the point, man."

George didn't say anything for a while as Will scouted around for any missed casings. "Will?"

Now, he looked up. "Yeah?"

"I'm not sure I could kill a person."

Will laughed. George wasn't sure he liked the sound of it— too much pressure behind that valve. "Oh, I'm pretty sure you're not going to have to kill any people, Georgie."

"Really?"

"Yeah, really." *Because I don't think we're going up against humans.*

Will straightened up and grabbed a handle of the cooler. George grabbed the other side and they walked back toward the Will's Jeep. A crow called. Life was already flowing back into the absence created by the thunder of guns.

* * *

WHEN WILL GOT back to his office, the message light was flashing on his machine. (Cellular phones were little more than bulky pocket clocks back in the hollows of eastern Kentucky. The mountains just inhaled the signal and never gave it back.) He thumbed the "play" button and got the County Sherif's scratchy voice. Tommy Ward always sounded like he was just this side of quitting, but everyone knew he couldn't leave that job. After all this time, no one else in the county would run against him. "Will, ah, this is Tom Ward. Can you call me when you get this? I need some extra hands."

Will dialed the county seat. "Hi, Marlene, it's Will McFarlan down in Shard. Can you find the Sheriff for me? Yeah, I'll hold her." A couple of dry minutes passed and a voice came on the line. The quality wasn't great. Sounded like a patch-through from a car radio. "Will?"

"How do, Tommy?"

"Fine, fine. How's your little slice of heaven? Your house pitch into a sink hole yet?"

"The house is fine. The jail slid into a pit the other day. I'm actually callin' you from underground right now."

"Cute, Will." He paused a second. "Listen, we got ourselves a situation up in Roanneville's gonna' require some extra hands. Can you tear yourself away?"

Roanneville was at the very northern tip of the county and a good hour and a half through the back country, but it was a respectable town in terms of population. They even had a Walmart. "'Course, Tom. What's going on?"

"Illegals. We been monitoring a good-size operation for about three months now. The coyote's a local boy name of Howard Kent. He's got a contracting business, drywall and such."

"He ain't running illegals for that, though."

"Naw, but it's my guess he started out that way. Probably, picked up one or two of 'em every so often on a job and picked up a little Español to boot."

"Got to talkin' with his new compadres about how they got to the states and figured he could turn the same trick?"

"Exactly." Tommy yawned. "Anyways, he's been stepping up his little operation. We got him going and coming with this big

172

ole' cargo van he uses at least three times in the last month alone. Now, usually he takes them right to the job site and best we can tell that's 'cross state lines into West Virginia."

"Usually?"

"He's been holdin' 'em in the Super 8 in Roanneville. We got a tip from the Chamber maid that there was, and I quote," Tommy threw on a crackling hill country drawl that made Will's eyes want to water, "a room stuffed so full a' beaners you can smell the cologne and hair grease from the lobby."

"Nice." Will shook his head. "Why's he holding them like that do you think?"

"Probably some kinda contract job in Pike County or even over the line into Beckley if there's enough of them. Maybe's he had to get a couple of loads for this one."

"Tommy," Will said. "Ain't this something for the Staties?"

The Sheriff chuckled. Will could imagine him brushing crumbs from his belly onto the floor of his prowl car. "Well Constable, it *will* be something for the State Police to be sure, but not until after we've made the bust. They can have the whole mess then when it's all over but the paper work. You see, it'll all have happened so fast there just wasn't time to call them in."

"You just stumbled upon all this from an anonymous tip."

"Right."

"And there hasn't been any continuous survailance over the past few months."

"Exactamundo."

Will shook his head some more. "Okay, Tom. When do you need me up there?"

"You got anything needs tending to in Shard?"

Will paused. "Nothing immediate."

"All right, then. We're set to pop in two hours. That give you enough time to get up to Roannville? I got four other cars all scattered on the back roads around town so we won't clump up and get seen by no one. So, let's say you and me'll get together at the shopping center on Route 40."

"That works."

"Hot damn, Will. See you in two." Tommy hung up.

Will put the phone down and took a deep breath. Welcome to the shit-kicker jamboree. Yee—as they say—haw.

THE BIG INDIAN Chief rumbled through the hills toward Roanneville. The air outside of Shard was sweet and cleaned the sulphur out of Will's sinuses. Every time he left town he marveled at the difference. It was amazing what you could get used to. The road hugged a creek for almost half the trip to Roanneville. Every so often Will took his eyes off the road to take in the sparkles from the water. It was dumb to look at anything but the road in front of you when you were riding a motorcycle—too many deer just wander out, loud pipes or not—but he was hoping he'd catch sight of a great blue heron. Besides, the sun on that laughing water as it rolled over jade-colored rocks was too gorgeous not to look. Oh! And there was his heron—tall as his chest and waiting, a patient, lethal stick until some fish or frog got in range.

He wanted to smile but this job was giving him an ugly feeling. Maybe that was why he wanted to be distracted from the road by the pretty creek. Anything to keep his mind off what he was about to do. It wasn't busting Howard Kent that bothered him. Coyotes were often as not sub-human trash making their living on the desperation of others. He'd heard stories of rape and murder in the desert. If you didn't pay the price the Coyote wanted, it was just as easy to take it out of your flesh as it was your life savings. And who the fuck cares about a bunch of wet backs, right?

Will didn't know how to solve the problem of illegals coming into this country. It wasn't right to break the law and take jobs from Americans who could use the work at a decent wage. And it made him sick that some of the big companies were taking advantage by paying illegals little to nothing with no benefits and sometimes in dangerous conditions. It wasn't like they could form a union or complain to OSHA. He'd read about a meat packing plant in Midwest that got busted for having a huge workforce of undocumented people, including a large group of children. When he thought about it, he wondered what he would do if he lived in a place with no work and no future. (Well, if he lived in one he couldn't leave anyway.) He'd do what half the population of backwoods Kentucky had been doing for generations: pick up stakes and move to where the work was. Problem with the illegals was that when they picked up stakes, they moved over an imaginary line that striped their humanity, like walking over a bad spell.

Will leaned into a bend and upshifted on the way out. The Indian got the idea and put on a little extra. The leaves blurred to sheets of wavering green in his peripheral vision. Will thought about the stories Daddy used to tell about the coal wars back in the early part of the Twentieth Century. The miners went on strike to protest bad pay, perilous conditions, and the dept-vortex known as the company store. The companies brought in Itallian immigrants to die for next to nothing down in the black holes punched in the mountainside. And when they petered out or went on strike themselves, the companies brought in trainloads of blacks. Those poor sons of bitches got caught between the company *and* the miners. Will gunned it down a straight stretch, the engine roaring off the trees and rock outcrops. He wondered how many bleeched ribcages still fingered the sky back in these woods.

By the time he pulled up next to Tommy Ward's patrol car in the parking lot out back of the Walmart, Will's mind had cleaned itself out. He was here to work. Maybe he could make sure the bust went down smooth. Tommy's boys sometimes liked to play it a little rougher than they needed to. Tommy hopped (as well as his gut would allow) out of the car and gave Will a warm handshake. Rough calluses pushed into Will's hand. (Tommy's hobby was spliting wood. He had a pile out back of his house near as tall as the roof line. Reminded him of his hero—Ronald Regan.)

"Constable! Damn happy you could come up and join our little swarree."

"Tommy," Will said. "Wouldn't miss it. When we set to go?"

"Ha! All fired up and ready to pop?"

Will squinted up at the sun. "Yeah, I suppose I must be." Tommy Ward was practically shucking and jiving on the pavement he was so juiced up. This was as big a deal as he'd seen in years. Finally something to give the job some edge. He'd have stories to tell for years after this one. "Super 8's just up the street a bit, right? They all still there?"

"Kent pulled in last night with a final load of them—well, *final* 'cause we're going to make it final. Our man on the steakout counted another half dozen or so. I got Steve MacMillan watching 'em."

Will nodded. Steve was a good guy, a little older and cool; reminded Will of Stu Redman from *The Stand*. He'd taken the deputy job because the pension was good and he had three young children. Most of Tommy's boys were little more than grown-up high school bullies who'd gotten tired of mailbox baseball and cow tipping. If things got stupid, Will could look to Steve for help. "How many in total?"

"We put it at between fifteen and twenty."

"Jesus, in one room? How long they been there?"

Tommy turned toward the motel as if he could survey through its walls. "Few days at least cept' for that last bunch."

Will put his hands on his hips and looked at his boots. "How many armed?"

"Oh, you getting uncomfortable Constable?"

"C'mon, Tommy."

"Just ribbing you, just ribbing you." He put on a lisp, "You're always so sensitive… Anyways, way I figure it, just our coyote'll have a gun. They don't like the cargo to be carrying."

"Right."

"You can bet a few of them've got knives or razors hid on them somewhere, though, so watch your ass all the same."

Will had a thought. "Tommy? You or any of your guys speak Spanish?"

"Nope, but I brought my universal translator." Tommy patted his holster. "Don't worry about it, Constable. Them beaners'll get a look at the heat and our badges and hit the floor like sacks of shit."

Will ran it through is mind. He'd taken a couple of semesters of Spanish in school but that was a thousand years ago. He couldn't do much more than kick down the door and shout, "Please! Where is the bathroom?"

The car radio squawked. *"Sheriff? This is MacMillan, over?"*

Tommy reached in and pulled out the hand mic. "Go, Steve-oh."

"Two-bears get here yet?"

Tommy handed the mike to Will. "Right here, Mac." He handed it back.

"Can you all come on over to my position? There's something going down in that room. Over?"

Will was already walking around to the patrol car's passenger side by the time Tommy Ward said, "We're on our way, Steve."

THE THREE OF them squeezed into the cab of Steve MacMillan's big pick-up truck. A pair of binoculars floated on the dashboard amid a tide of food wrappers. A couple of day's growth of stubble darkened Steve's cheeks and it smelled just a fart shy of an animal den. Steve pointed to the room on the far end of the motel and whispered as if they could hear him from this distance. "Those curtains been closed most of the time I been out here, but about five minutes ago I seen 'em kind of smash up against the glass like someone pushed into them."

"Well, shit," Tommy said, "there's got to be at least a baker's dozen of them in there. Somebody probably just tripped over somebody."

"Yessir, but then I seen one of the illegals at the window. He was trying like lord a'mighty to get out, but someone pulled him back. It happened real fast, but I saw it."

"Tom we need to go," Will said.

Tommy Ward didn't even try to conceal the excitement in his voice as he grabbed the hand mic off the radio and squawked it. "Gentlemen, this is your Sheriff. We are go in one. Come back, please."

A chorus of scratchy voices squawked back, *"Ready, over."*

Steve MacMillain started up the truck. Will reached down and fingered the snap off the hold-down on his holster. Tommy Ward let out his breath and thumbed the mic, "This is Sheriff Ward. Three…two…one…*Go!*"

When it was all over, Will wouldn't remember the truck jouncing over the curb or Tommy Ward almost flattening him as they all piled out. He wouldn't recall the purple eye makeup on the woman behind the front desk or the look of satisfaction on the face of the chamber maid, nor that her feet were bare. There would be no memory of the other cops pounding in a second after them, the rasping of their breath or the tromp of their boots. Somehow Will ended up on point and was the first at the motel room door. His memories started with his foot against the door.

Everything leading up to then was flash-fried by what he saw afterward.

At first he thought they were all sleeping. Then the blood on the wall, a cheery splash of crimson that couldn't be more than a few minutes old, registered in his peripheral. So did the smell: the loosened bowels of fourteen men. Men, that was funny. Half of these bodies had housed teenage boys. Will walked into the room, stepping over the outstretched hand of a dead man. Will's eyes moved up that arm, over the blue denim work shirt, rolled up at the elbow, past the shoulder to the neck. Did some woman press her lips to that spot his final night with her? Did some child wrap her arms around the strong column of her father's neck as he carried her to their front door? Will's eyes traveled further, pulled toward the man's own. They were whited over, seeing nothing. Maybe seeing everything. His jaw was clenched shut.

Someone called his name from the door. Will put up a hand to silence them and realized it was full of gun. He holstered *Smaug* and stepped over another man, another, another. He found the coyote, Howard Kent, with his lower half shoved under the bed. Had he been trying to back into this hiding place? He clutched a nine-milimeter semi-automatic in his left hand. Will leaned down. Someone used his name again. This time he ignored them. Will snifed the gun barrel. It hadn't been fired. He glanced up. Kent's white eyes painted him with nothing.

Will stood up. White eyes like a handful of ivory chips tossed over the ground. Twenty-eight blank television sets that had played some secret, terrible show. Now they played milky reflections of one man standing in the middle of the room while six others crowded the door. Will stepped over more limbs and torsos and made his way to the blood spatter on the wall. From what he could tell everyone was intact, so where did this come from? He could smell the copper in the air as he drew near and almost tripped over his answer. A huge man, all work-carved muscle, sprawled on the floor. Will grimaced. This one had swallowed his own hand up to mid-forearm, dislocating his own jaw and tearing the skin at the corners of his mouth. His throat had burst and the artery sprayed the wall.

Something rustled in the corner.

Will's left hand flew up in a stop, stay back flat for the other cops. His right filled with dragon. He stepped over the giant toward the sound, over by the window. There was someone behind the window curtain. He thumbed back the hammer with glacial speed and held his breath. There were fourteen dead men in this room. Whatever hadn't died was behind this curtain. Four other hammers cocked behind him and a shotgun racked a shell. Oh, shit. Those idiots might shoot him, but he was already reaching out for the edge of the curtain. Will yanked it back and his breath caught.

A Latino boy, maybe a year or two older than Childe Howard, hugged his knees on the floor. He rocked a little back and forth, his eyes boring holes through the fabric of this universe and seeing...something else. A roseary was intertwined in his little fingers. He had dirt under his nails. For a moment, Will thought he had some kind of weird punk thing going on with his hair—the roots were dyed platinum blonde. But then he got it and a little involuntary "Oh," escaped him. The kid's hair was in the process of turning ghost white. Will made *Smaug* safe and called over his shoulder. "It's a kid." He crouched down. "Hey, amigo." The boy stared into and past Will Two-Bears McFarlan and rocked, rocked, rocked. "Que pasa? Que pasa?"

Will almost thought better of it, then reached out and put a hand on his shoulder. The boy was freezing with shock, all his blood pulled to his core. The boy's eyes stayed away, but his lips parted and breath shaped a word. Will leaned in to hear it. "What'd you say, pardner? Que?"

"Avispa."

* * *

THE SUN HAD slipped below the shoulder of the mountain by the time Will was able to slip away home. He hated riding after dark. The criters came out and the Indian's headlight wasn't worth much. He'd already scared a small heard of deer back up the side of a draw as he rumbled around a corner. Orange eyes in the halflight, frozen on him and then scattered apart like sparks from a campfire. You'd think the damn things would know enough to run from a sound like a motorcycle, but they had gotten used to people. He supposed it was kind of pretty when he thought about it, but he was feeling a little too scoured to do pretty just then.

There had been fifteen of them in all, including the kid he found. That one breathy word was all they got out of him. He'd fallen into some kind of catatonic stupor by the time the ambulance got there. Tommy Ward had called in the Staties after all. He wasn't about to screw around with protocol with a bodycount to consider. It took an hour for them to get there: two suits and two uniforms, all with crew cuts. Tommy and the suits went off to one side to talk—rather the suits took Tommy around the corner and reamed him a new one. He came back hat in hands, twisting the rim and red as a July strawberry. The suits did some poking around and picture taking and when the county M.E. arrived they did some ordering. Will and the rest of Tommy's goon squad spent the afternoon stacking corpses. It took two van trips and one in Steve MacMillain's pick-up to finish the job. All those white eyes.

The other men were baffled by what they'd seen. Was it some kind of contagion? Poison the M.E. had guessed, gas pocket of some kind maybe. He'd know more after the autopsies. But he wanted Tommy and his men including Will to keep an eye on themselves and call in they started feeling "symptomy". Will rounded a corner and spooked a crow out of the road. What the hell kind of a symptom was reaching into your throat so far you blow out your main pipe? And how exactly would he call that in? He fogged up his face plate with hot giggles.

Will flipped the shield up and fresh air whoosed in, cooling his head and pulling tears from him eyes. He'd kept his mouth shut when the staties took his statement; told them just what he'd seen in that room and not what he thought had caused it. Was the Poompiliad as close as Roanneville? No, he didn't get that feeling, didn't get the sense that it had been in the room, not directly. He didn't know how he knew this. It didn't feel like when the spider filled his head with images, visions of the Wasp's progress across the plains toward Chicago. But Will did have a taste for the thing now, and its impression had been in that room, its influence. It wasn't here but it was preparing the way.

Will kicked the bike down to second gear and pulled over. He put the kickstand down and pulled off his helmet. He scrambled down the bank and stood at the creek's edge. The shakes hit him hard, racking up through his ribcage and grabbing his shoulders. Will tried to take in slow, easy breaths, but his throat tightened.

180

He doubled over and retched. It took him down to his knees. For a while he kneeled at creekside, listening to the water as it sluiced away his sick.

Chapter 25

LORAINE WANTED SEX. She'd pushed back from her computer an hour ago with the realization that she could either stay put for another second and lose her mind, or go for a walk and get her shit together. This is what happened to her whenever she worked too long. It wasn't her fault—sometimes she'd just lose track of how long she'd been crunching away at the keyboard. Childe was such a good boy about feeding himself and taking care of the dog, days could go by before she took a break beyond the odd can of tuna and then collapsing into bed in the wee hours. She could always count on her body to remind her before she fainted away from hunger or sleep deprivation. Now that she was in her mid-forties, she could add sudden attacks of sexual hunger to the selection of body clock alarm sounds.

She'd told the Kiddo she was going for a walk and asked if he'd like her to take the dog. Childe replied from deep within the spine of a Harry Potter novel that Darwin was already outside somewhere. She shrugged and pulled the back door closed. The moratorium on solo missions for the Amazing Ninja Dog had ended without much fanfare. She knew it would. You couldn't keep a decent mutt away from the emerald halls of the forest and the battalions of squirrels within, nor screenwriters with a bad case of the hottsies. Barring a hot bath with a battery powered friend, a long walk was always a good choice. That and her dirty secret.

Loraine aimed for the trailhead that emptied out in their backyard and plunged into the cool dark. It was early evening and just chilly enough that she could have brought a jacket, but the air braced her skin and helped clean away some of the cobwebs. She tromped over roots and the odd fern, the house receding over her shoulder and the trail in front of her only half seen.

She hadn't had sex with anyone since they left Hollywood. That had been Steve Winslow, the effects guy from her last movie. Not a real catch in the looks department, but as long as she was being honest with herself, neither was she so much anymore. (They had giggled the whole time, though, and that was more important in her book. A great bedroom giggler was Loraine.) She had never been a beauty per se, but back in her day she'd been cuter than hell. No one did flirtatious winking better than Loraine Duchamps Howard. And with the right outfit and makeup engineering, she managed to get her fair share of attention.

More than anything she got men by making them laugh. Funny women are strange creatures, exotic. It's the men who are supposed to do all the joking around. Women who could joke with the boys were crass and manish. (That was her mother talking, of course, but mothers' voices stay forever, even when we learn to ignore them—like that involuntary reaching for a cigarette twenty years after you've quit. You catch yourself doing it, feel a little pain and move on.) She'd caught Childe's father with her sense of humor. On their first date, Terry Howard had laughed so hard he'd sprayed martini all over his steak.

Steak and a martini: that was pure Terry. He had this old-fashioned advertising man from the sixties thing going, with slicked back hair, sharp suits and a pack-a-day habbit. Never mind that he was a studio CPA, forever scurrying around after the director and reminding him how far over budget they were. He always had a martini at five and another at seven and, oh what the hell and why not, another at seven-thirty. Terry had surprised Loraine into marrying him, kind of snuck up on her really. One day they were just dating and screwing and generally having a good time of it. (Lots of bedroom giggling and sneaking off the set for nooners.) The next, there he was on his knee, the sun shining off his lazer perfect hair and the rock he was holding out to her. She'd accepted almost out of a sense of novelty.

Childe made the scene nine months after their wedding night on the nose. Terry had wanted to make a Terrance Jr. out of him, but Loraine had vetoed the living hell out of that one. She sat him down with a freshly squeezed martini and read him *Childe Roland to the Dark Tower Came* by Robert Browning and threw in a blowjob for good measure. Now, as she thought back on it a wry smile twisted her lips. Terry had been a decent enough man, but he was such a doofus. He used to squeak with he came. This high-pitched whining noise would issue from his sinus cavity. It reminded her one hell of a lot of the noise Darwin always made when he was in the midst of a decent doggie yawn.

It was that doofusness that had finally crept into their Hollywood bungalow after eight years and placed a pillow over the marriage's face. One day Loraine just woke up and realized that out of that funny sense of novelty she had allowed herself to be packaged into a life that didn't feel right. She still did her work and made her living, she had her son and he was the light of the world, but at the end of the day she felt like she was Mrs. Terrance Howard, not Loraine. She'd allowed Terry to put her in a nice pink dress, pearls and heels, and stick her in a corner with a smile and a pitcher of martinis because it was funny at first. But eight years of the same joke will kill any punchline no matter how good.

Quick fade and here she was in the middle of nowhere Kentucky, raising her son and emailing screenplays to her agent, Charlene McGiveron back in Hollywood. The move had been a fantastic decision. Her work had improved not only in substance but volume as well; with almost nothing to distract her, Loraine was turning out a new script every other month. Charlene was selling them as fast as she could churn them out, and the money was better than it ever had been. Childe's college was already in the bag and if she sold another couple of screenplays by December, she'd take them on a month long tour of Europe or maybe Australia. Kiddo loved those that great big flying fox bats and they were supposed to be like pigeons over there.

All in all she was happy as she'd ever been, but the novelty of this situation, as great as it was, was beginning to wear thin and soon so would she. Loraine new herself well enough to expect that thinness of the soul that comes when tedium sneaks around the corners of life. Much like the yellow wolf of fog sneaked around the corners of London houses in *The Love Song of Jay Alfred Prufrock*. Had that also been Browning? "Nope," she said aloud. "That there's an Elliot if I ever heard one." The signs of that wolf's predation were already showing. She'd put on a few pounds in the last month or so and her concentration was slipping at the keyboard. That special window past the LCD flat-screen and into the scene itself had been fogging up a bit lately. Even Childe, her precious boy, was beginning to get on her nerves more often. Some of that had to be her insistence on him staying closer to home after their experience in the woods.

The memory of Darwin suspended in that gigantic spider web tumbled Loraine out of her mind and back onto the trail. Since that day, she had come a long way around to the explanation the good Constable gave them about the mind's tricks and the local orb weavers, but goosebumps broke out on her arms nonetheless. And speaking of the sneaking of carnivorous canids, these woods were full of freakin' coyotes. Was she being a doofus herself, taking a walk on her ownsome, or was this a formula for a bad retelling of *Lil' Red Riding Hood*? Perhaps a B-movie plot wherein our heroine—a frightfully sexy MILF in her early forties—finds herself attacked by a giant cross-dressing coyote/spider on a path in the deep, dark forest only to be rescued by a handsome lumberjack. Coyote-spider? No thanks. Lumberjack, yes please—preferably one bearing a resemblance to Hugh Jackman... Or, just Hugh Jackman would do. He didn't *have* to be a lumberjack.

Loraine sighed deep and long. This was her brain telling her it was almost time to leave Shard. She'd never really had the notion that they were going to say all that long in the first place—just a few months, a year at most. Their time in Shard was to be something of a transitional sabbatical between their lives in Hollywood with Terry and their lives...where? Now, that was rub: how should she choose where to end up?

Finding Shard had been easy. Loraine smiled as she passed through a bar of slanting sun, the light illuminating a halo of her curly blonde hair. Shard had sort of found them when she thought about it. She been putzing around with the idea of a project on Harriett Tubman, and was digging around on-line looking for a town in West Virginia called Sharp Creek that had been a stop on the underground railroad. She mistyped Shard instead of Sharp and was about to start her search over when a headline from an old news article caught her attention: "Seventy-Five Dead in Mine Explosion." She read on and learned the story of the ghost town with the fire under its streets.

Loraine spent the next hour digging for more information on this funny little boom town gone bust in coal country. The computer screen glassed over and soon enough she was looking through into a strange, empty place with abandoned Victorians that bled smoke from smashed out windows. To her surprise she uncovered that there were actually people still living in Shard and that a person could get a ridiculous deal on a nice house in the woods as long as said house was on the right side of the fireline. By then she was ensnared. Shared was caught between poles, life and death, creation and destruction, suspended. It was that feeling of suspension that resonated so powerfully with her and moved her hand to pick up the phone and call her realtor.

Now that sense of floating between lives was leaving her and a feeling of being drawn onward was beginning to rise in her middle. But where oh where to go with herself and her lil' boyo? Loraine stopped on the trail and put her hands on her hips. Didn't matter. The universe would send her in one direction or another, just as it had when it sent her here.

She took a good look around and got a faceful of late summer forest. Dark tree trunks swayed in the evening breeze, deep green leaves (reds and golds soon enough) shifted and splashed heavy sun dapples at her feet. God *damn* but it was pretty here. Where ever she and Kiddo ended up, trees would have to be part of the bargain.

The breeze brought a tang of sulphur. A change came over Loraine's round face, a furtive sort of hardening. Her eyes sloted left, right. She dug into her pocket and pulled out her dirty little secret: a pack of Marlboro lights. She lit up and took a drag on her cigarette like a man crawling out of the Mohavi would take a pull on a canteen. The smoke stung her throat a bit at first—she only smoked about a pack and a half per year—but then the nicotine hit and her shoulders relaxed. Every pore in her skin seemed to open up a bit. She smiled and shook her head. Retarded habbit, but mizz Looraine Howard did love her smokey-treats. And to hell with anyone who said it didn't make you look a million times cooler. Not that she'd ever let anyone see her doing this, especially not Childe. He'd caught her a couple of times in the past, but instead of nagging or clipping articles about lung cancer he just shook his head and walked away from her. Oh, and hadn't that stung like a sonofabitch, those little shoulderblades moving away from her, the sweet neck stretched a bit because of the dear head that hung low.

She took another drag and looked around. That was one of the wonders of smoking, it gave you *almost* nothing to do—sort of forced you to stop and smell the roses, even while you were poisoning their air. At least she didn't feel so horny now. A few minutes ago she was ready to hump the nearest most likely looking tree trunk. Now, she was merely considering how embarrassing it might be to get caught jerking off (jilling off if you went to a wymyn's college) in the woods. She was in Appalachia—it's not like it would be the first time someone got off in them thar woods. There was an entire sub-genre of bad jokes about the very subject.

Loraine laughed out loud and scared a bird from its perch in the corner of her eye. She turned to look and caught her breath. The leaves of a small scrub maple had turned arterial red. She blinked and realized they weren't leaves, but hundreds, maybe thousands of cardinals perched in the branches. "Holy crow," she whispered around her cigarette and giggled at the unintentional pun. A shift rippled through the crimson mass as if her laugh were a stone dropped in a pool of blood. A rain of black beaded eyes watched her. Loraine had of course seen a flock of sparrows dense in a tree before. Had the misfortune of parking her car under one as a matter of fact, but she had never seen cardinals like this.

She wished she had a camera. Childe would freak out if he could see this. If she had her cell phone on her she could have at least taken a crappy shot from its little camera, but you couldn't get signal anywhere in Shard so she'd become used to leaving the house without it. Wow, though. She just stood and stared and they just perched and stared, another flocked ripple moving over the surface of the blood sphere every now and again. She smoked and remembered that flock of sparrows that had rained shit down on her car during a fifteen minute stop into a drugstore. She'd come out to find her Acura with a new paint job and those little sparrows just cheep, cheep, cheepin' away… That's when it hit her: the cardinals were silent. They hadn't made a single peep.

Loraine glanced around again. The evening sun was rolling down the other side of the ridge. The sky was still bright, but the forest floor was dipped in purple shadow. It had crawled halfway up the tree trunks, contrasting the brilliant red of the birds that much more. The brilliant, silent birds that were just watching her and that she hadn't noticed on her way here; the brilliant, silent birds that didn't startle when she tromped her way into this part of the woods. Loraine grimaced at the smoke from the end of her cigarette. She put it out on the bottom of her shoe and then stuck the butt in the cuff of her slacks. (Her dad had told her they'd done that in the Air Corps and she'd picked it up. Trashing one's lungs was one thing, trashing the rest of the planet was something else.) When she looked up the birds had moved to another tree. A closer tree.

Loraine jumped. "Jesus," she whispered. What the fuck was going on here? She was struck by the idea that it might be fun to watch them explode out of their roost in fear of a primate waving her arms and shouting. Loraine did just that. "Hey!" The flock rippled, but stayed put in a tree about twenty feet away. "You lil' bastards ever work with a guy named Hitchcock?" She took a step closer, feeling better to be on the offensive, better to just be moving instead of standing slack jawed. She raised her voice, not digging the shrill edge she heard, but forgiving it. She was scared and wigged out after all. "He's something of a portley fellow! Very DISTINCT shadow!" The birds stared at her, a thousand tiny black eyes like a mist of oil droplets. Loraine stopped. "What the hell?" This was getting beyond a little creepy and into extra creepy.

The birds fluttered in perfect unison and shifted from their roost to another tree without a single peep. In spite of her fear, Loraine gasped, "Wow." They moved more like a crimson fog than a flock of birds, floating into the branches and settling right away. Those oil-drop eyes reflected a thousand tiny Loraines. She lost the urge to frighten them. In fact, she lost the urge to do much more than get out of there. Loraine backed up a step, then another. A stick snapped under her heel and enough adrenaline dumped into her system to make her fingertips hurt. She stumbled and the stumble became a pivot and she had her back to them and she was running, running, her feet skimming over the ground, her breath coming in locomotive chuffs.

She ran this way for as long as her lungs would hold out. Embers flared in the pits of her chest behind her lower ribs. A spear point dug into her side. She didn't know how long she'd run, probably not far but she recognized this part of the woods. She'd come this way before. Yes! That was the trail that led back to her yard. She was only a quarter mile from home. Little black spots squirmed in her vision and her heart began to take on a stoney quality she didn't care for. Loraine made herself slow to a shambling fast-walk, her hand pressed to the stitch in her side. A minute later, she saw the fallen log with the lichen where she sometimes stopped to tie her shoelaces before beginning any walk in earnest. She was almost home.

Loraine slumped down onto the log, put her head between her legs and just breathed for a few minutes. She didn't want to go back into the house in a state of panic and scare Childe. She wasn't even sure what she was so afraid of in the first place. A flock of quiet birds? How do you explain that one? Yeah, I got really freaked out by a bunch of cardinals that didn't make a lot of noise—scared they were going to poop on me, you see. She shook her head and drop of sweat tumbled off her nose and shattered at her feet. Had she had some kind of a panic attack? God, she was spending *way* too much time in her office.

"Mom?"

Loraine let out a little yelp and turned to see, "Kiddo. Whatcha' doin'?" He was walking up the path toward her.

"It's getting dark."

"Yeah."

"I guess I got a little worried."

"You did, huh?" Just being around him was calming. Her heart had slowed and the evening chill had doused the heat of fear from her skin. She smiled and he smiled back, but it was sheepish. "You got a little freaked out from readin' Harry Potter again, didn't you?" She pronounced "Harry Potter" with a heavy Brittish accent, dropping the "H" and emphasizing the "Ts".

The Kiddo looked at his feet. "Yeah, a little. It's those Dementor things, they're scarey."

Having read all the Harry Potter books, Loraine remember the Dementors well—terrifying mixtures of the Grim Reaper, zombies and cops. She always thought part of Rowling's genius had been her ability to take pieces of the everyday and mix them with the magical. The Dementors were just to the left of everyone's age-old vision of death. They didn't have the scythe, but they had the same tailor. They also had the same interest: your soul. Sometimes Loraine wondered how parents could let their younger childen read those books. Rowling got pretty damn dark between mugs of butterbeer and teenage witch crushes.

"Yeah," she agreed. "They are pretty scarey." She patted her thighs once and stood. "You wanna' go in, make a frozen pizza and watch Indiana Jones?"

A sly smile spread on Kiddo's cheeks. "Can Darwin have a piece?"

"Only if you scrape off the sausage. I *really* don't feel like wearing a gas mask." Her boy—the light of the world—laughed and the last bits of stone cladding fell off her heart. "C'mon then," she said, throwing an arm over his shoulder and turning them back toward the house. "Let's devour el food de junk and raid us some lost arcs."

"Ooh, not that one. I like *The Last Crusade* better. It's got Sean Connery."

She threw on another bad Brittish accent. "All right, Moneypenny. We'll watch that one, but I've got to get M's approval first."

"What?"

"Oh," she squeezed his shoulder, "you're cinematic education is woefully incomplete."

The walked back up the path and disappeared into their cozy rancher as the sun disappeared around the other side of the world. A large holly bush standing just off the path shimmered in the gloom. Eight long branches burst from its middle, kinked and curved down to the ground. The branches slimmed and sharpened at the ends. They pushed against the earth and uprooted the body of the bush. Each waxy green leaf turned black as coal and flattened, merged. The great spider, Yïn, stood and considered the boy and his mother. This place in the world had worn almost through. A bubble that was a mix of the world above and the world below was expanding out from the portal in Dampf's lair, creating a zone where reality had begun to splinter. The woman had almost crossed out of it on her walk, so Yïn had become the birds and stopped her. Another quarter mile and she would have walked back into the solidity of the world above untainted. Yïn didn't know what might have happened if Loraine Howard hadn't then turned. Would she have seen a difference in the air behind her, sensed something off? She might have, and then she might have braved the weirdness to come back for her son. That could not be allowed. The boy was necessary as was she. Everyone left in Shard had a part to play, even if it was just to die.

A raccoon strolled by in the dark, oblivious to the motionless spider. Yïn speared it with her front leg and pulled it in. She injected her venom and began to take the animal apart, contemplating its flesh with her manibles. Yïn didn't need to eat, she just liked to. Warm yellow windows reflected in her eight black eyes. Inside the house, she could smell the oven warming up. The dog barked once, muffled and playful. Yïn liked Darwin. Perhaps she'd keep him as a pet when this was all over. She chewed through the racoon's ribcage with a sound like a wet wicker basket being crushed. Maybe she'd just eat him.

Chapter 26

T.R.'S MOTHER SMILED, which was really kind of amazing considering the hole in old Jean's head. The other leg in Shard's famous pair of Jeans couldn't smile or frown. His face was pretty much gone.

T.R. had spent most of the day waiting for them to come home crouched in the upstairs hallway under the wall of family portraits. Every time he looked, they showed a trauma from his childhood. The time he'd walked in on his parents having sex and his father chased him from the room with a giant erection. The day he pooped his pants just before leaving the house for his first day of school and how his mother made him go anyway with a full load in his trousers. Each of these lovely memories was captured for the ages with the magic of KodeCOLOR. And like the extra photographic touches you could get for a few bucks more at the Sears—an airbrushed zit here, a gause filter for grandma's wrinkles there—these images had their own special something. The lines next to his mother's screaming mouth were deepened, her brow sharpened. The pearl of pre-cum at the end of his father's turgid cock caught the light just so. It resonated nicely with the fat tears on little Tommy Ray's cheeks.

And they came with their own soundtrack, too: the buzzing.

The *fuck*ing buzzing in his head had been unendurable. At one point he drew a cold bath and dunked his head under, hoping to drown the wasps trapped in his skull. The acoustics had changed, gone all deep and round, but it was just as bad. For a moment, T.R. considered just leaving his head under the water until he ran out of breath. In the end, he reeled back against the wall tiles, panting, his tears of pain and frustration mixing with the bathwater. Not long after, he got his father's deer rifle from the closet.

As soon as his fingers wrapped around the steel and polished wood, the buzzing decreased as if some benign hand had reached into his mind and turned down the volume. It was still there, still so awful, but at least he could think a little. And what he thought about was a place to hide for the ambush. His mother always said simplicity was best, so T.R. just leaned up against the wall next to the front door.

After a time, the day darkened and the pickup truck pulled up, its lights spraying the front of the house. There were three door thunks—the one on the passenger side always needed a second slam after that fender bender a couple years back—and the sound of footsteps on the walk. The screendoor, never to slam in the morning again, squeeled back on its hinges and his parents slumped into the house.

His dad got the first bullet to the back of the head. It made a neat little hole right below the adjustable strap on his baseball cap and blew his brains out through a giant, ragged one that took away his face. Ugene Dalton's memories, hopes and dreams, not to mention his entire set of teeth, his nose and eyes arced across the living room and splashed down on the couch. It was where he always plopped down after work anyway. His mother got out a, "Huh?" as she turned and T.R. put a slug through the side of her head. It did about the same amount of damage to her skull as Gene's, but because the bullet entered through her temple and exited just behind her ear her face was left intact.

She didn't die right away, though. Through some ballistic miracle, enough of Jean's brain was left for her to keep drawing breath for almost a quarter of an hour. T.R. could have finished her off but he was frozen with revulsion. Not so much by what he'd done but by her singing. Jean lay on the floor in a puddle of her own pee and gray matter, singing at the top of her lungs. One word, over and over. *"La, la-la, la, la, la-lahh!"* She had this big goofy grin on her face and sounded just like a little girl skipping down the street on a sunny day. *"La, la-la, la, la, la-lahh!"* T.R. wanted to tell her to shut up. He wanted to rack another shell and make her shut up, but he couldn't. He backed up against the wall, eyes wide and watched her sing her little ol' heart out. After about fifteen minutes and just when T.R. started to get the shakes, her singing began to die away. As her voice faded her right foot began to shudder, flopping around on the hardwood floor like a gutshot rabbit. A minute later she was still, her eyes wide and staring, the smile stuck fast to her face.

T.R. dropped the rifle and it clattered to the floor with a huge noise. He wanted to jump, but he was still frozen. *That singing.* His mother's singing like he imagined she must have done when she was younger than half his age. It rang in the empty halls of the house. T.R. could feel it collecting in the corners, swirling in little eddies. It occurred to him that all those little fragments of voice could flow back together. One day he could be walking from his bedroom to the bathroom and all of a sudden, "*La, la-la, la, la, la-lahh!*" would ring out.

And what about Daddy? T.R. managed to stick out the toe of his boot and touch his father's left foot. Gene had fallen forward, so T.R. could easily see the waffle pattern on the bottom of his workboot. A coin of dirty pink bubble gum was stuck in the sole. It was somehow obscene, like a pair of soiled pink panties around the ankle of a serial killer's victim. T.R. couldn't stand the site of it. He rushed forward, grabbed his father by the belt and hauled him over on his back. Gene's bulk was liquid and heavy, like turning over a sack full of soaking wet blankets, but T.R. was running on adrenaline and flopped him over with a grunt. What little color T.R. had in his cheeks drained when he saw his father's face, or lack thereof. He sank to his knees with a hard *clunk!* but didn't feel it. There was a ragged crater where Daddy's face used to be. T.R. could see some of his tongue gleaming like an exotic sea creature and a piece of one molar hanging on for dear life.

"*Ahhhh,*" his father sighed.

T.R. gave a screamy little shout and crabbed backward until he rammed into the wall. He peered at his father, waiting for Gene to sit up and turn that raw mess toward him. He couldn't talk, so T.R. imagined he would just point one of his calloused fingers at his murderer. When it didn't happen, T.R. became curious. Were his parents really dead? He wasn't so sure. Momma had done all that singing and she was still smiling and Daddy had just done what he done, so maybe...?

"Maybe they're, like, lobotomized."

A swath of relief pasted T.R.'s face. It hadn't worked. He hadn't really killed them. But shit, that had been his homework. The movie screen had told him he had to kill them. Except the buzzing was gone, so he must have done something right. Maybe it was enough to just get them out of the way. That was it, must be. So, not an A+ but perhaps a B or B-. He grabbed at his crotch. Sure enough, his days-old hard-on was still going strong, but he guessed he could handle that for now. But what to do with them? The Outrider said to take them to the teacher's house. That was that dried up old bitch Charlotte Najarian. Why couldn't T.R. have scragged *her* ass first? A thought occurred to him: maybe she was supposed to take care of them now that they were lobotomized.

He glanced over at his mother and away again just as quickly, but not fast enough that he didn't register the spreading stain at the crotch of her cacki work pants. He could smell the shit in the air now, like being inside one of those blue port-o-sans; "shit booths" Daddy called them. People shat themselves when they were dead. Who the fuck was he kidding? He hadn't lobotomized them. He'd blown their fucking brains out. Everything that made up Ugene Dalton was cooling in a curdled pile on the sofa. Maybe T.R. should get it a beer from the fridge; turn on the game. T.R. barked out a single, screamy laugh. No, no, they were alive. You didn't sing at the top of your lungs when you were otherwise, unless of course the whole coir of angels deal worked way different than he always imagined.

"Doesn't matter," he said out loud. "They gotta' go to the teacher's house one way or the other." First thing was first, though. T.R. got up and walked into the kitchen. He rummaged in one of the counter drawers and came out with a flat-head screwdriver. That fucking screendoor was coming off the hinges before anything else.

HE WAITED A good three hours before moving them. Shard was sleepy all day every day, but it was completely passed out by 9 P.M. on a work night. T.R. didn't want to risk running into Constable Will and having to explain the condition of his passengers.

T.R. had set the Jeans up next to him in the cab of the pick-up. Daddy was seatbelted in with the shoulder strap, so he pretty much stayed put. The middle seat had been a bit of a problem because it only came with a lap belt; no shoulder harness. T.R. couldn't stand the thought of Momma knocking out the teeth in that frozen smile of hers the first time he had to hit the brakes. It wasn't a problem if Daddy joggled around a bit in his seat as they tooled along, the empty socket of his face dripping into his lap, but T.R. wasn't about to pry Momma's teeth out of the console if he didn't have to. Besides, last month Dadddy had finally broken down and bought that satelite radio. He tried to make a shoulder harness out of duct tape, but it kept pulling free without anything to wrap it around. (Riggor mortis was setting in and she wanted to curl up like a bug.) There was a ringbolt sticking out of the back wall of the cab in the bed of the truck. T.R. made a rope of duct tape stretching from the ringbolt through the little slidding window at the back of the cab and wrapped tape around Momma's head.

T.R. switched on the pick-up's headlights and walked down the driveway a little. He lit a Marlboro and tried to squint through the windshield. He smiled around his cigarette. It was perfect. Just Shard's famous Pair of Jeans out for a ride with the fruit of their loins—The Dalton Family on a Sunday drive, at night, on a Tuesday, with holes in two-thirds of their heads. A laugh burped from T.R.'s lips and he got moving.

The drive was uneventful. T.R. kept his eyes on the road, afraid that if he looked over, his parents would be staring back him—Momma with that too-big grin and Daddy with that big wet nothing. T.R.'s window was down as well, the smell of coal smoke and sulphur welcome over the smell of shit and cordite. He ran over a split in the pavement when he turned onto Mrs. Najarian's street and something splashed into Daddy's lap. T.R. guessed it was probably what was left of his tongue, but wasn't interested in deep investigagtion.

He pulled into Najarian's driveway behind another pick-up and shut off his engine. It was one of those old International Harvesters. He'd seen it around, everyone had. It belonged to Cyrus MacCoy. T.R. could actually smell whiskey radiating from bed. What the hell was that old booze runner doing here? Mrs. Najarian hated most people, especially a low class sort like Cyruss. He was the same as any nigger drug dealer in her opinion. T.R. knew this because she had elucidated her feelings on the matter with the class one sunny October afternoon during sociology hour.

For a moment he sat listening to the engine tick. The night was quiet and good. The stars weren't out but it was warm so that was okay. It was the end of August and already getting pretty cold at night this high up in the mountains. Might not be the Andes or anything, but you could freeze your nuts off in Shard once summer decided to ditch. There wouldn't be many more even as warm as this one.

T.R. reached for the key and almost turned it. He could leave. He could drive to the town limits, maybe dump his folks at the old mine offices on the way, and just…vanish. He could find somewhere new to start. Join the Army or maybe that new Cyber Opps unit the Air Force was running out of Florida. Seemed like their recruitment ads were always popping up on the hacker sites he visited. He could leave this burning trash pile behind him, heaped with the bodies of his parents and his past and never be Tommy Ray Dalton again.

He closed his eyes and laid his head on the steering wheel. The Outrider would find him. Maybe not right away, but one day T.R. would hear the rumble of a chopped-out motorcycle or worse—he'd look down some lonely road at dusk and see him coming with no sound at all, just floating that big bike down the center line. Besides, the buzzing in his head was still there. It was less since he—he glanced over at Momma, she grinned back—*lobotomized* the Jeans, but those hornets were still honeycombing his brains. Only the Outrider could get them out. He sighed and bonked his head once against the wheel.

It took him another twenty minutes to get the Jeans inside and situated at the kitchen table. The front door had been open and the house stood empty. In fact, T.R. had never been in a place that felt so devoid of breath or human touch. He'd spent his fair share of time screwing around in the empty buildings of his home ghost town. In the other houses you could feel the presence of the people who used to live there, but this place felt *scoured.*

He turned on the little fluorescent strip over the kitchen sink and washed his hands. (Daddy had slipped a little as T.R. had been folding him into the chair and as he was stabilizing him, T.R. had put his hand in something.) He turned off the tap and turned around. The right word was ghastly. T.R. was a ghoul in a nightmare. His parents glistened in the low, colorless light, their bulks hauling at the air and space around them as if they were as heavy as dark stars. T.R. gripped the counter behind him. The bones in his legs were gel. His throat clicked. The stories had it all wrong. When you sold your soul, you didn't get to enjoy life and

197

end up in hell when your time was finally done. No, no, hell didn't wait. It came and found you.

The basement door swung open.

T.R. couldn't move. He smelled them before their white faces hung in his peripheral vision, reeking of trash and bloating rot. They filed out of the basement and shuffled across the kitchen floor; standing in a semi-circle framing his parents, it was like some demon's joke of a family portrait. The fluorescent light glowed on hands, throats, faces. There was Cyrus with the hole chewed in his cheek, the flesh around it raw and puckered. Bill Owens stood with his big workman's hands at his sides, swaying next to his daughter, Maggie. Her feet were bare and one strap of her gingham dress had slid off her milky shoulder. T.R. used to fantasize about what he would to do to young Maggie if he ever got her in a quiet corner, but now she was a mildewed manakin. One of her eyes was missing and the other clouded over like dirty silk. He guessed the almost headless thing next to her was her mother Lizzy. The innertubes of fat around her upper arms and the glitter nail polish fit well enough, but it looked like her last meal had exploded in the back of her mouth. Luther Becket's little boy, Ricky, stood next to a creature so blackened from the waste up that identification would be impossible. Well, maybe dental. The thing's lips had been crisped off giving it a permanent grimace; it was missing a couple of teeth. Smack in the middle of this little town meeting stood Charlotte Najarian, her white arms streaked with grime. She placed a gentle hand on each of the Jean's shoulders.

Time stretched out. There was no question in T.R.'s burning, buzzing mind as to what these creatures were. Cored out. Dead. Walkers. These were the outstretched fingers of the Outrider. As if to confirm his thought, all their mouths, except his parents, dropped open with an audible crackling. A voice issued from the gaping holes as if from a set of speakers—*his* voice.

"You have done well."

T.R.'s poor cock sprang to full, painful attention. The wasps in his head crashed from one side of his skull to the other. He howled and fell to his knees in supplication. A little whimper escaped his mouth as tears squeezed from his eyes. "Ow," he said and sniffed. "Ow."

"Now," the Outrider said through his puppet chorus, "whitness my miracle."

T.R. winced open his eyes. Najarian cracked open his mother's mouth and clamped her own down over it. Maggie Owens burrowed her face into Daddy's ruined maw. Silence descended. The chorus swayed like bamboo, touched by the breeze of another's will. T.R. thought he heard something rustle, something muffled and wet. The teacher and the girl straightened. Najarian's lips were moist, fresh from a long kiss. Maggie's face was masked in gore. In the color-thieving light, she looked like she'd been bobbing for apples in motor oil. The smile was still on Momma's face, but now her teeth were parted. Daddy looked, well, the same. He kicked one heavy boot out hard, knocking into a table leg. Momma began to jerk, her hands spasming open and closed, little explosions of fingers. And as if they were hauled up from the napes of their necks, Shard's famous Pair of Jeans stood.

T.R. wanted to scream, but the world was going dark around the edges. He could feel the sharp edge of the counter rucking up his back, scraping the knobs of his spine as he slid down to the floor. It was more abstract than painful. The thud of his tailbone onto the lenolium floor was a distant boom of thunder as his teeth clicked together. His vision tunneled to a point on his mother's left eye. As he lost consciousness, T.R.'s last site was that of his mother's eye clouding over: the lens of the Outrider's spyglass. His last thought was a quick prayer to anything that would listen. *Please don't let me wake up.*

IF ANYTHING HAD been listening, it ignored his plea. T.R.'s eyes fluttered open some time later and the kitchen came swimming back. For a blessed moment, he didn't know where he was or what had happened then the pain from his groin and his head yanked him all the way back and he let out a little cry. He scrambled up to his feet, wincing at the scrapes on his back. The kitchen was empty. It was like they'd never been there at all. Even the chairs at the kitchen table had been pushed back in. T.R.'s eyes widened. Maybe it hadn't happened. Maybe he'd had some kind of episode, some kind of sleepwalking deal and had ended up here. Except, he sniffed, dreams didn't smell like the inside of a refrigerator where some kid has gotten trapped and smothered.

And there was another piece of evidence   anchoring   his nightmare to reality: a message on the table.

It wasn't written out on paper or drawn in a smear of spilled salt, but it was easy enough to read. T.R. walked up to the edge of the table and put his fingers on it. A bottle of gin sat like a blue glass pillar in the middle. Momma drank it sometimes—used to drink it sometimes—in gin tonics when she was feeling fancy. Daddy usually got some on those nights. But this wasn't her brand. She liked the stuff in the clear glass bottle with the red lettering. This one was squared off and Windex blue. The message was clear enough, a reminder to pay a visit to George Rhodes. A long kitchen knife lay next to the bottle, the exclamation point at the end of the note. T.R. picked it up. The wasps in his head dulled to a low hum and his rigid dick deflated a little. He looked out the window; it wasn't quite dawn yet but he could feel the light crouching on the other side of the mountains. Tomorrow night, then. For now he needed rest.

T.R. grabbed the bottle of gin by the neck and used the point of the knife to flick off the fluorescent light. He walked down the hall toward the front door. A floorboard creaked behind him. T.R. turned around. Maggie Owens stood on the stairs about three risers up, her bare feet dainty in the gloom. The shoulder strap of her dress had slipped farther down and one small breast was almost completely exposed. T.R. could see a mole just above the crescent of a gray nipple. It reminded him of the new moon with Venus just off its shoulder. Her jaw creaked open and the Outrider's voice issued forth.

"He dies under your knife, but the woman lives for me."

T.R. clutched the gin bottle and knife in his sweaty hands. He was terrified he might drop them. He nodded and whispered, "Okay."

Like an after thought, Maggie's left hand drifted over and pulled up her dress. Her other hand dug into her panties and began to busy itself. T.R. grimaced, but his traitor cock thudded. The Outrider's voice came again from her gaping mouth, "This is yours when you are finished."

Chapter 27

WILL'S EYES FLEW open and he sat up in bed. The dream had been bad, real bad, but had stolen itself clean from his memory, leaving only a stew of sweak-soaked sheets. A minute passed in the dark, Will's breathing slowed. It was just after 4:30. He was certain something had happened, or would.

Amy muttered in her sleep and rolled over. Will looked over at her inviting sillouette and wondered what she was doing here. Last he remembered she had been talking about going back to her trailer. Wanted to get an early start on the day, something to do with mineral analysis. He guessed they both drifted off talking about it. His eyes followed the delicate tracery of ink along her shoulderblades. He sighed and rubbed his face.

Will swung his legs out of bed, pulled on a pair of jeans and padded into the kitchen. He wasn't getting back to sleep now. Didn't really want to come to think of it. Consciousness was a closed closet door and sleep was on the other side, but there were strange, muffled groans coming from in there. What the hell had he been dreaming about? He switched on the fluorescent light over the sink and squinted at the yellow-white light, his pupils going from night-cat huge to pinpoints. He didn't suppose the details of the dream mattered. His mind had plenty of tensions to roll over and mold into big scarey beasts. It's not like he didn't know what was coming: a fight with the devil.

His naked arms and shoulders broke out in goosebumps and the memory of that little boy they'd found with the dead migrant workers came to him—*Avespa*. "Yeah, avespa," he whispered, "Jesus." Maybe that's what had been back there in his mind's closet, ranks of dead Latinos, or maybe it was just an image of George Rhodes accidentally blowing his own foot off with the gigantic automatic rifle Will had given him. He wasn't about to go back on that decision, but it sure as hell wasn't a clean one.

Training the town drunk how to blow the wings off a fly with a machine gun was one of those lesser of two evils kind of things.

Will went through the atuo-dance of making coffee as his mind walked his troubles. He filled the caraf with water and looked out the window over the sink. The sky was only just thinking about throwing some light over the hills, and his motorcycle sat dormant in the driveway. No skin-walking giant spiders resembling his father sitting on it this morning. Well that was good at least. Will turned off the tap and sighed.

He could leave. There it was. He could throw a change of clothes into the saddle bags and get the fuck out of dodge. He could putter his little half-breed ass over to Lexington and get a job as a security guard or even go to the Police Academy. Better still, he could find a job in a library. Hell, why not get out of Kentucky altogether? Maybe move north, get away from the poverty and ignorance that seemed the south's Civil War legacy. He could go as far as Boston, maybe, find a woman who was interested in him as something more than a sex toy.

He turned and filled the back of the coffee maker, the sound of the water was loud and hollow in the still kitchen. He slipped the caraf back into place and thought of the rest of the people it his town. Will tried to remember the last time he saw someone other than George at the "shooting range". He scowled as the coffee maker growled out steam and French Roast, the noise a perfect sound track for the look on his face. Jesus, when *was* the last time he'd seen anyone? Sure there were only a handful of folks left, but he usually passed the time of day with at least one or two people everyday as he made his rounds. When was the last time he'd been to Tooley's Grocery? He could at least count on losing a good half an hour to old Meg Tooley everytime he went in there. She was opening up later and later these days—God, she had to be like what, eighty, eighty-five?—but at least she would have a handle on how many of them were left.

Will's mind played back over the scene at the little village of cabins and doublewides in the woods. The Owenes and the Beckets were gone. Cyrus had gone missing, but his truck was still parked outside of Missus Najarian's house. According to Erica's story, they were all dead and Will was inclined to believe her, missing bodies or not. Who did that leave? There was himself and George, of course. Erica and Amy, but they were newcomers.

202

There was that little weirdo, Tommy Ray Dalton and his parents, the Jeans. Loraine and Kiddo. And then the other kids: Maddy and Patty Wilkerson and their mother and father, Silvia, who everyone called Silver, Bob. There was chubby Howard Sams and his folks, Rich and Georgia. That brought it up to how many, seventeen? That only felt about half right.

Will poured himself a cup of coffee and took a long inhale of steam. He imagined the caffeine molecules riding the vapors into his brain and lodging themselves between his synapses. He had a thought: he'd run a census. See just how many people were left in Shard. Jesus, he was the damn town constable. He should know that already. What had George said the last time he was in his weekend retreat at the jail, that there were only around thirty people left? They'd been leaving in dribs and drabs ever since The Fire, but in the past six months or so the exodus seemed to have accelerated. Will whispered, "It's like they knew it was coming."

The phone rang.

Will's shoulders jumped in his skin and he almost dropped his coffee. He grabbed the phone off the wall before it could ring again and wake Amy. He checked the clock on the microwave: 4:51am. This would be bad. "Two-Bears McFarlan," he said.

"Will, it's Tom Ward."

Will forced calm, even took a sip of coffee. "Mornin', Tommy."

"Sorry to call you so early. Didn't get you out of bed, though, did I?"

"Naw, I was already up making some coffee. Bad dream. What's going on?"

Sherif Ward sighed long and heavy on the line. Will could imagine him sitting at his desk in a cone of light from the single desk lamp, running a hand through his sparse hair. "It's that thing with the migrant workers."

Will remembered the hotel room filled with bodies. Fourteen men and teenage boys, eyes whited-out. That one big fella who'd reached all the way down his own throat. The boy, *Avespa*. Will brought the coffee cup up to his lips and realized that if he didn't put it down, he was going to spill it all over himself. He set the mug down on the counter and steadied himself for it. "Okay, Tom. What's happened?"

"They're gone, Will."

203

"I'm sorry, come again?"

"Gone. Taken we think. I got a call from the Staties just a few minutes ago. Looks like someone stole 'em out of the morgue."

"What the hell for?"

"Now how in heck would I know? All's I know is apparently it was some kind of inside job, because there was no evidence of B an' E. They're questioning the staff now, but they got no leads."

Will's throat clicked. "What do *you* think?"

"I haven't had time to really think about much of anything. We had a real bad morning ourselves."

Will could hear the sadness in his voice, the age. "What is it, Tom?"

"Well, you know we were going to give over that little boy we found to social services, but they didn't have a single opening with any of their foster families. You know they send the kids to the work farm over in Monroe if they can't find a bed for them? Me and Marlene decided to foster the little guy until we could track down his people back down south."

A warm smile bent Will's mouth. That was Tommy Ward through and through. "That was mighty good of you, Tommy."

"Yeah, yeah." Will could imagine him waving his hand as if to brush off the compliment. "Poor little fella, his name's Miguel by the way, had a bad turn earlier last night. Real bad. Woke up from a nightmare shouting this one Spanish word over and over."

"Avespa."

Quite on the line a moment. "How'd you know?"

"He was saying it when we found him, remember?"

"Oh. Yeah. Any idea what it means?" Ward sounded like the other side of exhausted.

"No," Will lied. "My Spanish always sucked."

"Hmm. Anyway, Marlene took him to the kitchen to get him some warm milk or something and, uh, while she had her back turned…"

"Jesus, Tommy, what?"

"He grabbed a kitchen knife off the magnet strip by the counter and drew it across his own throat."

"Oh my God."

"Oh, Will, there was so much fucking blood. I—I slipped in it. Marlene was just screaming and screaming."

"Tom, I'm so sorry. Is Miguel..?"

"No, thank the sweet lord Jesus and all the apostles. Cept' Paul. He was just plain mean sometimes."

"You got him to the hospital in time, then?"

"Yeah, it wasn't as bad as it looked. They got the poor little guy all stitched up and then sedated him all to heck and back. He's on the psyche ward with a couple of junkies and a few senile old folks. Keepin' him under observation. Breaks my heart all over just thinking about it." He was quiet a second, then, "I just can't imagine what it would take to push a young boy like that to do something so..."

But Will knew. They both did. Tommy Ward had been in the same room he had. How long had Miguel been sitting in there with those fourteen dead men? He'd seen whatever had killed them. Had the poor kid stared into their empty faces until his mind cracked and his hair went white? "Tom what can I do? Do you need me up there? Just say the word." Even as it was out of his mouth, Will knew two things: One, Tom Ward wouldn't ask him to come up. Two, he wouldn't have gone anyway, couldn't have. There was a fight at home that needed tending.

"Naw, Two-Bears, you just stay put. You got your own town to take care of. I'm just letting you know because the Staties might want to talk with you a bit more. That and I guess I'd like you to keep your eyes open."

"For what, a dozen or so gardeners and construction workers that don't quite fit in or breathe?"

Ward chuckled. "Something like that."

"Tom, did the M.E. get a chance to autopsy any of them?"

"No."

They said the pleasantries and hung up. Will finished his coffee and put the mug in the sink with a dull clunk. Jesus, what the fuck would The Pompiliad want with a bunch of illegals? Will's mind filled with the spread of dragon wings. At least he was on the side with the really heavy artillery.

"You're up early."

Will yanked a smile from somewhere and turned around. Amy was standing in a pair of baggy boxer shorts and nothing else. They were hers. She had drawn little skulls and crossbones and a few biohazard symbols on them with a sharpie. Will knew this because she'd done it last night at the dinner table when conversation had gotten dull. Her tattoos looked like strange,

205

secret hyroglyphs in the low light. "You say it almost like an accusation."

"I am. It's unnatural to get up before the sun." She yawned. "Monkies are diurnal."

"Want some coffee, Cheetah?"

"God, yes, but weren't we talking about monkies? Cheetahs are cats. Don't mess with a girl before her morning drugs."

"Cheetah? Tarzan's chimpanzee?"

He handed her a full coffee mug and she leaned back against the counter. Will did his damndest not to stare at her boobs. It wasn't easy, what with the star bursts framing her nipples. That and it was a little chilly in the kitchen this morning. She took a pull of the coffee. "Ah, that's good," she said. After another sip, "You know chimps aren't monkies, they're apes."

"Right. I bet they get up early, though."

"Doesn't matter. It's still disgusting not to be sleeping at this hour."

"Thought all you scientist types liked to get up early. You know, get into the field and not waste a second of the day."

"I'm a geologist, babe. Rocks can fucking wait." She focused on him. "Who was on the phone?"

"What? Oh, county sherifff."

"Po-leece bidness at four-thirty in the morning? What about?"

"Remember that thing I told you about? Those mirgrant workers."

"Yeah."

"Someone stole their bodies out of morgue. They're just gone."

"Really?" All the sleep left her eyes. "That's freakin' awesome."

"Think so?"

"Well," she looked at her coffee, "not really. I mean it's terrible for their families and all that jazz, but that's so Stephen Kingy. Who do you think did it?"

Will almost blurted it right there, but held his tongue. Amy was leaving. There was a chance she could get out of Shard without having to play a part in any of what was coming. He wondered about Erica. Her work and whatever was going on between her and George might keep her here long enough to get caught up in it. "It's not something I can talk about, Amy."

She walked up pushed her hip up against his crotch. "Really, Constable?"

He tweaked a nipple and she jumped back with a yelp. "Yow, your fingers're cold!"

"Amy? How long have I got you?"

The smile fell off her face and her body language went from sleepy-sexy to all folded in on herself. Will wished he had a t-shirt to offer her. She turned around and put her mug down on the kitchen table. She put her palms on the wood and hung her head. "Will, this thing we're doing is fun, right?"

"Yes. Hell yes."

She pushed off from the table, the ink on her shoulders swelling and receding like waves. "Do we really have to have this conversation?"

Will walked up behind her, leaned over and wrapped his arms around her. He pulled her against him. Her skin was warm against his naked chest and belly. "Don't worry, tough guy," he said. "I'm not getting all *oogy* on you. I just want to know how long I get to enjoy this, this…whatever-the-hell-this-is."

She leaned her head back against his shoulder and sighed. "Seriously? You're really not getting all teenage girl on me, right?"

"I'm cool. We're both grown-ups. This is how grown-up monkeys play."

"Okay," she said, twisting around in his embrace and pressing against him. "You have me for another three or four days. My work's just about done. I'll file my report in the next day or two. My supervisor at Blackstone will read it, make recommendations to his bosses and then they'll send me somewhere else, or tell me to bring the lab back home." With each sentence she popped a button on the fly of Will's old Levis. Amy reached in and grabbed him. "Oh, you *are* an early riser."

He took her on the kitchen table. They made a hell of a racket and her coffee mug spilled and shattered on the floor. Both of them shouted their orgasms as the sun threw light across the eastern sky. All the while, Will thought *four more days. Just keep it away for four more days.*

Chapter 28

ERICA SIPPED HER coffee at the kitchen table and thought about the gigantic diamond she had held in her hands just a day ago. Was she really going to break the law, risk everything? She rubbed her thumb and index finger together. She could still feel it, heft its weight in her imagination. And according to Amy there were more of them, maybe thousands more. Yes, no question. She'd throw the dice for this. But there was an even bigger gamble in her life now. She watched him turn around with a steaming pan of eggs over easy.

"One or two," George asked.

"Two," she said.

He lifted an eyebrow and slid them onto her plate. "Big day today?"

"Not really. Just woke up really hungry is all."

George served himself and sat down across from her. In the week since he had quit drinking, George had gained almost ten pounds. His hair had regained some thickness and his face had filled out. When he moved around the kitchen, Erica could see the muscles in his back under his shirt. It might have been twenty some years since he'd played high school football, but his body wanted to go right back to its old quarterback shape. His hands no longer shook when poured coffee or served them at table, and he no longer smelled like something was wrong with him on the cellular level.

George caught her staring at him over the rim of her coffee mug and his cheeks burned. "What?"

His blush was contagious. "What? Oh, I was just wondering how you're, um, doing."

"Since I stopped? It's okay, you can say it. I'm not going to be doing any of that twelve step stuff, but I know I've got to be honest about it."

"Really? I thought that was the only way to stay clean—the twelve steps." About every three years or so Erica's father had made an attempt at sobriety. He would tumble right off the wagon within a couple of months usually, but the meetings and steps had been the only thing that worked even for a little while. Once, he'd held on for thirty-four days. He came home stinking of whiskey and barged into her bedroom, braying about his thirty-four day chip. He'd sprawled his reeking weight across her bed crying; his sobs turned to snores about a minute later. Erica had been about thirteen.

"They're just tricks," George said. "They work because most folks don't have any emotional self-awareness. Hell, most sober people only go through life with a semblance of consciousness and drunks are worse. So you need tricks to keep them on the straight and narrow."

"And you don't?"

"I don't mean to sound all arrogant and everything. I just don't think the magic would work because I know what's going on backstage. In the end, it's all about being honest and giving in."

"You going to do this all by yourself, then?"

George's face was hot and he wanted a drink. "That's the only way to really do anything, isn't it?" He took a breath. "Listen, it comes down to this: I'm a junkie for booze. I'm wired for it. I was wired for it on my first birthday and I'll be wired for it on my last. I have absolutely no power over that fact except to never forget it and just give in. It's when people talk themselves into forgetting that they fall off the wagon."

"That's sounds like a lot of twelve step stuff."

He grinned and Erica's heart slammed in her chest just once. "I know. See, I've got the truth behind the tricks. I don't need the other stuff. Besides, where the hell am I going to find a meeting around here?" He picked up his fork and pointed at her plate with it. "Now, you eat your eggs, or I will. I'm sure you've got a big day of running people out of town."

He winked at her and tucked into his eggs. Erica felt this absurd warmth at watching him eat. He looked super real, like his outlines were sharper than anything else in the room. She'd never been in love before. Was this that? She sipped her coffee and thought about a trick of her own that often worked in legal proceedings. Sitting across the settlement table from an opponent, she found she could read the emotional state of another person through his or her body. Nose scratches and knuckle cracking told volumes where verbal communication obfuscated. It was no great discovery; people had been reading each other's body language for ages, but instead of watching someone else for how he or she was feeling Erica had learned to watch herself. It was a good trick. She'd spent so much of her life controlling herself that she'd lost touch with her emotions. Sometimes the only way she knew to calm herself before a big day in court was to take a moment and invite her body to show her how she was feeling. If her fingertips were shakey, she needed a beta blocker. If her eyelids were heavy, she'd been billing too many hours and needed a stimulant.

She'd never done a physical check-in around her feelings for another person before, but figured it would work. She took a discrete deep breath, pretending to sigh as she looked over at the morning paper next to her then invited her emotions into her body. It started in her tummy—a deep thrumming warmth. The corners of her mouth twisted up and the corners of her eyes wrinkled. Her palms got a little damp. She stole a glance at George, reading The International Herald Tribune on-line on her barrowed laptop. They'd been having meals together like a married couple for the past week, but she never noticed how fine a jaw line he had, or how his shoulders spread. And George was brilliant, there was no mistake there. Like a lot of northerners she was used to thinking that a southern accent equaled ignorance, but when George talked about books, or psychology, or just about anything it was like tasting honey with her ears. She closed her eyes and opened them again. He was staring at her.

"You okay?"

"Huh?"

"You're breathing heavy." George's brow drew down. "Erica, you feeling alright?"

She laughed. She was feeling fine. Better than fine. She wanted to stretch and roll around naked in this feeling. The room was extra bright and her blood was hot. Jesus, she'd come to the asshole of America and fallen in love. When she spoke, it felt a little like it was coming from someone else. "I just had too much coffee. Got the jitters. I think I'll go take a shower."

"Oh, okay." George jumped up and grabbed her plate to take to the sink. Erica breathed in a swath of his scent as she rose from the table and her nipples stiffened so fast it was a little painful. She shook her head at herself. How long had she been feeling like this and just doing her usual Mendez Mega Bitch repression thing? She walked up the back stairs without a word.

George scraped the food off her plate and sat back down. He glanced once over his shoulder as the water thudded a little in the old pipes. He hoped she was okay. Erica seemed so wound up sometimes.

She called down to him, "George?"

"Yes, ma'am?"

"There's no hot water."

"Really?" That was weird. "Okay, I'll be right there!"

He hopped up and took the stairs two at a time. When he got to the bathroom she wasn't there. He guessed she'd retreated to her room, not wanting to be seen in just her robe. He stuck his hand under the water and found it hot. Maybe she just hadn't waited long enough. The floorboards creaked in the hallway. George said over his shoulder, "It's fine now. You can have your shower." He turned around and there she was. George's breath caught: caramel skin, the sweep of her belly and breasts, the triangle of her sex. Her toes. Her toes were pefect. Her eyes laughed and craved. "Wanna' join me?"

* * *

FOR A LONG time they held each other in a rocking slow dance under the steaming water. When she slid her hand down their bellies and wrapped her fingers around him, George had to grab the shower curtain rod and spread the other hand against the cool tile to steady himself. Swimming in delight, George was thrilled and relieved that his equipment still worked after all the poison he'd pumped into himself over the years. And there was gratitude for Erica, oceans of it. He found her mouth and they kissed, George's eyes closed and dreaming, Erica's open and searching his face. She found no guile or mal intent.

Was she doing something incredibly stupid? Not having a romp in the shower with the hunky inn-keeper, but allowing her heart to swing open like this? She was happy, thrilled even.

Before, it was like her skin had been electro-magnetized and covered in razor blades and rusty nails. Letting go for George was like cutting off the current and now all that tetnus armor was falling away. And her body was reacting to him to like she was a teenager. At home she kept a bottle of KY in her bedside table and another little bottle in her purse in case she ended up going to someone else's place. When she did have sex, it was because it was a good idea, a dose of something necessary like a vitamin. She'd stopped getting wet enough on her own years ago. But with George, *Jesus.* She was going to have to remember to rehydrate when they were done. He laid a finger along the length of her and she gasped. Erica moaned into his mouth and her knees buckled.

After another minute, she reached out and clutched his shoulders. "Bedroom," she said. "Right now." She whipped aside the shower curtain and grabbed his hand. They ran naked and steaming down the hall like a couple of kids truant from the bath, leaving wet foot prints on the hardwood. In the back of his mind, George could just make out his mother's outraged voice. Something about the water eating through the varnish maybe? Sounded like her, but he couldn't really make out the rest or worry about it now. He was chasing the most beautiful woman he had ever seen into the bedroom. She splashed down onto the duvan and rolled over with her arms stretched out to either side. George stopped at the foot of the bed and took a moment to drink her in.

"You know boys fantasize about this kind of thing from about age eleven, right?"

Erica slid her eyes along the length of him. "Same for us girls. Now, come *over* here."

"Yes'm."

They spent all morning in bed. Laughter and talk filled in the chinks between love making—sometimes languid sometimes fevered—as their minds and hearts began to lock hard into one another. George lay on his side staring at her face. "I can't even begin to imagine the evolutionary processes that'd be necessary to eventuate a bone structure like yours."

Erica smiled up at the ceiling, eye closed. "Mmm, you get that from a Halmark card?

George brushed a loose strand of her hair out of her face. "You know I can practically feel the oxytocin re-wiring my head around you."

"Oxy-what?"

"Don't worry, not oxycontin, oxy*tocin*—it's a neural transmitter like saretonin. It's the way the brain forms really powerful emotional bonds."

"Damn," she said. "Again with the romantic talk. You just don't give a girl much of a chance to chill out do you?" She turned and winked at him. "Really, though, I like it when you talk like a big nerd."

"Oh, yeah?"

"Yeah," She got up on one elbow. "For one, you seem to know a little bit about just about everything. And two, your accent in just plain hot."

"Wot?" he brayed in terrible Cockney, "this one? Blimey!"

She stopped his mouth with hers but pulled away before they got wrapped up in their bodies again. "George?"

"Erica?"

"Why'd you quit drinking?"

He scanned her face. "You worried I did it for you?"

"Yes."

George sat up and leaned against the headboard. He laid his hands in his lap. "I've thought a lot about why," he said. "I didn't do it for you. A person can't tie a thing like sobriety to another person. That can't work."

Erica let out a breath she didn't realize she'd been holding. "Why then?"

"I think I did it," George cherry picked his words, "because I felt something coming." Great, spreading wings filled the chambers of his memory. The rattle tap of spearpoint legs and the far away drone of insect swarms echoed in his mind.

Erica startled him with a hand on his arm. "You're shaking."

George snapped out of it. "What? Oh...I am." He was tempted for a second, just one second, to lie to her. There would be none of that with Erica. Even if this thing they'd fallen into together lasted only another day, he would never lie to her.

"You okay?" she asked.

George took a deep breath and looked over at her. The planes of her face sweapt into his mind and brushed away the terrors. "I am," he said, nodding. "No, I'm good." Her eyes were so dark. He could see himself and the room reflected in them. He wondered if Erica could see herself in his. She filled his mind, it only made sense that she would show in his eyes as well. He was still afraid to say *I love you* but that's what he was feeling when T.R. stepped into the room and racked a shell into his daddy's rifle.

Erica and George sat up bolt straight, eyes huge.

T.R. stood in a slanting bar of dusty sunlight, a pale spector. Deep circles ringed his eyes and his mouth hung open just a little. His clothes were streaked and filthy. He leveled the gun at George. Erica tried to move in front of him, but George grabbed her by the shoulders and kept her rooted. For a moment, she forgot to be terrified and was instead furious with George that he would restrain her when she was trying to protect him. Then the wraith with the gun spoke:

"She ain't yours. She's the Outrider's."

George's eyes narrowed, "What'd you say?"

T.R. pulled the trigger.

Erica didn't hear a sound. There was no moment of flinching or impact. There was just the release of George's fingers from her arms and the strong smell of cordite. He lay back on the white pillow, blood pouring from the side of his head. Erica became aware of the sound of her own heart beating, then her breath. Slowly, the volume turned up and she could hear screaming. When it filled the world T.R., stepped forward and hit her in the back of the head with the butt of the rifle. Erica plunged into nothing, grateful.

Chapter 29

THE SUN SPREAD over Will's shoulders like the arm of an old friend. They sauntered down Oak Street together, Will glancing at the shuttered brick houses hunkered in weedy yards. This was the part of Shard dedicated to the mine workers and their families. The houses were small and simple, nothing like the grand Victorians over on the north side of town. The smouldering coal seam zigged and zagged under Shard and had left this portion relatively untouched. But without the mine to support their inhabitants, the rows of solid brick boxes emptied as sure as they would have had the fire rose up in the night and gutted them. In fact, only three blocks over it had done just that. The brick shells still slumped against each other, their roofs long gone, the sun and moon lighting grassy living rooms. Most of the buildings on Oak were still in good shape, though.

The only way you'd know the street was deserted was the lack of cars at the curb and high grass in the yards. And the silence. There were no children playing or dogs barking, no flap of clothes on the line losing moisture to the high blue sky. There was only the sound of Will's Chucks on the pavement, his hand brushing his jeans as he walked, his breath. A sparrow trilled a few notes and it was as loud as an aria in an opera house. Will closed his eyes and stood still a moment. The tang of sulfer was strong here, but like a smoker he was used to the slight burn in his nostrils and throat. An afternoon breeze toyed with the hair that peaked out from under his Kentucky Wildcats cap. A cloud passed over and the red behind his eyelids dimmed; the warm arm of the sun slipped off his shoulders. The sparrow, or whatever it was, stopped singing and Will opened his eyes.

He rounded the corner onto Hill Avenue and the houses plumped again. Hill was where many of the town merchants had lived. You couldn't earn enough *as* a coal miner to buy a big house, but you could earn enough *from* the miners to do so. Will passed a three story number with white gingerbread trim that had belonged to the Dearborns. Shirley and Mainard Dearborn owned the *Watch N' Wash* laundrymat where you could watch your favorite soaps on coin-opp TVs while your underwear tumbled behind you. Will remembered watching *Kimba the White Lion*, his legs dangling over the edge of a hard-plastic chair while his mom talked with the other women who'd come to try and wash the soot from their men's clothes. Kimba always managed to stay pure white, but no matter how much bleach they used the women of Shard were never able to beat back the coal dust. Will's nose wrinkled with the memory.

"You look like your pa."

Will stopped and looked up a short flight of stone steps to the porch of an old Arts n' Crafts style house. Every inch of the deep front porch was crammed with bookshelves and they in turn were crammed with mostly nothing. A few cans of soup here, a bag of rice or box of brownie mix there broke up the monotony, but there was little else. Will knew there was refridgerator just inside the front door with a few extra pounds of ground beef and maybe some frozen shrimp for Friday nights, not that there were any Catholics left in Shard. This is was what passed for Tooley's General Store. When the fire shuttered main street most of the merchants picked up stakes, but Meg Tooley just picked up the stock and moved to higher, or in this case less smokey, ground. Will dug her out of the shadows between a couple of bookshelves, rocking in her old wicker chair. She squinted bright eyes back at him. "Now you look more like your ma—facing straight on like that. Got those Cherokee cheekbones. She was such a pretty thing, your ma."

Will smiled. When his hands (and mind) had been too little to hold novels, Meg had comic books for him: *Superman, Green Latern*, and *Batman*. As he got older, she began to horde used books for him. Before the fire, when the other kids were out running the streets, Will sat in the storeroom at Tooley's and ran the jungles with Mogli. Meg always gave him a big discount on the fragrant and sometimes waterstained old books for an hour or two of chores around the store.

He lifted a hand to her as he climbed the steps. "I suppose it makes sense," he called, "me baring a resemblance to my parents."

Meg waved him off. "A changling like you? You oughta' look more like the fairies who left you in the bassinet."

Will stepped into the shadow of the porch. He leaned down into the scent of old woman and chamomile tea...and whiskey. He gave her a peck on a papery cheek. "How's business, Meg?"

"Might be good," she said. "You buying something?"

"I'll take that brownie mix off your hands if the price is right."

"Hunert dollars," she deadpanned.

Will put his hands on his hips and sighed as he peered out into the yard. Meg's lawn was in good shape. "You'll have to stand me the money, I'm afraid." He looked back at her. Wizened, sharp-eyed old crow—could she have mowed the yard herself? Will smiled a little, imagining her trundling around the yard on a riding mower behind a big pair of sunglasses.

"Care to sit for a spell, William?"

"Thanks." Will took off his cap and folded into the rocker next to Meg's. For a while neither of them said anything, just stared out at the neat patch of green. Hill Avenue was a border street, the last of Shard's asfault clothing on the southeastern end. Across the road from Meg's front porch, the land tumbled off and down a good seventy-five feet before a new border. The same creek that flowed near Amy James's Winibago just off the mine office parking lot slid by at the bottom of the hill. It was well below their site line, but Meg and Will knew it was there. Each thought of it in turn. If they held their breaths and the wind stilled completely, chance was they might hear it.

Will elected to speak instead. "You never really answered my question."

"'Bout business?" She took a sip of high-octane "coffee". "It's been bad even for this place."

"Yeah?"

"Most usually I can count on a visit from at least three or four folks a week, but your pretty cheekbones are the first I've seen in days."

Will nodded. "Meg? Would you ever leave?"

"My house? Laws no. I own this place outright. You talking about that lawyer lady? She's been out here, oh yes, talking about relocation stipends and whatnot. I told her it was lovely having a fresh face on the porch to jaw with, especially one as pretty as hers, but that she was barking up the wrong maple if she thought she could get rid of Meg Tooley."

Will smiled and held up a hand. "No, I didn't mean Erica. I was just thinking: what if some of natural disaster was coming? Oh, wait, I know—what if The Fire moved over this way? What would you do?"

Meg cocked a whispey silver eyebrow. "I'd burn."

"C'mon, Meg, seriously now—what if you *had* to leave?"

She eyed him. Will felt a little like a shiney bottle cap being scanned over by a jackdaw. "Why you asking?" she said at length. She could see the worry on his face, the fear, though he tried to hide them both. He was frightened for himself, but there was more concern there for her. "You're a good boy, William." She chuckled. "Listen to me, like you're still sitting in the back of my shop all of eleven years old. You're a good *man*, Mr. Constable. Do you have something you need to tell me?"

"Maybe," Will sighed. "I'm not trying to be difficult. I promise, Meg. I'm just trying to get a sense of whether or not you'd budge...I guess...I guess if your life depended on it."

Meg had her answer on the tip of her tongue but held that raskle still. William wanted an answer, a real one, so she was going to give it a minute to percolate. She stared off past the front yard into the tree tops. They were low across the street, their trunks having to stretch that much higher for the drop off in the land. When she was a younger woman—a real honey if you wanted to know—she and Mr. Tooley had gone sledding down that hill after a fierce snow storm. She'd been afraid because the drop was steep and the creek cut through the pure white at the bottom. It was frozen over, sure, but that ice was hard and so were the rocks that jutted from it. Mr. Tooley was a clever young man, though, and pushed the snow into a ramp. She could still remember that look he gave her when he hopped on his sled. *It'll work, darlin'. You watch.* She'd never been so randy for him after he gave her look, so excited by just the idea of her man being brave and foolhardy. She'd stolen his chance and gone first. Meg whooped and jumped out over the drop, hugging her sled to her chest and belly for dear life. She slammed into the slope and shot down it like an iron ball through a greased cannon. Meg hit that snow ramp and launched through the cold air. Her blue knit cap flew off and landed on the ice, but she cleared it with room to spare and a executed beautiful landing. She stood in the sudden silence and looked at that blue hat sitting on the ice, then up at her husband, Clemson.

Meg found her way back to the present and looked at William Two-Bears. He was a good man and she was happy to have him looking out for her and the rest of Shard. There was something about him, some deeper responsibility. He didn't do his job because he felt like he had to; he did it because he was the right person. It was run around thinking, she knew, but it was true. William Two-Bears McFarlan was the constable. It was simple that way.

"I don't think that I could leave, William. I'm sorry."

Will sighed and closed his eyes. He sat back in the rocker and listened to it creek over the old porch wood. His mind wandered a bit. How many times had this chair rocked back and forth? A hundred thousand? A million? What if a little generator had been hooked up to it and the power stored in some kind of long-lasting capacitor—could the accumulated power have run the street lights? He heard Meg take a sip of her coffee, felt her eyes not on him, respectfully giving him his thoughts. The wind soughed through the tree tops across the street. Will opened his eyes and imagined long lines of wind turbines marching along the spines of the mountains, their great rotating blades looking like some kind of alien walkers. They did that in a few places up north in West Virgina. The end age of the coal age was coming. No more fires. No more Shards.

Will patted his thighs. "Meg, I gotta' get moving."

"So soon, William?"

"Afraid so," he said and stood. Will walked to the edge of the porch and paused just before crossing the barrier from shadow to sun. He snuged his cap down and turned to the storekeeper. She winked at him and for a second Will could see a young Meg Tooley sitting there, younger than he was now, in the full bloom of her twenties. The image was gone as quick as it had come, but Will's blush remained.

"William? Will you tell me what's troubling you? Mayhap I can take some of the weight off'n your mind."

He hesitated a moment, considered what good could come of it, what bad, and shook his head. "No, thanks, Meg." He turned to go and called over his shoulder, "I'll come back for that brownie mix."

Meg Tooley watched William Two-Bears walk down the porch steps. The sun painted his shoulders and brought out the red in that old cap of his. She truly felt sorry for him. Sun or not, the constable looked cold.

* * *

MEG DOZED AWAY the rest of the afternoon, slipping in and out of dream and memory. At her age sleep came when it wanted and she wasn't about to refuse it when she could get it. She skipped through her life and time like a little girl crossing a creek on wobbling stones. For a time, she ran her store, a ten-year-old William Two-Bears McFarlan devoring some classic comic in the store room. Then she skipped backward to a hot night with Clemson in the meadow a mile or so into the woods—"Our Place" they'd called it. Then forward to the present and she opened her eyes to long purple shadows and cornflower blue sky.

The first of them shambled over the rise across the street— Meg blinked and sat up in her rocker—a man in jeans and a white-tee shirt, moving like he was drunk or tired or both. But where had he come from? There was nothing on the other side of street beyond the drop-off and creek but miles of deep woods and old mining roads. Another nodded into view, his head bobing up over the little hill's horizon line. He was dressed similarly and moved as if only his legs worked, the top half of his body slack, his head lolling to one side. The first one had cleared the little weedy strip on the opposite side of the street and paused at the cracked asphalt of Hill Avenue. Another head bobbed into view, another and another and another. Before she knew it, there were at least ten men all done up in boots and denim and—she squinted—it looked like they were all Mexican or from somewhere south of the border.

They stood, gently swaying at the edge of the road. There was a strange emptiness to their eyes. Meg couldn't really make eye contact with any of them (not that her eyes were that good anymore anyway) but they seemed to be looking straight at her. That in itself was strange. She knew the afternoon sun was in their faces from that angle and that she was all but invisible back in the shadows on the deep porch. Who in heck were these people?

Meg Tooley ended her long and lustrous life by calling out, "You gents lost?"

A shudder rippled through the group and their boots shuffled across the stone river separating them from the town of Shard. They moved through the yard, long shadows thrown out behind them like capes. They bunched and climbed the porch stairs. Meg was still as they came, she watched and understood. Her hands iched for the twenty-two rifle leaning in the corner behind her rocker but she let it be. Meg had walked the earth long enough to know what was simple and true: you can't kill what's already dead. They filled the porch with their weight and emptiness. Meg closed her eyes and felt her Flexible Flyer against her chest and the sharp winter air on her cheeks. She jumped the frozen creek and met Clemson on the other side.

Chapter 30

GEORGE RHODES MOANED into his pillow. This had to be the worst hangover of his life. No, wait, that couldn't be right. He'd quit drinking. He'd quit drinking because he needed to get bright. He needed to get bright because something terrible was coming. Something terrible was coming and he would have to step up, stand up and fight next to Will. Fight for the town and for the people in it. His people. "Erica?" he slurred.

George's eyes flew open. Orange afternoon light flooded; memory was right behind it. He began to sit up but something held him to the pillow. His blood had congealed and glued him to the bed. His eyes widened. He had bled a lot. A dark patch spread away from his point of view onto the sheets and stopped about a foot away. George could feel his scalp trying to open as he pulled away from the pillow. "Fuck it," he said and yanked himself upright. The world teetered and grayed on a wave of pain and sick heat from the side of his head. George dug his hands like talons into the bedding as tears squeezed from his eyes. After a few moments the pain subsided down to a low burning. He tried his legs and they worked well enough for him to wobble into the bathroom.

A few minutes later, the world was clearer as was the deep gash running along the left side of his head. The bullet from the Dalton's kid's .22 rifle had creased his scalp and knocked him cold, but he was all right. George dabbed alcohol at the edges of the wound and hissed like a broken gas line. He put down the cotton swabs and alcohol and looked deep into his own eyes. Little bastard had said something before he'd shot George in the fucking head. George put on an eery approximation of T.R.'s backwoods drawl, "She ain't yours. She's the Outrider's." Outrider. Could the kid have meant the big bad ugly that was coming? George knew in his gut that it was true before he even asked himself the question. Well, Dampf had its agents in Shard. It only made sense that the Pompiliad would too. That white face hanging in his kitchen window the other morning—Maggie Owens, he had thought. Could she have also been part of this? Who was he kidding? They were all part of this coming battle, this last stand, all of Shard.

George gripped the edges of the sink. The ceramic cooled his hot palms. Every inch of him was screaming to get moving, to run outside and find Erica. He felt like a racehorse twitching in the stall before the gate went up. God only knew where that kid had taken her…what me might be *doing* to her. Nothing. He wouldn't do a damn thing to Erica except stash her. *She's the Outrider's.* And when he'd said that, T.R. had looked, what, abashed? No, outraged. The little punk had been outraged that George Rhodes had his hands on the Great Outrider's property. T.R. wasn't going to lay one unnecessary finger on Erica. But where would he take her?

Again, George focused on the man in the glass: a little worse for wear, but clear-eyed. This man was better, stronger than the man in the glass just a few days ago. You could almost see through that other guy. This George Rhodes was all the way here, but he still wasn't ready. "I don't know enough yet," he said.

* * *

HALF AN HOUR later, George hunched over Erica's laptop and drummed his fingers on the kitchen table while the screen filled at glacial speed. An odor of gun oil and fresh coffee mingled not unpleasantly. The M16 lay on the table next to a steaming cup of nuclear-strength java. He had the computer hooked to his landline and it was like trying to siphon an ocean of information through a coffee straw. You could do it (hell, everyone used to do it and was thrilled about it) but it took forever. Finally, the page loaded and George sat back. Filling the screen was a Wiki entry on the Tarantula Hawk. Order: Hymenoptra, family: Pompilidae, a sleek, blue-black wasp about the size of George's pinky finger. The wings were a rusty red, the color of dried arterial blood. There were several paragraphs on this charming creature. George began to read, his hand crept over his mouth and his eyes widened. "Holy shit," he muttered.

223

Twenty minutes later, the screen was populated with multiple windows: text and pictures of spiders, dragons and wasps, oh my. George had absorbed over fifty pages of text on everything from the emerald wasp and trapdoor spider to the number nine's signifigance in Chinese culture as it related to moon dragons. Now he had at least an idea of how Erica might be hidden but not where.

He sat back and absently rubbed his head. The pain from the wound was helpful in keeping his mind straight. George wanted to panic. He wanted to grab the M16 and go roaring out into the golden afternoon sun, but that wouldn't help him find Erica. He needed help. George leaned forward and started closing windows on the screen. No wait, he paused, not that one. He needed that one for effect. He yanked the landline connection and plugged it back into his telephone. A minute later he was listening to the phone ring at the police station. Three rings, four—the old Bakelite handset creaked in George's fist, five rings. "C'mon, Two-Bears, you dirty injun, pick up the fucking phone." George stared out the kitchen window at the fading light. Gold had melted over to molten orange, purple wouldn't be far behind. Looked like the search for the prettiest lawyer in Shard was going to happen without the aid of the sun. Eight rings, "Shit!" George slammed down the receiver. Looked like it was going to happen without the aid of the Constable as well.

George walked over to the sink and poured himself a glass of water. An almost desperate thirst had crept up on him. He downed the glass in three giant gulps, his Adam's apple leaping. Through the kitchen window the easy hand of summer dusk had come and drawn out the shadows like taffey. The light was strange now, full of half seen things, thin. George became aware of the sulphur backdrop on the air. He was going to need everyone he could find to help him search. He would go door to fucking door in this burned out little hole and drag them out with their hunting rifles and their flashlights. They'd all tell him "no" at first, thinking it was just George Rhodes on one of his sad benders, but he'd make them listen. Either that, or he'd make such a fucking ruckus that eventually Will would show up and then *he* could convince the good citizenry to lend a hand.

An image of blood-rusty wings filled his mind like evil smoke. The cruel, stupid eyes of the Dalton kid and his tone of almost prissy disgust, *She ain't yours. She's the Outrider's.* The little smiles she had tossed at him over breakfast like shining gifts over the last few days. The way she looked at him, *Wanna' join me?* Their laughing between moans and sighs. The feel of her smooth shoulders against his chest when she'd tried to block T.R.'s shot. She was in the dark somewhere, some hole, imbolized, terrified. Maybe in pain. George's hands were shaking. Every little boy plays this game: he's the handsome knight and must save the beautiful princess from the evil monsters. Half-burned out thirty-something ex-drunk instead of a handsome knight, black M16 instead of a shining sword. The princess was still beautiful and still needed saving. The monsters were probably worse than anything he'd imagined as a child.

George walked over to the hall closet and pulled out a knapsack. He stuffed it full of the spare ammunition clips Will had given him for the M16 and a few boxes of the two and half inch long shells. They reminded him of little rockets. Well, if he ran into T.R. he would do his best to send that little fucker straight to the moon. George slipped on the knapsack and grabbed the heavy flashlight off its wall charger next to the phone. He was about to pick up the rifle but stopped himself. Breathe, George, think. What have you forgotten? Don't feel. Just think. "She'll be dehydrated," he muttered, and pulled a plastic water bottle from the cabinet over the fridge, filled it at the tap then slipped it in the pack. What else, what else? George dashed out of the kitchen and up the back steps in four great strides. He swung into the bathroom and grabbed the first aid kit; into the pack. *Now*, he was ready. George bounded back down the stairs and almost shrieked in surprise to find Will Two-Bears McFarlan standing in the kitchen.

"JESUS, HE FUCKIN' shot you, Georgie?" Will said, blinking. "In the head?" They sat at the kitchen table, George's knapsack next to the rifle. George had given Will the whole story, but Two-Bears kept coming back to that part. George was losing patience. Every time the red plastic second hand on the clock over the stove ticked it felt like a stress bomb going off in his chest. "Yes," he said, slowly, evenly, "T.R. Dalton shot me in the fuckin' head." George exhaled. "He also stole my girl, so can we please, like, mobilize goddamnit?"

Will blinked again. He'd had a pretty strange day himself. He had been all over the populated areas of town taking his census. The results had left him scraped raw and detached. "Mobilize?"

George pounded the table with his big paws. "Yes, damnit! Get moving! You know, fucking get out there with the hounds and shit? WE HAVE TO FIND HER."

Will sat back and put his hands up. "Well, yeah, right. I mean, of course."

"What the fuck does that mean, William? Of course? Yeah, right?"

"What do you want me to do, man?"

George stood up so fast his chair fell over with a bang. "Let's go round up everybody and do a house-to-house search, or whatever the hell you paramilitary motherfuckers call it. We need to get everyone and their mom out lookin' for Erica." George saw the look on Will's face and a deep crease ran through his forehead. "Why's this so hard for you?"

Will's shoulders slumped. "'Cuz there ain't nobody left, man."

"What? There's at least twenty or thirty folks still around. We can…" He trailed off as Will shook his head back and forth.

"No, Georgie. I been trying to get my head around it all day. I walked every street in town today—even the one's with smoke pouring out of 'em—and I saw three people, not including you." He counted off his fingers. "Meg Tooley and Loraine and Kiddo. That's. Fucking. It. After the fourth or fifth empty house—well, outside of the usual empties—I started to get a little freaked out. I was poundin' on those front doors like it was the end of the world." Will winced. Talk about your bad choice of words. "After a while I just started walking into people's houses." He paused, eyes far away. "George? I found plates of food that had been left out. The TV was still on at Marty Patrick's place." He sighed, running his mind over all those empty houses. "Meg Tooley and the Howards. That's it."

George shook his head once. "What, seriously?"

"I guess I saw one more if you want to count Darwin."

George had a crazy image of a stodgey naturalist from the 1800's. "What? Who?"

"Kiddo's dog?"

"Right," George shook his head again and righted his chair. He sat back down. Both men stared at the table, their eyebrows bent in what would have been a comic angle were it not for the gravity of the situation. George said, "Is Amy still here?"

"Don't know. Saw her this morning, but I didn't get as far as her Wini on my rounds. I was going to check there after I stopped in on you." George took a warm hit in the guts from the look on Will's face as he said, "I'm really happy to see you, Georgie."

"Where did they all go? I mean the Wilkersons? That fat kid Howie Sams and his folks?"

"Georgia and Rich."

"Yeah. That old witch Missus Najarian? Come to think of it, she hasn't scowled at me in weeks."

"Hasn't scowled at anyone. The Pair of Jeans is missing, too."

She ain't yours. She's The Outrider's. George rubbed his head. "Well, at least we know the fruit of their loins is still around." The light outside had gone from blue-gray to deep velvet purple. The kitchen should have been full of the sound of crickets tuning up in the yard but there were none. A single firefly flared and streaked like a match, and then the evening was still. George whispered, "Where'd they all go, man?"

Will looked up at him. "Everyone's cars are still in their driveways."

George blinked.

"Yeah, man," Will said. "I think they're all still here."

WILL DROVE ERICA'S rental up the street toward the Howard's house. George sat shotgun with the M16 propped between his legs like the world's most obvious Freudian joke. He stared through his reflection in the dark glass into all those dark, flowing woods. The glow from the instrument panel turned his face an unhealthy greenish white. The plan, such as it was, was to get the Howards and then collect Amy. They'd regroup at the police station and figure out next steps. Will had jumped up at the kitchen table and blurted this out. Talking about what he'd seen, or rather not seen, during his census of the town helped to purge the weird residue the experience had left behind in his head. George had almost smiled with relief; finally his responsible friend, The Constable, was back in action. Now as they pulled up in front of the little rancher at the edge of the woods, Will muttered under his breath, "Please let them still be okay."

George reached for his door handle and Will put a hand on his arm. "Stay with the horses, Tonto."

"Are you fucking with me, Two-Bears?"

"No, you and your giant automatic penis stay here and make sure nothing makes off with our wheels."

"But—"

Will dropped his voice into cop, *"But nothing.* I don't want you coming in there with that cannon. You're freaked out as it is and you look scarey as hell, George. It's going to be hard enough getting Loraine to just agree to throw her son into a car and roll out. You showing up looking like the last twenty minutes of *Platoon* will not help matters."

Will popped his door and was halfway out of the car when George said, "Will?"

"Yeah?"

"Charlie Shean, right?"

"Huh?"

"I remind you of Charlie Shean from *Platoon*, right? It's just that I don't wanna' be Tom Bearinger. He was *such* a dick in that movie."

For a second Will wanted to smile and cry at the same time. Looking in at his best friend—dashboard werelight picking out the gash in his head, the machine gun throwing an oily gleam—he was struck with a powerful feeling. It thrummed in his chest like a mini electric generator: they were going to win. Will gave a sideways smile, "I was thinking more Willem Dafoe," and closed the door. He could hear George's muffled voice at his back, *"Dude! Willam Dafoe fucking dies!"*

Will quick-stepped it up the flagstone walk and raised a fist to knock on the front door. He brushed it with his knuckle and the door pushed open a few inches. His skin crystallized into gooseflesh. He dropped his hand to *Smaug* and thumbed open the safety snap on the holster. Will pushed the door open all the way with his left hand expecting a drawn out screech of hinges like some B horror movie but all he got was the gentle *haaahhh* of the carpeted inner hall under the door's bottom edge. The hall ran for about seven or eight feet before breaking right into the kitchen and left onto the family room. The front hall was broken by two doors, one a coat closet, the other a powder room. He couldn't remember which was which.

He did remember Loraine's injunction against shoes on her white carpet. "If you don't mind, Constable, I'd rather you not leave your footprints as a momento of your visit." Will had unlaced his Chucks and left them on a rubber mat by the front door. He looked down now and saw Loraine's grown-up hiking boots and Kiddo's kid-sized sneakers on that same mat. Maybe he was just being paranoid. Maybe when Loraine showed him out after he'd run his litte census earlier she'd just neglected to close the door all the way. After all, it wasn't like people in this town worried very much about hermetically sealing their houses. But that was bullshit and he knew it. Loriaine had been welcoming enough—offered him a root beer and crackers if memory served—but some distraction kept dragging her face toward the big sliding glass doors that made up one whole wall of the family room. It was like she knew something was out there, or some part of her did.

The Kiddo had been his usual bright and charming self, but something was different there, too. Sitting on the floor, playing with Darwin while the grown-ups talked, Will got this kind of, well, *glow* off the kid out of the corner of his eye. And every time Childe had met Will's glance, the boy seemed galvanized, calm but ready.

The urge to call out to them surged up his throat and died. Thinking of Darwin just now had brought it home: no barking. The deep-voiced beagle sang out a raucous greeting every time someone came to the door. Now the house breathed silence into Will's face like a defiant drunk. *Whut you got on me, ocifer? You don't got shit.* They were either gone or they were here and couldn't talk. Will did something then that most city cops wouldn't think to do. He closed his eyes and took a great breath of air in through his nose. He got the thin background tang of sulphur (always sulphur) surfing the deep wet of a humid summer evening, the scent of a dog who's just about due for a bath, old burned popcorn. There was something rancid—dead mouse behind the wall or road kill fetched up in a corrugated drainpipe. His eyes opened, hardened.

Will moved into the house, eyeing those two hallway doors, the muscles on that side of his body tensing as he padded past each one. As he got closer to the light from the family room he could make out muddy footprints on the carpet. He didn't stoop to examine them, but there were three people here who hadn't wiped their feet, one without shoes, one in sneakers and one in big old work boots.

He rounded the corner and the living room spread in a tableau before him. Will didn't remember hauling leather and leveling *Smaug* on the scene, but his gunsites were before his eyes, tracking off one horror after another.

Loraine stood frozen, her eyes huge. Lizzie Owens stood behind her, her meaty arms wrapped tight around Loraine, one pinioning her arms to her sides, the other around her upper chest, a thick hand clamped over Loraine's mouth. One bare leg sinewed around Loraine's right leg like a cellulite-dimpled tree root. She was enveloping Loraine as much as holding her fast. How she was balancing was impossible to see. Erica had told Will of the dead woman in the trailer, the one who had a shotgun in her mouth. He had found nothing, of course, and here was why. Lizzie had gotten up and walked away. Her face hung just over Loraine's left shoulder, her eyes bleached white. He couldn't see the back of her head, but something told him (the rotten smell, perhaps) that there wouldn't be a lot to see. Shotguns didn't leave much behind at close range.

Will followed Loraine's hurricane lamp gaze and shifted *Smaug* to cover the other nightmare in the room. Sitting in a beautiful chair constructed of graceful wood and leather bows was a timeless classic: young boy on the lap of an adult. In another time and place this could have been a beloved uncle telling a story, or even Santa and a hopeful child. But no, not here, not now. Childe Harold sat stiff as a board, beads of sweat shining on his bloodless face. Cyrus MacCoy was playing the part of the beloved uncle this evening, holding Childe to his lap by gripping the back of his neck. Kiddo was trying to recoil from what was in front of his face, but the man's hand was like bridge cable encased in old, crumbling cheese. Cyrus held his other hand in front of the boy's face, palm up like a little landing pad for the biggest fucking wasp Will had ever seen.

It filled Cyrus's wide hand, deep blue/black and slick with moisture. It passed its antenna through its cerrated mandibles and scraped its back legs over its wings, drying them. It seemed sluggish as if it had just woken up or emerged from hibernation. Cyrus tilted his face toward The Constable and Will put it together when he saw the hole chewed in his grub-white cheek—that thing had been in Cyrus's mouth. Childe's eyes were the size of liberty silver dollars. Even from across the room Will could see the boy was focused on the stinger. It was an inch long spike, and as if the little monster it was attached to sensed the attention, a drop of black venom blossomed at its tip. Childe whimpered.

Will's entire body went numb. His fear crested and washed him away. What was left was a stone pylon in the shape of a man with a gun. He whispered, "Cyrus, let go of the boy."

Cyrus tilted his head, the bruises below his eyes standing out in sharp contrast to the palor of his face. Fissures of purple black ran in the veins under his skin as if some terrible drug addiction had collapsed them. The tip of his nose had turned black with rot and his lips had gone a fishy green-white. Those lips bent into a smile and one white eye winked. Will was suddenly, ridiculously glad he'd gone to the bathroom at George's before they left because had he not he would have pissed himself right there on Loraine's nice white carpet. It was not Cyrus who had winked at him, but someone who was looking *through* Cyrus like a closed-circuit TV camera. Will knew who that someone was.

He thumbed back the hammer and the big pistol made three very loud clicks. At this range he couldn't miss, wouldn't miss, and the better part of Cyrus's head would vaporize. Will wondered for a moment if he could end it all right now. Would killing Cyrus while the, the *enemy* was inside him kill the enemy as well? No, it wouldn't. Will could feel its essence staring through Lizzie Owens. Even the wasp seemed to be channeling the real evil in the room. So many eyes on him. In his chilled state, Will imagined what it would look like to the viewer—insectoid, like a wasp's compound eyes.

Three quick shots if his aim was perfect: Cyrus to the head, Lizzie to the head and then the wasp. Cyrus would fall to the side and the wasp would either fall with him or take to the air. Either way, it would clear his field of fire so Childe wouldn't be in danger of being hit. Either way it was bullshit; no one was that good. And besides, Lizzie's head was already mostly blown out and she was still standing. Will didn't know what to do.

Something banged against the big sliding glass door. Everyone in the room twitched. (Will's trigger finger, which lay along the chamber of the gun and *not* on the trigger, not yet, also twitched.) Will slid his eyes to the side. A bird had flown out of the dark and smacked into the window. It was fluttering around against the glass. He squinted. It was a bright red cardinal. For a moment, it seemed to lock his stare with its own beedy oil-drop eyes. Before anyone could react another cardinal smacked rudely into the glass. It fell to the ground, dazed, shook itself and then started fluttering against the glass like its brother. Another *bang!* and another orangey-red kamakazi bludgeoned into the glass, this one hard enough that a tiny crack caught the light like a single neon thread. Another second went by and a wall of roiling red filled the night as hundreds, maybe thousands of cardinals careened into the glass, some of them fell dead in a growing drift at the bottom sill. The noise was like booming hailstones in a sideways rain. The birds themselves made no sound at all.

All those eyes on Will, staring, impelling, chips out of the night itself, black as... His eyes widened. Black as a spider's eyes. Will dragged the gun around in a stiff-armed arc and squeezed the trigger, *Smaug* roared, the glass shattered, and a bloodstorm exploded into the room.

* * *

TWENTY MINUTES EARLIER, Loraine was sitting on the couch reading a copy of *The Week*. Childe and Darwin lay on the floor across from her, Kiddo with his head propped up on Darwin's back, while reading a graphic novel that was probably too violent for a kid his age, but what the hell, it was Batman. If being a mother had taught her anything (especially the mother a child who's father had elected not to remain in his life after the divorce) it was never get between a boy and his superheros. She peered at him over the edge of the magazine and stole over his curly hair, his eyelashes, the little divot of his upper lip quivering ever so slightly as he read the dialogue.

"Hey, boo-boo," she said.

Kiddo smiled but didn't look up from his book. "I know," he sighed. "You're lovin' me like crazy again."

"Ooh, tough guy."

"Mo-*om!*" He shook the big comic book for emphasis. *C'mon lady, this is the best part.*

She blew him a kiss and went back to *The Week.* This was *her* favorite part, the double-page spread toward the back that featured six or seven houses up for sale from all over the country. They were grouped by a different theme every issue and this week's was *Houses on the Maine Seacoast.* Most of the properties ranged from a million to over five in some cases, but in the lower left there was always the "Steal of the Week". It was a renovated lighthouse jutting out from a sharp point of land. The photographer had snapped the shot just as a wall of crashing foam had leaped up almost half as high as the house, the sun throwing rainbows around it. Loraine lingered. She missed the ocean. Granted this was the wrong one and the weather in New England was, well, fucking horrible, but something about this place was yanking at her. She looked at Childe. Could she uproot him again so soon? It wasn't like there were a lot of kids around here to play with and the school consisted of one crabby old lady. The only real friend Kiddo had was that pudgey kid, Howard Sams. A real sweetheart, always ma'am this and ma'am that, and boy could he put away the brownies.

"Hey," she said, "boo-boo."

Childe levered the graphic novel down with a *whap!* and stared at her. "May I help you?"

"How would you feel about living in a lighthouse?"

Childe, who had come to expect his mother's flights of fancy to come to fruition about a third of the time, remained skeptical. "A lighthouse? Like for ships an' stuff?"

"Well, let's see," Loraine read, "Property for sale includes three bedrooms and one bath, an oil room and a stucco keeper's quarters."

"What's a stucco keeper?"

"Not stucco keeper—stucco quarters for the keeper. The lighthouse keeper."

"Oh." Childe heard the sound of crashing waves in his head as he fell asleep each night. He blinked. "Where is it?"

Loraine smiled. Gotcha. She peered over her bifocals, what Kiddo called her "granny glasses" and said, "Point Maddox, Maine, United Federation of Planets."

"Maine, huh?"

"Yeah. I think you'd like Maine. It's a lot like Mendocino but without all the pot."

Darwin, who had been dozing on the edge of his humans' conversation, popped his head up and looked toward the front hallway. Loraine noticed. "Looks like the amazing Ninja dog smells prey." She frowned and checked her watch. "It's almost eight o'clock."

Childe brightened, "Maybe it's Will again."

"That's Constable MacFarlan to you, young man." And then to herself, "Maybe he forgot something." Calling on someone in Shard after eight o'clock on a week night was akin to showing up at midnight just about anywhere else. There was a knock at the door, more a rhythmic scratching, knuckles brushing the wood.

Childe popped up, "I'll get it."

Loraine raised a hand in protest, but he was already gone. Instead she said, "Stay, Darwin," as the dog got to its feet and made for the door after his boy. Darwin regarded her over his shoulder. Hi tail waved a question. "Stay, buddy-roo." Loraine listened for Will's voice as Childe opened the door. From around the corner she heard her son say, "Hey, man, what are you doing here?" then a sound like someone falling against the wall. The door slammed open. Shuffling feet. Childe cried out, *"Mom!"*

Loraine didn't remember crossing the floor. She surged into the hallway and into the waiting embrace of Lizzie Owens. In the darkened hall she had time to glimpse a smaller figure tussling with Childe who had given off calling for his mother and commenced grunting as he struggled and fought. Behind them the silhouette of a man filled the open door. Rancid, heavy air pounded in Loraine's nose as Lizzie's sausage fingers palped her face searching for purchase. Darwin was barking, roaring at her feet. He slipped into the forest of shifting legs, caught one of the smaller intruder's bare feet and bit down for all he was worth. There was a wet crunch, like a bag of moist twigs being trod upon, but it didn't register with the attacker. The shadowy figure caught hold of Childe's wrists and began to bend him to the floor. Kiddo howled in pain as something began to give in his wrist. It audibly *creeked* as his assailant bent him down.

Out of the corner of his eye, Childe saw the heavy workboots of the third intruder clump over the threshold. The stench was astonishing. Once when Kiddo was much smaller, Daddy took him for a picnic in one of the city parks. Daddy had been chatting with a pretty lady with big hair and tight clothes when Childe had wondered off. He found a cooler that looked just like their's next to a big green dumpster. Childe had bent down and opened the lid to find the week old corpse of a cat. The cloying reek in the hallway was like that. He was sure he would faint from the smell. The world began to gray and Childe thought *Good thing Darwin likes to roll around in dead stuff or he'd be puking his guts out all over Loraine's precious white carpet.*

The thought of his dog galvanized Kiddo. A dump of adrenaline gave him enough energy to shout in the voice of a much older person, "DARWIN! RUN! GO, BOY! OUTSIDE! GO OUTSIDE!" He was almost sure the dog wouldn't listen to him, compelled to stay and probably die trying to help his masters.

The beagle threw his master a look of depth and inquirey that lasted only a moment then bolted. He dodged the groping hands of the man in the workboots and plunged out into the night, barking and howling in his most operatic doggy voce. There was a scent in the back of his brain that equaled *help* and *power.* The smartest of dogs will go fetch a human if another is in trouble. A hundred thousand years of symbiosis with homo sapiens sends them to find the next available upright monkey when things get really dicey. But instead of going for the road, Darwin raced around the back of the house and into the woods.

Carried on the humid summer air, a fount of glorious smells flooded his forebrain—new growth, tannins, animal spoor, prey and predators—but Darwin shook it off with a rattle of his collar and tags. He pressed his nose to the earth and found the scent he was after. It was a strange smell, not something he could taste but more a line of direction he could feel way, way back behind his dialated brown eyes. It was far, but growing stronger as he trotted along in the pitch dark. Somewhere over the darker line of a ridge a coyote sent up a howl. Darwin froze, head cocked. A chorous of howls answered. Darwin's hackles bristled and his teeth shown in the gloom. Let the forest dogs try to get in his way tonight, just let them try.

Time to a dog is forever; it does not shift. When Kiddo was gone from Darwin, it was always forever. When he played or ate or slept it was also forever. And so forever passed as he traversed the forest floor, sometimes thrusting his way through tangles of briar (earning a nasty, flaring scratch on his soft mussle), sometimes tearing along a well worn deer trail. Time didn't matter. He was what he was doing. Darwin was The Finder and always had been. And so it was forever before he found the source of The Scent and no time at all. Darwin stopped and sat. He barked once, loud and urgent. A great, complicated shape rose up in the night, unfolded.

Good dog.

* * *

GEORGE WATCHED WILL push the front door open with his left hand, his right falling to the butt of that gigantic revolver of his. (Big nerd actually named it after the dragon from *The Hobbit*.) Something was wrong. He sat forward in the passenger seat. Sweat popped on Geroge's brow and stung the gash on the side of his head. *Shit, shit, shit.* What should he do? Should he get out and back Will up or stay in the car? He became very aware of the smell of gun oil and tightened his grip on the M16.

George took a deep breath and weighed the options. He could go in behind a trained policeman pointing an automatic weapon with which, admittedly, he had become a very accurate shot, and run the risk of accurately shooting the wrong person. "Stop it," he said to himself. It was Shard. No one locked his or her door, and these folks probably just didn't close their's well enough. The door had come open a little, big deal. Still. George rolled the window down and listened. He counted thirty-mississippi and calmed some more. George let his arm dangle out the window and drummed his fingers against the door. They would collect the Howards and go back to the police station. George could imagine them spreading a map of the town out on Will's desk and figuring out the best place to begin the search for Erica.

George leaned back and squeezed his eyes shut. Erica. He grimaced. He was sitting in a fucking car, doing fucking nothing, while Two-Bears fucking chit-chatted with the fucking Howards. His drumming against the metal door started to sound more like the death throes of a squirrel than jazzy finger beats. He opened his eyes and stared at the open front door. Man, did he ever wish he had a Bombay Saphire and Tonic in that bee-bopping hand. Where the hell where they? It had been at least a minute.

Something wet touched his hand.

George shouted a nonsense word composed of many vowels and yanked his hand back into the car. It was followed by a pair of muddy paws and the tip of a snuffling nose. Darwin. *Je-SUS.* George looked out the window and into the beagle's eyes. "Are you fucking kidding me, dawg?" Darwin whined and yapped at George. He backed off from the car door and turned in a little circle. He barked again and looked at the house. George smiled at this funny little dance, his brow folded. "What's up, doggy-dude? Did the Well Creature finally eat Timmy?" It was a joke, but the words cut through the fog. George looked back the house, that gaping front door. It had been too long.

A shot.

* * *

THE ROOM FILLED with red wind. The cardinals blotted out everything. Will held up his hands to ward off the multitude of little beaks and clawed feet, but the birds did not touch him. They flew around in a great swirling mass of disturbance then organized, congealed on Lizzie Owens, Cyrus MacCoy and the wasp. Lizzie and Cyrus changed in an instant from horrendous, albeit recognizable forms into red, writhing shrubs as the cardinals began to shred them. Loraine and Childe stood out in pale contrast against all that furious, blurring red. A second later and each was expelled, tumbling toward Will, as the limbs that held them were reduced to little more than bone.

The three of them backed toward the hallway. Will had the fleeting impression that Cyrus and Lizzie were on fire; what was left of them flailed like willow branches in a slow breeze. Aside from the busy susorous of wings and beaks, there was no sound other than their breath and thudding hearts. Will's mind rushed back to him and he shoved Loraine and Childe toward the front door. *"Go! Go!"* he hissed. He was pretty sure he knew what was saving their collective asses, but he didn't want to stick around and have tea with it afterward.

Will gave a last look at the dimishing shapes covered in a crinkling mass of feathers and pin-prick black eyes before herding Loraine and Childe into the front hall. He watched the Howards shoot out into the yard like a couple of corks from a champaign bottle and then he heard it—the distinct click of a doorknob. Time slowed. Will turned on his heel. A troll stood in the hallway right behind him, short and fat, stinking. It had been hiding in the dark powder room. Will pulled a double take. It was Howard Sams and in a strange parody of what a real kid might do, a living kid, Howard stuck his tongue out at the good Constable. Surfing that thrushy board was another giant black wasp.

Will started to bring *Smaug* to bear, but it was happening too slowly, the huge pistol weighed a thousand pounds. The wasp's delicate wings flickered into transparency, the air they disturbed feathering Howard's bangs. Will had just enough time to realize the boy was grinning around that impossibly long tongue. Every detail flashed into perfect clarity: the mold at Howard's hair line, the obsidian glint off the wasp's marble-sized eyes, the flex of its legs as it began to rise into the air.

Howard staggered back as if an invisible boxer nailed him with a triplet of lightning-fast jabs to the body. He gulped the wasp back into his throat and put a hand on the wall to steady himself before taking a step forward again. Blackish ooze bloomed on the front of his t-shirt in three dinner plate-sized patches. Will didn't waste his second chance and leveled the .357. He took the top off Howard's skull neat as a meat clever and a million times as loud. The boy flew backward a couple of yards. And got up.

A hand clamped down on Will's shoulder from behind. He began to turn, to roll *Smaug* around, when George's voice cut through the ringing in his ears. "Fuck outta' here!" They ran, Will half staggering with shock, back to the car. Will could see Loraine and Childe's faces through the windshield in the back seat, Darwin on Kiddo's lap. Will threw himself behind the wheel; George thudded into the passenger seat, pulling the still smoking M16 in with him. Will got it then: the invisible boxer had been a quick squeeze from the machine gun. Georgie had saved his life. He hadn't even heard the shots.

Childe screamed, "Ah, *Jeez*, Howard!"

The troll was back at the front door, staining the rectangle of dim light. Its head was reduced, flattened. Childe sobbed just once, a horrible choked sound that did more hurt to Will's heart than any of what had just come before. The body of Howard Sams teetered on the front stoop, one chubby, bare foot raised and then he was gone. George blinked rapidly three times. "The hell was that?" He'd caught…something, a flare of giant hooks that reminded him of that old grappling arcade game that lowers down and snatches a toy from the bin. Except it came from behind Howard. Will threw the car into reverse and twisted over the back seat as he hauled down the driveway, the Subaru's transmission whinning. "What *was* that?" George demanded.

"Yïn," Will said.

Chapter 31

THE POMPILIAD DREAMED. Over the past few days and nights, angular shadows crawled up and over its face, dust fell on its shoulders and hair, its unblinking eyes. Barn swallows and bats dropped guano around it. Nothing would stay over its head except beams of dust-solid sunlight. No roving insect investigated its fingers clamped white over the leather knobs of its knees; no cob used any outcropping as anchor for its web. On the second day, a solitary mud dauber wasp floated down to pearch on the back of its hand. It stayed as the sunbeam clock threw its glowing arms and spots around the barn. In time, the wasp rose and flashed as it passed through a ray of sun. It slipped through a gap in the planks like a crack between worlds. (Hours later it found a baby bird, a cardinal, alone in her nest and stung it to death.) The Pompiliad was still. The Pompiliad dreamed.

It dreamed an unfolding story through the eyes of its swarm. It levitated with a thousand cold intellects little more than apetite and drive, *its* drive, as they moved from place to place. One day they populated an old pine tree, waiting for instructions or opportunity. Another, they carpeted the pews of the abandoned Methodist Church, the heavy sulphur smoke drugging them quiet for a time. And the story found characters: the teacher, the moonshine man, the hill people, the migrants—all added eyes through which the Pompiliad could look. It sent these characters on to find more and they did, stinging out the lights of their old inhabitants, laying in new tenant riders. And there was its servant: the poisonous young man who was himself little more than need and aimlessness. It was eating the servant alive from the inside, coring him out, but he was a young human. He would last until it no longer needed him.

His part of the story was especially interesting. The Pompiliad had watched with detached amusement as the servant crept into the drunk's house and dispatched him before taking its Queen. If the Pompiliad could be said to have anything even like emotion, it felt a pull toward this woman. She was strong, physically resilient, possessed of DNA coding granting her fine mind and limb. It would secret her away in the nursery, and through her hatch a generation of world eaters. When the traitor lizard was dead and its ridiculous pet arachnid food for the swarm, the Pompiliad would impregnant the woman at its leisure and *change* her. It imagined her new beauty: pendulous, swollen, straining, eyes as empty as chunks of coal, body a factory.

The Pompiliad dreamed about a Queen and an army.

It awoke soon after moonrise. Time in the old barn stoped. Every snowy spec of dust froze in space, each sliding beam of saphire moonlight stilled, and every living thing from the barn owl roosting in the far corner to the tiniest microbe in the dirt floor died. A gentle rain of feathered and many legged things pattered into the dust as the Pompiliad gained its feet. Long arms swaying at its sides, back hunched, it trudged to the motorcycle and threw a leg over. The bike was covered in a thin layer of dust. It kicked up the stand and righted the chopper, but there was no slosh of gasoline from the fuel tank. The bike had been out of gas for more than seven hundred miles.

The Pompiliad blinked its black eyes and the chopper roared into life. A moment later and those eyes had changed, covered over by large black sunglasses. It didn't bother backing out but clamped down the front brake while gunning the engine. The back tire ground out a plume of sterile dust that choked the barn and burried the bodies of a thousand dead things. The bike whipped around to face the big double doors and the Pompiliad let go of the brake. It smashed through into the thick summer night and layed down a line through the hay toward the highway.

South now. A fat gibous moon hung over its shoulder like a focilized skull. The road reflected in its dark lenses. South. The air was redolent with hydrocarbons, sweet grass, and the tang of skunk. South. The porch lights of farm houses slid by. In the refridgerators of those closest to the road the milk curdled, the eggs bloodied and the children's dreams turned sour. South. The star Antares, the heart of the Scorpion, hung over a dark horizon. The Pompiliad smiled, remembering Scorpios all too well. South.

And Shard by morning.

Chapter 32

WILL STOOD IN front of the four by four wall map. It was marked with a small splotch of streets surrounded by wooded hills that were overlaid with a maze of old mining roads. His arms were crossed over his chest like a man appreciating a museum piece. George stood next to him, tapping his foot and readjusting the way he held his own arms every few seconds: hands on hips, crossed arms, behind the back, again on hips. Will grabbed a push pin from a cluster in the lower left corner of the map and stuck it roughly in the center. "This is us here," he said.

"That's terrific, Magellan, but where's Erica? That's what I need to know." George faced Will with a look just bordering on lost. He was doing his best, but much more of this farting around and he was likely to go running into the night shouting her name.

"I don't know, man. If we had about a hundred more people, I'd say we should do a pattern search, but it's just me and you."

"I'll help look," Childe said from atop his mother's lap. He was much too big for lap sitting, but Loraine held onto him like grim death from her seat in Will's desk chair. Darwin was busy sniffing around the open holding cell. "You'll stay right here," she said.

Will didn't like the look in her eyes. Loraine was walkin' and talkin' but she wasn't really here. She'd been spooked plumb out of herself. He needed to talk with her, make her see what was going on here. It wasn't going to make things any less spooky—more so, he was sure—but she needed to know she wasn't alone in this insanity and that her bunkmates in the asylum were really quite nice. Hell, knowing that George knew what was going on was what had kept Will from losing his shit after he met Dampf. But they didn't have time for that now. Loraine would just have to learn on the fly, because right now they needed to fan out and search for Erica. And Loraine and Kiddo couldn't stay here by themselves.

Will scanned the map for a long, quiet moment, the others' eyes on him, and turned around. "Okay," he said in pure cop, "here's how we're going to handle this: each of us gets a walkie and everyone over the age of fifteen and with less than four legs gets a gun. Loraine, I'll show you the basics before we head out." She opened her mouth to speak, but Will held up his hand and something in his posture or the tilt of his head did the job. She closed her mouth and waited. George's eyebrows went up and he thought *You don't need to see our identification. These aren't the droids you're looking for.* Will continued, "George, Loraine, Childe and Darwin will be one team. I'll head up to the mine offices and see if I can't fine Amy at her RV. If she's there, we'll form team two. If not, I'll be on my own." Will turned toward George. "Like I was saying before, if we had enough people we could do a pattern search and just carpet bomb the whole town with eyeballs, but since we only got two points of search, we need to think about likely spots and hit those first. If we don't find her at any of those places," he put a finger on the map and drew it out in a concentric line, "we spiral out until we do."

The Constable turned back around, "We check in on the walkies every five minutes." He eye-locked each of them for each word, "Every. Five. Minutes." Will could see Loraine was still waiting to freak out and refuse. And there was no better way to get past this, either for or against, than to get past it. He took a deep breath and said, "Okay, Loraine, your turn."

Loraine nodded as if to an opponent in a debate. "I'm not going anywhere but to my car and then right the hell out of this town. I'm going to take my son and my dog and drive until I see enough lights to convince me that the population is in the hundreds of thousands." She paused for a moment, "I'm thinking Lexington…maybe Cincinnati."

George broke in, "And what about Erica? You just going to let her get killed or, or, or *worse?*"

Will put a hand on his friend's shoulder. It was a bit like touching a live wire insultated with a thin film of rubber. George shook it off with a noise just shy of a growl. "No! Damnit, no! Loraine, I know you're not from here but you have to help,"

George spread out his palms, "you have to. That little bastard T.R. could have done anything with her."

Childe who had been studying his knees looked up, "T.R. took your girlfriend?"

"And shot me in the head," George said, holding back a curtain of dirty blonde hair to show the streak of coagulated blood running from just behind his temple to just over his ear. "You have to understand that this isn't the big city. This isn't a place with a population that numbers in the hundreds of thousands. People actually help their neighbors here. I mean what did me and Will just do for you back at your house?" Even in the midst of this rant George paused, "Okay, it was mostly Will, but you get the goddamned point."

Loraine kissed Childe on the ear and whispered, "Hop down, sweetheart." He slid off her lap and Loraine stood up with an audible pop in each knee. She extended a finger like a fencing foil and took a step toward George. Loraine was five-three on a good day in heels and George was over six feet when he slumped. The scene reminded Will of a greeting card he once got with a tiny Chihuahua staring up at an enormous Great Dane, *You're only as small as you feel!* Loraine jabbed that finger at George and said, "You don't get to tell me what's right and what isn't, George Rhodes. I'm terribly sorry that hoodlum hurt you and took miss Mendez, but I *will not* endanger my boy, understand?" Loraine drew up like a preacher with a fist full of the good news. "I am a *mother*. My first duty is to the protection of my son. That is the natural order."

Will's head dropped. Okay, George would go get Amy and they would be a team. Will would search alone. He was about to announce this new configuration so they could just get on with it when Childe's voice interceded, "Things have changed, mom."

All three adult heads swiveled like SETI dishes finally catching that alien signal. "What'd you say, sweetheart?" Loraine asked.

Childe Howard, scruffy headed and tall for his age regarded his mother with plain eyes, "Thing's are different, now, mom. Don't you see that? The natural order, like you said? That's changed, too."

Loraine walked over and put her hands on his shoulders. She spoke gently, but a reed of fear was woven just under her voice.

Loraine *did not* want to hear what the light of her life had to say about how things had changed. No they hadn't. Things— whatever "things" meant—were as they always had been. The sun rose in the east and set in the west. The earth was round and Republicans were evil. Nothing had changed. "What I see, young man, is a town full of crazies that isn't safe anymore. I don't know what, what *hysteria* has effected these poor people, but this is no place for a twelve year-old."

"It's not hysteria, mom. It's him." He frowned. "Or *it*, I guess."

The whites of Loraine's eyes showed a little more. "Stop talking in fantasies, Kiddo." She squeezed his shoulders a little too tight. "We talked about 'magical thinking', remember? There's a difference between the real world and your imagination. And—"

"Howard Sams was dead, Loraine," Childe said.

"Don't call me Loraine," she hissed. "I'm your mother."

She dug her fingers into his arms, but Kiddo spoke even and true, "Howard Sams was dead. That other man had a giant wasp living in his head and that fat lady was also dead."

Loraine let go and began to turn away. Childe grabbed her wrist and spun her around. Pink circles stood out on his cheeks and his eyes were glassy with tears, "No! You listen now! Red birds came in and ate those bad people. Mr. George and Constable Will shot Howard Sams and then he *got up.*"

Loraine was shaking now and all the color had drained from her face. George and Will shared a look, but let it play out. Will had been planning on bringing Loraine up to speed but a hell of a lot more gently than this. Apparently, her son had other ideas. Shit, they probably didn't have time to be gentle now that he thought about it anyway.

Finally, Loraine managed a horse whisper, "You're just a kid. What do you know?"

Childe erupted, "I know that we saw a giant web in the forest! I've met the thing that made it." He jabbed a finger at Will. "He used its name when we were pullin' away from the house." Now Childe dug his fingers into her arms. Loraine was looking everywhere but her son's eyes. The light of the world was proving a tad too bright at present. He shook her, tears streaming down his face. "What'd Constable Will call it, Loraine?"

"I don't remember."

"Mom? I love you. What did Will say its name was?"

"Dunno'." She muttered and sank to her knees with a little moan.

Kiddo went down with her, but kept his hold on her arms. "Mom," he whispered. She was crying now. "Look at me, okay?" She did and smiled as if she hadn't seen his dear face in some time. Loraine wiped a tear from his cheek. Childe wiped one from hers then pinned her eyes with his own. "What's its name?"

Loraine squeezed her eyes shut and frowned like a little girl, her lower lip stuck out and quivered. "Yïn," she said at last and opened her eyes. "Its name is Yïn and it's a giant fucking spider, okay?" She reached forward and hugged her son. "I'm so sorry about Howard, Kiddo." For a long time they held each other, kneeling on the floor and crying softly. After a little while, Loraine looked up at Will. He saw two things in her face that filled him with relief: acceptance and sanity. She also looked like ten years older. She whispered, "What else do I need to know?"

* * *

"A DRAGON? SERIOUSLY?" Loraine said as George drove her and Kiddo in Erica's rented Subaru. He had been laying out the rest as they rolled over darkened streets toward the movie theatre—Childe's suggestion as a starting point.

"Oh," George said, "You can get your head around a giant shape-shifting spider but a dragon's what, too far fetched?"

Loraine sat back in the passenger seat. Childe and Darwin were in the back. The boy spoke up, "Wow, a dragon? I mean, I saw Yïn in the woods that one time, but I didn't know there was a dragon." Awe crept into his voice. "Was it really big?"

"Well, I was kinda dr—confused at the time, but I'd say it was big. I remember having to crane my neck a lot."

"Wait," Loraine said and turned around to face her son. "You already knew about the spider? How come you didn't tell me?"

Kiddo just looked at her.

"Would you have believed him?" George said quietly.

Loraine faced forward. "No," she said. "I wouldn't have." She looked back over her shoulder, "I'm sorry, Kiddo. I guess I'd believe you now if you told me Darwin was really a robot under all that fur."

Kiddo threw on a flat Austrian accent and lowered his voice, "Sarah Connah? Woof."

"God, it bothers me that you've seen *The Terminator*."

George smiled. He couldn't help it. "What self-respecting twelve year-old boy hasn't seen *The Terminator*?" He glanced at the twelve-guage pump shotgun propped against the door next to Loraine. Will had shown her how to use it before they'd split up, but if that thing didn't blow her on her ass the first time she fired it, George would be amazed. "Man, I wish we had a few terminators workin' for us right about now."

Loraine brushed a finger along the stock of the shotgun. "What else is there for me to know?" She said. "Other than those people? Will there be more of them? What's with the wasps in their mouths?" She shook her head. "God, I feel like everyone knows more about what's going on than I do."

"Well, you're the mom," Kiddo said as if that explained everything.

"All I know is what I've seen," George said. "There's a big fuckin' dragon—pardon my french, Kiddo—under the mines in a cavern full of jewels. It called itself Dampf and said its giant spider buddy was called Yïn. They're guarding a doorway between our world and a different one. In this other world there are some monsters trying to get to into this one. This would be a very bad thing. One of these monsters—which are apparently giant shape-shifting wasps—has already come through. The dragon called him 'The Pompiliad'. He wants to open the door and bring all his buddies over here. We're supposed to help Dampf and Yïn keep him from doing that." George took a breath.

"Dampf? Yïn?" Loraine asked, "What's with all the German?"

"I'm guessing they can call themselves whatever they want. They're older than German or English or Martian for all I know. I think Dampf is like 'damp' as in Firedamp. It's coal mine speak for a pocket of combustible gas. You know that whole thing about canaries in coal mines? The poor little suckers are more susceptible to the gas fumes from a firedamp, so they crap out before the people do. I'm not sure what Yïn means."

"Yes and no," Loraine said, staring through her own reflection in the window.

"What?"

She looked at George, "Yah unt nine. Yïn. Get it?"

George smiled in spite of himself. "Cute."

"What about T.R.?" Childe asked.

"Yeah, him," George said, his fingers creaked on the steering wheel. "I'm not sure what's going on there, but I get the distinct impression that he's workin' for the black hats on this one."

"Black hats?"

"Bad guys, honey," Loraine said.

"Oh."

George continued, "When he snatched Erica," his voice wavered just a bit on her name, "he said she belonged to the 'Outrider'. I figured he was talking about The Pompiliad."

Childe thought for a moment. "Is T.R., you know, like Howard and those other people? Dead an' stuff?"

"I don't think so, buddy," George said. Poor little guy didn't just lose his best friend, he watched him die twice and get up. And speaking of poor *big* guys, how didn't George himself feel after blowing away a small child with a big gun? He felt like he needed a drink was how he felt. And he felt like he could do it again. Something in his hindbrain told him that thing wearing Howard Sams wasn't Howard Sams. George didn't think it would be too far a stretch for him to unload on another one. And as far as T.R. was concerned, there would be zero hesitation. Maybe he'd start with the kneecaps. "T.R. looked really wrong, sick, and I get the idea that anyone who gets in good with the Pompiliad probably doesn't do very well in the end." George hoped like hell that whatever sickness was coursing through T.R. like bad electricity hadn't found its way into Erica. "God, I need a drink," he muttered.

"What?" Loraine asked.

"Nothing," George pulled the car over and killed the lights. He left the engine running and checked his gear. He still had the little knapsack with the flashlight and first aid kit. The M16— which he had begun to think of as the Incredible Boom Stick— was in the hatch back stinking of cordite and machine oil. He grabbed his walkie and thumbed the talk button. "Will."

The radio squawked back, "You're a minute late."

"Try to keep your pantyhose dry about it. We're just down the street from the theatre." George's nose wrinkled, "Man, the sulphur's really strong down here."

"Say again all after theatre?"

"Nothing," George said. "Listen, we're going to check it out. I'll call back in five."

"Don't be late this time."

"Won't. Where're you?"

"About two minutes from Amy's Winibago."

"All right, man. Good luck."

"Thanks, Georgie. Be careful. Out."

"Out," George said. The walkie-talkie made it difficult to be sure, but he thought there was something odd in Will's voice. Loraine articulated it for him. "Doesn't sound like he think's she'll be there."

"No," he said, "It didn't, did it." George stared out into the night and let his eye rove along the main street. There were a hundred hiding places behind those boarded up windows and T.R. could be in any one of them, training his rifle on them right now. The gouge in George's head throbbed. He half-turned in his seat, "Okay, here's how we're gonna' do this."

* * *

WILL DROVE THE Jeep Cherokee into the weedy parking lot outside the abandoned offices of the Shard Mine Co. He knew what he'd find before he even got there and wasn't happy to be right. Amy's RV was gone. When he'd left her this morning, there had been some smell on her, some intention that got behind his eyes just a bit. Not enough at the time to put him on alert for her, but enough so now that he found her gone it wasn't a surprise. Well, good, maybe that was one less person he'd have to worry about.

Will killed the engine and got out of the jeep. He swung a big MagLite around the lot. A group of red eyes flared at the edge of the woods. Will's breath caught in his chest and then let go. Deer—just a small herd of deer. He moved the light on and the deer crashed off into the undergrowth. Will walked over to the empty spot that had been occupied by Amy's rolling apartment-slash-laboratory. He got a flash of her sunbathing on that rock, smiling at him in bed, bending over the kitchen table, tattoos writhing. God, what a wildcat. But now she was gone. Will kicked a pebble and tracked it as it skittered across the broken macadam. She would probably have been able to pick that little sucker up, squint at it and tell him exactly what it was made out of. Will smiled. Amy was gone and that was fine.

* * *

AMY JAMES WATCHED the Jeep turn around and trundle out of the parking lot from the upper corner office of the Shard Mine Co., crimson brake lights flaring like a couple of robot eyes in the dark. Behind her on the dusty floor was a sleeping bag, camping stove and a serious backpack stuffed with rope and other gear. If Will kept looking, he'd find her Winnie abandoned on a mining road about three miles into the woods. Not far enough back that it would never be found (at least she didn't think so, but around here who the hell knew) and then the worst would be suspected. She had ransacked the inside of the Winnie so thoroughly it would appear as if an entire tribe of meth fiends had gone over every inch of it and made off with its owner.

Amy waited until the sound of the Jeep was a distant hum and the sound of the night—crickets, a night hawk's call, frog songs— found their way back into her little squat. Her eyes had already gotten used to the moonlight pushing through the filmy windows. She plopped down on the sleepbag and dragged her pack over. It made a loud rasping on the gritty concrete floor and sent up a cloud of mildewy air, but she barley noticed. She unzipped a large side pocket and pulled out the diamond sphere she'd taken from the cavern. A low jolt of pleasure ran up her arms and settled, humming in her gut. Amy held the huge crystal in her lap and stared into its milky heart. Moonlight found her eyes and washed all the color away. Her face was empty.

She planned to wait for first light before starting out for what she had begun to think of as The New Mine. It would take her a while and some serious muscle power, but she could probably haul at least another five of these amazing diamonds into the light before the day was through. Amy turned the sphere over and over in her lap. That subtle buzz of pleasure, a liquid cold that did not chill but invigorated like negative electricity, spread down through her pelvis and into her legs. Soon she was suffused with it and began to rock gently back and forth. Something moved in the corner, but she didn't care. It was probably just a mouse. If it came near her jewel she's simply grab it and bite its head off. Even if it was a coyote (she'd heard them howling at night) she'd just use her rock hammer and gouge out its eyes or even bite its throat until her face and short hair were tacky with blood. It was her jewel and that was final. There would be no taking it away from her.

Amy pushed it into the hollow of her belly and a low moan slid over her lips. She was taken with the urge to strip and rub the crystal all over her skin, rolling it along the curves and divets of her body. The very idea sped her heart and gave her the shakes, but if she took her hands away from the diamond to unlace her boots or pull off her shirt she would lose skin contact with it. The pleasant cold throbbed in her every pore now and began to drag at her eyelids. She was tired, so tired. Careful to keep her hands on her jewel, Amy lay on her side and curled around it. She fell asleep and dreamed nothing.

The hours crept by in the warm summer night and the world wound on its way outside, but in Amy's little keep time was told only by the travels of the moon over the floor. It slid up to Amy and outlined her, stealing the colors from her painted arms except for one tiny patch on the back of her shoulder. It winked in the light like a scale of mica. Amy's rib cage rose and fell, rose and fell, the sphere grasped tight to her belly with hands that looked more like claws in the strange light. The moon moved on, sparking a second flake of mica on the back of her hand, and a third behind her ear. The moon moved on and so did Amy James.

Chapter 33

T.R. SAT ON the cool earthen floor of Missus Najarian's cellar
and tried not to think. When he thought about stuff he heard a
voice and that voice sounded a lot like his mother. Tommy Ray
Dalton did not, as did many of the yocals around these parts, fall
off a hay wagon yesterday. He knew it couldn't really be his
mother's voice. She was dead. He understood that now. He put the
bullet in her himself. He hugged his bony knees to his chest. It
was nice down here in the basement, peaceful—when his
goddamn dead mother wasn't nagging him, anyway. Something
about being in their den or whatever (hive would have been more
accurate) kept the buzzing in his poor skull at bay and even kept
the throbbing down in his priapic member. The smell was terrible,
of course, but it was safe. This was where they'd been sleeping?
Would you call it that?

T.R. glanced around the room. The only light came from a
hissing Coleman lattern he'd found hanging from a hook near the
top of the steps. They didn't need it to find their way around, but
he had almost fallen and broken his fucking neck getting down
here with the Outrider's slut. She was a little thing, sure, but solid.
T.R. was thinking that some serious gym time went into making a
bod as tight as that one. The dishwater glow from the lattern
illuminated her in the corner. Well, illuminated her face anyway.
The rest of her was kind of covered up. He grimaced with the
memory.

As soon as he'd gotten her down the stairs, they'd, well,
swarmed him, the stinking walkers—Najarian, the Owenses and
the rest. They'd taken Erica's unconscious bulk from his
shoulders and spirited her toward the back wall. They'd been
doing some digging, enlarging the cellar, a little renovating in
their off hours. There were holes gouged in the hardpacked earth
all around the cellar walls, their sides roughly hexagonal. Some of

them were neatly stacked with only a thin partition between. T.R. was sure they should collapse, but some sort of coating caught the light. Glue, cement? Something.

He stood at the base of the stairs, swaying, exhausted and then suddenly marveling at the blessed silence in his head. The buzzing was almost gone. A smile spread across his face like an overheated child's melodramatic relief when he walks into airconditioning after a hot day's play. T.R.'s hands stole to his crotch—yep, still hard as a rolling pin, but not so bad it was like he was going to bust his own sausage casing.

A wet scratching, crumpling noise was coming from the back of the room. He wanted to see what they were doing. Some goulish sensibility told him they might be eating her and he had to make sure she was in one piece for the Outrider. He clumped up the wooden risers and grabbed the Coleman from its nail by the door. With each step up, the buzzing grew louder, his face more contorted; as he moved downstairs, the buzzing grew more faint. It was as regular as a volume knob. T.R. held the lattern up and sprayed the cellar with hissing white light.

A little crowd of walkers was busy at the intersection of the east and south walls. They had Erica propped up in the corner. T.R. could just see her face—eyes closed, mouth hanging slack. That swampy squishing sound was very loud now, and then he saw what they were doing he understood why the hexagonal cells were able to stay up. They were cementing her in place. Charlottte Najarian—her skin now mottled as a moldy squash—leaned forward, jaws stretched to the breaking point and took a huge bite out of the hardpacked earthen wall. She began to chew with rapid, machine-like quivers, her jaw spasming on her load of dirt. The half-burned one that T.R. was pretty sure was Luther Becket was on his hands and knees, the bow of his arched back flexing as tarry muck pumped out of his mouth. He layed a thick bead in a half circle, penning Erica into the corner. He was already up to her knees. Najarian leaned forward and added another layer of processed earth to the cell. The others were working from her chin down, closing the sides in around her in a gluey hug.

T.R.'s sense of time was pretty much gone down here in the dark, but it felt like they'd finished at least a half an hour ago. They had stood and walked away, each shuffling for one of the hexagonal holes. They'd wriggled into the shoulder-wide cells head first, but somehow managed to turn around. The mud clotted tops of heads crowned just inside the lip of each cell like a nightmare birth canal. And there were more than when he first met them in the kithen upstairs. He hadn't noticed the extra tenants before—at least fifteen of them—because he'd been distracted by the construction crew. All told, there had to be something like twenty or twenty-five. It was like most of the town was down here. Now, with his back propped up against what seemed like the only section of wall not honeycombed, T.R. tried to keep his mind clear while he waited for whatever came next.

It ain't right, what you're doin'.

"Shut up, Momma," he whispered. "You ain't real anyway, so just shut up."

Bad enough you did for your Daddy an' me the way you done.

T.R. wound his fingers into his greasy hair. "Shut. Up."

Now you gotta' go and hurt this poor lady, too? And for what?

T.R.'s voice was getting smaller and higher pitched, as if he were aging backward. "Please be quiet. I just need some rest is all."

You think some heavy-metal rocker gawd is gonna' make you into a prince?

"Outrider'll reward me." T.R. grimaced as soon as he said it, remembering Maggie Owens raising her dress over her scabby knees.

Sure he will. Just like the devil always pays up on his debts. You just have to say goodbye to your enternal soul.

T.R. squeezed his eyes shut. "You," he said, "are dead. I killed you myself. I shot you with Daddy's rifle and it sounded just like the *fucking screen door slamming!*" He took a deep, shakey inhalation. "Now, I may not be able to get you to shut up, but that don't mean I have to listen to you, you nagging bitch." He flapped his hands in an expansive gesture, "So go on! Talk all you want. I just won't hear you no more."

T.R. cocked his head, his eyes wide open but there was no retort. There, ha, he'd done it. He'd even managed to silence her goddamned ghost. He blew a long, stinking breath out into the dark. Hadn't even realized he was holding it. He barked a screamy little laugh into the gloom. Erica gave a tiny moan from her

254

prison. T.R. guessed his laugh had worked its way into whatever dreams she was having. He hoped for her sake they were good because he didn't expect she'd find life on this side of consciousness very appealing. His cracked lips pulled back, revealing a smile in the same way wriggling white things are revealed when you tip over a rock. "Just you an' me, good lookin'," he said.

"YOU HAVE BETRAYED ME," Chorused throughout the cellar. T.R.'s heart slammed in his chest. The voice, *its voice,* came from all around him. He panned around and saw them: they'd pivoted their heads so their faces stuck out of the cells, some of them were upside down, others sideways, all of their mouths hung open, unmoving. And all those empty white eyes. The Outrider's voice issued forth as though they were little more than an organic PA system.

T.R. stood up and held out his hands. "I don't understand," he cried. "I've brought you the woman. I shot the man she was with, the drunk." But he understood his failure the moment it was out of his mouth. Back in the movie theatre, the Outrider had given him specific orders. He'd been told to use his knife on George Rhodes. His knife. "I killed him, though," he said. "I put him down like a—."

"Quite." The Outrider's whisper, harmonized through the strange chorus, silenced T.R. even more than a roar would have. *"Your new weapon is a poor substitute for the old blade. The drunk draws breath. He searches for my prize with the child and his mother. Go to your temple and find them there. End them there."* The voice ceased with a sigh and a low rasp as the chorus turned their faces back into the earth.

T.R. stood. His temple. The theatre. There were plenty of knives in Najarian's kitchen upstairs. He wimpered aloud at the thought of rising back into the buzz, but it had to be done. Denying the Outrider would be like denying the coming of a hurricane. For those foolish enough to do so, no mercy.

* * *

THE LAST TIME George had been inside the old movie theatre he had been younger than Childe Howard was now. He remembered it fondly: the rows of red velvet seats, the old-fashioned stage before the modest-sized screen. You could still smoke in theatres back then. The story from the projectionist's booth wafted down on a cone of swirling blue-white. Shard didn't get a lot of first-run pictures, so his mother took him to see *The Ten Commandments* with Charleton-cold-dead-hands-Heston his own bad self. They played it every year a few weeks before Christmas.

Now, the beam of George's flashlight wafted on swirls of sulphur fumes and dust. The reek of mildew and old spent matches replaced buttered popcorn. George played the light down the center isle. A black strip ran along the middle of the ancient red carpet. The flashlight's white disk flared over the stained canvas movie screen and for a moment George could almost imagine Moses shielding his eyes from what was then an extremely cool special effects burning bush. Old Chuck Heston'd be proud of George now. Just look at that big machine gun he was toting. "From my cold, dead hands indeed," George muttered. Something skittered in a far corner. The rats hadn't left Shard just because of some little underground fire. People should be so resilient.

Erica wasn't here. She could be up in the projectionist booth, the offices, or behind the screen, but that was pretty much it. He'd already checked the offices and the booth—nothing but cobwebs over cobwebs—so that just left the maintenance space behind the screen. He already knew she wasn't there either. If Erica was in here, even if she couldn't talk for some reason—yeah, for some reason—George knew he would just *feel* her somehow. It didn't make any rational sense, but the days of wine, roses and rational thinking had joined the Dodo in the lounge of Ain't Ever Fucking Coming Back to Shard. George sighed in the dark. Somewhere under his feet a dragon—even he was still having trouble with that particular gem—slept and kept watch.

He should just beat feet back to the car and regroup with Kiddo and Loraine. He'd left them there and told them not to come in under any circumstances. Will might think that they need to stay together in little fire teams just like something from one of his adventure novels, but George wasn't about to go waltzing around in the dark with an M16 and the Howards to worry about as well. It was too easy to imagine blasting a few rounds at some noise and realizing he'd just blown off Childe Howard's left arm.

Nuh-uh, no way. The kid had whined a little about it, but Loraine had been perfectly happy to stay put.

Didn't matter anyway. This place was as dead as dead could be. And not the kind of dead where you get up and walk around with wasps in your head. A flash of goosebumps zipped up his back and George began to shake a little. What if there were more of those things waiting for him behind the screen? Will had said that everyone in town, *everyone* was missing. What if missing meant they were like those things at Loraine's house? An image of the Sams boy flashed across his mind, his eyes whited out, that giant hornet riding his tongue. George heard a strange clacking noise and realized his teeth were actually chattering. His feet had frozen him about halfway down the isle. The circle of illumination from his flashlight wiggled on the screen.

Okay, okay, he was being a bit of a chicken-shit here. But part of his mind had injected the idea—no, the absolute certainty—that at least ten of those (oh, go ahead and think it) *zombies* were waiting for him in the dark. That little fat boy had gotten up after George put three rounds in him at no more than six feet away. He'd gotten up. Howard Sams had gotten up. Will had taken the top half of his skull off with that giant hand-canon of his and Howard Sams had gotten up. The circle of light on the screen was really juking and jiving now.

"Cut it the *fuck* out!" George hissed at himself. Being scared like this for himself was one thing, but he had Erica to worry about. If their situations were reversed she wouldn't just stand here shaking, trying not to piss herself. She'd storm back there, check that George wasn't shoved in some corner somewhere and leave so she could continue searching. He was wasting time, hiding behind his own cowardice. He was better than that. Jesus, he'd quit drinking almost cold turkey not a week and a half ago on the strength of his own will. He could get control of himself now and go find his woman. George took a deep breath. It shook going in but came out smooth and even. He set his jaw and took a step forward.

A pale hand shot out from between the seats just above the floor. It was filled with a ten-inch carving knife. The blade sliced through George's left Achillies tendon like piece of wet cord. White phosphorous flared up his leg and blinded him. George shouted a nonsense syllable and pitched forward, the flashlight rolling out of his hands. It caught on a chair leg a few feet away and stopped, throwing a weird jag of light up the aisle. George managed to roll over on his back while he struggled to unsling the rifle, but he was tangled in the shoulder strap. His eyes widened as T.R. crawled from between the rows of empty seats where he'd been waiting, half his sallow face illuminated by the flashlight. He didn't waste time getting to his feet, but scrambled over George's body. He pressed the knife-edge to George's throat, his face hanging in the dark over George's like a malevolent planet. George could feel the blade part the first layers of skin with a thin sting. Worse he could feel the club-hard erection in T.R.'s pants pressing against his thigh.

"I told you she ain't yours." T.R.'s breath, stale and wet, gassed over George's face. "She's the Outrider's."

George didn't speak. His muscles were locked with adrenaline, the pain from his severed Achillies tendon threatened to take his consciousness. More than anything, he was afraid to move his Adam's apple with the slightest whisper. T.R. was practically *leaning* on that knife. His body felt fevered and wire strong. George was afraid that if he talked he would cut his own throat.

"Oh, you ain't got nothin' to say? I guess you shoulda' died the first time I came calling." He smiled and leaned in even closer, his hard-on digging into George's leg. "I'm kinda happy you didn't die, really. The Outrider told me to use my knife on you, but I didn't listen. The Outrider always knows what's best." T.R. reared up and held the knife two-handed over his head. "Now I'm gonna—!" A loud *thock!* like a baseball thrown hard against a brick wall and T.R. tumbled to the side.

* * *

LORAINE WAS JUST fine with George's decision to leave her and Childe in the car. Kiddo had of course protested at first, saying that he and Darwin could help sniff Erica out just like in the movies, but she was having none of it. (He'd caught her tone and shut it down fast.) It was reckless enough to be sitting curbside while George went into the theatre to search. She had half a mind to just slide over, turn the key and get the hell out of Dodge. But, as her beautiful, wonderful and now a little scarey son had said, things were different now. They couldn't leave Shard. She knew that as surely as she knew the sun would come up in the morning. The world wasn't as she thought it had been. There *were* monsters and, it seemed, heroes to fight them. And frumpy, fifteen pounds overweight, middle-aged Loraine Howard was one of them? Seriously? Oy.

Well, as far as that went, she could be the hero who stayed in the rear and kept watch. It wasn't quite as glamorous as charging in with the light brigade up front, but hell with that. She had a twelve-year-old and a beagle to look after. Hanging out in the car and trying to remember what Constable Will had told her about handling the shotgun was about the most heroic she felt like being at present. Pump it once all the way up and back. Hold it in tight to the shoulder, aim and squeeze the trigger. She kept remembering that scene from *Aliens* where the good-looking solider teaches Sigorney Wever how to use a gun. Loraine laughed to herself. If this little script was relying on her to save the day by blowing away all the bad guys, they were just royally fucked.

"What's funny?" Childe asked from the back seat, sleep pulling at the edges of his voice.

"Nothing, honey. Just thinking 'bout a few things."

"Yeah," Kiddo said. He stretched and turned around to look out the back window. "How long's mister Rhodes been gone do you think?"

"Oh, the grammar. I'm guessing no more than five min—." A shriek ran up out of the door of the theatre and into the night. Loraine and Childe stiffened. Darwin lifted his head, ears perked. Loraine's eyes flicked off the car keys dangling from the steering column. She turned around and grabbed Childe by his shirt. "You *will stay right behind me*, understand?" Childe had never seen her like this before. He smiled. "Yes, ma'am."

* * *

THERE WAS NO Special Forces flourish to their advance. Loraine ordered Childe to hold onto the back of her belt while she marched them straight past the empty lobby and into the theatre. (Dawin had stayed in the car without a whimper of protest. He'd never seen Loraine like that either.) She held the shotgun in front

259

of her more like a big stick than a rifle; her face was set, brow drawn down, teeth clenched. She waded into the gloom and saw that creepy Columbine wannabe' Dalton kid lying on top of George. Loraine Howard, frumpy, fifteen pounds overweight, middle-aged screenwriter from Hollywood California assessed the situation in about a half a second. Dalton knew where Erica was; they needed the little fucker alive. She pulled back and let fly with the stock of the heavy rifle. It connected (*thock!*) against the back of T.R.'s head and sent him sprawling. George looked up at the valkerie outlined in the white glare of his flashlight. "Holy shit, Loraine."

* * *

GETTING KNOCKED OUT is often more of a gray-out than a total loss of consciousness. When Loraine whalloped T.R. he'd gone sprawling and all the juice had run out of his muscles, but he was still aware. That little bitch-boy, Childe, and his mother set T.R. up in one of the movie theatre seats. Everytime they moved him it felt like liquid metal sloshed around inside his head, but he was still too out of it to yell out from the pain. Worse still, the damn buzzing was still there. In fact, being half unconscious was like turning down the volume on everything else in the world so he could really appreciate that godawful sound.

While Loraine and Kiddo busied themselves with T.R., George worked on his tendon. (Kiddo had run back to the car and come back with Darwin and the first aid kit.) It hurt like a smouldering coal under his skin, but he breathed through it. That realization he'd had about giving in to the misery of not drinking seemed to be working with the pain as well. He just didn't fight the flaring stab in his ankle and that made it somehow manageable. That and a few extra cc's of adrenaline can do a world of good. (And to be honest, a part of him was wondering if he could get away with taking a swig from the isopropyl alcohol in the kit.) He sloshed some rubbing alcohol over the wound, expecting it to retaliate with a fresh onslaught of hurt, but it just cooled his skin. He guessed his pain sensors were overloaded. The bleeding was minor, just a slow seep. T.R.'s cut had been surgical and deep, but George didn't think it severed the tendon all the way through. If that had been the case it would have rolled up behind his calf under the skin and so far the back of his leg was stil normal. George wrapped it up with some gauze and an ACE bandage.

Loraine had just finished binding T.R. to his seat with a length of orange extension cord Kiddo had fished out of the office. His head lolled on his neck like a milkweed pod in the wind. George tossed the kit over to Loraine. "Here, smelling salts." She rummaged, pulled out a little ampule and cracked it under his nose. The ammonia hit and T.R. rolled his head to one side, "Buhhhh," he slurred. Loraine chased his nose with the salts and he jerked away. "Buh!" His eyes blinked and focused. "Fuck outta my face with that shit!"

Loraine hopped back a step. T.R. took in all three of them, yanked at his bonds a couple of times to test them and sat back. He smiled at Childe, "When I get loose? I'm gonna' fuck you in your eye socket."

Loraine saw fear stain the edges of on her son's face. She drew back and delivered a resounding smack to T.R.'s cheek.

"Ow!" T.R. stretched his neck at her like a snapping turtle, eyes just as reptilian. "Bitch, I'm gonna'—"

She turned her hand over and backhanded him. The sound bounced around the empty theatre, a single clap. Tears squeezed from T.R.'s eyes. Loraine held her reddened hand up and a question on her face. T.R. flinched away, "Okay, okay." Loraine lowered her hand and soothed in an airy, 1950's flight attendant voice, "Tell us what you did with Erica, or I'll dig your eyes right out of your skull."

T.R.'s lips pressed together and turned white. He looked at George, Childe and finally Loraine. They were serious; they meant to have the information out of him. And as if to dispel any doubt he might have, Loraine added, "Childe, honey, see if you can find your old mother a bucket and a rag. I'm pretty sure I saw a closet marked 'Janitor' back behind the candy counter." Childe took off up the aisle without a word.

"What you gonna' do with that?" T.R. asked. "Clean me to death?"

Loraine tilted her head to one side and bestowed her best Mother Teresa smile, "No sweetheart, I've been working on a screenplay about Guantanimo Bay and I've been itching to see if waterboarding works as well as they say it does."

"Hey!"   T.R.   shouted, "That's against the Geneva Conventions!"

George barked a laugh. "Are you for real?" He shook his head. Nothing was for real anymore. Stupid question. He pegged T.R. to his chair. "Where's Erica, you little creep?"

T.R. turned his head away. Thought about it and turned back to George. "You think I'm more afraid of you," and to Loraine, "or of you, than I am of him? Of the Outrider?" He chuckled. "You don't know what you're dealin' with."

Loraine recognized the crappy bravado for what it was. How many times had she written that line or ones like it? Childe's voice floated back to them, "I found a bucket, but I don't know where we're going to get water."

"Try the little bathroom next to the projection booth," Loraine called. "Just turn the faucet and wait; sometimes the water will take a long time in an abandoned place like this."

"You ain't gonna' get no water outta ' them pipes," T.R said.

"He's right," George said. "Closest water's probably going to be that creek in the woods a few hundred yards across the meadow."

"I know," she said, toying with the broken smelling salts ampule, testing the edge against her thumb. She winced as a drop of blood bloomed. She showed it to T.R. "I just wanted to get Childe out of the room for a minute. He doesn't need to think of his mother this way."

"What way?"

"This way," she said and dropped down on T.R.'s boney lap, facing him, her pelvis pressed against his belly, pinning him down even more. She entwined a claw into his hair and yanked his head back. T.R. started to thrash, but Loraine brought the ampule up to his right eye and stopped. "Hush," she whispered. "You have one chance to save this eye. You need to answer my question and make me believe you. This close? I'll know if you're lying."

George couldn't hear what Loraine was saying, and he wasn't sure he wanted to. This middle-aged writer who looked like she hadn't spent more than twenty minutes in the sun in the past year had turned out to be the hardest bitch George Rhodes had ever encountered in truth or fiction. His mother would have loved her. No, that wasn't fair. Loraine wasn't being hard because it was fun or out of some spite. In fact, from everything he'd ever seen of her, this performance was counter to her nature. She was galvanized. Maybe the strangeness of everything that was happening was finally sinking in and pushing her into an emergency state. Maybe she was just pissed off that this little fucker threatened her boy. Either way, George was damn happy she was on his side.

T.R.'s eyelids fluttered as the residue from the ammonia in the little tube wafted up. "You ain't gonna' do it. You ain't got the stones." That last was more a question than a statement. And once again, Loraine recognized a bad movie line when she heard it. This kid was just that: a kid, and he wasn't fully in the moment, didn't grasp the reality of the situation. Loraine questioned her soul, and found she could do it. She took a breath and muttered to herself, "Close your eyes and think of England."

* * *

CHILDE HOWARD STARED at the dry facuet in the little powder room next to the projectionist booth from just outside the open door. He wasn't about to go in and *stay* in if he didn't have to. Besides, he could barely see as it was and figured he would hear the water if it ever came out. The chances of that happening were pretty slim, as in no freakin' way. Loraine just wanted him out of the way, and you know what? That was totally cool by him. She'd gone into full-on Sarah Connor mode and he didn't feel like hanging out for that. A minute passed, another, and he was just about ready to pack it in and come down when T.R. started screaming. "Oh, God," Childe said. That was his mother doing that. He hugged himself in the dark as competing emotions roiled in his chest—fear of and for his mother, and pride. She was doing this for him. Then a little shame because he was glad, and he loved her for it. He was the one who told her how everything had changed, how it was all different now. Sounded like ol' Loraine had taken that and gone whole hog.

* * *

FIVE MINUTES LATER, Loraine stood back from T.R. and surveyed her handy work. He slumped sideways against his bonds, his boney chest chugging like an old freight train. His left eye was half-lidded and glassy. His right was a red hole. The eye itself lay on the theatre floor, wherever it had rolled to a halt. Loraine's right hand was slick to the elbow. T.R. had bled a lot, but less than she was afraid he might. Wouldn't do if he passed out or expired before he gave them Erica's location. And he hadn't yet.

"Loraine," George said.

She threw a look over her shoulder. In the glow from the flashlight she looked like an extra out of *Carnival of Souls.* "He's gonna' tell us."

"I hear you, but c'mere a second."

Loraine walked over and plunked down in a chair, sending up a small puff of dust and mildew. She wrinkled her nose. "Man, it reeks in here. You can barely smell the sulphur over the mouse shit."

"Guess I stopped smelling the Fire a long time ago. I mean, I can still smell it, but I don't notice it much anymore."

T.R. hitched a sob and moaned on the exhale. He'd go into shock soon if he hadn't already. Loraine craned her neck back up the aisle. "You think Kiddo's doing okay?"

"He's fine. I saw him stick his face in here a few minutes back, but he's hanging out in the lobby. Darwin trotted up there to be with him."

"I don't blame him for keeping his distance," she said. "George?"

"Yeah?"

She lowered her voice so T.R. wouldn't hear. "I can't believe I'm doing this. I fainted when I dissected a fetal piglet in high school. Went right over and clonked my skull on the lab table. But here I am playing Torquemada."

"How you doing?" George looked at T.R. "He going to crack or do we just forget it?"

Loraine looked at him. "Think through what you just said. We 'forget it' and you can forget Erica."

George looked down.

Loraine pulled a deep breath and, the air came out shakey. "I'm not sure I can keep doing this. I dropped that little piece of glass I was using for one."

"And for two?"

"Jesus H, George! I just dug a kid's eye out of his head. Me. I did that." She sat back and shook her head.

"Right," George said. "Shift two coming on for duty." Before she could say anything in protest—and Loraine wasn't sure she would have—George hauled his bulk up. He braced himself on the backs of the row of seats in front of him and limp/hopped toward T.R. He gripped the carving knife T.R. had used on his achillies tendon. In the back of his mind, George was pretty sure it was already too late. So much time had gone by since the afternoon. An image of Erica flashed in his mind—that smile when she said *Wanna join me?* With a detachment that reminded him a lot of how it used to feel when he was tanked on gin, George realized he might kill a young man in the next few minutes. His hand just happened to be at eye-level as he passed Loraine. She grabbed his wrist.

"Loraine, let go. This has to hap—"

"Shut up a second, handsome." She leaned in and squinted at the knife. "George? Who's C. Najarian? Is that—that's Kiddo's school teacher, right?"

"Yeah. Yes, why?"

Loraine sat back and smiled in the gloom. "It's engraved on the knife. Twenty bucks says Erica's stashed at Najarian's house."

Fire lit George's chest and shown in face. He turned to T.R. about to ask if it was true, but already had his answer. The boy was terrified, his remaining eye huge. His head shook back and forth. "Please," he said. "You gotta' kill me now."

Chapter 34

WILL WAS SORELY pissed off at his deputy. George hadn't made contact on the walkie-talkie in over—he checked the dashboard clock—eleven minutes which was exactly six minutes late, or more than twice the amount of time he was supposed to go before checking in. Will thumbed the talk button three times. On George's end, three impatient clicks should squawk alerting said deputy that he was, in fact, lousy at his job. Nothing. Will slammed the walkie-talkie down on the passenger seat. "Shit!"

He stared through the windshield at a crumbling Victorian. The porch drooped at the steps like a swollen lower lip. The front door stood open to the flies and mosquitos, though Shard didn't have very many of the later. Will always figured the fumes from The Fire acted like the world's biggest backyard tiki torch. A tarnished yellow light burned from deep inside, past the front hall. This was the most likely place to start: T.R.'s house.

For a minute he just sat and stared, listening to the engine ticking as it cooled. If T.R. was in there he'd have to know Will was out here by now. In a town as tomb-quiet as Shard, a ladybug couldn't pull up to the curb without announcing itself let alone a two-ton Jeep with a rusty muffler.

But that wasn't the problem because T.R. wasn't in there. Will could feel it. His senses were so turned up the slightest change in the wind or air pressure would shrink his balls. But the night was dead-still, the clouds low. The stars hid behind a blanket of dark purple, little gods that didn't give a sparkly fuck what happened on a blue dot parsecs away. Will wondered if they had impossible creatures on the planets that orbited them like Yïn and Dampf. Did they have alien nightmares about demons like The Pompiliad? Maybe Earth was like Shard: too far away, too small, too damaged to matter. Will whispered to himself, "They got dragons on Alderan?" The sound of his own voice textured his skin with goosebumps.

He was stalling. Sitting here thinking about stars and muttering to himself because he was scared to go in there. It wasn't T.R. that he was worried about. Will would have been happier about going in if he knew it was some burned-out teenager with a .22. That, at least, would be a known quantity. And more than anything else, it would be something killable. He closed his eyes for a second and the image of Howard Sams rushed up out of the dark to meet him: ghastly white skin, puffy sausage fingers reaching... Will shook his head to clear it. He pulled *Smaug* and flicked open the heavy chamber. Six .357 caliber copper eyes stared him in the face, their primers like tiny pupils. He snapped it closed. Aiming for the head, like in the movies, didn't seem to cut it. Howard had gotten up after Will had taken most of his head *off.*

"Giant-flock-of-carnivorous-fucking-cardinals'd do it, though," he muttered. "Too bad I left my giant-flock-of-carnivorous-fucking-cardinals gun back at the station."

Will grabbed the walkie-talkie and clipped it to his belt. He jerked open the car door and pushed out onto the street. Okay, step one completed. The front door of T.R.'s house sprayed that weak yellow light out at him. His foot weighed about eighty pounds as he hauled it over the curb. Step two. The two upstairs windows, dark now, looked out on the yard, on him. His rubber-soled Chucks made almost no sound as he took one step, two, three up the short walk. He raised his pistol in a two-handed grip up next to his head. He hadn't had time to clean his gun since he fired it earlier that night and the tang of cordite still wept from the metal.

Will put his foot on the first step and made himself breathe. He pushed off and put his other foot down on the second step, wringing a hideous creak from the old wood. He froze and flashed his teeth in a wince. He raised his foot again and extended it like a ballerina. Will got an image of himself sneaking like a caracature, stepping on every loud board and shaking like a leaf. Would he step on a rake next and have it fwap up in his face? Whatever was in that house knew he was there already. "This is retarded," he said and settled his weight on the steps.

Will Two-Bears McFarlan took a breath and shouted, "ARMED POLICE!" He stepped up to the front door and broadcast into the house, "Lay down on the floor with your hands on your head!" He didn't for a moment expect anything in there to comply with his order—it was just the closest thing to a battle cry his cop training had to offer under stress. Will didn't do the peeking-around-corners-and-checking-sight-lines Miami Vice thing, he ran straight back through the living room toward the kitchen. He leveled *Smaug* and let off a thunder-blast as he passed what might have been a person standing by the couch. The top of the standing lamp exploded and fell over like a cartoon solider. He didn't stop to look but kept on toward the light source. He jogged around the corner into a hall with a mirror hanging at the end, saw his own reflection and blew it to hell without thinking twice. Will was smilling now, grinning like a wolf. Going in guns blazing *felt good.* He burst into the kitchen and there it was: the corpse of what had to be Rick Becket sitting at the table just as prim as you please. Will had to guess it was Rick because the top half of its body was completely charred. The stink was amazing, but everything smelled like fire and brimstone anyway. Rick's neck crackled as he turned his head toward Will.

Will leveled his hand-cannon, "Just one of you, huh?"

Rick's jaw unhinged and his tongue unfurled; the Wasp that rode it was as big as a man's thumb.

Will took three steps *toward* Rick, "Uh-uh, buddy," and used the barrel of his gun to shove the wasp back down Luther's throat. Rick gagged and but that was all the protest Will allowed. He unloaded the remaining four bullets into Rick's head directly through his mouth. The first vaporized the wasp and a good portion of Rick's neck. In spite of Will's firm grip, the gun kicked up and back with every trigger pull and thus destroyed the rest of Rick's head from jaw, to nose, to forehead. When the gun dry clicked, Will stepped back, deaf and hauling in breath after breath. What was left looked less like it had been shot and more like someone had fed the top half of it into a wood chipper.

Will didn't wait around like one of those cows in a horror movie. He snapped open the chamber, reloaded with a blur of fingers and shells and whipped it closed again. This was the part of the movie where the hero (or large breasted blonde, if you prefer) gets it in the back by the other badguy/monster.

Will faced the door into the kitchen and listened. He didn't especially like having his back to what was left of Rick Becket, but that hunk of overdone steak wasn't getting up again. The trick seemed to be not just blowing away the entire brain but the wasp as well. It was like the wasps were driving them. A shiver ran up and over Will's shoulders. *Note to George Romero*, he thought, *head shot alone not enough*. The house was stone-quiet. Will held his breath and listened for the slightest tick or creak. Nothing.

The walkie-talkie on his belt brayed, "Will. Hey, Will! Two-Bears, you there or what?"

Will fumbled the walkie off his belt and thumbed the talk button, "I'm here, Georgie." He wiped his brow with his wrist and blew a long, shaking exhalation. "I'm at the Jean's house. Where're you guys? Everyone okay?"

"We're fine," George crackled. "We're in the car now headed over to old Charlotte Najarian's place. We found T.R. Or, rather he found us. Anyway, we left him—what would you call it, Kiddo?" Will could hear the boy offer, "Secure?" Then George again, "Yeah, we left him *secure* as a psycho-killer extension corded to a movie theatre seat, or a bug in a rug, whichever you please. Anyway, we're pretty sure Erica's at Najarian's. We oughta' be there in about five minutes."

"On my way," Will said and looked at the mess he left at the table. "And Georgie, be careful. I ran into another one of those things like the Sams kid. Had a big wasp in its mouth, uh, and everything."

"Jesus. Who was it?"

"Pretty sure it was Rick Becket." Will paused a second and thumbed the talk button. "Listen, George? I want to make sure all three of you can hear me."

Loraine and Childe Howard chimed in, "We're here. We hear you."

"Yeah, right here, Constable Will."

"Okay," Will sighed. He didn't like talking this way to a kid, especially one who'd just seen his best friend, well, the way he'd seen him. "You have to kill the wasp and take the person's head off," he said and winced. Will glanced back at Rick, gone from the shoulders up. "Remember with Howie Sams we just got him in the head a couple of times and he kept coming? I'm not even sure what happened with the wasp. Anyway, Rick's down and it was because I took his head clean off *and* killed the wasp."

Silence from the walkie-talkie.

Will frowned. "You all copy me?"

"We heard you, Will," George said. "We're just throwing up."

Will smiled. That they were joking meant they weren't beat. Not even close. Which was good because he had the idea this was just the beginning. "All right, I want you three to wait for me just down the block from Najarian's place. George, I know you want to storm in and see if Erica's there, but I'm begging you, man, don't do it until I get there." Silence. "Loraine? Don't you let him go in until I get there, you here me?"

Loraine came on, "Oh, I won't," she said and for a moment Will wasn't sure he was hearing the same woman he knew. That Loraine Howard was dowdy and a little hippy-dippy, totally laid back. Will had attended a lecture, a kind of cop continuing education credit course in Louisville a few years back on Special Weapons and Tactics. The admin had been a decent enough guy, affable, but there had been an edge to his voice like his mind was ready to deploy around a situation like a machine. Loraine had that sound now, like she was tensed and ready but tired.

"See you in five," Will said. "Over. Out."

He clipped the walkie back on his belt, holstered *Smaug* and jogged toward the front door. It was standing open and the lights from the Jeep sprayed into the living room. Humidity and car exhaust had found their way into the house. He could smell cut grass and the hydrocarbons of burning fuel from the car and the mine below. God Shard was weird—all the contrasts of destruction and poison on top of the clean and natural. Maybe it made sense that it would be some kind of nexus point between worlds. Will loved this town, had since he was younger than Childe Howard, and it broke his heart. Made sense, though, he guessed. A thing so beautiful and isolated from the rest of the world had to have a cost. He just wished it wasn't so damn high.

He stepped off the front porch. A white hand reached from under the steps and snapped shut around his ankle. Will pitched forward and caught himself in a painful push-up with a surprised, "Shit!" Young Luther Becket scrambled out from the crawlspace, all flailing limbs and grasping fingers. He flowed up Will's body and pushed his open mouth right next Will's ear. In a strange moment of stillness, Will could hear the wasp rustling forth from the back of the dead boy's throat.

Luther's little hands were strong as iron clasps and he seemed to weigh three times what he should. Will could only move his head. In another second, the wasp was going to chew a hole through his cheek or bore into his ear and he'd become one of those mindless things. Will Two-Bears McFarlan stopped breathing. He felt the pornographic caress of the wasp's antennae against his face. For a moment he almost smiled. He couldn't believe what was about to happen, but he could at least face it head on. He snapped his head to the side facing Luther and stared into his gaping maw, open much wider than was possible without unhinging the jaw. The wasp was enormous. It brushed Will's lips with its mandibles and he opened his mouth. Luther's fingers, arms and legs constricted, even more. A tear squeezed from Will's eye as he felt the little monster poke its head and thorax past his front teeth, felt it step onto his tongue. Will bit down, slicing the wasp in half.

The taste of tar, acid, rot from the underside of a hundred dead logs filled his mouth and nose. He would have eaten an oily clod of dirt to cleanse it. Luther recoiled and Will spat the still spasming insect back into the boy's mouth where its lower half was already dying. In its death throes the wasp's abdomen stung Luther's tongue, the inside of his cheek, the roof of his mouth and soft palette. The boy rolled away from Will, clawing at his own face and grunting. Luther hooked the insect's remains from his mouth and stood.

Will gained his feet and drew *Smaug*. The headlights from the Jeep gave him a white aura and illuminated his target: Luther Becket, slow now and confused without his driver. Will leveled his gun at a boy who should have been able to grow up, get a job, fall in love. Two-Bears spat in the dust and cocked the hammer back. "C'mere," he said.

Chapter 35

THE NAJARIAN HOUSE stained the night. The once elegant Victorian used to sit on the corner like a prim southern belle in a hundred yards of bubbling crinalin, all perfect landscaping and gingerbread. But sometimes evil shows its mass and bears down on a place, begins to push it through into somewhere else. Will parked the Jeep across the street and leaned against the door panel. How in hell had he not seen it before? The house was fucking *leering* at him, daring him to charge in and save the day. It would be okay, all he had to do was his best and the universe would take care of him because that's what was fair and right and bullshit. The house was like a slow-eyed teenager, egging Will into a fist fight while hiding a switchblade behind its back.

Headlights flashed to his left.

Will waved at the Suburu squatting a few houses down. The doors flung open and what was definitely *not* the A-Team piled out. Two-Bears couldn't help but smile for a second—Loraine, pear-shaped and hard with her (and it *was* hers now) 12-gauge at port arms; Kiddo, gallumping along in that awkward puppy gate, his limbs getting too big for his brain, a long kitchen knife in his belt like he was playing pirates; Darwin trotting behind, game as hell. And dear George, who after half a life of poisoning himself had gained back much of his vitality. Will had forgotten how tall his friend was and now that George had gained some weight, the spread of his shoulders was impressive. He looked like a football player again. Limping a little, but steady enough. The M16 was strapped across his back like he'd been born with it. (Well, to be fair, just about everyone from around here was born with some kind of firearm near to chubby little hand—can you say G'bless America?) The A-Team they weren't, but damn they might rate at least a B+.

Will leaned back against the Jeep and crossed his arms over his chest. Kiddo drew up next to him and copied his posture right down to the disaffected smirk. Loraine stared at the house. George stared at Will.

"She's in there man. We gotta' move."

"I know it, Georgie, but I reckon she's not by herself."

Kiddo asked, "How many people used to, you know, live here. In Shard, I mean?"

"Before The Fire?" George said.

"Yeah, and after."

"There were almost a thousand folks in this town during its heyday," George said. He didn't like having his back to the house, felt like flies on his neck. He faced it and continued, "I suspect there were about thirty-five or forty of us as near as last month." He took a big inhale of night air, filling his chest with honeysuckle and sulphur. "That sound about right to you, Sheriff? Around forty?"

Will was checking the cylinder of his revolver. He spun and flicked it shut with a flourish he'd practiced in alone his office hundreds of times. "It was exactly thirty-three not two weeks ago."

Loraine spoke up, "You think most of them are in there?"

Will considered, nodded. "Maybe. I think it's a little less more like. Folks seemed to've been drifting away from town over the past several days, not many, but some. When I went around the other day, there were a few cars missing." He paused and shook out his hands. "But not enough to make this easy. There could be one or two of them in there, which is bad enough, but I get the feeling this is some kind of, I dunno'."

"Nest," Loraine said.

"Hive," Kiddo corrected.

"Sure, hive. That fits," Will said. "Freaks me out just a little more than I already was, but yeah. You sure Erica's in there?"

George shrugged. "She has to be."

Will looked at him a second. She has to be or what, Georgie? "Well, we can't just go in there blasting away. There's every chance we'd hit her by accident."

"Where's your pet nightmare giant spider when we need it?" George said.

"I'm sorry, my what? My pet? Are you fucking kidding me?" Will blushed. "Sorry, Kiddo. Sorry, Loraine."

She waved him off, "At this point? Oh, please."

"Seriously, though, Will. Can't you, I don't know, summon it or something?"

"No, George, I really can't. Besides, I got the feeling Yïn's probably back underground with the dragon." He shook his head. Knee deep in quasi-possessed living dead and Will still couldn't get his mind around a dragon. "I think that's where we're going to need to get to if we get through this."

"Why?" Loraine asked. "I mean, can't the *dragon* take care of itself?"

"If that were the case," Will said, "I doubt any of us'd be here right about now."

Darwin nosed the air and let out a yap toward the house. He looked up at Childe, his tail high and ears perked. "What's up?" Kiddo asked. "You smell somethin'?" Childe took a deep pull of night air and his brow crinkled. He took another to be sure. The adults were arguing about who would go in which door or something when Kiddo interrupted, "Hey, guys?"

Loraine turned, "Not now, honey."

"No, mom, seriously. I think I smell smoke. Darwin does, too."

George put a hand on his shoulder, "That's Shard, buddy. You're pretty much always going to smell some species of smoke. You ought to be used to it by now."

Kiddo shook him off. "No, Mr. Rhodes. It's not the same thing." He looked over at the Najarian house. "I think maybe that house is on fire."

Will glanced over at the front porch while taking in a lungful of air through his nose. Something was burning and it wasn't underground. He squinted and thought he caught a flirt of yellow through the kitchen window, like a woman in a dress rounding a corner. "I, uh, I think Kiddo's right."

That's when the parlor windows blew out in a spray of little stars. The eyes of the house lit orange and flashed at them. The heat ran across the street and blew the hair off their foreheads. Will felt the spit on his lips dry, his skin tighten.

George screamed, *"Erica!"*

And everything went right straight to hell.

* * *

ERICA NEVER FELT the butt of T.R.'s rifle connect with her skull. One moment she was watching herself writhing in the agony of George's murder—the very picture of a hundred thousand women on the news in Gaza, in Iraq, in Harlem, beating their chests and shrieking for the loss—the next moment she was here. Here was nowhere: a vast dead plain of gray hardscrabble under a low, leaden sky. Everyone who has ever walked in a field of flowers or lay down in grass would know the place simply because of what it was not—it was the wastelands and it was forever.

She walked toward the horizon, away from the memory of George's shy smile in the morning over coffee at his kitchen table, the Appalachian caramel of his voice. Her feet threw up little puffs of steel-colored dust as she trudged away from George's strong hands on her body, the fine lines next to his eyes, her smile reflected in them. Head down, arms down, hair lank and swinging, Erica moved away from him because if she tasted even a trace of the feeling she'd found, she would go mad. The whole side of his face had been a sheet of blood and he had been still. Erica loosed a cry, a flutter of pain like a sparrow finding an open window in a warehouse. The strange atmosphere enveloped the sound and dropped it to the earth.

She looked up. Earth. Did this place qualify for that descriptor? No, this was Planet Elsewhere. The clouds flowed in and out of each other in random currents, more smoke than vapor and with no wind to push them. Erica's eyes followed an upside down creek of cloud toward the horizon. Now she marched with her head back and her mouth wide open, eyes on the roiling sky. George would've known what to call a cloud formation like that. Here was this guy living in the middle of nowhere who seemed to know a little something about everything. His mind emptied out on the pillow.

Erica stopped and squeezed her eyes shut. A gutteral sound, like a hit to the stomach, lurched over her tongue. She shook her head to clear it of George, but he stayed, he held her. If she'd had a knife she would have opened her own chest to tear out the aching, beating thing. She opened her mouth to scream and opened her eyes.

It was good that she had stopped. What she thought was the horizon had been an optical illusion. She had marched herself to the razor edge of a high cliff. Erica gasped and looked down. A hundred feet down, a thousand feet, ten thousand and then... Not blackness, not darkness. Not even death. It was beyond the end of those things. And it pulled. "Look, ma," Erica whispered. "The Abyss."

There was no central mass on which to focus, no tendril of color to differentiate a swirling eddie from a still pool. It wasn't even the color black as she had always understood it. Even the deep behind one's eyes in the midnight dark is shot through with images, flashes of the mind. This was pure nothing. Erica imagined this was what a black hole must be like, something so powerful that not even light could espcape. But instead of a star slowly unraveling its glowing plasma wrapper at the event horizon, Erica felt the outer layers of herself begin to strip and flow over the edge. She got a flash of George's face, scowling over some op-ed piece in the *Times*, and felt it fall away into the chasm.

Her right foot dislodged a pebble and she watched it tumble and flip out of existence. Would it be so easy if she followed? Could she skip the process of slow stripping at the edge and cease this pain imediately?

A deep cold rippled up her spine. Something, someone was behind her, its presence pushing a mass of decrepitude and frost. Its foosteps were heavy, like those of a giant; she could feel their bass thud in her feet and chest as it approached. Erica felt the shape of a man invade her peripheral vision, but could not bring herself to look. It was tall, but bent at the shoulders, dark hair cascaded like tar. She heard the creak of leather. It was silent as the abyss below.

After a long time, Erica heard herself whisper, "Can I help you?"

It made a sound that might be classified as laughter. It made Erica's teeth hurt. "Help me?" The Pompiliad considered, "You will. It's true."

Erica wanted to look at it full on, but fear bridled her. The skin on the arm nearest this *person* was alternately hot and cold, clamy and desiccated. "Huh-how will I help you?"

"Your body will be a cornicopia and give birth to new gods." It turned its great dark eyes on her, "Many gods." Erica's spine was stiff as glass, her joints frozen as it lifted a limp finger to her cheek. Sickness and sleep pulsed off it like stink. Her eyes grew heavy. It would be so easy to slip over the edge. "Go then," the Pompiliad said. "Fall away into nothing. We don't need your mind, just your perfect machine." The finger caressed her jaw line and dripped down her neck, over her shoulder and traced the swell of her breast. Her nipple hardened and burned.

She sensed a change and was able to look over. George stood next to her, his good, strong hand on her body. But this wasn't George. His touch made Erica feel like she was set free of some self-manufactured armor; this creature's contact made her want to bury herself in steel and stone. It was wearing George's likeness like a salesman wears a suit. Deep within her an ingot began to heat and glow red. Her blood warmed and her eyes narrowed. She turned to face it full on and the human mask dropped away.

A bruise-colored blur burst from its shoulders like an eruption of nerve gas. It was accompanied by a low, thrumming buzz that got into Erica's head and twisted like a knot. The arms melted into the torso and six chitin spears thrust through the rib cage, segmented and became insectile legs. The waist cinched thin as Erica's wrist as if some invisible lariat yanked tight. The clothes melded with skin and all turned a slick, hard black. The head elongated and cruel pincers gnashed the slow air. Twin reflections of Erica bent in its obsidian crystal ball eyes. Her gaze drew down and along the obscenity at the end of its abdomen: a foot-long chitin dagger dripping with some viscous fluid.

When it spoke, the sound was like sheet metal blown over sand. *"You will help us. You will mother us. You will be queen to the hive."*

She threw up her hands and backed off a step. A piece of the hardpan cracked and slid away from under her heel. Erica glanced back in time to stop herself from backing over the edge. Somehow the giant wasp-thing had herded her toward the abyss. She hadn't even noticed moving before now. Maybe she hadn't. Maybe the strange ground had reconfigured under her. All horrors seemed possible here. "Wait!" she tried, her mind side-slipping into lawyer mode, "If you need me to help you, how can you throw me over the edge?"

The terrible pincers clicked and stuttered off each other like castanets. It thrust the air with its stinger, but Erica had no more room to back off. Her brow drew down. It was laughing at her. That ingot in her gut grew hotter.

"We don't need your mind," it repeated, *"just your perfect machine."*

Erica looked down at her feet and realized for the first time that she was naked. She felt no need to cover herself, she wasn't cold and the thought of feeling shame in the face of such abomination was absurd. Her brain began to run over this jibberish about her mind and machine, began to find pattern. It if could throw her over the edge into that great nothing and still have her body then it followed that anything that happened here had nothing to do with her body. It was a dream, or a nightmare, or some coma universe. Either way—"This isn't real."

Erica's head snapped up. She faced her doubled self in its eyes and repeated, "This isn't real. I'm not really here." The wasp retreated a couple feet, floating under a flickering cloud of purple wings. Erica advanced a step away from the edge. "This is all in my mind, is that it? Some dream? And you want me to toss myself, *my mind*, over the edge into that, that shit?" She turned and spat into the abyss. "You disgusting *puta madre*. What? You get my body after you convince me to empty my own head?" The Pompiliad retreated further and seemed somehow smaller, the volume of its wings muted. Erica advanced on it, her dream-muscles taught and her fists clenched into hammers. "You killed George, didn't you? It wasn't really that kid at all. It was you." Hot tears burst over her eyelids, flowed over her cheeks and hit the ground with a sound like nails on tin. "I was just starting to find my life and you took my one true good away from me."

The wasp halted and blurred. Again the figure of George Rhodes stood tall and beautiful before her. Erica gasped from the pain in her chest. "Cruel," she whispered.

"We will still have your machine, but now you will have to live through it," it said. "We came here as a mercy."

It became still and its skin turned gray as the dust at their feet. Cracks zig-zagged up from its boots to its head. A shudder ran the length of it and it fell apart in dirty chunks like a shattered mud statue. The wind picked up in a fierce gust and grabbed every last piece of grit, blowing the Pompiliad away. When the wind died down, Erica stood alone in a world of her own making. She thought of George again, *her* George not some demonic replicant, and felt more heat from that ingot. It was white now.

"Wake up, chica," she said to herself. "Wake up."

And for a wonder, she did.

* * *

ERICA'S EYES OPENED to near total dark. She could make out the earthen cellar and the old wood stairs leading out. What light there was spilled down from wherever they led, a kitchen she imaginged. Her arms and legs weren't bound, but she was encased in something that restricted her movement to just a few inches here and there. An open strip at her eyes allowed her to breathe and see out. It was like she was in one of those mummy sleeping bags but standing up. Her eyes widened as she made out the holes in the walls and their inhabitants. Most of the cellar was honeycombed and each cell was stuffed with a person. Some of them were slotted in like bodies in a morgue, but about half were facing out, their heads tilted up or back depending on whether they lay on their backs or stomachs. Those who faced out had white, empty eyes like the *people* she had seen at the little village in the woods.

Panic rose in her throat and wanted to flutter out in a scream, but she bit down on it. Bit her tongue pretty good, too, and the blood filled her mouth with iron and anger. This was the world of physical things (perfect machines) but she had brought that glowing piece of steel back with her. She drew on it now and pushed against the mud casing, but it was thick and hard. Her brain began to run over everything she had: the creature in her mind, the things in the walls. Wasps. They were like wasps. How did wasps build nests? Her mind threw a Discovery Channel image of a yellow and black insect daubing mud in little rows to construct cells for its larvae. They chew. Oh, Jesus. She was going to have to chew her way out.

She shoved her upper jaw forward in a ridiculous overbite and was just able to get the leading edge of her teeth on the bottom lip of the eye slit. She began to scrape, slowly and carefully at first. Erica Mendez wasn't about to go through the death of the man she loved and an escape from dream-hell just to die because she chipped her damn teeth. She had to make it. That thing was coming and it had plans for her *machine*. A piece of the casing crumbled into her mouth. It tasted like old, stale dirt and her mouth filled with saliva so fast her glands hurt. She spat it to the side and glanced at the staring faces of the wasp people. They were still. She was able to get more of a purchase now and took a serious bite. A piece of mud-cement the size of a pie plate tumbled away. She stifled a little cheer. She could get her whole head out now. She tapped her chin against the crust and a felt another large section give way. It wasn't dry yet! That was it. If she'd stayed unconscious for what, another twenty minutes, there'd have been no chance.

A few minutes later, Erica was stepping away from the shattered cocoon, padding barefoot toward the stairs. Her bare skin was covered in grime and goosebumps. She placed one foot on the lower riser and stopped as her eye caught on something. A small pyramid of old paint cans squatted behind the stairs. At their base, a smaller can. She glanced over her shoulder. Multiple pairs of cotton eyes stared back, but made no movement. She caught the smell now: rot, sugar, slime and damp. She reached through the risers and grabbed the little can. She brushed the dust off the ancient lable but her nose already told her what was inside. Paint thinner.

Erica found the kitchen empty and dark save for the single fluorescent strip over the sink. That little fucker with the gun must have left it on when he brought her here. Where was he now? She shuddered thinking of his hands on her naked skin. The house was utterly silent except for her breathing and the thunder of her pulse. She found a rag hanging over the handle of the oven door. She opened the refrigerator and found a mostly empty bottle of white wine. She smiled. It was fancy grape juice not wine. She emptied it into the sink and then poured in the paint thinner. She scowled at the rag then splashed some of the paint thinner—the fumes making her grimace—onto the rag before stuffing one end of it into the neck of the bottle. There: her very first Molotov cocktail. Wouldn't Momma be proud?

She grabbed the box of matches (Diamond Head – Strike Anywhere!) and scratched one against the counter. The smell of sulphur flared in her nose as light flared from the single flame. It resonated with what she held in her belly. This would be for her and for George. Another smell came to her then, overpowering the match. The stink of damp rot and cold flowed over her shoulders. A riser creaked behind her. Erica spun around to find a man in his early thirties with dark, close cropped hair. He was huge, at least six and half feet tall and damn near half as much across the chest. His thick, muscular neck showed a ragged wound as if it had burst open from the inside. His eyes were blanks. He reached for her with powerful hands, grass stains on his fingers and lines of black dirt under his nails.

The match burned her finger and Erica gave the luckiest flinch of her life. She made to bat out the flame with her other hand, but it was full of Molotov cocktail. The guttering match caught the rag and it burst into bright flame. Erica let out a, "Whoa!" and backed up a step, holding the bottle out in front of her. The wasp man advanced a step, his fingers flexing. He meant to take her back into the dark.

"No! No more!" she shouted and threw the bottle at his head. It connected and shattered. Liquid flame cascaded over his face and shoulders and within seconds his entire torso was engulfed. A black column of acrid smoke pounded the ceiling and spread out. The wasp man still stood but couldn't seem to find Erica through the flames. She grabbed a chair from the kitchen table like a lion tamer. This was her only shot. Erica screamed, *roared* and charged him. She powered into him and he tumbled down the stairs, a pinwheeling torch. Erica noticed the latch on the cellar door. She slammed and locked it. "Burn, you fucks!"

No more screwing around. She bolted for the front door. A slim door stood off to one side. Coat closet? She took a moment to wrench it open and there was the ubiquitous raincoat that all flashers must wear when streaking out into the haunted Appalachian night. She was just zipping it up when the paint cans at the bottom of the stairs exploded, shattering the glass in all the front windows. It felt like a giant had picked up the house a few feet and dropped it back down again. Erica grabbed the front doorknob and yanked it open. George Rhodes stood there, the real George Rhodes.

Neither of them said anything for a moment and then they both said, "Oh."

Chapter 36

THE VICTORIAN BURNED and the little group of survivors watched it from across the street. The lawn was long and the street was wide, but the heat made it almost intolerable. George stood behind Erica, gently draped around her. She leaned into him, but kept watch on the house. She half expected them to come crawling out, writhing in fire, but unstoppable. There were flames in her eyes. George muttered quietly in her ear, explaining everything, holding nothing back. She listened and nodded. Nothing was impossible in this strange place, not after what she'd seen. She could feel a part of her mind ranting, counter arguing, attempting control over these insanities, but let it be. By the time George got to the part about the spider and the dragon that rational voice sounded as if it came from down a long hall.

The fire licked along the old wood siding, outlining the gutters and belching windows. The intricate gingerbread and moulding stood out in flickering relief. About twenty minutes after Erica and George ran from the front steps, the glowing roof collapsed with a deep *fwoom!* Childe Howard looked at Will and asked, "What should we do now?"

Every face turned to Will. For a moment he felt pushed at, angry. He wanted to say *How the fuck should I know?* Instead he let his mind run over the available data. "Erica," he asked, "how many of those, uh, people were down there?"

George hugged her a little tighter. "I'm not sure," she said. "There could have been almost twenty of them, but about half of those honeycomb cells were empty."

Will nodded, considered. "Okay, to be safe we gotta assume we're dealing with about twenty to twenty-five more of them."

"That doesn't add up," George said. "Remember Will? We just talked about how there were no more than thirty-three people even left in Shard. We saw three get taken out at the Howard's

283

house, you took down Rick Becket over at the Jean's and their psycho kid's all trussed up in the movie theatre. That's five down from thirty-three right there, leaving twenty-eight. If Erica torched close to twenty of them that leaves less than ten."

Will shook his head. "No. I'm pretty sure that leaves more like twenty-four."

"But—"

Will held up his hand. "You remember when I had to go out of town to help the Sheriff a little while back with those migrants? There were fourteen of them and they'd all been killed. Eyes were whited out when we found 'em." He looked at his Chucks and shook his head. "Jesus, one of them bust out his own throat. Trying to get the wasp, I guess."

Erica looked up.

"Anyway," Will continued, "they all disappeared from the morgue. My guess is they came on down here."

Loraine got an image of fourteen souls shambling through the woods at night, making their ponderous way to Shard. "It's so lonely," she said.

"What?" Will asked.

"Nothing, Constable. You were saying there were closer to twenty-four of them left?"

"Right, yeah. So, what I think we need to figure out is…" He trailed off, head cocked. "You all hear that?"

Kiddo said, "Is that—?"

A motorcycle rumbled around the corner five blocks up the street. The single headlight lanced through the dark and picked them out like deer in a field.

"It's here," Will said. "It's the Pompiliad."

The engine revved, staccato and echoing off the dark houses.

George hissed, "Fuck do we do?"

"Run!" Will shouted, already moving around the front of the big Jeep. "Go! Get in your car and head to the jail. It's the safest place. George, Erica, you're with me."

Loraine nodded and sprinted toward the Subaru, grabbing her son by the elbow as she went. Kiddo picked up the pace and Darwin zipped along ahead of them. The cyclopian headlight disfigured their shadows on the pavement in front of them. Loraine had her keys out and ready. No fumbling at the ignition while the monster drew down on them like those idiots in the movies. She slammed into the driver's seat, heard Childe thunk shut his door and laid a respectable strip of rubber on the pavement. "Okay, Kiddo?" she asked as she rounded the corner and floored it.

"Yeah," he said, panting. "Yeah, I'm okay. So's Darwin." Childe twisted in the seat. "I don't think it's behind us anymore."

"Good." Loraine took a left on Main.

Childe looked up and down the street. Constable Will's Jeep burst out of a side street and came to a rocking halt in front of the jail. He was just able to catch one of the doors opening before the Subaru went over a little rise in the road and he lost sight of them. "Mom, we gotta go the other way. The jail's back there."

Loraine's face was lit from below by dashboard werelight. She looked as stern as a statue of a saint. "Not us, honey boy. We're splitsville."

"But what about George and Will and Erica? We can't leave them!"

"We can and we are. We did more than our part by helping find Erica." She saw the stop sign that marked the end of Main Street and the beginning of the two-lane feeder road that wound along the creek and through the mountains to civilization. They were a scant two hours from arc sodium lights and bad food. Solid things. "We'll call the police and send them back to Shard when we get to the first real town."

"But the Wasp Man's going to kill them, Loraine! For fuck's sake!"

Loraine's shoulders dropped a little. It wasn't his curse or that he made her feel guilty. Nothing about getting her son away from that bedlam could make her feel like anything less than mother of the year. What got her was the adultness of it. Little Childe Howard, her honey boy, had aged into something like manhood in the space of a few hours. She'd protected his physical body—he didn't have a scratch on him—but his innocence was toast. She sighed, "Constable Will can take care of himself."

She stopped at the intersection. Front: deep woods that plunged down to a black water stream. Right: one of the old mining roads, single lane gravel track that led into the hills, tall green weeds fringing its crown. Left: gravel bled into two-lane blacktop, the faded double yellow line stretched into the night.

Loraine began to turn and stopped as the headlights pushed back the dark. Childe whispered, "Uh-oh."

Walkers, at least six or seven of them. Loraine recognized the Dalton's boy's parents. Everyone called them The Pair of Jeans. They were lugging a piece of rusted pipe across the road—no, it was an old transaxel from a car or a pick-up truck. (Loraine was no engineer or mechanic but guessed that thing had to weigh five hundred pounds.) There was that nice old lady who ran Shard's pathetic excuse for a general store, Meg Tooley. Her long gray hair swung down in her face as she bent over and dragged a fallen tree, the root ball trailing clods of fresh dirt. Jesus, had she pulled that out of the ground? It was as big as a streetlight. A few more were blocking the road with various detritus from town or the woods.

"Mom," Kiddo whispered. "What do we do?"

Loraine was already slotting the gear selector into R. The back-up lights sprayed illumination behind them and her hopes of getting back to the jail died. Four or five more of them had already blocked the road behind her. One of them, she couldn't tell who, was pushing an old car all by himself. There were no tires. He had his fish white hands splayed on the back bumper and his back arched so deeply that his belly nearly dragged the ground. His plaid shirt had come untucked and in the dim light Loraine made out the shine of an appendix scar.

She threw the car in D and thanked whatever gods were getting their jollies messing this hard with them that Subaru made cars with all-wheel drive. She sprayed gravel as they bounced to the right and up the mining road into the labrynth. After about thirty yards, the trees ate the sky and the only sound was the hum of the engine, the pop of gravel under their tires and the hiss of the weedy strip caressing the undercariage. Loraine hoped that one of these roads branched off and would lead them back to the feeder road by some other route, or even over the ridge and onto another road.

After a few minutes of quiet, Childe said, "You know they made us go this way, right?"

For about half a second, she felt like smacking those beautiful blonde curls right off the top of his head. "Yes, I know." Loraine breathed. "There was nothing else I could have done."

"We could have gone to the jail with everyone else."

Loraine had the urge to laugh and say *Young man, I'll turn this car right around!* but it died as they came to the first fork in the road. Loraine pulled to a stop. For a while, they just stared at the identical gravel tracks leading into more night. "In the old cartoons, you'd spit in your palm and then hit it with your index finger," she said. "The bigger lugi-half was supposed to point the way."

"That's nasty, mom."

"Okay, which way then, smart guy?"

"Left."

"Why left?"

"Feels like it's leading away from town."

"Thought you wanted to go back to town."

"I do," he looked out the window. "But if we end up back in town, you'll just turn around again. Saves time this way. So, left."

"Good 'nuff," she said and pulled forward. She stopped again as soon as the headlights shown full on in front. A giant spiderweb stretched across the road. It caught the light and held it like a thousand, twinking moths. Childe could actually see the goosebumps on his mother's forearms. This wasn't just some pretty, gossimer weave. Each strand was as thick around as airplane cable. There'd be no driving through that. "I guess we go right," she whispered.

* * *

WILL ALMOST SMASHED the Jeep into his motorcycle as he screeched to a stop outside of the jail. For one icy second he was sure it wasn't his bike but the low-slung chopper The Pompiliad was riding. Will had only gotten a look at the headlight when the chopper rumbled around the corner a minute or so ago, but he remember what it looked like from his dream—black, cinch-waisted, a machine version of its rider's true face. But the Indian Chief, his father's bike now his, was white and gleamed like pearl in the headlights from the Jeep. Calm gelled over his thoughts. He glanced in the rearview mirror. The chopper's single glowing eye burned a few blocks back.

"Go, go, go," he said, piling George and Erica out of the Jeep. He slapped them both on the butts like a couple of wayward calfs, but they were already moving like, well, a wasp was after them.

They shoved inside. Will turned the key in the steel door and slid a bolt as thick as a big man's thumb. He took a few steps back and unholstered *Smaug*. George unslung his M16.

"Look at you, Rambo," Erica said. "Got one of those for me?"

George raised his eyebrows. "Will?"

Will kept his eyes on the night outside, but said, "Sorry, guys. We had a shotgun but Loraine's got it. Did you guys see her and Kiddo?"

"Yeah," George said. "They were hauling ass up Main when we came 'round the corner. I think she's making a break for it."

"Can't blame her," Erica said. "Maybe that's what we should have done."

"I don't think they're gonna get very far," Will said. "That thing out there and its little militia won't let them."

Erica nodded at the windows. "Can it, they, you know, get in here?"

Will threw a little half smile at her. "Not without a rocket launcher. This old jail was built before the unions got any real hold in this part of the world. Coal town uprisings were common and violent back in the day. There's double thick wire mesh on all the windows, the walls are cinder block and the roof's fireproof. The front and back doors are solid steel. I've even got a little food stockpiled in the pantry." His eyes went away as he remembered cooking hotplate omelettes for him and George too many nights to count. They'd eat and play chess while George sobered up. "We should be okay in here for a while."

"What happens when the food runs out?" Erica asked.

Will turned around and poked his best friend in the shoulder, "We eat George."

George grinned and gave him the finger.

Erica walked over to the window, her arms crossed over her chest. It was a warm night but she was a little cold in just the raincoat. George asked, "Will, we got any clothes for Erica? I'm not feeling very southern or gentlemanly making her walk around in just that coat."

"Matter of fact, we do. I got some spair stuff in back. Least a pair a jeans and a tee-shirt. I'll go look in a minute." He walked over and stood next to Erica. "He out there?"

"I don't see him, but that's doesn't mean he's not there." She squinted hard into the night, as if her will could be a flare against the dark. "He was right on top of us, right?"

George joined them. "Maybe he broke off and went after Kiddo and Loraine." He shook his shaggy head. "Man, I hope they made it out."

Will set his teeth and backed into the room. "Okay, class, let's take stock."

Erica and George turned around. Will took a good long look at them: dirty, tired, hurt and standing. He surpressed smile. "Okay, we got two guns and plenty of ammo. We got food and water."

He sat down at his desk and clunked the big pistol down on the blotter. He loved them; that's why it pained him to lie like this. He had no intention of staying put in this little fortress for any longer that it would take for them to get their act together. They still had work to do. The fight was outside and he had a feeling that eventually it would be underground. His job now was to manipulate them both around to helping him. It was the right thing to do in the bigger picture, but it made him feel like his skin was covered in oil. Right now their eyes were still showing a little too much white, but after he got them to back down a notch or two, they could start planning together. For one evil second, he wished he had a little something for George to drink.

"Georgie? How you feeling?"

"Like my foot was half cut off and I haven't had a drink in eight days, nine hours and forty-three minutes." Erica put her arms around him and squeezed. George got a whiff of her hair, and past the mingled smells of stale earth and paint thinner he could still smell her. "I'm doing okay, though."

"Erica?"

She didn't let go, but turned her dark eyes on Will. He didn't know what he was seeing, but Will could feel she'd brought back some of the abyss with her. "I'm all right," she said after a little while. "My head's reeling with all of this, but I'm okay." She looked at the floor, "I'm better than I would have been, anyway. I had a dream when I was down there all cocooned up. Think it was more than a dream, really. I saw that wasp man, thing, whatever the hell it is. It wanted to use me, my body to make more things like it. It was going to," she trailed off remembering that obscene

289

stinger jabbing the air, dripping. She looked up at Will and had he been standing he might have taken a step back. "We have to kill it."

"Agreed," Will said. "But I don't get the notion we can do that the same way we did with its zombie buddies."

George took a deep breath. "Will, I think we need to call in some help. Sheriff Ward and his boys can be down here in, what, an hour, two at most? We don't have to do this by ourselves."

"Yeah," Will said. "We do. Listen, we can't just stand outside the mine with twenty of Tommy's guys and wait for The Pompiliad to come. Even if we flanked out with the Staties there'd never be enough of us. We can't beat this thing with boots and guns, man." Will took off his baseball cap and ran a hand through is hair. "Try to imagine it, okay? We end up backing down into— Jesus jumped up Christ, I'm gonna say it—the dragon's lair, then what? Tommy and his boys get one look at Dampf, or shit even just lil' old Yïn, and they'll freak right the fuck on out."

Erica pulled away from George and put a hand on his chest. "I know cops," she said. "They'll unload with everything they have."

"And Dampf," Will finished, "will kill them."

George walked away from them and looked out the window—just dark, no movement. "What keeps it from killing us, Two-Bears?"

"It called on us, man. It's asked for our help. You stood in front of the damn thing yourself. It didn't kill you then. And, hell, Yïn could've wasted any one of us whenever it wanted to. Aside from some basic mind-fuckery, it actually saved our asses a couple of times."

George turned around. He was a big man, but right now he was reminding Will very much of a little kid about to hold his breath to get his way. "If the bug and the lizard are so hardcore, what do they need us for? Seems to me like we'd just be getting in the way."

Will sighed. "George, I just don't know. You act like I know more than you do in all this, but I haven't seen or done anything you haven't seen or done. Why's this all hit me so different than it hits you?"

"Cuz I'm scared, you half-breed dipshit!"

Erica looked at Will, but he was still.

George went on. "This *hits me different* because I've got more to lose than you. I've finally found someone. I could sell the house and leave tomorrow if I had the chance. You'd be happy to stay here forever, wouldn't you? You'd just sit back and re-read some novel another forty-five thousand times. Don't you get it, Will? You can leave, too, man." In two steps George towered down from the other side of the desk. "You don't have to keep paying back the universe for some imagined slight by staying in pergatory. You're a smart man. You could go anywhere you want and start a real life instead of this bullshit in-between crap."

Will stared at his friend, felt his anger and his love. With what he was about to say, he worried about the placement of the gun on the desk between them. "A new life." He nodded at Erica, "An amazing woman, someone to love and who loves you. I would never, *ever* stand in the way of you having these things, George Rhodes. But to get this prize you have to pay first. You have to do this, whether you're afraid or not. You have to go out there and into the ground. You have to fight and you have to win, or Erica and your new life, wherever it may be, are going to die."

George stood back and opened his mouth.

Will surged up behind the desk and cut him off. "No, Georgie. No. You listen to me now. This thing, this Pompilliad isn't some bad man. It's a demon or something worse. If you leave and it gets past Dampf and Yïn, it'll open some kind of seal and more of its kind will come through. They'll crawl all over the world and soon enough," he stabbed the air between them with his finger, "no matter *where..you..go*...one of them will come and destroy everything. You think you're getting out of Shard? You think you're bugging out of a dead town for greener pastures? Yeah, for a little while, maybe. But eventually it'll all look like Shard, including the poor dead fuckers walking around being eaten from the inside out." Will closed his eyes and pinched the bridge of his nose. He took a long, deep breath. "If you're lucky, you might even get to watch Erica's body get used like some kind of breeding factory as you die."

That's when his best friend hit him.

Erica didn't make a sound. She sensed this drama needed to play out. The cavemen had to hit each other with rocks until they understood one another.

Will sat down hard in his chair and rubbed his jaw. George had pulled his punch at the last second or he wouldn't still be conscious. "Hope you broke your paw, dickhead."

George flexed his hand, "Nope."

"You gonna' hit me again?"

"Nope."

"You gonna' cowboy up?"

"Well, I have to, now, don't I?"

"Yup."

"Your jaw hurt much?"

Will smirked. "You kidding? I thought a fly landed on me."

Erica rolled her eyes.

"You sat down pretty fast. Must'a been a big old horsefly."

"Nah, it was nothing," Will said. "Course you do it again, I'll shoot you."

"My gun's bigger."

Erica shouted, "Oh, for the love of God!"

The phone rang.

They silenced. All three of them huddled around the desk. The blinking light on the phone winked on and off like an eye. They all knew who it was. It rang for a full minute before anyone spoke.

George said, "It's for you, Will."

"I'm not here."

Erica shook her head and picked up the base of the phone, careful not to the let the handset fall. She turned it over and popped the cord. The phone stopped ringing. Three sets of shoulders fell at the same time. "See?" she said, setting the phone back down on Will's desk. "That wasn't such a big thing."

The phone started ringing again.

Erica lept back as if it would shock her. "Madre de dios."

"Yeah, doubt it," Will said. "Fuck this." He picked up *Smaug* just to have it in his hand and then answered the phone. "Joe's pizza." He winced. Not at the voice, but at the silence. If a black hole could make a sound, or a lack thereof, it was in his ear now. It was a thousand nails on a thousand chalkboards, a million bites of tin foil and the instant after his mother's last breath.

"The sow and her piglet already rot."

Will began to tremble, not just shake but really boogie. One bitter winter about five years back he'd edged out onto some rotten ice over the creek. A big old dopey mutt had fallen halfway through in a misadventurous rabbit hunt and Constable Will had risen to the occassion. Will had fallen through, too, of course, and both of them had to be rescued by the dog's owner. He was an older man with the presence of mind to extend a long branch over the ice instead of his life. Will had shuddered under a blanket the rest of that afternoon. The dead cold the phone exhuded was worse. It made his bones feel thin.

"The sow tried to run, but we caught her. We stung her. Our maggots feast."

Will's eyes grew heavy at the sound of that ancient, ageless voice. There was no dramatic tone, no emotion, just depth. It was like being spoken to by the Marianus Trench. A growing part of him wanted to lie down on the desk, close his eyes and let the cold flow over him like that thick creek water. The Pompiliad could have George and Erica. It could have Will. It could have Shard. He just wanted to cease.

His shoulders slumped and his gun hand dropped against his leg. Will felt the heat from the metal. It was only ambient room temperature, but it was warmth, life. It flowed up his arm, a branch extended from the shore, and pulled him back. He blinked away a blurry rime of frost from his corneas. He looked at George and Erica. They were holding hands.

"I don't believe you," Will said. "I think they're still around, and I don't think you have them yet. You don't have us yet either. If you did, you wouldn't be calling and fucking with me." Will squared his shoulders. "What do you want?"

Silence from the line.

"Know what?" Will said and dropped the phone. He leveled *Smaug* and purred, "I've always wanted to do this." George and Erica moved away and covered their ears. The metal dragon roared and the phone exploded in a satisfying spray of plastic shrapnel. George's mouth hung open in an O. Erica was laughing. Will deadpanned. "Goddamn telemarketers."

"What did it want?" George asked.

"To mess with us. Said it had killed the 'sow and her piglet'."

"Loraine and Kiddo?"

"That's my guess."

"But," Erica said. "You don't believe it."

"Nope. Know what I do believe?" Will paused for a second, remembered that cold, that moment when he *wanted* to give up. "I believe The Pompiliad will get in here sooner rather than later and that we need to get our collective asses in gear. This thing's too badassed for a couple of swingin' dicks and their lawyer."

George asked, "What do you want to do, Sheriff?"

"I think we need to get ourselves underground. And one day you'll stop calling me Sheriff." Will smiled at Erica and dialed up his drawl. He was going for charm but had the opposite effect. "Y'all feel like meetin' a real Kentucky dragon?"

Chapter 37

ERICA PEEKED THROUGH the steel mesh covering the windows. Deep night rushed up against the glass. "I don't see anyone," she said. "I think we can just walk to the Jeep." She passed a second in silence. "It's weird. Shouldn't there be like a zillion crickets singing? They've been keeping me up half the night since I got here, but I don't hear any now."

George walked over and stood next to her, head cocked. "Yeah, that is weird. Will, can you think of a single summer night in this town when the bugs didn't make a huge racket?" Will didn't say anything. George turned around to find his friend stifling laughter. "What's with you, injun boy?"

"I just think it's funny that out of a wasp demon, a giant spider and a dragon, what's gettin' you is quiet crickets." Will shook his head. "Who the fuck cares why the crickets aren't singing? Maybe Yïn ate them all, what do I know?"

Erica looked at George. George put a hand on Will's shoulder. "You okay, man?"

Will covered his friend's hand with his own. "No, Georgie. Not even a little, but I'm going to cowboy up and do this anyway." Will nodded his head and walked over to the window. "Okay, so I want you two in the Jeep. About a minute later, I'm going to hop on my bike and follow you. Those walkers—if they're around—don't hoof too fast, but don't let 'em box you in either."

Erica said, "We've all seen *Night of the Living Dead*, Constable."

Will smiled. "Keep this one, George. I like her a hell of a lot."

"Where're we headed? That shaft?"

295

"Yeah, we're going to see Dampf. This thing started with the dragon and I've got a pretty solid feeling it's going to end there, too."

"What do we do if we get there and a bunch of those fucking things are guardin' the gate? What if the Pompiliad's there?" George shuddered. "Jeez, it creeps me out just saying *the name*."

"If there's walkers, you blow their freakin' heads off. Don't forget to zap the wasp while you're doing it. They *stay* down when you kill both the horse and the rider."

Erica looked at him. "Horse and rider?"

"Yeah, I get the idea that the bodies are just that, bodies. The wasps are doing all the thinking, what little thinking they seem capable of." Will changed gears. "Now, the climbing gear's still in the back of the Jeep from when we went on our little spelunk the other day, Georgie boy. You remember where we tied off, right?"

George nodded.

"Erica," Will faced her. "You okay with sliding down about three stories worth of rope? Cuz' you're going to have to be."

"Climbing wall."

"Huh?"

"There's a climbing wall at my gym. It's not three stories high, but it's big and you have to repell down. I do it three times a week." She smiled. "After cardio."

Will took her hand. "Marry me?"

George took her hand from Will's. "Mine."

"Right, right. Okay, so you guys get there and get into the cave. I'll be right behind you."

"Why aren't you just coming with us?" Erica asked.

"Because," George said, "he knows that if we split up there's a better chance of getting it done. Whatever 'it' turns out to be. If we're together and the Pompiliad blows up the Jeep or turns us to stone or whatever, it's over. That about right, Constable?"

"Yeah. That's right. But if it makes you feel any better, I'm the one who's going to be all ass out in the wind. By contrast, you too are riding around in an armored car. I don't even have my helmet here. It's at home."

"Are you pouting, Sheriff?" George pinched the air with his fingers. "Just pouting maybe a little bit?"

"Guys?" Erica said. She was staring out the window again. "I think if we're going to do this, we need to do it now. There's a bunch of a really unhealthy looking people coming up the street."

Will squeezed in next to her. Sure enough, about six or seven of the Pompiliad's puppets were slouching and shambling up the street toward the jail. They were far enough away that Two-Bears couldn't make out their faces, which was just fine by him. He knew well enough that these things weren't the people they once were, but it still hurt shooting his neighbors in the face. "Erica's right. We need to do this. Lemme' go grab those clothes for you."

A minute later, George and Erica were piling into the Jeep. Will didn't burn any precious time repeating instructions. He gave his best friend a look that said what he needed it to then nodded at Erica. She leaned through the window and planted a kiss on his cheek. "For luck."

"Star Wars," he said.

"Star Wars?"

Will smiled. She wasn't perfect after all. "We'll work on it."

George's eyes widened. "Shit, Will, you better…"

Two-Bears started moving before he even turned around. He would not a waste a second looking over his shoulder at what George saw. He jogged around the front of the Jeep and threw a leg over his motorcycle. The Jeep roared into life. Will shouted, "Go!" over his shoulder as he kick-started the bike. The Indian threw a welcome growl as Will twisted the throttle and spun a trick turn-around. His headlight illuminated Meg Tooley and his heart broke. Her skin was slatey and tissue-paper thin, her eyes yokeless eggs. Her once shaking hands clawed the air in slow, steady rakes. The others were still a good block away. Now that he knew how to time it, Will could wait for her jaw to crack open, for that gray tongue to slide out with its rider. He reached down for his gun and let his hand fall away. "I'm sorry Meg," he whispered and rode off toward the woods.

* * *

GEORGE ROLLED UP the windows as soon as they were out of the parking lot. He felt the pull of the rear view mirror like there were magnetic chips in his pupils, but kept his eyes on the road.

He wasn't about to fuck everything up over something stupid and right now it was taking everything he had to keep his panic behind his teeth. If anyone had a drink, now would be a terrific time to share. Really great. He took a corner at Main and S. Mine Streets, headed for the border woods and the old gravel track that lead to the shaft. "Did you see him," he asked Erica?

"Yeah, he got on his bike and fish-tailed it around like Evil Kinevil or something."

"Show off," George said, talking more now to himself. "He'll probably go around the long way. Take Hill Avenue to the woods road and then go down one of the branches back to the shaft." He grew quiet a moment. "No one knows these roads better than Will Two-Bears."

Erica got an image of Will bouncing along the paths and mining roads under the black silhouettes of vaulted trees—a knight errant on his white horse, galloping toward the dragon. But where was the other; where was that black knight? George slewed around another turn and they rocketed toward the woods, only two blocks over from the old movie theatre. Outside, a raked-out black chopper stood at the ready, waiting for its rider. No kickstand kept it from falling over, the bike balanced like a dime on its edge, impossible and perfect.

* * *

T.R.'s BLEEDING HAD slowed to a trickle. What that witch had left of his poor eye dangled on his cheek and itched like a line of busy ants. He rocked in and out of consciousness, shock acting like waves of anesthesia. He knew there was pain; it was just happening to someone else. The constant hum of wasps in his head had even grown distant. Everything had been destroyed. His great plans to ride out of Shard and into the world at the right hand of its conquerorr. His dreaming grasp of becoming the dark prince of all he surveyed. In the dank gloom of the theatre he laughed at himself, a sound like old syrup over rocks. This is why adults so often think teenagers are daffy, this grand sense of melodrama. That's what happened when you were all emotion and no logic, no brain to cool things out. The joke was that it took a stroll through a corner of hell to turn Tommy Ray Dalton into a grown-up. Fuck, man, most guys just went to college and got a job.

"I still have a job for you."

T.R. tilted his head up as the movie screen glowed into life. A silent, old-timey street scene juttered in browns and whites across the mildew-stained canvass. But instead of women in their frilly Sunday best or men in pressed overalls and suits, the street was peopled with walkers. Their clothes were filthy and ragged, feet dragged and arms swayed. The flickering camera zoomed in on the marquee over the theatre where drooping, crooked letters proclaimed a double feature: *THE LAZARUS BOY and LOVE NEVER DIES.* The point-of-view swam through the front doors, past a dead man slumped over the candy counter and through the swinging door into the theatre proper. The screen showed a theatre with empty seats save one, and a screen that showed a theatre with empty seats save one—on and on like facing mirrors, creating a tunnel to infinity.

The camera floated down the isle past the lone movie-goer and flipped around to face him. A 1920's era T.R. stared back through the screen. A razor-straight part cleaved his gleaming hair and he wore a starched white shirt with little round collar wings. The camera panned back and refocused over his shoulder at the back of the theatre. T.R.'s mind swam with confusion. It was like he was looking through the back of his own head. The door swung open and two figures walked in—a tall man with slumped shoulders and lank hair holding the gloved hand of a young girl. Dressed in a gingham skirt she he had to be no more than thirteen or fourteen. The man wore a coat and tails, his top hat grasped in his other hand. T.R. felt them come down the isle behind him like the tide come to claim a paralyzed man left on the shore. On the screen they advanced down the isle toward him and stopped. The screen went out and the theatre was plunged into perfect, velvet black.

T.R. knew what was behind him: his master and his intended, young Maggie Owens. Only he didn't want Maggie anymore, not like he'd last seen her at Missus Najarian's house. She wasn't the taught little hottie running around town in a pair of cut-offs and a t-shirt tied off so you could see the sweat roll down her flat, tan belly. She was a walker now, emptied out. Really just an extension of The Dark Rider, like a finger on his hand. T.R.

guessed he was almost as far gone. The thought of her as she had been sent a spark along his still erect penis. He almost moaned with the agony, but the fear of making a sound in this tomb sewed his lips shut.

The sussurous of bare feet on grit as someone suffled around in front of him. There wasn't much space between his boney knees and the next row of seats. Someone was standing right in front of him, not breathing. T.R. sucked in a quick breath as if ready to take a plunge into a deep pool. Fungus, rot, sharp stench of corrupt tissue. Soft, dry lips brushed his mouth and he jerked his head away. The Pompiliad caught hold of his skull from behind and the buzzing became thunder. T.R. thought he was screaming but couldn't hear himself. A dainty hand pressed down on his crotch and his entire lower body roared in pain. She leaned in again, but this time her sweet, teenage kiss found his empty eye socket and the wasp crawled through into his brain.

The buzzing ceased.

The Pompiliad and Maggie Owens walked back up the isle. The swinging door allowed for a flash of dim light—really a lessening of dark—and then it was just black. The muted roar of the chopper shook some dust from secret places and then faded into the distance.

After a time, a field mouse slipped from its nest in one of the seat cushions. Its oil-drop eyes were quick and clever, its humped little back glossy. It had done well on the beetles and various bits left by the big animals that made this place. Now, it smelled something new. One of the big animals had been in here, but was now still. Sometimes they had things, good things for nesting or eating, and being a field mouse means being curious—cautious, but curious. It slipped along the tops of the seats and stopped about six inches away, testing the air with its nose. It froze, no, this thing was wrong. This wasn't... The mouse couldn't move, turned to stone in its terror.

T.R. opened his eye and stood up, tearing through the duct tape like it was wet tissue paper. He left some skin behind him, but didn't mind. There was no mind to bother. The buzzing was gone and his poor, painful dick had deflated. These, too, were moot. He wouldn't have minded anymore anyway. T.R. Dalton no longer existed. The husk that clomped up the isle toward the fragrant night was nothing more than the single directive planted in him by The Pompiliad: kill William Two-Bears McFarlan.

Chapter 38

WILL ALMOST WIPED out as he rounded a sharp bend deep in the labrynth of mining roads around Shard. The back wheel sprayed gravel as the big cruiser tried to squirt out from underneath him. The headlight jounced, spraying flashbulb glimpses of skeletal woods—a thousand faces in the leaves, a thousand grasping hands in the branches. Will dug in his heel hard and let go just as the bones began to do interesting things. The bike found its center and he rumbled on.

He wasn't far from the shaft, from the dragon and safety. Dampf would take care of everything. They'd lost the battle in town, but the war would be decided in that glowing cavern below the fire. He just had to make it there without getting himself killed. Wouldn't that be funny, the fate of the world decided upon a bad turn in the mountains? A big root snaked across the road (really just a gravel path overgrown with tall weeds) and Will stood up on the pegs to better take the shock. Oh, his poor bike.

Dad would've been *pissed* that he took the Indian into the woods like this. Nothing to be done about it, though. The town was full of walkers. Will shook his head. Hard to think of them like that, walkers, zombies. Jesus, they'd been his neighbors, his family. But he had to think of them that way. That had not been young Luther Becket he'd plugged back at the Dalton place, it was a puppet. And that hadn't been the puppet's father he'd wasted in the kitchen a few minutes before. Chrissakes, he'd spent half a day next to Rick Beckett clearing snow on the mining road that led from town proper back to their little village. Rick kept trying to pay Will with canned tomatoes from his garden. No, that really hadn't been Rick and his boy. Him and the rest, they were gone. They were walkers.

After he'd separated from George and Erica, Will zipped around a group of them standing by the t-juntion where Main Street merged with the highway feeder road. They'd dragged a bunch of junk over to block the way, but he'd been able to scoot around and onto the gravel track. Will had recognized an old axel that had been sinking into a clump of weeds in front of the old Jefford's place since he was a kid. It was weird to see it moved like that, as if it had come alive and rolled over there all by itself. Even though the axel movers were standing right next to it, swaying, tracking his progress with radar dish faces as he passed, Will couldn't reconcile that they'd done the moving. There was no feeling of life to them at all. It was like driving past a clutch of headstones. At least he knew where they were. Back there in the dark, behind him. *Get thee behind me, you freaky sonsabitches.*

He took another sharp bend, downshifting and keeping his wheels about him this time. He didn't expect to run into anything in the woods. They were all in town. And with this thought in mind, he almost plowed into the back of Lorain's Subaru. Will shouted, "Shit!" and slewed the bike sideways. If he'd been on blacktop, he'd have gone over the side and through the Subaru's back windshield. Gravel pelted the bumper loud enough to hit his ears over the engine.

Will shut off the bike and silence pounded. There was no sussurus of wind, no insect song. He pulled his pistol and stage whispered, "Loraine! Kiddo!", then thought better of it. Wasn't like he was being stealthy driving around a hog like the Indian. Will walked around the car, but it was empty. The driver's side door was open and hanging by a hinge. He ran his fingers over the crimped metal where the door would have met the car. Something had ripped it halfway off the frame. The shotgun he'd given Loraine was lying on the ground. There were no footprints. Not even a paw print from Darwin.

Will got back on the bike and gunned the engine. He needed to move. He knew damn well who'd taken the Howards and their dog. The shaft was close, just over the next rise maybe. He could be there in another five minutes. He feathered the brakes as he topped the rise, throwing ruby light over the giant spiderweb that clung to the Subaru's front bumper.

* * *

WILL STOOD BEFORE the shaft and tried to make his legs move. George and Erica's Jeep was parked a few feet away, a line of mustard-colored rope tied off at the bumper and slipped into the mine. At least they'd gone down voluntarily. It gave Will some courage. His friends were waiting for him inside. It wasn't just a god-monster and its pet nightmare spider—which, by the way, had kidnapped a mother and her kid, not to mention the family pooch. Two-Bears never trusted Yïn. She always seemed on the edge of disobedience, as if the dragon barely had her controlled.

"I need to move," he said to himself.

He clicked the Indian's headlamp on and pointed it down the throat of the shaft. The ever-present line of smoke drooled up into the night. It would run the battery down to shine the light without the engine running, but he could always jump it off the Jeep when they came back up. The thought stopped him. Even now, in the face of ultimate craziness (seriously, he could wake up in a psych-ward in another minute and not be surprised an ioata that the whole thing had been a hallucination) he didn't just hold out hope for victory, he assumed it. Will shook his head. The uber optimist. Sure.

Ten feet into the shaft, the rope slipped off into the side cut and disappeared down the rabbit hole. The light from his bike faded to little more than an ivory blush on the dusty ryolite walls. He grabbed the line and planted his feet on either side of the opening. It ran at a sharp angle for about ten feet before dropping straight down into…what? He gritted his teeth, tasted metal and sand. His gun was going to have to stay snapped in its holster while he rapelled then dangled in open space like bait on a fucking trout line. Will thought about calling out to George and Erica but stopped with his mouth half open. Best to come in with some surprise on his side just in case they weren't all friends anymore. Had he ever been a friend to the dragon? Closer to a press-ganged recruit.

Each backward step was a silent deliberation. *Look ma, the world's first Native American Ninja warrior.* He bit down on a gasp as his foot reached the end of the angled shoot and dangled in space. Damn, did he wish he had gloves. If he had to zip down the line like some Navy Seal or something, he was going to leave most of his palms on the rope. Really, just fuck it. Will Two-Bears McFarlan let out a breath and hopped backward into gravity.

For a moment, he hung suspended in emerald gloom, the green werelight dazzling him. The rope slung tight under his butt and took his weight, but his hand did, in fact, already hurt like a mofo'.

Will kicked out, spun himself around and sucked in a breath. His father was standing right in front of him, upside down, boots sticking to the roof of the cavern like he was, well, a spider. Dad winked a bloody, pupilless eye. Will's heart slammed in his chest and the world reeled, but he got his head together fast. If he passed out now, he'd fall some three stories and maybe do more than knock the wind out of himself this time. It was just the spider fucking with him yet again. Just a bad joke. Actually, kind of a good sign. If Yïn wanted him dead, he would be.

Will sighed, "If I could get to my gun, I'd totally shoot you."

Yïn flipped him the bird and smiled. She reached behind herself and rooted around, eyes slotted up and to the right (or rather down and left) as if looking for something in her back pocket. She nodded to herself and yanked a cable of silk out behind her and stuck one end to the roof of the cavern. Will watched as his dead father decended, his body changing in rude bursts, until a huge spider placed all eight claws on the strange metal ground. It sounded like someone dropping pebbles on a frying pan. Yïn detached and reared up to mark him with her alien eyes. She waved a razored foreclaw. "Right, right," Will muttered, "C'mon down." He began a grunting descent. "Jesus, I can actually feel my hair turning gray."

After what felt like a long time, his hand and butt complaining with every inch, Will's Chucks touched down. "That's one small step for man," he whispered to himself. "One giant cluster-fuck for blah, blah, blah." He shook his hands out and blew on them. Yïn's pincers jigged in and out in what Will had always assumed was giant spider mirth. Still, he couldn't shake the whole psychotic gardener coming at him with a big pair of shears gestault. "Yeah, yeah, some of us can't pull five-hundred pound test filament out of our asses." He flexed his hand, making sure his fingers would do what he needed, then hauled leather so fast even the spider was caught off guard.

Yïn stopped laughing.

"Where are my friends, fucko?"

Can't kill me.

Will winced. The voice in his head wasn't speaking English or anything even close to language as he understood the concept. If static or wind or lightning could talk it would sound, *feel* like this. "Maybe not," he said. "But I bet I'm close enough to really mess you up." He ratcheted back the hammer. "Wanna' check?"

Yïn's mandibles twitched. A smile? Will scowled. The spider waved a pedipalp and turned, its claws throwing that weird staccato around the cavern. Will walked behind it, wondering just exactly where you were supposed to plug a pony-sized spider from another dimension. Were its brains in its thorax? Did it have a brain? Jesus, the last time he saw this thing it was a flock of birds. He shook his head and lowered the gun. *Smaug* felt leaden and stupid brushing against his leg, but he wasn't about to put it away. They rounded an emerald column—the joining of a stalactite and stalacmite that stretched toward the dark ceiling—and stopped to take in the tableaux.

A rough-hune block sat before Dampf's bed of diamond spheres. Deep scars gouged the sides where the dragon must have clawed it from the wall. Dampf was nowhere to be seen. Childe Howard and Darwin sat on the block. Kiddo was tousling the beagle's ears. George, Erica and Loraine stood nearby, an amiable trio. They could have been talking about sports or discussing the weather. Will's eyes blured and stung. "What the *hell* is going on here?" he shouted.

Childe looked up and shouted back as if he hadn't heard, "Hey! Constable Will!"

Erica smiled, "There he is."

Loraine squinted in the half-light and beamed.

George brayed, "Howdy, Sheriff!" He trotted over, big amiable golden-retriever of a man, and slapped Will hard on the shoulder. "You made it. Boy, we were getting' worried."

Will stammered. "You were getting worried?" He pushed past George and walked over to Loraine. "What the hell happened to you? I found your car and the shotgun. It looked like you'd been abducted by aliens."

"Oh, that," she said.

"Yes?"

Childe piped up, "Loraine totally blew a gasget back there."

"Yes, thank you, Childe," she said over her shoulder, then faced Will again. "He's, uh, actually sort of right. I, um…for a minute, I couldn't really figure out how to, um, work." Loraine, with a deep blush on her round face went on to describe the scene after she almost ran into the giant spiderweb. She had put the car in park, set the brake and started to cry. Nothing like hysterics, just a slow, steady leak.

"Kiddo kept trying to talk to me, but it was like I wasn't really even there," Loraine explained. "I dunno', I guess I just got to this point where I realized—and I mean, I really got it—that all of this was happening for real. My brain just needed to shut down for a few minutes while I processed everything." She sighed, considered. "Maybe it would have been different if we'd made it to the highway. We just kept getting deeper and deeper into the woods and I could *feel* that we weren't getting any closer to the road."

"And then you hit the web," Will said.

"Right and I stopped. Just stopped." She nodded over Will's shoulder at Yïn. "That's when the big ugly came." She shuddered. "Jesus, I get that it's on our side and everything, but I can barely stand to even look at it." She leaned in. "Makes me feel like I need to pee."

Will put a hand on her shoulder. "I'm not much of a fan either. You see the dragon yet?"

"Ha! I still can't get over that. No, I haven't. The spider just led us down here. Shit, carried us. That's why I dropped the shotgun, I guess. It kind of just peeled open the car and scooped us all up. Kiddo kept tellin' me not to worry and the dog's actually wagging its tail and whining like when I make hamburgers." She shook her head and looked at her feet. "By the time we got down here, I was back to myself and feeling pretty okay about everything considering. I mean I guess I've hit acceptance? Does that make sense?"

"Sure. I think it's about the only way any of us could possibly deal with any of this." He winked at Kiddo. "'Cept maybe your boy, there. Kids've got elastic for brains."

She smiled. "Yeah, Kiddo's imagination is his armor. I'm just hoping mine holds up when I do see your dragon."

George sauntered over. "I fainted when I met it."

Will smirked. "You were loaded."

"I know. You'd think that would've helped."

George nodded toward the stone slab, "That's new."

"Yeah?" Will said. "Guess you're right." He looked at his friend—his scary smart friend. "What's got your hackles up, Georgie boy?"

"Look like anything to you?"

Will watched Childe lean over and kiss his doggie on the snout. "Flintstones park bench?"

"Okay," George said. "Maybe it's nothing. Just kind of reminds me of something is all."

"Something you don't like."

"Right."

Will slapped George on the shoulder, the one with the M16 strapped to it. "Know it looks like to me? A good place to crouch behind and lay down cover fire."

Erica walked up. "You really think guns are going to do any good against, um…"

"Beings," Lorain offered. "Beings is a good word for them."

"Right. Fine. Beings. You think guns are going to work against *beings* like that?" She pointed at Yïn.

"No," Will said. "I really don't."

"Then what..?"

He held up his hand. "I think they'll work against the walkers. I know they do. You just have to hit them right and we already covered that."

George slipped an arm around her waist. "She's got a point, man. Even if we can hold back the rest of the town what are we supposed to do against the boss?"

A voice like the jangling of crystal whispered from the rocks, *"You'll do nothing, George Rhodes."* Will's gut went tight and his mouth set. Erica's muscles tensed. George scanned the cavern. Loraine ducked her head into her shoulders. Kiddo pulled Darwin close to him. *"Humans for humans. Angles for demons. Djin for djin."* The giant pillar of rock shivered and the humans stopped breathing, each and every one, as the great dragon unfolded out of it.

Dampf towered over them; its wings stretched and filled half the cavern. Its huge head, all spikes and thousand year eyes, curved over on the end of a neck like a tremendous question mark. That low, heavy jangling voice came again, the sounds of planet shards rubbing against each other in a quasar, *"Dragons for wasps."*

"Holy mother of God," Loraine whispered.

"We are older than that, Loraine Howard. So much older."

Erica's mind cleared. All thought, all emotion was plowed under by a single wave of terror. It passed over her and only the essence of Erica remained. That pure person saw the dragon and smiled. "Beautiful," she said.

Will finally put his gun back in its holster. The part of dragon would be played tonight by Dampf not *Smaug*. His fear that something was off, something wrong melted away with a look into those eyes. Everything would be more than okay. They were so going to kick the Pompiliad's ass. He started grinning like a kid. He nudged George, "Eh? Eh? We're totally going to win, buddy."

George scowled and muttered, "Where is it? Where is it?" His eyes ticked off the dragon's body. "It's gotta' be there."

Will started to feel a little like George was shuffling baseball cards in church. "Dude, would you pay attention?"

"Yeah, sorry."

Will took a deep breath and stepped forward on shakey legs. "Dampf," he pitched his voice to cross the distance. "We're the only one's left. Everyone else in town has been taken over by The Pompiliad."

The dragon tilted its head toward Two-Bears McFarlan. George thought it seemed amused. *"I know, Constable. I know everything. You have done well."*

"Done?" George shouted. "We haven't done shit. We just survived."

Will glared at George and spoke up fast, "Dampf, what do you want us to do?" He felt Lorain's hand slip into his and squeeze. "How do we help?"

"Fight the swarm, little Constable. Fight the swarm so I may save my energy for The Pompiliad."

"Swarm?" Erica whispered. "What's it talking about?"

"I think—" Will started and stopped, head cocked to one side. "You hear that?"

Dampf began to fade back into the stone column, but Will's attention was on the strange sound from the other side of the cavern. "Sounds like sacks of potatoes or something."

"Fight the swarm."

George unslung his rifle. "It's them," he said. "It's the walkers. They're dropping through the hole in the ceiling."

Will's eyes widened. "Okay," he said, "everybody back behind that slab." They scrambled and tossed themselves over the low redoubt. Erica, Childe and Darwin and Lorain huddled in the middle with their heads down. Will and George looked over them from the ends. George looked stoney, calm. Will thrummed with energy and fight. He pulled *Smaug* and said, "Take their heads clean off, Georgie. There's only a few of them left."

"We can take 'em," George said. He pulled the bolt on the M16 then blinked, said, "Shit," and clicked off the safety. "Okay, now we can take 'em."

Will smiled. He popped up from behind the slab and sighted as the first of them rounded the giant pillar. It was one of the migrant workers, stumping along on a broken ankle. Another came after, Meg Tooley, but her brittle bones had shattered when she hit the cavern floor. She dragged herself along with her hands, her legs a useless, twisted train. After her, there were another five or six and now they looked like a proper scene out of *Night of the Living Dead*, the fall having ravaged their limbs. They crawled and limped, broken arms outstretched, some dangling. "Wait'll they get closer," Will said. "Wait'll they show the wasps."

"I got the three in front," George said.

"Okay," Will breathed. "Okay, okay, okay."

They were coming. They were close. Meg Tooley opened her mouth.

* * *

I SHOULD BE yelling something, Will thought as he squeezed the trigger. *Some war cry or something.* His gun filled the cavern with light and noise, but silence had hooded his mind. Will's ears registered but did not hear as his first slug caught one of the migrant workers in the cheekbone and sheared away the entire left half of its head. In the stuttering flashes from George's M16 Will made out the wasp inside the migrant's head. It was struggling, dying. The walker went down. Meg Tooley dragged heself over it like a salamander over a rotten tree branch. George had already put two in her but the machine gun was hard to steady even for a natural like him, and he'd done little more than break her collar bone and shread the shoulder. Will let her come on. *Just a few more feet and it's over, Meg. Just a few more...there!* She swiveled her head and gave him a perfect view of the wasp on her furred tongue. *'Night, Meg.* The .357 bucked and old Meg Tooley was still.

Will glanced at George—he was squeezing off bursts, the rifle looking as much like a fire-spitting magic wand as a gun. But he wasn't doing much, just wasting ammo and driving them back a few paces. George's mouth was set in a snarl. Will waved at him, but his friend lived at the end of his rifle now. Erica saw what Will was trying to do. She pulled her fingers out of her ears and wapped George on the leg then pointed at Will. George pivoted like a piece of clockwork and for one frosty second Will was sure his best friend was going to open fire on him. Will held up his hands and George shouted, "What?!"

"Put the selector lever in single shot like I showed you!" Will yelled back. "Use it like a hunting rifle."

"Look out!" Loraine said as a woman she thought she recognized from over on South Ave drew near. "Look out, Will!"

Two-Bears felt the adrenaline rise in him but shut it down. He took a long slow breath, turned and waited for the woman—it was Jean Dalton—to get within a finger's grasp of him. Her lips reminded Will of over-ripe plumbs. They split and revealed the spikey wasp. Grimmacing, Will raised the pistol and put the barrel an inch from her mouth. He fired. She died for the second time in as many days. He had four bullets left.

George didn't wait to make sure Will was okay. Two-Bears wasn't about to miss at that range. George flicked the selector all the way down to single shot and sighted along the, long insectile barrel. There were three of them coming in from the right; each staggered about three feet apart from the others. George breathed in, out, in, held it...fired. The round tore through the teeth and lips of the first walker (he didn't recognize the guy, which made it only slightly easier). On the same breath, George rolled the rifle sight an inch, squeezed. The second walker's head came off.

George   blinked.   Something somewhere inside his own head
started screaming.

The third walker in the line could have been anyone. Its face
was hamburger, like someone had set off a cherry bomb as a sinus
cure. But still, something about this one was familiar. *Fuck it. And
fuck you, too, buddy.* He fired but the slug plowed through the top
of the man's head. The wasp, clearly visible in the raw hole that
used to be this poor slob's mouth flicked its irredescent wings and
took to the air like a puff of evil smoke. The wasp's tickled
George's peripheral vision then disappeared.

Will caught what happened with the now headless walker. He
planted one hand on the top of the rock slab and vaulted over. Just
as the wasp was chewing its way through its host's decapitated
head, Will jammed *Smaug* against its cheek (its white-out eyes
rolling toward him) and fired twice. The wasp was vapor. The
vulnerability of Will's position rammed home as young Maggie
Owens clamped her dainty hand onto his shoulder.

Will cried out as her fingers taloned into him and the bones in
his shoulder ground together. It was his gun arm and *Smaug*
clattered to the floor, empty. Somewhere far off, Kiddo shouted,
"Will!" Maggie's rose petal mouth yawed in a grostesque train
tunnel as she leaned in to give the good Constable a kiss. She
stopped and jerked back a step. Darwin had crushed her ankle in
his jaws and shook her back and forth for all he was worth.
Supernatural circumstances or not, Maggie was only a hundred
pounds soaking wet. The sturdy beagle dragged her back a few
steps before she reached down and picked him up by the tail. He
thrashed at the end of his tail, breaking a few of the small bones,
and throwing whinning shrieks. Maggie tilted her head and leaned
in toward his open mouth, the wasp climbing up from her throat.

George pirouetted and trained the M16 on the walker-girl. He
took a breath, held it—and jerked the gun back as Childe Howard
jumped in and obscured his shot. "Kiddo! Fucking move!" But
the boy was tearing at Maggie Owens, tears of rage and fear
streaming down his face. He pounded her on the back and ripped
at her hair. It came out in chunks, but did little to stop her. With
her free hand she grabbed hold of Childe by the throat and bent
him to his knees. Now she redirected again and began to lean her
gaping maw toward his face.

Loraine surged up from behind the block, stone silent, the intent on her face louder than any lion's roar. She saw Childe jump up to go after Darwin too late and now she would see her only son die. Yes, she was certain, she was just a couple of feet too far away to make it in time. Maggie Owens's tongue slipped from her mouth and the wasp flared its amethyst wings.

And then Maggie was flying.

Loraine stopped in her tracks, her tennis shoes making a little *freep!* on the metallic deck. She watched open mouthed as Maggie dropped her son and the dog then levitated straight up, rotating like a leaf on the wind. When she reached the ceiling, Loraine understood. They all stared up and understood. Childe let out a "Yeah!"

Yïn.

The great spider hauled the thing wearing poor Maggie Owens's body up a line of silk. The wasp tried to escape, flicking off her tongue into the air, but Yïn spat a glob of venom at it. The poison struck dead on and dropped the wasp in a steaming heap at George's feet. He jumped back a step and spat on it himself just for good measure. Yïn reeled Maggie in and speared her with two of her free legs. Everyone turned away as the spider made short work of the last walker. Except Loraine. She gathered her son into her arms and watched as the avatar of her own intent unmade the evil thing.

Will picked up *Smaug* and stood, rubbing his shoulder. The floor of the cavern was littered with bodies, but none of them moved. He ticked his eyes off Childe, Loraine, Darwin, Erica and George. His family was here and unhurt. The swarm was gone and they were still here. He felt like crying and throwing up and dancing. He shook his head and smiled. "That was some fancy shootin', Georgie boy."

George held the rifle with shaking hands. The adrenaline dregs were already pulling at his guts. Still, he smiled back. "Don't tell me about good shootin', man. You were Jesse James, Billy the Kid. You were Han Solo, Constable."

"Holy shit, George."

"What?"

"You called me 'Constable'."

George began to chuckle, but it died on his lips as his eyes grew wide. "Look out, Will! Look out, now!"

Will began to turn just as the wasp that had elluded George's rifle moments before alighted on the back of his hand like a black snowflake. It wasted no time in jabbing its cruel stinger between the bones of his middle and ring finger. Will crushed it with his other hand, but the poison was already in him. Fire raced up his arm. He held up his hand and watched as the veins turned cobalt.

"No!" George screamed. "Oh, no! Ah, God. Ah, no!" He raced over to Will just as Two-Bears slumped to the ground. George caught and guided him gently to the ground. The others clustered around but no one spoke. George rasped at them, "Back up, damn you! Give 'im some space."

Will started to convulse as the black poison traced back his blood. It slipped up under his shirt sleeve and ran toward his heart. His teeth clenched hard enough to crack a filling loose. Rolling on that sea of pain he was aware of the little piece of silver on the back of his tongue. There were no thoughts, no emotions, only pain and pain. George's sweaty, unshaven face filled the universe like an anguished moon. He was shouting something, something. Then he was gone, shoved aside and replaced with eight smaller, more pefect spheres. Obsidian planets rose over his death with cold observation.

Yïn could smell the poison in the little Constable. The wasp was dead, the swarm gone, but its venom would still take him even with no rider to steer his corpse. It was a toxin much like her own, eternal and powerful: death as elixir. Not even she was immune to it. She looked at the little Constable, felt him fade and pulled an image from his head. Yïn, the trixter, the storyteller made her decision. Her pincers jigged.

George got up, fists ready but Erica grabbed his elbow. "Look," she whispered. "Look what it's doing."

Yïn skinwalked. A young woman with long, black hair and high, round cheekbones knelt over Will. Her brow was smooth and her eyes clear and fast. She was dressed in a simple apron and jeans, the kind of thing a waitress in a diner might wear. A sob caught in George's throat. "That's Charlotte. Will's mom," he said. "She looked like that when we were kids." She glanced over and tipped George a wink.

Charlotte Two-Bears took Will's savaged hand and placed her mouth over the wound from the stinger. The poison singed her lips. She began to pull at it, slow and deep. The black sludge began to back out of Will's veins, returning them to their normal healthy blue.

* * *

WIND ON HIS face, smelling of tannins and rich forest soil. Cool and clean, not a trace of hydrocarbons, no coal smoke. Warm sun on his shoulders. Will opened his eyes on the little clearing where he'd first met Amy James. She'd been sunbathing naked on a granite outcropping, the same one warming his butt through is jeans. Trees waved in the breeze, their new leaves like jade chips. A few wild daffodils splotched the long grass like discarded candy wrappers. This couldn't be now. This couldn't be Shard. This close to the shaft, his nose would be full of sulphur. And this looked more like spring time than the end of summer.

"It's not, Shard, you're right."

Will turned his head at a familiar voice. His mother sat on the other end of the rock, dressed like she was headed off to work. "And you're not my mother."

"Good guess."

Will shifted so he could face her comfortably. "Well, pretty easy. Mom's been dead almost as long as dad. You really dig on messing with my head through my parents, don't you?"

She smiled and shrugged. "It's something to do. A way to bond."

"How come you're talking? You don't talk."

"I talk all the time. I talk with pictures and ideas, actions."

"Where are we?" Will's face fell. "Shit, did I die?"

"In a sense."

"A sense? So, I'm dead."

"Ha!" she barked. "No, you're not getting off that easy, I'm afraid. More to do. Always more to do." She fixed him with a hard stare and there was nothing of his mother in those black eyes. "I, however, am finished."

"What's that mean? You're finished? And if I'm not dead, where is this?"

"Just your mind, little Constable." She waved an arm in a wide arc, "This is all from you. A good place to show you."

"Show me? Show me what?"

Yïn closed her eyes and breathed in the redolant air. "Everything," she said, and the air above and behind her began to shimmer. Will looked into it and saw spinning stars, galaxies pinwheeling, colliding, combining, civilizations rising and falling in supernova as common as thunderstorms. And more, and more, and more. It entered him, changed him, and made him new. Yïn vanished.

* * *

WILLIAM TWO-BEARS MCFARLAN came back to consciousness just as his mother staggered back from him. Yïn was everywhere in his head like the scent of strange perfume on skin. He knew this woman wasn't really his mother; just a last joke from a funny monster. But she didn't look funny now. Blackened blood vessels mapped her face and arms. Yïn tried to change back before the poison took her away, but didn't have the strength. She lay on the cave floor, an amused smile on her face, and closed her eyes on the universe. *Finally*.

* * *

"IS SHE DEAD?" Erica said.

"Yeah," Will answered after a little while. "She's gone. She took the bullet for me. Pulled that shit right out of my body before it could get to my heart. "

George put a hand on his shoulder. "That's your mom, right? That's Charlotte?"

Will had been so angry at the spider for impersonating his father, messing with his head like that. This, though—somehow it was more like a gift. "No, Georgie. My mom's been gone a while. That's a faery." He smirked. This horrendous, mind-bending monster, this most terrifying of all the old fears, *a spider*, had been a Faery. In his heart he knew that was the closest to true. At least that would be how he chose to remember her. It was a shame she was gone. He would have liked to start calling her Tinkerbell. That *really* would have pissed her off. She'd have laughed, though, he bet. Or, whatever, done that heinous thing with her pincers.

"Hate to break up the family reunion," Loraine said. "But I think we're still in trouble." She pointed up as a clunky motorcycle boot and leather clad leg sprouted from the hole in the ceiling like a questing root.

"You all feel that?" Ercia said. "It's really cold." The last three words came out on puffs of steam. She wrapped her arms around George and whispered. "Keep me warm big fella."

"You first," he muttered.

The Pompiliad slipped through the hole and hung suspended in space above the cavern floor. Not by rope, but by the cloud of blurry air behind it. Its wings thrummed with a bass that shook their ribs, but it kept its human form—a dark angel on insect wings.

"Will?" George asked.

"Yeah," Two-Bears said in slow, measured tones. "Let's get back behind the slab thing." He waved them toward it as he backed up a step at a time, "Go, go," always keeping his eyes on the demon. It's what that thing was, could only be. And if they lost now, it would cover the world with its kin. Will stumbled over a corpse. His blood vessels began to vibrate as if he were touching a live wire. He felt shifty, unsteady. The poison's after effects? Maybe. The Pompiliad was looking at him. "Dampf!" he shouted and then jumped back behind the stone with the others.

Will hudled next to Loraine and Kiddo. Darwin let out a whine and licked at the base of his tail. Will gave him a pat on the head, more for Kiddo than the dog. He craned his head up over the edge of the stone. The great column of rock from which the dragon had unfolded was still. "Dampf?" he called in a harsh whisper. "The swarm's gone. Dampf!" Nothing.

"Uh, Will?" George said, and nodded at the rifle in his lap.

"Not yet, Georgie," he said. "Dampf said she'd take care of this part of it."

Erica touched George's forearm. "I don't think bullets are going to do anything against that."

The thrumming from those giant insect wings pushed at their eardrums. The Pompiliad hovered in closer, its arms and legs hanging lip as Spanish moss. Erica stole a look at George. If the dragon didn't come, she'd take his rifle and kill every one of them. Or at least try. Quick shots to the head and then herself. None of them had walked the ghost plane with this thing, or stared

317

down into the abyss. None of them really knew what was coming if they lost. She leaned in and placed a feather-light kiss on his neck. "Love you," she said.

George looked into her eyes. The great Wasp was very close now; he could feel it as much as hear it swooping in for them. He closed his eyes and waited. The pain in his severed achilles tendon was there to meet him, flaring up from a dull throb to a respectable cymbal crash. His head was still killing him from T.R.'s first attempt, and on top of all of it he hadn't had a goddamn drink in days. Days. He kissed her back, just once on the forehead. "S'cuse me a sec'," he said, got up and walked around the stone slab.

"Hey!" George shouted, "Bug-fuck!"

The Pompiliad froze and hovered in the air twenty feet off the floor. It put its eyes on George and for a moment he wanted very badly to turn around and run. Never mind that there was nowhere to go, his guts and everything attached to them were simply repelled. He stood his ground and sighted down the M16. Back at the quarry he had bulls-eyed soup cans at twice this distance. The Pompiliad's palid face was as big as the full moon at the end of his rifle. It smiled as he pulled the trigger.

Nothing happened.

George's fingers grew numb as the gun eminated deep cold. He hissed in a breath and yanked his hands away, but instead of clattering to the floor, the rifle hung as if he were still holding it. George backed up a step. The cold intensified and turned the hair in his nose to spikes. His corneas fogged. He blinked to clear them and backed up as fast as he could, throwing himself around the corner of the slab and back next to Erica. His cheekbones and nose were scraped red with frostbite. A weird, keening, shrieking note filled the cabin as the M16 approached absolute zero. The Pompiliad tilted its head to one side, raised a long hand to its lips and blew a kiss. Its breath waved through the air and touched the weapon. It exploded. A triangular piece of iron that might have been a part of the bolt landed at George's feet with a clang.

The thrumming grew louder and ceased as hobnailed boots clocked down on the top of the slab. None of them turned to look. It was standing right behind and above them, staring down at their unprotected necks. Even Darwin squeezed his eyes shut tight. Their hearts slowed under the weight of all that cold and death.

"You cannot shed another's blood on the threshold." Dampf's jangling, crystal voice floated down on them. *"Or, do you wish it closed forever?"*

The Pompiliad turned its head, greasey hair whipping from side to side. "Show yourself, dragon."

The pillar unfolded like a five-story origami tower, wings and tail, claws and scales, eyes telescoping back into forever. The Pompiliad looked up at the great dragon. Its frown burst through with chiten shears as it eyes bloomed into segmented obsidian orbs. The rest of its thin humanity fell away like dead leaves. "Nor can you," it rasped. "I will fly back into the world and lay a new swarm. It will take longer to do on my own, but time is only time. This world will be devoured, and we will come back for you in unending number."

The dragon's mouth yawned and a furnance glowed orange from back in its throat. Dampf roared a ball of roiling fire. It speared through the air and stopped just shy of The Pompiliad, filling its empty eyes with a hundred little fires. The Pompiliad held its ground. The fire boiled and spat, a miniature sun but the wasp was untouched. After a time the flames retreated back into the dragon's mouth.

The Pompiliad loosed a sound that made Childe Howard think of garbage cans knocking together. Loraine imagined a pile of bodies—like those from the grainy films of the deathcamps at Buchenwald—being bulldozed. George heard his mother breaking every glass in the house as she threw them on the kitchen floor. Erica heard a storm of papers rushing against each other in a high wind. Will heard his father coughing. Darwin heard coyotes. It was laughter.

"You can't kill me! You can't shed anothner's blood on the threshold!" It laughed and laughed. "For me the door will close and for you it will open!"

A shudder passed through the dragon. Its wings pulled in as it diminished. A moment later, a young girl stood at the base of the rock altar. She was dressed in overalls and had blonde pigtails. Her cheeks were round and dirty, her feet bare. She squinted up at the giant wasp through one eye. "No," she said in a pure hills accent. "I don't think this stalemate's gonna hold. You're right on that one." She turned and eyed the hole at the top of cavern. "That's gotta' go first." She pulled in breath, her chest swelling,

swelling and then let it out in a great scream. The humans covered their ears and cowered even lower behind the rock. On the heels of the sound a tongue of blue-white flame licked across the air and filled the hole. It danced there like propane caught in a bottleneck. The little girl turned back, but the hole stayed alight with werefire. "Try flyin' through that, buddy."

"We can stay here forever," The Pompiliad said. "But your pets will die in time. Even if they eat one another. Their blood will spill on the threshold and my kind will come through."

The girl considered. "I could kill you myself and then re-seal the doorway."

"Once a blood law is broken there is no magic great enough."

"There is one magic. New blood for old. Innocence for sin." She nodded to herself and hopped up on the slab. Now she stood toe to claw with the giant insect. "It's long past time you died, filth. Long past."

The Pompiliad flexed its stinger but did not strike. If the dragon shed its blood, all the rest of its kind would flow through the broken portal. If it shed the dragon's, then the portal would seal forever. As it thought, the little girl reached out and grabed the thin stalk connecting the wasp's abdomen to its thorax in her chubby hand. She twisted then, just once, hard. The Pompiliad's broken body fell, its legs beating against the slab, gouging deep furrows in the stone. The girl lifted her foot and brought it down on the wasp's head. She crushed its eye and ichor splashed out onto the stone.

Dampf smiled down on the little humans. She blew a warm, gentle breath out over them. Will and others began to stir as the paralyzing cold evaporated. They found the strength to stand and move. George tripped over the jagged blade of metal from the M16 that had landed in front of him and managed to get to his feet again. The humans clustered to one side, clutching each other.

Dampf hopped down and stuck her hands in her pockets. The remains of the demon-wasp were little more than a pile of sharp angles and seaping wreckage behind her. Will looked at it and shook his head. "It was so easy for you."

Dampf rocked back on her bare feet, "Yep. Killin' the Pompiliad was never gonna' be the hard part. I was more worried for y'all with the swarm and everything. I couldn't risk sheddin' blood in here, but you could. No rules broken there."

"But you did," George said, staring hard at the little girl. His eyes scanning below her face for something. Where was it, damnit? They all had one. "You got its blood all over the place."

"Yeah," she said. "Kinda' had to, though, right? Y'all were gonna' die eventually anyway and that woulda' counted as me shedding your blood, too."

Loraine pointed at the diamonds. "Look," she frowned. "They're getting...*thin*."

"Yeah," Dampf said. "I gone and shed its blood, so now the rest of 'em are gonna' come through."

"You said you could re-seal it!" Childe said. "Something about new blood for old, right?"

George moved over a step or two and stood next to Kiddo. "Quit helping," he said.

"Huh?"

The dragon-girl smiled and showed off a grin of meshing fangs. "S'right. I can re-seal her nice and tight. Alls I needs is some virgin blood. Just like all them old stories."

Loraine's eyes opened wide. "Wait, what?"

Now the little girl's fingernails sharpened and slid from her finger tips. Her pupils blossomed and filled her eyes. "Dragons and virgins," she said, her voice lowering, scraping over itself. She beconned to Childe. "C'mon over here, boy."

Loraine moved in front of her son. "No!"

The little girl's skin darkened and split like the glaze on an old vase as it textured with scales. Her pigtails straightened and angled up into horns. Her pug nose pushed forward into a long snout. "No use," she said. "They're coming."

"Mom?" Childe said.

She reached behind her with both arms and grabbed him, keeping her face to the horror sprouting in front of her. Even as she protected him she understood the futility. "Not him," she said, her voice flat. "No."

A gruesome hybrid of girl and dragon stood next to the altar. It reached over and shoved the mess of broken wasp over the side. "Climb up here, child." It turned its gaze to each of the adults in turn. "It's the boy, or it's your world." It pointed a hooked claw at the diamond pile. They had become gray, whispy. Behind them, a black mass, like a cloud of metal filings, boiled and whirled. "You see," Dampf said. "The swarm. A million Pompiliads instead of just one."

George moved over and stood next to Will. Erica said, "What are you doing?" George ignored her and whispered into Will's ear. Two-Bears jerked back and stared at his friend like he'd gone mad. "It's what we have to do, Will," he said. "It's the right thing." Will looked from Loraine and Childe to the dragon and back to George.

"Choose little Constable," the dragon growled. "Choose now."

Will looked deep into George's eyes. "You sure?"

George nodded. "Positive."

Erica's hands flexed open and closed at her sides. Her shoulders bunched. "I can't—I can't see this." She turned away, tears streaming down her face.

Will took a step toward Loraine. *"Don't you fucking touch him!"* she spat. Will lunged and grabbed her. He was trained and she wasn't. He had her in an arm lock in less than two seconds. Loraine's throat caught, closed. The strength ran out of her legs and Will guided her to the ground, whispering "Shhh, shhh. It'll be okay." She made muttering, mewling sounds behind shut eyes and felt like a bag of angry snakes under his hands.

George moved in and snatched Chlide by the wrist. Kiddo yanked his hand away, surprising the hell out of the big man. "I can walk just fine, Mr. Rhodes." Tears, hot and angry flowed down his cheeks. "I know what I need to do." Together they walked over to the altar. Childe Howard threw a leg over and boosted himself up. He shot a look at Will, "Don't you hurt my mom. Don't you hurt her."

Will choked back a sob. "I won't, Kiddo."

Childe lay down and closed his eyes.

"You save your world, boy," the dragon-girl said.

George moved in close, his eyes searching, searching. His hand crept up under his shirt. There! Right there! Plain as day! His voice shook, "You said there was another way to seal the door, dragon." Dampf turned as George struck, stabbing with the shard of broken rifle. It plunged into the weak spot on Dampf's left breast and pierced its heart. "*Your* blood must be shed."

Dampf reared up and back. It knocked George to the side and clawed at its chest, but the metal shard was buried deep. The ancient magic of iron poured into every cell and filled the great dragon with endings. It staggered back and slumped against the wall. Its head roved back and forth and one claw hand caressed the emerald wall. A moment passed and the dark light went out of its fathomless eyes. Dampf slowly faded, its wings and tail, talons and head, teeth and horns changed shape one last time and only a pile of coal was left.

Will let go of Loraine and stood up. She ran over to Childe and pulled him to her. He cried quietly into her chest while she rocked him and hummed. Erica walked over to George who stood staring at the pile of coal, rubbing a sore shoulder from where he'd fallen. "You knew the whole time?" she said. George craned his neck to look at the diamond pile. It had solidified again. "I didn't know if I could kill it," he said. "But I remembered what it said, and I remembered my myths. They always have a weak spot." He took her hands. "Besides, if I'd been wrong it still would have killed Childe."

"And you," she said.

"And me."

She laid her forehead against his chest. "Jesus, what *is* this life?"

"Yeah."

Will walked up, "I totally should have figured that out first."

George smiled, "Oh, yeah?"

"Have you ever even picked up copy of *The Hobbit*? Do you know how many times I've read that?"

"Actually," George said. "I never read it. I was thinking about all the Norse shit I read in high school. *Hafnir and the Dragon*, that kind of thing. It's always iron and it's always in the weak spot. Just couldn't see it until I got in close."

Tears filled Wills' eyes. He threw his arms around his friend and they crushed each other. "You're such a badass," Will said, pounding him on the back.

"Constable."

Will let George go and turned around. He was already squinting when Loraine's fist connected with his nose. He blinked and backed up. It didn't hurt too bad, but the message was more than conveyed. She was looking at the gun in his holster. "I should kill you." George opened his mouth to speak, but she held up a hand. "Both of you. I know what you were doing now and I know I should forgive you, but I can't. Not for a while, so don't you ask me." She glared at Will. "Get me and my son out of this filthy goddamn hole."

Will turned to look at the hole in the ceiling. The blue-white fire had gone out.

* * *

WILL MADE THE initial accent. He expected it to be hell after the grueling physical trial they'd all just endured, but the climb was easy, fast even. He put it down to hysterical strength, like the little old lady lifting up the Cadillac. He must just still have been flying on endorphins or whatever. In another minute or so, he would crash and crash hard. Probably sleep for a couple of days, getting up only every now and again to drink water, eat handfuls of potato chips and pee. Getting the rest of them up was just a matter of tying a rope sling at the bottom end and securing the knot tied to the Jeep's bumper. All he had to do was back it up nice and easy and they had their own little elevator.

They all rode in silence as the Jeep jounced over the forest floor. Soon enough it found the twin ruts of the old mining road and the going became easier. The sun was coming up now and filled the woods with gray light. Sentinel trees slid by the windows, past five staring faces all replaying their own private horror shows.

Will dropped Loraine and Kiddo off first. She didn't say a word as she trudged—looking about a hundred years old—up the walk to her house. Tomorrow she and Kiddo would leave and never look back. There was a lighthouse in New England with their names on it. Kiddo hopped out and held the door open for Darwin. He trotted right after Loraine, broken tail crooked at a painful angle. The boy looked at his mother and then leaned into the car. "Constable Will? Mr. Rhodes?"

Will turned around from the driver's seat. George said, "Yeah, buddy?"

"I forgive you guys even if mom can't yet. I mean, I get it. I was scared but I get it."

Erica leaned over quick as a fox and kissed him on the cheek. "You're an amazing guy, Childe Howard."

Kiddo blushed so hard George thought his hair would go from blonde to red, but still he had deep circles under his eyes. "Go on in, buddy." George nodded up at the house. Loraine was glowering down at them, but something in her face had already changed, loosened.

A few minutes later, it was Erica standing in the door of George's house looking back at the Jeep as the two men talked. George stood next to the driver's side door and Will half leaned out the open window. The sun was just clearing the tree line and it felt like Shard was in for a little Indian summer. They could have been just a couple of guys talking about the weather instead of… What were they all now? Survivors? Something more than that.

"You got enough first aid stuff to take care of that ankle?" Will asked.

"Enough to get me through a few hours of sleep before we go. We'll hit an ER on the way."

"On the way?"

"We're leaving. I'm getting out of Dodge with the lady over there. Think I'll like Manhattan?"

"It'll like you, Georgie."

George put a hand on Will's arm. "You should leave, too, man. This place's well and truly dead."

Will stared through the windshield. It was going to be a fine day on this old street. The Victorians stood proud in the long morning shadows and there wasn't much sulphur on the air. "I 'spose your right," he said. "But not before I get a long, long nap." He turned back to George. "Just come by the house before you go, right?"

"Of course."

"'Cause you got unpaid parking tickets."

"You're leaving now, yes?"

"Bye, Georgie." Will waved to Erica and drove off.

* * *

WILL WAS STILL waiting for the endorphins to wear off and for that wave of exhaustion to crash over him, but it wasn't happening. He puttered around the kitchen for a few minutes, emptied the dishwasher and thought about making himself some eggs or something. But he wasn't hungry and he wasn't tired. He was thrumming. At one point, he leaned against the kitchen table, crossed his arms and just beamed. Everything was beautiful. The light streaming through the window, the way it caught that one stubborn drop of water hanging from the faucet. Man, even the way the air felt on his skin! If this was how he felt every time he helped save the world he was going to do it more often. He shook his head and headed to the shower. A shower'd be great.

T.R. was waiting for him in the hallway. As soon as Will walked by, he struck out with the long kitchen knife. The blade glanced off Will's shoulder blade and knocked him forward. He spun around grabbing for his gun, but *Smaug* was empty. Will threw the heavy pistol at T.R.'s head. There was an audible crunch as it pulped his nose, but it didn't even slow him down. T.R. shambled forward, his mouth unhinging. Will could see the gleaming black head of the last wasp as it crawled up from T.R.'s throat.

Will's mind flooded with thoughts of Yïn. If she were here, she'd turn into a flock of cardinals, or just wrap the walker up in a bundle of silk and make short work of him with her pincers. But she wasn't here. It was just little Constable Two-Bears McFarlan. Two-Bears. Two-Bears. Two-Bears. Will looked at his hands, but they weren't hands anymore they were huge paws, covered with thick brown fur. He felt a strange sense of doubling as he split down the middle.

Outside of the house, everything appeared tranquil. The Jeep sat in the driveway, its engine ticking as it cooled. A bluejay scolded a squirrel from its perch in an old juniper tree. A die-hard cicada began its rhythmic call. As a single puff of cloud passed near the sun, a terrible harmozied roar shattered the morning.

Epilogue

IT TOOK A long time for her find her way through the smouldering dark. The ground beneath Shard was fouled with angry heat, but it wasn't enough to singe her new hide. Nothing could burn her. She could walk the rims of Mercury's craters— these inflamed tunnels were time consuming, nothing more. Time was different now. Once her master, consuming *her*, it was now insignificant. And so eventually, her scaled snout lead the way through the burning maze from the mine offices at the top of the hill to the cool, green glow of the cavern and the diamond bed. There she curled her long tail around herself and closed her eyes. She could hear them buzzing on the other side of the threshold, but they'd not come through. Not so long as she guarded her new lair.

* * *

IN THE DARK below a burning town, a dragon sleeps. Its horns are long and sharp, its talons razored spears, and the tattoos on its skin a vestage of human life already forgotten. In the light above a burning mine, a spider keeps watch. Sometimes it rides through empty streets on the back of an old motorcycle looking every bit a young man in a red baseball cap. Some days the man is absent and the woods are patrolled by two great Kodiac bears. Sometimes it's a flock of crows, or a cloud of iridescent butterflies. It always watches its town.

And the green shoots creep in and clothe the Victorians. The animals make their beds in engine blocks and desk drawers. The summers rise and rot, the winters freeze and break. The spring and fall set color-fire to the woods. And Shard slips back into the mountain.

The End

Washington, DC
October 8, 2009